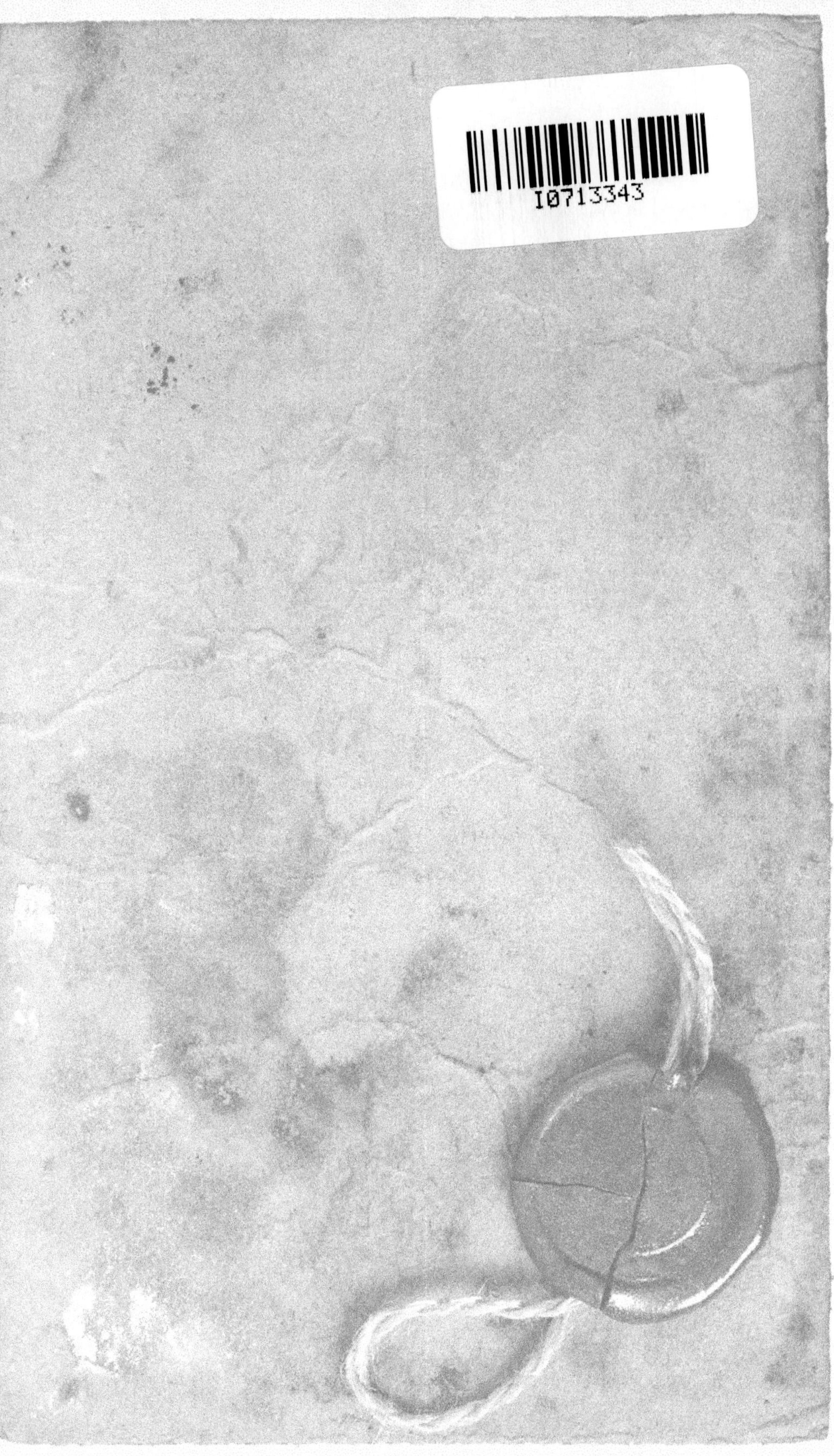

THE COST OF SECRETS

Wordalicious
PUBLISHING

THE COST OF SECRETS

Sasha Penno

Author's Note

Shapeshifting isn't a new phenomenon; it has been the stuff of legends since prehistoric times, when humans began attempting to understand the natural world and their place in it.

The ancient Greek gods often took different forms to suit their own, usually carnal purposes; Zeus managed to appear as a swan, a shower of gold, an eagle, a bull, and a satyr in order to seduce various women.

Odin in Norse mythology could fall into a trance and send his out his soul, to adopt the form of another person or creature.

Native American shamans also used the trance state to allow their souls to wander at will, taking on the form of whatever creature they needed, to travel on their spirit journeys.

Even the Bible speaks of God appearing in pillars of cloud or fire, or as a burning bush…

I've always loved folk tales and legends. Norse and Scottish folktales, the Greek heroes, legends of the Canadian First Nations peoples and the Dreamtime stories of the Australian First Nations people all fascinated me from an early age.

The Scottish legend of the Silkie in particular, the mythical beings capable of *therianthropy* – changing from seal to human form by shedding their skin captured my young imaginings long before shape-shifting protagonists arrived on any modern author's page.

Although this is strictly a work of fiction and all characters are fictitious, the issues facing the planet – global warming, over-fishing, food security, pollution of our oceans and the threat of extinction to the beautiful creatures that call the oceans their home – are very real.

In *The Cost of Secrets* I have paid homage to the now retired "Orange Roughy" our very own much loved icebreaker *Aurora Australis*, which was responsible for the safe delivery and return of our intrepid Antarctic expeditioners over the course of many years, as well as the amazing rescues the ship and her crew took part in during that time. To all who sailed in her and endured the stormy and treacherous temperament of the Southern Ocean, I give my deepest respect.

This novel is written in Australian English but acknowledges the Canadian characters who have their own references to everyday things like mobile phones and biscuits.

Sasha.

Prologue

Somewhere in the Southern Ocean – early hours of Thursday.

Sounds of distant crying pierced his dreams and woke him with a jolt. Dougal threw back the covers and peeled off his thermal pyjamas. Shivering, he quickly folded them and tucked them under the pillow, looking across at the small alarm clock he always kept at his bedside: 1:30 a.m. He would be back before the others woke, with luck. Padding noiselessly across the three-berth cabin, he shrugged his arms into the old black coat which had been hung up on a peg behind the outer door. He looked back at his young cabin mate, snoring softly in the other bunk, smiled fondly, and let himself out, quietly closing the door behind him. He silently climbed the stairs and opened the storm door to the outside world.

Out on the deck there was silence, apart from the constant keening wind and the thrumming music of the cargo-restraining wires; there were no crew members moving around the rear trawl deck. The vicious westerly squall blew his long silver-streaked hair around his craggy face, whipping it into his eyes. He swiped futilely at his mane as he approached the side of the ship.

The mewling was louder, loud in his ears across the wind-whipped water prancing under the sinking crescent moon's dying light. The eerie sound reminded him of the *pibroch* from his early childhood visits to his grandparents' house in the Orkneys; a lone piper would play the soulful lament each evening at the dying of the day atop the cliffs and the sound would float across the green tussocky *machair* grass on the shoreline to his ears as he mooched along the pebbles. It had made the hairs on his arms stand up then; the effect was the same, now. Phosphorescence danced fitfully across the sea towards him in the ship's ruffled wake as, naked footsteps whispering across the deserted deck, he reached and gripped the starboard rail and gazed away to the west. The sounds were borne on the spiteful wind that seemed ever present in these latitudes. Somewhere to the south, someone was in trouble.

Silently he finished buttoning his old coat, climbed over the cargo netting at the rail and dropped like a stone into the ice-cold sea. He kicked powerfully away from the single propeller at the stern and started swimming swiftly, away from the ship, in the direction of the lamenting song. Although the icy water took his breath away at first, he had always been a strong, swift swimmer, and his coat, while long, didn't slow him down at all. For, as he entered the water, the coat that clung to him like a second skin, *became* his skin; his upper limbs melded to his body, and his legs fused together. Hands and feet transformed into powerful flippers; with them he could exercise the powerful kicks necessary to propel himself away from the ship. He winced a little as he always did at transformation, as sinews and tendons stretched, bones shifted and rearranged, and dark fur covered his entire body. He had almost forgotten how much it tickled when long whiskers forced their way through his face. Anyone looking from the deck would never have seen a middle-aged man swimming away; they would have sworn it was a sizable bull seal with a grizzled head and whiskers, arcing effortlessly southwards through the wind-tossed waters of the Southern Ocean.

Bioluminescence coated and illuminated his outline, dancing and sparkling along his fur, casting a ghostly luminous blue silhouette of his sleek, powerful shape as he streaked through the freezing water. He surfaced for air, heard the cries, dived and headed, arrow-swift towards the plaintive sounds.

He located the source of the problem; there appeared to be miles of a vast lacy carpet of nets hovering hungrily, not far below the surface. Damned illegal fishermen! There was no stopping these people; criminal, greedy or just hungry, it made no difference. Even in his seal form, he was indignant.

Australia and the rest of the world had declared this part of the Southern Ocean as a marine sanctuary; he was sick to death of the ignorant, avaricious, or even desperate fishermen who chose to break the rules which other people seemed content to abide by. After all, that was one of the reasons he had signed up for this trip. Sea mammals were forever being caught up in the trade, innocent victims of the almost invisible nets. His concern was population numbers of the pinnipeds, and their sustainability in the Southern Ocean and on the numerous islands within the region.

Smaller whales, dolphins, seals, turtles, sea birds; nets were often the instrument of capture and destruction, and unscrupulous fishermen did not discriminate. Any mammals or turtles would be discounted as collateral damage and thrown back into the sea, for predators to devour.

When his large brown eyes had adjusted to the watery light, he could see such a creature; a young seal, cruelly entangled in a mass of net. The poor creature had obviously been after the fish trapped inside and had itself become a victim.

Ah, ye daft greedy wee beastie he thought, *chasing fishies that did nay flee from ye. Ye should ha' known better!*

Reaching the obscene mass, he started cutting through the strands closest to the seal with his teeth, freeing one flipper then another, until the whole creature was freed. He barely had time to caress the silky head before it arched away towards freedom. It was then he noticed that other seals had remained with their trapped companion, and they shot off into the depths with it, as it streaked away from its durance vile. He set off towards the surface.

He had been so intent on his task, he had neither heard nor felt the vibrations from a small outboard motor heading towards the net. A motor launch was running without lights and coming in very fast and bouncily across the wind-chopped water, perhaps from some larger trawler, and probably the same illegal fishermen who had set the nets.

Precious few seconds after he had freed the seal and seen it on its way with its companions, a brutal *thump* caught him in the back – and an excruciating fire blossomed in his chest cavity. The force of the impact violently pitched him forward and knocked his breath away. Searing, all-encompassing pain drove out all conscious thought except one—the need for air. He struggled to complete his ascent to the surface but discovered that his front flippers were now his only means of propulsion. His lower body wouldn't function! He wasn't going to last long at all in the frigid waters without useable limbs; he wouldn't have the strength to swim back to his ship now, steaming away towards the south-east. He would never make it before he drowned. And no one knew he had gone overboard. No one ever did when he went for his midnight swims. He cursed himself silently for a fool. This time he would not make it back to his ship. This time, something had gone horribly wrong.

A strange stinging heat in the middle of his chest brought him to realise the possibility that he had been shot; blood gushing or even oozing slowly from his wound would attract predators very quickly. As blackness starting nibbling at the edges of his consciousness, he found himself slowly sinking, and his body became entangled in the very net he had freed the young seal from. He flailed around, trying to avoid it, but thrashing just worsened the situation and he was well and truly snarled up; he was now trapped, and the seals had returned, crying in distress. He wanted to shoo them away, to warn them about the dangers of the huge risks they were taking, but he had no strength to either call or push them away. Shock, loss of blood and hypothermia would kill him; his coat and his fat reserves would not sustain him for much longer.

And then the nets started moving slowly, pulled inexorably towards the surface at an angle; something or someone was pulling in their haul. Perhaps he might not die tonight, after all. If he didn't drown first…

Chapter one

Earlier that week in Hobart

Late April, and the westerly wind bowled energetically across the Derwent, ruffling the water into loose white curls as it passed. The sunshine was kind, but winter wasn't far away; the stiff breeze was a brisk reminder. It ran reckless and restless fingers through the hair of the people standing loosely grouped behind the cyclone wire fence. They were there, either to embark, or to say farewell.

Professor Dougal Ferguson, one of the scientists bound for Macquarie Island, stood with his wife on the quay. His long silvering hair was tied back into a tail, but the wind still played havoc with it, whipping strands into his eyes. His wife was valiantly trying to control her own hairdo, one small, expressive hand holding her short straight dark hair in place as she laughed and talked, dark eyes sparkling. She was neatly dressed in khaki slacks, lemon silk tee shirt and a dark blue blazer. Her navy-and-lemon scarf fluttered vigorously in the capricious breeze. Dougal wore a highly visible yellow anorak; all the passengers were conspicuous amongst the crowd by their brightly coloured outerwear – yellow, orange, red. His trousers were a sensible navy twill, and he wore hiking boots; under his anorak he wore a long-sleeved polo shirt. At his feet lay a navy canvas duffle bag, with an ancient seal-skin coat thrown across the top.

"I do wish you would let me send that moth-eaten old thing to the op shop, Dougie," his wife teased, glancing at the disreputable-looking old black coat. "You know, one of these days I will, when you're not looking!"

"Over my deid body," Dougal replied, laughing but serious. "It's been wi' me a guid mony years the noo." His Scottish accent broadened out deliberately, which made Beth, his wife, laugh in return.

"Oh Dougie, I really don't see what your attachment is to the mouldy old thing; it looks so *tatty*! Why don't I buy you a new coat for your birthday?"

"No, Beth lass, leave well enough alone. I've nay need of a new coat. This'll do me right well enough, thank you all the same."

"Do you realise we have the same conversation, the same *futile* conversation, every time you go off on one of your wee jaunts?" There was a chuckle in her voice, which softened any sting which might have been meant.

He chuckled in reply. "Ay, I do, lass, and the answer's always the same, isn't it? Enough now. Let's not waste our time arguing aboot something we'll never agree on. Come here and let me hold you." He folded his arms around her, and silently they looked across to the ship.

***

The bright orange ice-breaker *Aurora Australis* had been towed downriver several days ago from her home berth at Kingston and was now berthed at No 2 Macquarie Wharf, Hobart, where the final provisioning was underway and nearly complete. This would be her final trip to the Antarctic bases before the southern winter, and there had been frantic activity aboard since late last week.

There was a well-founded rumour that she was to be replaced by a newer, more efficient vessel in the not-too-distant future, but for now, as for the past twenty-five years, she was still the main supply line between Australia and the Antarctic stations. Equipped with stern thrusters and a bow thruster, she was able to break through ice over a metre thick at low speeds and had been instrumental in the rescue of sick or injured expeditioners over the years, as well as providing the essential transport to and from the Antarctic continent.

Featuring fully equipped laboratories on board for biological, meteorological, and oceanographic research, *Aurora Australis* was very popular with Australian and international scientists during the Southern Hemisphere's summer months when the Australian Antarctic Division would charter her and her crew of twenty-four, for ocean-going research programs.

The ship and her crew had also taken part in maritime rescues when other research vessels had become trapped in the pack ice. She was as much a part of the Hobart maritime scene as the yachts which came streaming (or limping) into Constitution Dock at the end of the annual Sydney Hobart Yacht Race each December.

She was known as the "Orange Roughy" and was much loved by Aussies everywhere.

There was a flurry of last-minute activity on the dock and on the decks as the final preparations were completed.

Three helicopters were aboard and firmly lashed to the hangar deck floor, and near the helideck the all-terrain vehicles were likewise secured and confined, along with their fuel oil tank. A succession of twenty-foot sea containers packed with vast quantities of food, drink, medicinal supplies, weather balloons and every manner of goods and hardware likely to be required in the coming over-wintering season had been ordered, delivered dockside, hoisted onto the deck with the gantry, checked off, double checked, and secured. In the hold tanks, nearly one million litres of fuel oil had already been delivered and stored, to supply the needs of the bases in both the Antarctic and at Macca, as Macquarie Island was fondly called.

Nothing was left to chance when securing the cargo; people's lives would depend on it.

In the Screaming Sixties, the seas could be mountainous with blasting winds driving the frenzied waves across thousands of miles of unimpeded, merciless ocean. Any sloppy tethering or storage job this end could and would mean disaster and mayhem during a stormy voyage.

Although the ship was well-fitted with stabilisers to ensure a reasonably smooth and comfortable journey, it could still be tossed around by high-velocity winds and driven into vast watery canyons to have to plough its way up again through impossibly steep walls of water, where waves could exceed ten metres in height.

During one of those voyages, one "wag" of an Australian engineer had dubbed the ship "a chuck bucket" from one end to the other.

Passengers unused to sea travel would be the first to succumb to seasickness, confining themselves and their misery to their cabins; but on particularly rough crossings, even hardened crew members had parted company with their food on more than one occasion.

When a large, stable, reinforced steel-hulled ship started behaving like a roller coaster car in the peaks and troughs of the Southern Ocean, not many were able to withstand the urge to purge.

At present, serene as a swan on a millpond, with a reasonably calm sheet of water beneath it, the *Aurora Australis* was the epitome of reassuring orange solidity towering above the quay, radiant in the afternoon's sunlight.

***

Crew members had been scurrying like colonies of ants over every surface of the ship since early morning. They had already taken leave of their loved ones the previous night. Now it was the turn of the expeditioners, who had gathered on the quay, ready to embark; wives, children and other family or friends stood with them in small, loving groups. Leave-taking was never easy, especially for families with young children. For some who were parting for the first time, the farewells were prolonged and very emotional; for the more experienced travellers, farewells were quieter but no less charged with emotion. During the coming year, they would stay in touch, but for those with young families, it would be particularly hard; first steps would be taken, and teeth appear; laughing babies would become toddlers shy of a returning mum or dad.

All the families and couples had undergone the mandatory pre-expedition briefings and knew what to expect. But the heart often overrules the language of the head. Leave-takings were tough.

A twelve-month sojourn on the world's harshest and most demanding continent, and those weather-smashed islands deep in the Southern regions was a daunting prospect. Those who had to stay behind in the relative comfort and warmth of a Tasmanian winter, constantly aware of the absence of one of the family, were probably more daunted by this prospect than the expeditioners, who were eager to get underway.

For the passengers journeying all the way to the Antarctic, it would be a seven-day voyage, weather permitting; for those who would be disembarking at Macquarie Island, around three-and-a-half to four days' worth of discomfort on an open and treacherous ocean.

The expeditioners were not only scientists and rangers; there were tradespeople, plumbers, cooks, medicos, drivers, and all manner of sundry personnel necessary to maintain a level of relative comfort for all those living in the storm-tossed south. Some would start work as soon as they were aboard, but for others, not until they made landfall far away at the southern end of the earth.

***

Dougal bent his tall, lean frame to embrace his slim little wife; he marvelled at her resilience and beauty. In the shafts of afternoon sunlight, the finely chiselled planes of her heritage were revealed sharply; the high, broad cheekbones she had inherited from her Tsimchian grandmother from Prince Rupert Island on Canada's Pacific coast. Tiny laughter lines radiated from her slightly almond-shaped, dark brown eyes, and a full, loving mouth completed an exotic beauty, that at nearly fifty-five years of age she had not lost. He ruffled her short, straight, dark brown hair, tracing his finger over the few strands of silver starting to show there, and laughed when she lifted a hand to smooth her hairstyle back into place.

He bent his head to inhale the perfume of her hair, then kissed it. The tell-tale silver strands gave him a pang of guilt that he had largely been the cause of those, over the years. Although they had been almost brutally honest with each other during their marriage, he harboured two dark secrets from her. At this thought, he glanced across the top of her head at the young man nearby who was saying his own goodbyes to the beautiful blonde in his arms and smiled with genuine affection at him. Dougal's hair tickled Beth's face as he bent to kiss her. They stood, arms around each other, silent in their own thoughts, until the call came from the ship for the passengers to embark. Dougal and Elizabeth had parted many times before; but as they grew older, each parting seemed more difficult, as if they both knew that age and mortality was gradually creeping up on them both, and that each parting may well be the last.

"Sorry, my love, I'm leaving you again. But I promise, no more expeditions after this one."

We'll see, Dougie, we'll see. Look after yourself and remember to rug up against the cold."

He chuckled into the top of her head and murmured soft, loving words in Gaelic, which she recognised as "I love you, my dark-haired beauty." She snuggled closer into his warmth as he added in English, "Take care of yourself, Beth love. I'll talk to you next week when we're settled in at the station."

She gave him one last emphatic hug and replied, "You too! Now, get your boy and go play with your seals!"

He kissed her once more then gently pushed away to hold her at arm's length.

She looked back at him. His face was weather-beaten from all those years out in the field with his beloved seals, but he still had the same twinkling blue eyes she had fallen in love with so many years ago, and although his hair was rapidly silvering, she still thought him the most handsome man she had ever seen.

He leant in, kissed her swiftly on the cheek, and raised his voice to the young man nearby.

"Come away, laddie, kiss yon wee lassie goodbye. Time to go now."

***

Meanwhile, Jeremy, his Ottawa-born student had been standing slightly apart from the older couple, arms locked around his tall, blonde, and beautiful fiancée, Carrie. Their kisses were more urgent, more passionate — this was their first long time apart since they had met and fallen in love. Both were aware of the privations of the coming year, but Jeremy was so excited about his first expedition, Carrie had to smile at his boyish enthusiasm. She would not have denied him this opportunity for the world. She reminded herself that her life had been full of activity in the pre-Jeremy days; she had her work and her sporting interests to keep her busy and active, but she had lost her heart to this tall, blond, slightly gangly young man.

As they pulled apart, Carrie noticed that, even while they were exchanging promises of frequent contact, and more kisses, Jeremy's eyes kept straying to his mentor and professor, Dougal, almost as if he were awaiting the signal that it was time to go. She saw Jeremy frown slightly at the older couple, then turn his attention back to her. She felt no resentment at her man's restlessness; she knew he adored his mentor and was keen to get going on his big adventure. She wondered if it was to do with Jeremy's never having had a father. Certainly, he waxed enthusiastic about Dougal, and Beth, and had taken her to meet them on more than one occasion. Every opportunity he could, Jeremy would be off on field trips with Dougal, and always returned with renewed vigour for her. She felt her face heat as she remembered their explosive, lust-filled lovemaking at the end of those field trips. No, she wasn't resentful in the least.

Jeremy kissed her one last time, passionate, impatient.

"Look after Beth, honey? She's like a mom to me."

"Sure thing, sweetheart. Look after the boss, eh?"

"You got it! Bye, gorgeous, love you!"

"Love you too. Now get going, Jezz, he's waiting for you."

"I'll call you soon, hon, be good. Love you!"

"I love you too. Now go!"

And with this, Carrie pushed him playfully towards his professor, who was already carrying his gear towards the ship's gangway; she moved to stand closer to the small, middle-aged woman who had also been left behind on the dock. There was nothing to say as they watched the passengers filing up the gangway with their duffel bags and the odd personal item.

Carrie's hand crept into Beth's, child-like. Beth lightly squeezed the girl's hand in acknowledgement.

Nothing needed to be said.

Chapter two

Most of the families and friends waited until all the passengers were aboard. The engines had rumbled into life and *Aurora Australis* began to pull away from the quayside. Two long blasts of her horn echoed across the water to spectators who always gathered to see her go.

Beth and Carrie stood together as the passengers quipped and joked among themselves on deck. Beth understood what was behind it all, but for Carrie, it was the first in perhaps a long line of leave-takings in her future life; months of separation from her man loomed ahead. While police life didn't seem to faze Carrie one bit, this was a totally new experience, and one she did not appear to be enjoying; perhaps she had never been truly in love before.

As the two men had stalked up the gangway, Beth released Carrie's hand and put her arm around the younger woman's waist in a comforting way. She could feel the vibration of unshed tears through the woman's frame as Carrie fought against them; Beth gripped a little harder. Carrie's shaking arm curled around Beth's shoulders, and as Beth's head rested on Carrie's shoulder, Carrie tilted her head to rest on Beth's. They stood, locked as one on the quay behind the cyclone fencing, the tall and short, the statuesque and petite, the fair and dark, waving with their free hands to their men as they both stopped and turned at the top of the gangway, grinned wildly and waved back in excitement to their women before disappearing into the mass of faces already assembled at the rail for the farewell.

After the ship had pulled away from the quay, the two women watched a little while longer, then turned and started back towards the car park. As they walked, there was little conversation, but as they reached Carrie's car, Beth said, "Are you in a hurry to get home?"

Carrie answered immediately. "No. No, I'm not. Did you have something in mind?"

"I wondered if you would like to have a coffee with me. I really hate it when he leaves."

"That'd be great, thanks, Beth. I don't really feel like being alone yet, either. Where shall we go?"

"Do you want to try Salamanca Place? Or is there somewhere else you'd prefer?"

"No, Salamanca Place sounds fine. Your car or mine?"

"Why don't we take both; that way we don't have to come back here afterwards."

"Sounds like a plan to me. See you there." With that, Carrie leant in and planted a swift, light kiss on Beth's cheek, smiling at her through eyes too bright with unshed tears.

Beth returned the smile understandingly; she had been through this departure routine too many times to display much emotion anymore, but her heart was always heavy when Dougal departed on one of his expeditions. She felt a chill cross her heart; she uttered a silent prayer to the gods of the sea to keep her man safe.

"Right!" Beth smiled, unlocking and slipping into her car. "See you at the coffee shop."

Carrie followed a familiar route along Hunter Street onto Franklin Wharf, past Constitution Dock, veering right at the Mona Ferry Terminal onto Morrison, past Parliament Square, over Castray Esplanade and onto Salamanca Place. There were any number of cafes, bars, and pizza houses along this picturesque walk. The women parked their cars and ambled gently along. Eventually they found an open bakery, where they ordered cappuccinos and lemon tarts.

Sitting down at a table in the window, they gazed out onto the Salamanca Market site, neither initiating a conversation. Carrie looked through tear-filled eyes, images blurring before her; Beth discreetly gave the girl some space to manage her emotions and gazed through the window until their refreshments arrived.

The aroma of coffee roused both Beth and Carrie from their thoughts; the waitress settled their cups and plates with a gentle clink on the wooden table. The noise focussed their attention speedily, and the spell of introspection was broken.

Sipping hot coffee and sampling deliciously piquant lemon curd tart consumed most of their attention for the first few minutes. Smiles of mutual enjoyment crossed each woman's face.

Carrie broke the silence.

"Does it ever get any easier, Beth?" she asked in a husky voice as she dabbed at her mouth with a paper napkin. "I saw all those families, wives and small children who will have no husband and dad for a year. How do they cope? I mean, I know all about the Skype and phone calls – they told us about that at the orientation sessions before Jezz left. I guess they have to know if the ones staying behind are going to be supportive or destructive to their partner's success down there."

"Not really, pet, but you learn to deal with it, if you really love your man. And you learn to hide the grief better. And when you have children, if you ever decide to have children, then you learn to be strong for them."

"Do you and Dougal have any kids, Beth?"

There was a long silence, while Beth sat cradling her warm coffee cup between her hands and gazing into its depths before she looked up and answered. Her eyes glittered moistly.

"Not now, Carrie, but we did have a little boy, a long, long time ago." Beth's voice had dropped to little more than a whisper, and Carrie almost had to strain to hear the words.

As she spoke, Beth's voice gradually gained volume.

"Dougal and I met in '84, when we were both at the same university. He was passionate about his field, I was wrapped up in mine; it's a wonder, really, that we ever got together. But there we were, one evening, attending some really boring, dry university reception for the new dean, and our eyes literally met across the room. Sounds really corny and so cliché, but it's true. We found we could talk about anything. He was genuinely interested in my field, and I was fascinated by his. Anyhow, long story short, we married in '86, and in '89, Dougal was offered a fellowship in the Western Isles of Scotland, with his marine mammal research. By then, I was starting to scale back my professional activities, because, miracle of miracles, I was pregnant.

"Malcolm was born mid 1990…. D'you know, Carrie, he would have been twenty-five years old this June?" She turned the full force of tear-filled eyes onto Carrie, who sat, transfixed by the older woman's grief.

"Oh, Beth, I'm so terribly sorry; what happened?"

Beth lowered her eyes away from the younger woman's, and took up her sorrowful narrative, voice sinking back into the half-whisper as she strode, purposeful but painfully, through her memories.

"Malcolm, my wee man, was born in Scotland, just like his daddy. He was such a bonny child. Everyone loved him, especially Dougal's family members who were still alive at the time. Dougal came from Orkney, so he was happy to escape from the Western Isles each summer with Malcolm and me. I loved it there too. I was brought up on Vancouver Island, just across the strait from mainland BC, Canada, so it wasn't so different really. Different scenery, but the same treacherous coastlines.

"Malcolm was three years two months old, and was very independent by then; anyway—" A long, jagged sigh escaped Beth's lips as she shuddered with memory. "—anyway, that August, during the long summer break, we were up at Birsay, on Orkney. We were collecting shells on the shingle beach—they don't have sandy beaches there, you know," she added in a rueful aside. "Anyway, one afternoon we were on the beach and the receding tide had left a deal of the rock pools very full of treasures for a wee boy to find. He was always one for exploring and asking '*why*'. I didn't see him go, but my precious boy wandered away, along the high tide line, as I was collecting shells to make a mobile for his bedroom. Somehow, he must have tripped over some loose shingles; he hit his head as he slipped on a slimy seaweed-covered rock and into a brimming rock pool. He drowned."

From far away Beth heard the gasp of horror Carrie made.

"I heard a strange noise behind me, turned around, and ran across the shingles in bare feet. By the time I pulled him out of the pool, he was blue, and not breathing. I gave him CPR and tried to revive him, all the time screaming for help. I didn't carry a cell phone then, and I doubt if there would even have been any reception along that stretch of the coast. I tried so hard, but nothing could bring him back. I had to carry his wee body back across the shingles to the car and drive back to the house. I wonder sometimes how I did it. Dougal's family was hysterical. Dougal was heartbroken, of course.

"I was devastated. I felt so guilty, I just wanted to die, to be with my beautiful boy. The police got involved, and the coroner. I was interviewed again and again, and by the time they had finished with me, I felt like a murderer. I felt so *dirty* I never wanted to be touched or loved ever again." Beth slumped back into the chair, lost for a moment in her memories, eyes bright with the bitter tears which had welled into her dark eyes and slid, unchecked down her face.

"Dougal was loving and tender, but so angry, all at the same time. I felt he blamed me for being a bad mother, for letting his boy be injured like that.

"Anyway—" She interrupted her narrative to clear her nose, and streaming eyes. "—we went our separate ways for a year or so, each immersing ourselves in our work, after burying our child…"

She stopped in midsentence, drew in a juddering breath, and then added abruptly, "Sorry to burden you with all this ancient history. Do you feel like another coffee, Carrie?"

"Ah, okay, if you're having one…" stammered Carrie, caught off guard by the change of subject.

"Good." Beth signalled to the waitress who smilingly went off to produce two more cappuccinos.

"My treat."

"Thanks, Beth, you really shouldn't…"

"Nonsense, girl, who else can I treat now that Dougie's away to sea again?"

Carrie chuckled. "Well, if you put it like that, I guess it would be rude to refuse."

Her remark gained her the reward of a somewhat wry smile, and the two women found themselves quietly chatting and laughing at nothing in particular as they waited for the next round of coffees to arrive.

Over the second coffee, Carrie said, "Did you know, Beth, Jeremy looks on both you and the professor as long-lost parents or at the very least, as mentors? He speaks so highly of you both, but especially you. He lost his own mum when he was just a kid. I think he was in his early teens when she died. I believe she was Canadian, like him, like you, but from the East. Ottawa, I think. I don't think he had a particularly happy childhood, but he must have been really smart, because he told me he kept winning all these bursaries and scholarships, and he was able to finish high school and then go on to university. And then he lobbed up here, in Hobart, of all places."

Beth nodded, as though realising something. "Yes, he's a lovely boy. I've always sensed something sad about him, though. I didn't know his mother had died. What about his dad? Couldn't he help?"

Carrie shook her head. "Jezz said he never knew who his father was. He was pretty bitter about it when we met, but he's settled right down. The strange thing is, he's calmed down a hell of a lot since he met and started working with Dougal. He's picked up some of Dougal's mannerisms, and some days I even think they *look* alike." Carrie chuckled at the thought.

Beth smiled too. She was remembering the few occasions she had seen the two men together; she knew her husband was a charismatic person, but she didn't think she'd ever really noticed a facial resemblance between them, apart from how their hair seemed to stand up in a cowlick at the crown. She thought it was rather sweet and would be just a little flattering to the older man's ego, if Jeremy were copying Dougal's mannerisms, though. Something their own son would never be able to do.

Beth swallowed the last of her coffee, and excused herself for a 'bathroom break', as she put it. Carrie sat at the table, gazing out at the clouds which were gathering; it was probably time she thought about getting home, and she was a little concerned that Beth should be home before dark, or the storm, whichever arrived first. She suppressed a light shudder; her lips moved as she too prayed for a fair wind and a smooth voyage for the ship, but more specifically, both their men.

When Beth returned to the table, both women collected their handbags and went to pay the bill. Beth waved away Carrie's offered money.

"My treat, lass. You can pay next time, okay?"

Carrie nodded mutely and let her pay.

They stood a little while in the car park; neither woman seemed ready for solitude, or the reality of an enforced single status once more.

They solved the awkwardness by Beth offering Carrie a bowl of home-made soup and some crusty toast at her house; that was if the young woman was not busy with anything else.

Carrie laughed. "You must be psychic, Beth! I was just thinking how much I didn't want to go home yet, or at least be by myself just now."

Beth smiled ruefully. "It's therapeutic, just having company sometimes, girl. Come on, do you know where we live? Come have supper with me. Are you working tomorrow?"

Carrie groaned. "Oh yes, no rest for the wicked. I'm on duty tomorrow morning bright and early."

"Well, I promise I won't keep you up late. I'll have to be at the museum in the morning, myself. There's a huge backlog of artefacts for me to help collate and curate over the next few months. That will keep me busy and focussed. Come on, let's go."

After taking the first exit off the Tasman Highway Bridge across the Derwent, they turned left, heading northward toward Rose Bay. Dropping down almost immediately towards the coast, they pulled up outside a modest, slightly nondescript but immaculately maintained house and garden, facing Maranoa Avenue.

Carrie soon discovered that appearances were deceiving as they walked straight through the front of the house to the rear. The entire back area of the house had been gutted and modernised, so that a huge bow picture window on the left-hand side looked onto the river, almost due west, taking in the scenery on three sides and admitting the afternoon sun. Although it was late April now, the sun still had a bite to it. Carrie privately wondered how the inhabitants could stand the summer heat, especially as they were both from colder climates, but she didn't like to ask.

Beth, apparently, could read the girl's mind. "In the summer, we have steel awnings that wind down at the touch of a button. That keeps the worst of the sun out, but we love the sunshine. Coming from the frozen north, as most Aussies believe we do, we are kind of sunworshippers, I guess."

"The view is stunning, Beth!" Carrie recovered from her surprise and voiced her opinion. "But how did you know what I was thinking?"

Beth chuckled. "Human nature and practical observation, my girl. Now, how about some home-made vegetable soup and crusty bread for supper before you have to go home? Let's eat in the kitchen tonight. It's cosier."

Carrie smiled. Beth reminded her of her own mother, far away in Sydney. She cleared her throat.

"Um, Beth? Thank you so much for being there for me, and for Jeremy. I guess we're both a long way from home, and I know *I've* felt so much more at home here in Hobart since I met you and the professor, and Jeremy, of course! My own mum loves sunsets too. She still lives in Sydney and she always says the sunsets there aren't as spectacular as they are in the Red Centre. Something to do with the pollution, I'm certain of it. I don't miss her often, but there are times...." The girl's voice trailed away.

Beth could see Carrie facing up to the reality of a year without her man, and the girl was struggling. She walked up, put her hand on the girl's shoulder, in much the same matter-of-fact manner as she had at the dockside.

"Here, lass. Sit here on the bar stool while I heat the soup. The first time's the hardest, believe me, but it will get easier." She eased the young woman onto a low-backed stool and turned away from the breakfast bar where they would eat, to the cooktop. She allowed the girl time to come to terms with her situation. *She* knew it wasn't going to be easy for Carrie; *she* knew the long periods of separation had torn more than one couple or family apart. But she felt she had an inkling of the strength hidden beneath Carrie's soft exterior; the youngster would not be a good police officer if she didn't have a core of steel. The girl's strength would get her through—along with outside interests and some good company. Besides, Beth was very happy to have the girl around, herself.

Homely sounds on the other side of the roomy kitchen roused Carrie's awareness; she wondered, guiltily, if she should offer to help, but Beth was singing softly to herself, and Carrie was hesitant about disturbing the woman's industry.

Instead, she turned on her stool and looked around the large, modern room which blossomed out from the kitchen, and the view which flowed towards the river. She realised, suddenly, that she and Jeremy had only ever been entertained in the formal lounge at the front of the house, on the couple of occasions she had visited the professor and his wife. This was obviously Dougal and Beth's sanctum.

***

Two minutes later, Beth carried a laden tray of place mats, bowls, cutlery, and cups across to the breakfast bar. Carrie jumped up to offer help, but Beth put down her burden, smiled quickly, shook her head, and disappeared back to the cooktop from which mouth-watering aromas were issuing. Carrie smiled in response to the unspoken kindness as she placed mats and cutlery on the counter;

she knew she had eaten afternoon tea, but suddenly she was *ravenous* for home cooking. She could smell bread toasting, and the soup smelled *divine*.

Beth reappeared, carrying a huge pot of soup. "Can you put down a heat-proof mat for me, sweetie?" she asked, then gently deposited the pot onto the mat which Carrie had hastily placed in the middle of the benchtop. "I'll be right back with the toast. Do you prefer butter or cream cheese?" she asked over her shoulder as she glided across the kitchen. "No, don't worry," she called, "I'll bring both."

Soon they were sitting at the island bench, ladling out thick vegetable soup into bowls, pulling apart toast into small pieces to dunk into their soup.

"My dad used to call these pieces 'ducks', when I was small," Carrie reminisced. She smiled inwardly.

"So, is your father in Sydney too, Carrie?" Beth enquired.

"No, he left us quite a while ago. He couldn't stand the hustle and bustle of Sydney and wanted to return to the West where he was born.

"Mum didn't want to leave Sydney and her family, so they split up. I guess it happens all the time, but I was really very angry with him for abandoning us. Mum had a hard time making ends meet for a few years, but we got by. She discovered things about herself she had never known, and now she's a successful businesswoman. Perhaps if Dad had stayed around, she might never have discovered her inner strengths. It made it easier for me to move on, too."

Carrie stopped her reminiscing long enough to eat some soup and toast, then continued, "I guess that's one of the things that Jezz and I had in common when we started getting to know each other — we had both been abandoned by our fathers."

Beth nodded; her mother had never known *her* own father, either. She ate silently, while Carrie continued her tale.

"But in Jeremy's case, he never had a father to begin with. He said his mum would never tell him who the man was. It was one of the things that attracted us to each other, then bound us, when we realised we didn't want to be apart anymore." She dipped her head towards another mouthful of soup. "Kind of like you and Dougal, it seems to me…"

Beth swallowed hastily.

She said, "Except for those few really hard years after Malcolm, we've gone together all over the world, wherever Dougal's "crusades" have led him. We are never willingly apart when we can help it, but sometimes he takes it into his head that he must go off and save something…. Over the years, I have learned to go with the flow, and my skills are transferable pretty much anywhere. An artefact is an artefact. Fortunately, I'm passionately interested in indigenous cultures in general, so I can adapt to new places and new situations. My work at the university here is fascinating, and I have been hired to help collate and curate a new collection of Tasmanian indigenous art and artefacts.

"I thought the First Nations peoples in Canada and the USA had had a raw deal with the coming of the whites, but your Aboriginal people had an even more torrid time. It still makes me want to weep sometimes, especially when I'm handling such culturally sensitive materials. But I'm still learning about your indigenous people, and their histories fascinate me. There's always so much to learn."

***

The two women ate, laughed, and talked together until the sun had sunk, shimmering behind the hills across the river. They admired the twilight which Beth loved so much, watched the streetlights and house lights flicker on, delineating the line of the facing coast.

"It's almost magical, when you watch night falling this way." Carrie was almost whispering as she spoke.

Beth laughed aloud. "You see?" she cried joyously. "That's exactly why I love the twilight so much!"

She leaned across and kissed Carrie on the cheek. "Thank you so much for coming to share this with me!"

"It's been a real treat, Beth. It's been wonderful. I feel so much better."

"And now it's time you were away home, my girl. Go get some rest and stop worrying about your man—he'll be just fine."

Carrie stared at Beth in astonishment—the woman must truly be psychic!

Beth laughed at the girl's expression and gave her a swift, one-armed hug.

"Come by any time, Carrie. It's been fun. I'll see you out."

Side by side they walked to the front door and said their goodnights. Beth watched as Carrie walked down the front path to her car, waved once and closed the door.

Having had enough farewells for one day, she turned on her heel and went through to load the dishwasher, dimmed the main lights and sat down in the family room opposite the kitchen with a fresh cup of coffee. Her woven, hand-spun Tsimshian rug sat snug around her shoulders as she sipped her coffee reflectively, and watched the lights flicker on and off across the bay. Her fingers stroked the soft woollen cloth, woven by a member of her grandmother's clan, years before her mother, Selena, had left Kaien Island for Vancouver Island.

Beth checked off the colours in the rug, slightly faded after so many years, remembering their lessons and significance. *Black for invincibility and death of the negative, red for supernatural power and wealth, white for peace, harmony and balance, and purple for the wisdom of the ages.* Meditating on these a short while, and humming a little native tune from her childhood, she folded and returned the blanket to its position on the back of the couch, carefully smoothing out any creases, checked the outer doors and windows were locked, before making her preparations for bed. There was enough of an ambient glow from the lights across the water to find her way along the central passage towards the front bedroom.

"Dougal, love, take care for pity's sake." She rolled over and whispered to the empty side of their bed as she lay alone in the darkness. "May the gods of the sea protect you, my dear. Just come home safe, man."

She knew it would be difficult to fall asleep that night; it always was, on every first night her man was away to the sea.

Chapter three

"What do you mean, he's not there? Have you checked the bathroom?" the disembodied voice screeched through the mouthpiece of the phone, filling the silent, deserted cabin. "Where could he possibly *go*?" The last word rose to a yell. Heads were going to roll for this.

When Professor Dougal Ferguson was not in their cabin that morning, his student and cabin mate, Jeremy Munroe, the personable young Canadian, hadn't sensed that anything was wrong. His mentor firmly believed in a hearty cooked breakfast to set one up for the day's toil ahead; perhaps he had risen early to avoid the rush in the mess at breakfast. But when he arrived for his own breakfast, he had not seen the professor anywhere in the room. No one else had, either.

Jeremy quietly left the mess and made his way carefully along the slippery deck, down the corridor to their cabin and knocked, calling the professor's name. The door was not locked and swung open at his touch.

Empty.

Inside the cabin, Jeremy listened for tell-tale bathroom sounds — nothing.

A quick glance around the small room revealed nothing out of the ordinary, apart from a pair of thermal pyjamas tucked under the pillow on Dougal's bunk. Something was not as it had been the previous night, but Jeremy couldn't quite work out what wasn't right. He swept his eyes across the cabin again, but slowly this time, carefully; his eyes reached the cabin door — *that's* what was missing! The professor's tatty old coat was gone from the hook.

By now he was starting to sweat heavily, despite the intense cold. With a premonition of sickening dread, he lifted the phone to inform the captain of the man's absence.

It was his first time at sea aboard the *Aurora Australis,* and at this moment, Jeremy was wishing himself anywhere but here.

"Sorry, sir, he's not *here,* not in our cabin, not in the mess, not *anywhere I've looked!*" The protest came out as a strangled squeak. He coughed to clear his throat. "He's not here, sir, and no one has seen him at breakfast this morning either."

"Well, I'll be buggered!" came the terse reply. "Who would have thought it? Anything missing?"

"His glasses are still on the shelf next to his bunk, sir, if that's a help, and there's an empty mug. He has obviously been in bed; the sheets and covers are rumpled, his pyjamas are under the pillow and his slippers and clothes are here, but his coat is gone from the hook behind the door. His journals are here, neatly stacked in the locker… Can't understand it, sir. Perhaps he fell overboard…"

The scorching reply that came through the mouthpiece was so full of colourful expletives, that the young man jerked the phone away from his ear and held it at arm's length, staring at it, astounded. These Aussies could certainly curse. At length, the captain's voice came back down from the region of jet airliner decibels and the young man could just make out a muted babble. He put the phone to his ear once again, but cautiously.

"Well, lad," the ship's master barked, "I guess you didn't toss him overboard. Get back down here while we figure out what to do about this bloody mess of a situation."

Throughout this tirade, part of Jeremy's mind had been mulling over another problem; how on earth was he going to be able to tell Beth? And what would he say to her? Somehow, the prospect of dealing with the woman who had become like a mother to him, handing her such troubling and inexplicable news, worried him more than all the captains in the world yelling obscenities over a phone line. For one thing, he didn't *care* about all the sea captains in the world; he *did* care, and very deeply for the man who had mentored and guided his steps, almost father-like, and his wife. *They would have made great parents*, he mused. He made his way slowly and carefully down the companionway towards the mess.

***

On the roomy and brightly lit bridge, the captain hung up, and

32

sat back in his chair, shaking his head. *Damn, damn, damn, bloody damn! What a bloody mess! Almost within a day of Macquarie Island, and now we'll have to retrace our route to try and find the Scottish idiot! Shit! And it is a good bet that the man probably can't even swim. Not that anyone could last very long in the ocean in these latitudes…*

He kicked the console mounting in frustration, stubbed his toes and winced, then tried to breathe deeply. His second-in-command looked at him very strangely, then exchanged meaningful looks with the navigator. They knew something unfortunate had happened, but he would tell them in his own good time. He would have to assemble the ship's company, crew, and expeditioners in the mess for a debriefing. He put his head between his hands for a precious few seconds, trying desperately to *think.*

Come on, Peter, think! He hadn't been a ship's captain this long to stay disoriented. He took a deep breath, lifted the mouthpiece to the engine room and barked out terse orders, "All ahead full slow. Prepare to come about."

Dave, the engineer said, "Aye aye, skipper," wisely asked no questions, and the vessel began to slow. It would be a tricky manoeuvre to come about in these seas; the barometer was dropping rapidly, and they knew they were in for a "bit of a blow". The helmsman and engineers would have to work closely together to begin turning the large vessel in a wide arc across the increasing swell, while the navigator kept his eyes on the compass, and relayed the coordinates.

Peter turned to his second-in-command, John, and quietly asked him to give orders to the crew to conduct a cabin-by-cabin search of the ship; they were to search the holds, the equipment stores, the dog pens and the lifeboats, anywhere where somebody could hide, *or could have been hidden.* Then he ordered the junior officer to get everyone assembled on the mess deck in one hour, expeditioners included.

"Bob," he said to the navigator, "would you please plot our positions from around 22:00 last night until, say, an hour ago? It seems we have somehow lost a passenger."

His navigator looked up at him sharply, with eyebrows raised, then shook his head in disbelief and started calculating.

Peter paced up and down the spacious bridge, stopping to peer at the radar screens.

There was going to be a huge stink over this. He was master and commander of the ice breaker *Aurora Australis*, and of course the buck would stop with him. Although what could *he* have possibly done about a tall, solidly built, middle-aged academic deciding to go AWOL in the middle of the Southern Ocean!

All Captain Peter Gallagher really wanted, in that moment, was to complete a quiet and uneventful final trip to Macquarie Island, to offload supplies and the scientists he carried aboard, collect those he had delivered twelve months earlier, who had already overwintered and finished their year's posting at the station, then on to Antarctica for the same purpose. This was to have been his swansong; he was due to retire at the end of this voyage, but it galled him that his departure would possibly be under a cloud, not an honourable ending.

Getting to and from these remote outposts was a momentous mission entrusted to Peter and men like him; the captains were responsible, not only for the safe passage of their passengers and crew, but their equipment, and all the victuals, mechanical and medical supplies the bases would need, in order to survive the Southern winter ahead. There were no supermarkets in those latitudes, no corner stores.

By the time the vessel had been searched from bow to stern — on all the decks, the engine room down in the bowels of the ship, and the hold — there was no sign of Dougal Ferguson anywhere on the vessel. He had simply *disappeared* into thin air.

Peter Gallagher, experienced skipper, ran his hands through his white hair, till it resembled a startled bristle brush, took a calming deep breath, composed himself, and turned to the computer displays. He looked at the radar screen; three tantalising *blips* flickered on the screen. *Bloody hell!* Wait a minute! Why were there *three?* The large vessel they appeared to have been following for the past three days was obviously making for Heard Island, or the Antarctic coast — that much was obvious from the course the navigator had been tracking — and the ship off to the east was on the same course; that was a *Sea Guardian* vessel, he knew. He and Captain Lars had already had a chat since leaving port. But where had the *third* one appeared from, to the south-west, and when? They were being shadowed themselves. Curious and even more curious…

He turned to the communications officer and gave him the order to start sending out the distress call that would alert the authorities of their situation.

Calmly, Glenn, the communications officer, removed the cover from the DSC — Digital Selective Calling — device and activated it to start sending its text message to the Australian Marine Safety Authority in Canberra. It would transmit four times, and if there was no response, would change automatically to a different frequency where it would repeat the procedure until the message got through.

As he lifted the satellite phone from its cradle to try calling any passing or nearby vessels, he looked up from the bridge. He could see huge waves crashing over the deck as the ship pitched down into, and climbed up the other side of the steel-grey waves; the cloud cover was also too low, and the weather was deteriorating fast. Satellite phone would be no good. Shaking his head, he replaced the handset and picked up the transmitter for the HF band radio.

Meanwhile, Peter shook his head and pondered on the whereabouts of *Sea Guardian* and its quarry of the illegal fishermen who were currently in these waters. These fishermen spread vast acres of gill nets and long lines to scoop up Patagonian toothfish which sold on the markets of Asia and Eastern Europe for a pretty penny. Unfortunately, plenty of turtles and other sea creatures became tangled in the nets and drowned. He didn't have any sympathy with illegal fishers; in his opinion they were the scum of the earth.

Good thing one of the *Sea Guardian* vessels was in pursuit. *Aurora Australis* would have to ask them to heave to and help search the vast ocean — Captain Lars wouldn't be happy to have to stand down from pursuit of their quarry — but New Zealand wasn't too far away, and there was another *Sea Guardian* vessel based there, Peter knew that.

Oh! The media. Those bloodhounds would get wind of something amiss all too soon. Someone would let it slip that they had lost a passenger somewhere between their current position and where they had been the previous night.

Peter was aware that people went overboard all the time; passengers routinely seemed to get drunk and drop into the ocean from cruise ships. There was at least one case reported in the press every year, not to mention on all the social media he personally had no time for.

Losing a passenger; he was sure he'd be a laughing stock. Perhaps it really *was* time to call it quits. Although he *knew* he would miss the life at sea, the freedom, camaraderie of the crew and the interesting boffins he had met over many years in his career, he would have preferred not to leave his career with this kind of publicity.

The *Sea Guardian* boys would get some good publicity this time, he hoped. That organisation had had a very busy summer chasing the Japanese, and the Japanese whaling fleets seemed to hate it with a particular passion. They called the *Sea Guardian* crews 'pirates', each time they intercepted one of the many Japanese factory ships that proliferated in the Southern Ocean each year for 'scientific purposes', blatantly hunting whales in arrogant opposition to the maritime treaty which had been ratified by most of the world's nations.

From the news footage Peter had seen of some of their exploits, he wondered if perhaps some of the *Sea Guardian* personnel thought they were Errol Flynn!

God, I'm really showing my age now.

And speaking of age, what on earth could have possessed an intelligent man to go wandering around the deck in the middle of the night? *Damn the bloody man! What was he thinking? And how did he disappear? If he has gone over the side, he's a dead man, for sure.*

Peter's thoughts chased turbulently around in his skull; he could feel a headache brewing up like thunderclouds in their wake.

Peter sighed slowly and looked around him. His officers were a splendid team. The comms officer was busily at work with the HF radio, the navigator was plotting their course and determining where they had been; in the distance, the crew and expeditioners could be heard, footsteps and voices increasing in volume, doors slamming in the howling wind as they made their way to the mess, where he would have to voice his suspicions to them.

Wearily, like a man twice his age, Peter hauled himself to his feet, futilely swiped at his hair, ran a weathered hand over his chin, and walked down into the mess to meet the one hundred-plus ship's company.

This was not going to be a pleasant meeting, not pleasant at all.

He took a deep breath, steadied his swirling thoughts, and lifted his eyes to his audience.

Confusion met his gaze.

He cleared his throat.

"Thank you to all the crew for your efforts this morning, even though they appear to have been in vain. Get some breakfast if you haven't already eaten. No doubt you will have heard," — here he addressed the expeditioners — "that one of your number, Professor Dougal Ferguson, has apparently gone missing during the night. If he cannot be found, we will have to assume that he fell overboard sometime during the night."

A low, shock-filled murmuring percolated through the crew and the scientists and tradespeople; they were stunned.

"Jeremy here says nothing is missing from their cabin, except an old coat; even his reading glasses are still there."

Eyes swivelled towards the quiet young Canadian scientist, who lowered his eyes to the floor, and felt a burning creeping up his neck. He felt like a naughty schoolboy who had been caught in the act of smoking behind the shelter shed at school.

"Anyway," the captain continued, "this briefing is about what we'll do now." He took a deep breath. "We're already slowing and preparing to come about. The navigator is plotting our positions from last night until now, and we'll have to retrace at least part of our course to see if we can find him, or his body..." The word hung ominously in the air.

There were a few muttered curses of frustration; they were almost within reach of Macquarie Island, their first landfall, but they understood. They would all want at least the chance of being rescued if any of them were ever unlucky enough to slip overboard.

"In accordance with international maritime law," Pete's voice rose above the mutters, "we have an obligation to at least *try* to find our missing professor. We'll retrace our course to the point where Dougal was last known to be on the ship, or for two hours. Unfortunately, it's not probable that he could have survived in these seas, and the water temperature is not forgiving. Who was the last to see him last night?"

One of the crew, Jason, the cook's mate, replied, "He came in looking for a mug of hot chocolate around 2300 hours, skipper. He made his drink and took it back to his cabin, as far as I know. I didn't see him after that. I did the prep for breakfast, then knocked off and went to bed myself."

"Okay, thanks, Jason," Peter acknowledged.

Jeremy added, "I saw him when I turned in for the night; he was still reading one of his journals. He seemed okay then. I didn't hear him switch off the light…"

"Right. Thank you, Jeremy. The navigator will calculate our whereabouts last evening, and we'll steam back towards that point. You'll all have to be on the lookout for a body —" Here there was an ominous pause. "— or his coat or anything else he was wearing."

There was more muttering amongst the crew and the scientists who were en route to Macquarie Island; they had important jobs to do down there, meteorological observations to be made, and a myriad other things they would rather be doing than this. There was a transparent air of unease and sadness amongst the men.

"Look!" Peter Gallagher shouted. "I know you'd all rather *be* anywhere else, *doing* anything else at this time, but we have no option. It's the law of the sea."

There were nods of agreement, as none of them would like to be abandoned if one of them was unlucky enough to be swept overboard.

"Right," said the captain, "we've a little while yet until we really have to start searching, so I want you and you and you"—he indicated to a portion of the crew — "to take the first watch, while the rest of you get some food. It's going to be a long day, I suspect. I'll grab some breakfast and be up on the bridge. I need to make some calls. Anyone needs to come talk to me with any hypotheses or bright ideas, that's where I'll be."

Peter picked up a couple of buttered rolls and a mug of coffee, and walked out of the mess, bowed by Providence.

Chapter four

Babble broke out even before the door had swung closed behind the retreating figure. Those chosen to take first watch grabbed food, life jackets, harnesses, and binoculars, and left for their appointed duties. The others could stay and chatter like a flock of magpies if they wanted to; it was just too depressing. They had all liked the professor; some of the crew had sailed with him the previous year. He had been easy to get on with, always had a ready smile or an encouraging word, or was there to muck in with the rest of them when necessary. It was baffling. They turned to Jeremy, who was sitting alone, crumbling a bread roll in his fingers.

"What did you find in the cabin, Jezza?" asked one of the Australian crew.

"Everything was there, except for him and his old black coat. It was kind of weird, you know. Even his pyjamas were there, under his pillow. He'd obviously been in his bunk, because he was there, reading, when I turned in; the sheets were rumpled, but it was as if he'd just vaporised. The cabin door was closed, all his stuff was there, including an empty mug and his eyeglasses." The young man shook his head with a defeated air.

"You sure you two didn't have a lover's tiff, Jezza?" the Australian joked.

"Yeah, you could have offed him yourself!" another "comedian" chimed in, then, seeing the stricken look on the young man's face, added hastily, "Look, I was only pulling your leg, mate! No one thinks that about the prof. We all liked him. He was all right, for an academic type."

Jeremy shook his head. He was stunned; he had a terrible hollow feeling in the pit of his stomach. He could only stare at the two men in disbelief and horror.

Would the professor off himself, he wondered, *when we had work to do on Macquarie Island? And why? He looked enthusiastic at the dock, and he and Beth seemed happy enough together… And he hadn't said a word about anything that was troubling him…*

Because that's what it was looking like, a case of suicide. Suicide was a very depressing word, even to think, and yet he preferred his thoughts to the conversation he had overheard when some of the remaining crew members were bandying around their theories – woman trouble, debt, drugs, terminal illness, depression… *who would know?*

Jeremy got to his feet, donned his life jacket and a harness, and headed out into the brisk morning. He drew in several deep breaths of the salt-laden air and gazed gloomily out across the vast crashing rolls of grey-blue, stretching endless to the horizon. *How could anyone survive in seas like that?* He sighed, shaking his tousled blond hair, and headed off, cautiously, to the bridge. He was almost experiencing survivor guilt that *he* hadn't found the softly spoken Scottish academic, *his* professor; surely there was something he could do to help. By 9:30 a.m. he was certain his beloved mentor and friend was dead.

Jeremy's footsteps and the howling wind brought him stumbling to the bridge. He knocked and entered the spacious room, propelled by the wind at his back. The view from here would be stunning; but at this moment it was daunting, with the seas crashing and bashing across the decks as the ship slowed. The radar was still showing the blips, although one was further away than it had been before.

The skipper held up a finger and pointed. *Wait. Sit,* it said. He was talking to the communications officer who was selecting international distress channels to transmit the Pan message, which was the procedure in cases like this.

Jeremy sat, waited, and listened. It was the first time in his life he had experienced anything like this. Despite grief and disbelief, he was fascinated by the speed and efficiency of the crew, and with the large display of screens at their fingertips. The comms officer was transmitting the distress call on the HF band.

"Pan pan, pan. I have emergency traffic."

"Hello, all stations, hello all stations, hello all stations. This is *Aurora Australis*, this is *Aurora Australis*, this is *Aurora Australis*."

"My position is—" And here the navigator checked the chart

quickly and gabbled off a set of coordinates to the radio operator. " —
Latitude 51oS, Longitude 156oE."

"I have a man overboard, repeat man overboard. I require
assistance."

The communications officer then left the channel open to hear
any incoming offers of help; there were three blips on the radar; three
chances of finding the missing man, surely.

Peter Gallagher turned weary eyes to the youngster; he felt for
him. *Wonder who's going to supervise the remainder of the lad's research
now?* The lad looked shattered, lost.

"How can I help you, Jeremy?" he asked quietly.

Jeremy's attention snapped back to the captain.

"I was wondering, sir, if we'll still be going to Macquarie Island,
as per the original plan. It's just that…" His voice wavered a little; he
coughed into his hand, clearing his throat then resuming, stronger.
"It's just that Professor Ferguson and I were due to take up a six-
month research posting there over winter, along with the others."

"We'll get you there, lad, all in good time," came the gruff reply.
"Right now though, I must notify the authorities about what's
happened, we need to retrace our course to search God knows how
many miles of ocean, looking for a body… and I'll have to notify the
police in Hobart to inform his wife, or widow, of her husband's
suspected suicide. At least the message is out there, and if the *Sea
Guardian* boys are listening, they'll come to help. The satellite phone
is not all it's cracked up to be in these weather conditions, either, but
that's my problem, lad, not yours. Don't worry, we'll get you to your
precious wildlife."

Jeremy felt the familiar scorch of embarrassment rising up
through his neck to the roots of his fair hair.

"Sorry, sir. I didn't mean to throw more obstacles in your way.
I'm just concerned that, with the professor missing, it's going to leave
us a little short-handed down there for the winter, and I guess the
others will be impatient to be getting back to Hobart before the
weather really turns for the worse."

"Leave it with me, lad." Peter eyed the youngster warily — he
looked quite unwell. "Have you eaten anything this morning?" A
quick shake of Jeremy's head confirmed his suspicions. "Right! Well,
as your skipper, I'm ordering you to go to the mess, and get the

steward to fix you some breakfast. Okay?"

"Okay, sir, but…"

"No *buts*, lad, that's an order. Now get out of here!"

"Okay," Jeremy replied, and left the room.

As the door closed quietly behind the shaken Canadian, Peter and the navigator consulted their charts, and continued listening to the HF radio, waiting for a response.

The captain suddenly remembered something and spoke softly to his second-in-command.

"Best go and seal the professor's cabin, would you, John? It may be a crime scene, and we can't take any chances with the authorities. They'll be all over us, as it is. And get young Jeremy to collect his gear and find a berth with someone else for the remainder of the voyage."

John quietly left to carry out his duty.

So much to do, so little time. If they didn't find the body (and he was sure it *would* be a body) on this time-consuming sweep of their route, they would have to abandon the search. Personnel and supplies *had* to get through, and the meteorological forecast was not looking at all promising at this minute. They were in for a rough time of it. *Pity any poor sod unlucky enough to end in the drink in what was coming; pray to God there wouldn't be more before they finished their mission.*

Peter Gallagher, at that moment, was *not* a happy man.

He didn't have long to wait before a voice crackled through the speaker — it was Roddy, communications officer on *Sea Guardian*.

"*Aurora Australis, Aurora Australis*, this is *Sea Guardian*. Can we be of assistance, over?"

"*Sea Guardian*, this is *Aurora Australis*. We have man overboard, over. Our coordinates are 51oS, 156oE. Over."

Sea Guardian wasn't about to give away its exact position, being in pursuit of IUU fishermen who could be listening in, but Roddy came back with, "We are twenty hours away, *Aurora Australis*, over."

"Thank you, I understand. We're turning back now, to search along the run. Good hunting. Out."

Peter turned to Glenn, the communications officer. "They're too bloody far away. Keep transmitting, Glenn. Someone else, a passing vessel, out there might hear and help."

If all else failed, AMSA in Canberra would respond to the DSC and would send their specially equipped Orion to do aerial reconnaissance along their route.

What was interesting was that there were no responses to his Pan message from either of the other ships in the listening vicinity. Interesting, and suspiciously like someone trying to avoid detection or identification. When he mentioned this to Glenn, the younger man chuckled. "Yes, they're probably illegals; they'll want to lay low and hope *Sea Guardian* don't find them before they fill their holds and start for home. But Lars will! If *we* already have illegals on our radar, *Sea Guardian* will, too. They won't get away."

Over the course of that long morning, while Peter was preoccupied, the cook silently sent a plate of morning tea and a large pot of coffee to the bridge and shook his head later over the untouched food; he had been with this captain a while now, and knew his ways. When there was a flap on, Peter and his officers could stay on the bridge for countless hours at a time; Jason, the cook's mate, harboured a genuine concern for the captain's wellbeing, as the old man pushed himself a little too hard at times.

The cargo had been checked for signs of wear and tear; any loosened strapping or bolts had been tightened up and the equipment made safe again in the worsening weather. A few of the expeditioners had given up looking for their colleague; they were so ill with the pitching and tossing of the ship they had taken their pale green faces and their misery below to their cabins, to weather out the storm in their bunks. Remnants of the crew still moved cautiously about, lashed to the rails with harnesses; most were soaked to the skin beneath their waterproof outerwear, but they kept watch for developments or signs of trouble on the cargo deck.

Bob the navigator and Glenn the comms officer had closeted themselves with the skipper for most of the morning. Between them they had consulted tide and current charts, mapped a new course, and had contacted all the relevant authorities. Their actions had been text-book perfect.

Their EPIRB had been activated, their GPS was always active, so that the ship could be located by satellite tracking, and the AMSA had been contacted through the DSC. The listeners in Canberra had contacted the ship, and the Orion aircraft was already in the air, searching. The Orion would do an eight-hour sweep. AMSA would alert the Search and Rescue aircraft based at Essendon, Victoria, and it would be ready to go out on its direct orders if deemed necessary. The aircraft, a state-of-the-art Bombardier Challenger 604, had all the whiz-bang technology needed to locate something as tiny as a body floating in the ocean, if there was one to be found.

Aurora Australis's beacons had all been activated; the hardier members of the crew and passengers alike were on constant watch, lashed to the rails, visible in their bright orange life jackets, binoculars trained on the increasingly heaving seas for any sign of the missing man. They took it in turns to stand watch, rest and then relieve the watchers once more. All scientific work was suspended for the day; this was more important.

The expeditioners were able to get a first-hand insight into how emergency situations worked at sea; those who had not retired to their cabins, violently seasick, found it fascinating, but they stayed out of the crew's way, unless asked to join the watch on deck. Many of the stronger-stomached passengers found their feet drawn to the deck anyway; they had lost a colleague or fellow academic; the least they could do was to keep a vigil for him.

By the end of two hour's retracing, the seas were mountainous, and the captain and his officers had agreed that they were never going to see anything out there. The Marine Authority radioed to the ship that was no hope of anyone surviving in seas as wild and cold as these. The search was to be discontinued. Regretfully, Peter Gallagher gave the order to bring the ship about, into the teeth of a Furious Fifties gale, and they headed once more south-east towards Macquarie Island.

***

Jeremy gloomily recalled the previous evening when he and the other passengers had assembled once more in the mess after their early evening meal, to watch a documentary film on the place he would have called home for the next six months with his professor.

"Macquarie Island juts out of the Southern Ocean like a ragged torn piece of thumbnail, cast into the sea by some gigantic being."

The plum-mouthed narrator was aiming for a dramatic effect as he waxed lyrical in the voice-over, and Jeremy found it hard not to laugh.

"It has the unique distinction of being the only place on the planet

directly connected to the Earth's mantle at the end of the Macquarie Ridge … constantly buffeted and blasted by the tempestuous weather which lashes it mercilessly, as life clings doggedly to its surfaces. Howling Antarctic winds and raging tides have carved the landmass into bizarre, sculpted forms. The middle of the island lies low to the sea and is particularly vulnerable to high tides and wind-driven storms. The hills at either end of the island give the whole a strange carved bowl or saddle shape in cross-section."

Jeremy had wriggled a little in his uncomfortable chair, alternately fascinated by the scenery and amused by the slightly stilted BBC-like enunciation of the narrator and the narrative itself. He had twisted his neck around to gauge the reaction from the other expeditioners; judging by the way they either slouched or sat straight in their seats, they fell into two distinct groups—those who, like Jeremy, had never visited and who were interested, and those who, like the professor, had been stationed there before, had no doubt seen the slightly outdated documentary on previous voyages, and were bored. He had glanced across to the professor sitting beside him, then returned his attention to the screen and the slightly sermon-like quality of the narration.

"Lichens and tussocky grasses have adapted over millennia and somehow abound in this hostile climate, while the myriad birds and sea mammals that nest or colonise its rocky cliffs and shorelines enjoy a sanctuary these days almost untouched by predators."

The soundtrack became dramatic as the narrator droned on…

"a cruel and bloody time, when the seals and sea lions were hunted almost to extinction for their pelts and fat."

Jeremy winced at the graphic scenes of the hunters clubbing seals and pups to death.

"…but those barbarous days are long gone now, and the colonies have re-established themselves beyond their previously abundant numbers."

Jeremy sat straighter in his chair; this is what he was here for!

"The main scourge of the island remained long after the sealers' departure, though; rabbits, introduced by the sealers as a food source, and left to breed unimpeded. Rabbits, which destroyed habitat, ate the grasses and threatened to send the native species extinct. Rats and mice arrived too, unwelcome stowaways on the wooden ships."

In the neighbouring chair, the professor had noticed Jeremy's movement. He had leant across and whispered in Jeremy's ear, "Don't worry, laddie, we all have to endure this. It seems to be the cost of a berth on the voyage, but it really *is* informative. We watch the same doco every time. It's old but accurate. This bit's about us, laddie!" The older man had ruffled Jeremy's hair, laughed softly and returned his attention to the screen.

"The scientists who followed the sealers many years later have marvelled at the pristine nature of the place, and its value to scientific studies. They have brought in dogs to search out and destroy the rabbits and have begun an eradication program on the other rodents and feral cats, to protect the native wildlife ... and at the same time, these scientists and rangers have established for themselves a permanent station at the base of what they have named Wireless Hill on the northern end of the island; from here they can carry out their various tests, monitor flora and fauna populations, and do vital research into changing weather patterns and climate fluctuations, in the primeval environment and unpolluted air."

"Looks like a wild place, all right, Prof!" Jeremy had whispered.

"Although they arrive on the island each year, the population of twenty to forty scientists and rangers recognise their privileged role as temporary custodians of this lonely and isolated place; they take great care to remove all their waste, and they do not encroach on the nesting places and breeding grounds more often than to tag, monitor and study.

"As the whole place is inhospitable to humans, those who live there are not permanent fixtures; they ebb and flow like the tides, staying for six months or a year at a time, before returning to their homes further north. Their needs must be met by icebreakers and their crews who battle and navigate their ways through treacherous waters, icebergs, and astounding storms. Every single commodity a human could need has to be transported there by ship; sometimes even the bravest mariners and sturdy, thick-hulled ships are helpless before the might of the Antarctic's rage. Life at these latitudes is no place for the foolhardy or the weak of will."

Jeremy sighed as he remembered the hoots of derisive laughter and ragged applause which greeted the end of the documentary. Supper and hot drinks had been served, and then, for the most part, the passengers had departed to their cabins, to pack their belongings, to rest and prepare for their arrival on the island the next afternoon.

"Ah well" Jeremy observed aloud, "the best-laid plans..."

Chapter five

Elsewhere in the Southern Ocean
Early morning

Away to the south-west at dawn, the crew of eight illegal fishermen on the shabby little trawler *Santa Teresa* were preparing to haul in the nets they had laid out the previous night.

The captain, Jorge Gonzalez, was in the smoky little wheelhouse while his son Jeronimo was following his father's orders, to go below to hurry the crew along, to get to the deck and the holds, ready to salt and stow the fish as it came inboard. As Jeronimo entered the cramped, fuggy little mess, the four men who had been on duty the previous night had just woken up and were eating. They were talking loudly and jovially amongst themselves as they ate, scooping up a mass of eggs and beans into soft burritos, and shovelling in large mouthfuls without drawing a breath, or missing a word, it seemed.

A couple of the younger crew members, so-called "fishermen" who had drifted down from Colombia, were regaling their two companions with their tale of excitement whilst out in the motor launch late the night before; the older men were alternately listening to the young braggarts or talking amongst themselves.

Jeronimo opened his mouth to give the order to get them all moving, to haul in the catch, but one of the young men was in the middle of a tale.

"We fixed one of those thieves," young Ernesto was boasting, waving his food in the air. "Yeah, we fixed him good".

"Oh yeah, youngster, what did you do?" one of the older hands asked cynically. He had been at sea, fishing to feed his family, and make a little money on the side, for many years.

"I shot him!" Ernesto crowed proudly. He looked eagerly around him, seeking approbation in their eyes, and getting a couple of nods from his friend to confirm his story.

Jeronimo stepped forward into the mess. "Who did you shoot, Ernesto? A mermaid?"

Laughter erupted around the youngster, who blushed fiercely.

"No, no, it was a seal, a really big seal. It was down at the nets doing something with some other seals. I reckoned they were stealing the fish, so I shot it!"

Jeronimo stared at the youngster in alarm, then hurriedly composed his face to show no emotion.

"Why would you do that, Ernesto?" he asked quietly, almost silkily.

"I already tol' you, it was stealing our fish. They're our fish, not some furry thief's."

"You been walking on dry land without brain food for too long. Don't you know it's bad luck to kill a seal? They don't eat toothfish!"

"Yeah, bad luck for the seal!" guffawed the other stranger, leaning forward to clap a protective hand on Ernesto's shoulder. "What are *you* going to do, eh, Jeronimo? Tell your *papa?*" The man leant across the table towards him, almost intimidatingly.

"No. But don't go shooting at anything else, okay?" he shouted at the men, swinging on his heel to leave the room, momentarily forgetting why he had come. Suddenly the atmosphere had become stifling in that confined space, and Jeronimo needed clean air. A shudder passed through his muscular frame as he wrenched open the door to escape.

"Or what? Whatcha gon' do 'bout it, eh?"

Jeronimo heard the taunt as he left the room. He didn't even pause to make a reply. But he was determined that he *would* speak with his father at the earliest possible opportunity about replacing the newcomers. These new crew members were no fishermen; that much was for sure.

To kill a seal! Something deep inside him was thoroughly repulsed by the idea. Patagonian toothfish were a good cash crop, he knew that, and he figured they were not depleting the oceans with what they took. Their little vessel was not like those huge factory ships and the enormous fleets that raped the oceans until there was nothing left. Besides, his children needed food and clothing. But a seal… would a seal eat something as large as a toothfish? *No!* He knew seals would look for smaller prey. He felt the playful mammals had a right to exist, but his views were not always shared by older, hungrier, more desperate men. Anything that ate "their" fish was a rival, and something to be eliminated. Jeronimo shuddered. The two Colombians sported teardrop tattoos on their cheeks, and he knew what those signified; killing would mean nothing to them, obviously. How his father had ever been induced to give them a berth on this vessel, he was afraid to ask.

If you might not like the answer, better not to ask the question, he chided himself.

He shook his head and started along the companionway, then stopped abruptly, remembering his mission. Quickly retracing the few steps to the tiny mess, he poked his head around the doorway and gave the orders to start hauling in the nets.

"Bad luck to kill a seal, you know", Jeronimo remarked with a studied casual air, "almost as bad as killing an albatross."

He withdrew his head from the open doorway, but not before he had heard a collective intake of breath as the men within gasped and crossed themselves repeatedly; as he walked away once more, he could hear the murmurs of the two older men praying aloud to the Virgin Mary, their *star of the sea*, for deliverance from a watery grave, or worse, empty holds. He could also hear the sounds of breakfast being hastily concluded, coffee mugs clanging onto the table, plates tossed noisily into the wash-up bowl. He knew what those two thugs thought of him, but he really didn't care. On Captain Jorge's vessel, there were no passengers, and he had earned his right to be there; he wasn't just the captain's son. The older men respected him for his willingness to work hard and pull his weight; if others didn't like him, tough luck.

Back on deck the two other crew members were cranking up the elderly machines to bring up the night's catch, while his father kept a watchful eye from the wheelhouse.

Jeronimo in turn watched his father closely; he almost knew what the older man was thinking. They had been fishing these waters for the much sought-after and endangered Patagonian toothfish for more than a year now, father and son together, and the haul was usually lucrative and worth the risks of interception and the dangers of foul weather. The buyers at the end of each trip were hard men, and would drive a hard bargain, but they all knew that the rich people of Asia and Europe would pay good money for this commodity, and his father always held out for the best price he could wring from them. *Santa Teresa* was only a small trawler, and they had made little more than a subsistence living from fishing until they had entered the shady world of the toothfish trade. Certainly, the families of the crew had enjoyed a better quality of life in their villages because of their menfolk spending months at sea, and the illegal trade had paid off, until now.

On deck, the equipment was cranking up to haul in the nets. Even a small vessel like this could have up to a kilometre of nets strung out in the ocean and bringing them up to the surface and reeling them in was a time-consuming business, even with the aid of mechanisation.

Everyone knew his place; the captain was still in the cramped little wheelhouse but was bellowing orders through the open door. He commanded a higher view from his position and could oversee the procedure as well as steer the vessel; keeping everything (and everyone) in line was no mean feat for the man, experienced though he was.

Jeronimo, on the deck, was also watching the procedure carefully. This was always the moment of truth; if something went wrong with the motor, then a whole night's fishing could go for nothing. Nets had had to be cut adrift before when machinery failed; it was a costly exercise, and one his father could not afford and would not tolerate willingly.

This morning, as if the dark gods of the seas had heard his thoughts, the mechanism jammed, as one of the nets seemed to catch on something. There were muttered and shouted curses and a lot of heaving to free up the nets so the precious catch could be landed. The net full of writhing fish and drowned sea creatures swung precariously at the end of the spar, sea water streaming back through the mesh into the ocean. Men strained muscles and risked their lives to get the catch in, scrambling over the spar to free the net and take the strain off the gantry.

What came up out of the nets once they had heaved it clear of the ship's hull left them stunned and speechless. Tangled in the nets was a black shape.

"*Santisima Virgen Maria,*" Jeronimo whispered. "We've landed a seal!"

The large mammal was rolled unceremoniously from the nets out onto the deck. As the sea water drained away from it, something very peculiar and unheard-of happened. The seal's body changed in front of their shocked eyes. There was a collective gasp of disbelief as the entire crew watched the bizarre transformation. Superstitious and religious to a man, the crew crossed themselves repeatedly in the face of the inexplicable, for what lay on the deck was a *man*. The man was an *anglo*, and very obviously dead.

His limbs were covered by a long, dark coat. He sprawled untidily on the deck floor, head to one side; his face fish-belly white, with lips and eyelids slack and cyanosed, partially covered by long, tangled greying hair spilling onto the deck while the stupefied crew just gazed at it in utter and speechless terror. This was an omen of the very worst kind. The older men knew there would be no more fishing today.

"What are we going to do, Papa?" called Jeronimo to Jorge, who had leapt from the wheelhouse and was barrelling across the slippery deck.

"Throw him back overboard!" yelled the Colombians.

"But Papa!" Jeronimo protested. "We can't just throw him back into the sea!"

"No, they're right. We must get rid of him. Too many questions to answer if we're caught with a body. Throw him back into the sea!"

"But Papa!"

"Do as you are told, boy! This is bad luck to bring to our boat."

"How is he bad luck, Papa? How is he bringing bad luck to our boat? He is the one who has had the bad luck to die in our nets. He has not brought the bad luck to us. Ask the *estúpido* who killed a seal last night!" Jeronimo pointed a finger at the young man who had bragged freely about his exploits with the rifle. "Seals don't eat toothfish, you stupid land-walking *bastardo*, they eat small, small fish. Why did you kill it?" he screamed at the Colombian. "*You* are the one who brings bad luck to this ship, not this poor dead *anglo*!"

He and Ernesto faced off against each other, white-faced with fury. Ernesto's fingers were flexing as if he were looking for a knife; nobody spoke to him like that back in Bogota, not if they wanted to live. The Colombian clenched his fists and glanced at the captain. The look on Jorge's face was enough to make the young crew member change his tactics; the captain was plainly incandescent with rage.

"Oh, boss" Ernesto whined, "I didn't *know*… I didn't *think*—"

"Enough! Stop now! Your mother obviously mated with a donkey!" Jorge had had enough of this confrontation. He was furious with his son for challenging his authority in front of the crew, but he was equally furious with some unknown slut's stupid land-crawling offspring for bringing their voyage into danger and making the older men uneasy.

Jeronimo was not taking any notice of the insults being hurled around; he was staring in disbelief, certain he had seen the corpse's fingers twitch on the deck.

He tried to grab his father's arm, to make him look, but the older man shrugged him off and barked out orders.

"Throw him back into the sea! Now! This instant!"

"Yes, yes, captain, throw him back now!" one of the newcomers glared at Jeronimo and backed the boss. "This instant, boss. This instant! We need to keep fishing."

"But, Papa, he is *alive!*"

"*What*? *Where*? Don't be stupid! You're imagining things, boy! Nothing is moving; his chest doesn't move, he doesn't breathe. He's dead, you *idiot!*"

To the young Colombian he shouted, "and don't tell me what to do on *my* vessel. It's not yours yet! No more fishing today – we're going home!"

Jeronimo persisted, "But Papa, I saw his fingers move, I'm sure of it!"

"You *estúpido*," he shouted, turning on his son, "you are as bad as your *estúpido* shipmate. Get out of my sight! Both of you! You make me sick!" Turning back to the crew milled around the nets, he spat, "Throw him back, this instant! Do it!"

"No!" yelled Jeronimo. He strode forward and leant over the body. The coat shrouding the corpse interested the young man. He leant down and tentatively touched it. There was a sudden intake of air, hissing into the silence as the men started crossing themselves again. Such bad luck to touch a corpse, unless you were a midwife, a priest or the gravedigger.

Bending down further, Jeronimo examined the coat's back. He was sure he could see a spot of white on the dark fur. He squinted, looking even closer.

It wasn't a spot, it was a hole. He wondered how there could be a hole, such a neat small hole, in the back of the coat, when the rest of it remained untouched.

He put his index finger to the coat, and inserted it through the hole.

"Papa!" he called urgently. "This is a hole. It looks too even, too neat to be a tear from the nets or the hooks. Help me lift the coat!" he snapped at the crewmen.

They all took a step backwards, as if the corpse would rise and taint them.

Jeronimo wriggled his finger onto the flesh beneath the coat; he could feel a hole in the body's back.

"You!" he shouted, straightening up and whirling around to face the newcomer, Ernesto. "Kill a seal, did you? You killed a *man*, you stupid piece of dog shit. This is a bullet hole! You stupid son of a whore!" he hissed at the young man. "Do you want us all to hang?"

Ernesto produced a filleting knife from his boot and levelled it at Jeronimo. "Call me a son of a whore, you sea scum!" He threw himself towards the captain's son, murder in his eyes. "No one speaks to me like that," he screamed, "not if they want to live!"

"Grab him!" screeched Jorge. "He's mad. This is completely crazy! Stop!"

"Yes, boss!" came the male chorus, and the Colombian was grabbed; the knife was wrestled out of his hand. One of the crew kicked the weapon and sent it skidding across the deck. They hauled him below, to lock him up as securely as they could. The fight had gone out of Ernesto, as the madness faded from his eyes, but the hate in them remained. "I'll settle with you later," he yelled as he was dragged away.

Jorge and Jeronimo were left facing each other across the slimy deck. The body lay between them.

"Give me a hand, son", Jorge said quietly. "Now, before the men come back. We must toss it overboard before we sail. Too many eyes have seen this body already. Now, let's rid ourselves of it, so we can go home."

"But Papa," came the protest. "He murdered a man!"

"Enough!" Jorge repeated. "Do you think it would be the first man he's killed? Haven't you seen his tattoos? Just do as I say. Now!"

They moved to either end of the dead man, picked him up by hands and feet. Together they swung him to gain momentum, then heaved him over the side without further delay.

Tossing the body back into the sea was a bad omen, but to keep it on board, taking up precious space, and even more precious ice; to run the risk of having to explain its presence to maritime authorities, would be even worse for these men.

Jeronimo shuddered.

He realised that he feared the same fate befalling him; to be swept away by a freak wave, and not to be at least *sought*... No, the very thought made him shiver. He crossed himself swiftly, urgently, dipped his hand inside his tee shirt, and lifted out the gold cross on a chain around his neck. He raised the cross to his lips and kissed it fervently.

"Most sacred Virgin mother" he whispered, "Pardon us our transgressions, and pardon that man for the heartless bastard he is."

He slipped the precious cross on its chain back under his shirt, glared at his father, and leaned over the rail to watch the heaving waves for signs of the unwanted corpse. No-one had checked it for signs of life. Only those who had helped to physically lift the net inboard had approached it; they were all superstitious about death, especially a dead seal who appears from the sea in their nets and turns into a man in front of their very eyes. In the strengthening seas, the body floated momentarily, buoyed by the air trapped within the coat and then sank beneath the choppy waves.

***

As the illegal fishermen dumped him overboard, believing him already deceased, Dougal became vaguely aware of an unexpected warmth in the freezing water; two bodies, warm, furred bodies nudged and manoeuvred him between them, lifting him until he lay cradled in a hollow formed where their bodies touched. He had momentarily regained consciousness, but he knew that his lifeblood was ebbing away from the gunshot wound in his back; he could not last long, now.

Thank you, my brothers and sisters... Consciousness was ebbing, fast.

Rest now, grandfather... we will carry you home, came the gentle reply.

At the instant he had been tossed back into the sea with a resounding splash, the grey-brown seals had appeared from beneath the trawler. They had been trailing him ever since he had become tangled in the nets' fatal embrace and been pulled from the sea.

As his remaining life-force leaked away into the water, he surrendered himself to the seals' tender warmth. The universe danced diminishingly before his closed eyes, his dying brain fed his bursting eardrums with the threads of the haunting refrain of an old Orcadian folksong he had learnt as a child, as he danced in his delirium with his beloved wife one last time out amongst the stars and then… the universe winked out forever.

***

"Pan Pan Pan."

The distress message was squawking tinnily and continuously from the HF radio in *Santa Teresa*'s cramped wheelhouse as Jorge struggled to turn the vessel around and set course for home in the high seas.

He reached over to the radio set and deliberately turned down the volume; this day had been long enough already, and he had a throbbing pain in his back and side. There was no way he was going to respond to the distress call; the catch, such as it was, was in the hold, the body disposed of, and they were running for home. The mystery of the transformation from sea mammal to human would never be answered, Jorge knew; who could he speak to about such a thing, anyway? The local priest and other fishermen would think him *loco*, and anyway, he had broken the law by throwing the man back to the sea. Worse, he had probably broken some Divine law by not saying some words of prayer for the departed; the priest would take a very dim view of his actions, indeed. No, there was nothing to be said about any of it, but Jorge suspected he would brood on it for a long time. Never, in all his long years at sea, had he ever witnessed anything as frightening as that. He shuddered and winced at the twinge in his back.

The fish they had hauled up this morning were pitifully few, yet neither Jorge nor the other, older crew members were willing to lay out the nets again in that area, even though the Colombians argued loud and long about the captain's decision. The real fishermen were afraid that the corpse would return to haunt them from the depths once more. Better to cut their losses and go home. Although fish is cash, and hunger is the most powerful incentive to find food, Jorge was in pain and in an equally foul temper. In their part of the world, there always seemed to be more hunger than fish, especially in families that continued to grow each year. But the dead man was more than any of them had bargained for. His son's open defiance and confrontation on deck was almost more than he could bear, and he was determined to reach their home port and dispose of the ill-omened catch as soon as possible. It would be a while before the young man would be going to sea with his father again, Jorge decided. He was angry with his son's insubordination in front of the rest of the crew, and he would not tolerate such behaviour or let any man defy his captain, and soon there would be trouble at sea.

As if his father's thoughts had summoned him, Jeronimo pushed open the storm door and stepped over the threshold into the tiny wheelhouse, and noticed the radio had been turned down, but his keen ears picked up the urgent message. A Pan call meant something bad had happened at sea.

"What are you going to do about the man we threw back, Papa?" the younger man asked. "And are you going to answer the distress call?"

The captain shrugged, unwilling to talk to his son.

"There's nothing we *can* do, boy, without giving ourselves away. Someone else's problem, somewhere else. None of our business. You know only too well those *bastardos* from *Sea Guardian* will be all over us if we get involved, or if we announce our presence to them. You know what we do is illegal. Use your brains, if you have any!"

"What's the call about, Papa? Are they looking for that *anglo* we pulled in? And how come he turned into a man from a seal? Have you ever seen anything like it in your life before?" Jeronimo persisted.

Santa Maria, Madre de Dios, would the boy never stop with his annoying questions? Jorge took a deep, calming breath. It wouldn't be clever to lose his temper so far from home. His blood pressure was already high from this morning's events; his head was pounding, his back throbbed and his chest was now hurting.

"Probably. He wouldn't have lasted long in these seas, and at this temperature – it would have been a waste of time, anyway. And I have no idea what happened out there on the deck. I've never seen anything like it in my life. And there's no one I could ask about it. They'd all think I had gone *loco*. No!" he grunted. "We continue on our way home. Let the *anglos* waste their time looking for him. Better for us, eh? They won't be looking for us if they're busy looking for him. Those few fish in our hold mean at least some food in my grandchildren's bellies, eh?"

In an effort to pull himself out of his black humour, he reached across and slapped the younger man heavily on the shoulder, then spun him around and pushed him towards the door. "Just go and do your job, lad. Go and make those lazy crewmen of yours work. Let me worry about avoiding the *bandidos,* eh? And not a word to anyone ashore about the ghost from the sea, the dead one. It will have to be our secret. *Ours,* understand me? And tell those other good-for-nothings, those *bastardos* to say nothing about this morning, either."

The younger man looked back at his boss, his father; he *knew* the old man was right, and that their families had to be fed, but it just seemed so *wrong* somehow, to know that a seal had been dredged up in their nets, had transformed into a white man and then as unceremoniously been tossed back into the sea, like some piece of garbage. Jeronimo Gonzalez did not consider himself a particularly clever man, nor well-educated. He was just a simple fisherman, but he had been taught right from wrong, and his father had most definitely done the wrong thing this morning. In that instant, he lost some of the deep respect he had always felt for the older man. Fathers were supposed to be infallible.

"Yes, Papa," he muttered unhappily, "yes, okay." He turned to leave, then hesitated.

"Papa," he asked quietly, "just one question. Who are those men you've taken on as crew? They sure as hell aren't fishermen, they know nothing of the sea, and last night one of them was seasick. Who *are* they?"

Jorge turned and glared at this son; he had been dreading this question since they had set sail from South America. His son was too smart, by far.

"They're from a larger outfit, Jerri, they want me to work for a larger operation. They've been sent to see how much fish we take. If we run for home now, with only a small catch, maybe their bosses will figure we're no use to them and leave us alone. At least, that's what I'm hoping. The man I usually sell the catch to is just a small player. The big players want to cut him out of the operation. Understand? We have a small catch. Tough luck. We're heading home. End of story. Now go do your work, and let's get home, and put this morning behind us. Okay?"

Jorge reached across and squeezed Jeronimo's shoulder meaningfully, looking him square in the eye. "Say nothing of this to your wife or children. Above all, say nothing, I beg you, to your mother!"

"Yes, Papa, okay."

Jeronimo left the wheelhouse, pulling the door shut behind him and took several deep breaths. Straightening his shoulders, he trod down to the deck to ensure that the nets and gear had been properly stowed away for the trip back north, and to warn the crew to keep their mouths firmly shut. If the Colombians and their bosses were going to be unhappy, tough luck.

Unfortunately, Jeronimo hadn't counted on the murderous rage Hernan had been nursing in his twisted brain; pride and fury fuelled his strength, as the Colombian slipped away from his would-be captors, grabbed up Ernesto's rifle and stealthily crept back up on deck, furtively looking out for anyone else who would challenge him. The man saw two figures in the tiny wheelhouse and headed for them. That stupid fisherman and his even more stupid son were going to pay, big time, for their insolence, but he was cunning enough not to take them both on. He settled down in the lee of the machinery to wait.

***

The seals continued on their way, unimpeded by their burden or the tempestuous seas and worsening weather; unaware of the dramas unfolding above them. They headed south-east, cradling Dougal's dark and lifeless body between them. The bleeding had stopped as the flesh around the entry point of the fatal wound had become waterlogged and bloated, effectively sealing it over. The risk of predators was lessened, but always present. No telling when an orca might happen along, with a yen for a tasty seal-flavoured snack.

They flew through the water together in perfect harmony, always in the same south-easterly direction, until they could reach the Antarctic Circumpolar Current for an easier ride home to their colony.

Somewhere in the rougher, shallower waters near Macquarie Island, much later in the day, they parted in unison and allowed the body to fall away gently. They had spent most of the previous night fishing or being trapped, then following the nets in the early morning; they were tired, and they *needed* to feed more before returning to that outcrop of rocks at the edge of the Southern Ocean they called home. As they went on their way, they called to their families in the colony on the island, singing their lament and despair over the death of one of their own.

Dougal's dark pinniped corpse slipped quietly towards land, borne on the heavy incoming tide. Seals from the island's colony, keening loudly to each other through the chilly waters and alerted by an innate intuition which bound them all, then took over the task of shepherding the body towards a wave-carved outcrop of rock, where it lodged and nestled, trapped between two huge boulders. For now, this resting place would have to suffice… the crabs and other scavengers would make sure his body soon returned to the elements.

***

On the trawler, Hernan waited until Jeronimo had left the wheelhouse after the argument with his father, then he acted. He slipped silently to the wheelhouse door, poked the rifle's barrel through the slightly open door and fired. He was not sure if he had hit the older man, but it would give him a big scare, all right. He hid behind a piece of machinery, while the others came running. He would show *them* who they were working for! *He* was in control, now. Pounding footsteps along the deck, wait till they're all busy then slip back into the cabin. He considered throwing the rifle overboard, so no blame would attach to him or Ernesto, but clipped the safety on and got out of there.

Chapter

six

In the wheelhouse on *Santa Teresa*, Jorge had turned back to check their course setting when there was a deafening report in the tiny space. His hearing was muffled, he was suddenly very tired, and breathing heavily. There was a constant, sharp pain in his back now, and his chest felt tight. Jorge considered calling his son back to take over from him so he could go below deck to lie down for a few minutes, but his attention was arrested by the sight of an ominous *blip* on the tiny radar screen mounted on the bulwark. He leaned in closer, to try to figure out how far away it was; as he did, a sharp incapacitating stab of pain pierced his chest from back to front, and he lurched into the wheel, grabbing it for all he was worth, in order not to fall.

He could not breathe; his chest was on fire!

He opened his mouth to call Jeronimo, but no word passed his lips. Gripping the wheel for all it was worth, he slowly lost his battle to stay upright, and the wheel spun away from his increasingly loosening grip. Jorge crumpled to the floor, effectively blocking the space; he tore futilely at his shirt and tried to breathe. Black spots danced in front of his eyes as he lost consciousness; his last thoughts were of the man they had thrown overboard so callously. Surely this must be a judgement, his punishment from God.

Jeronimo, on the slippery deck, stopped abruptly from shouting his orders to the crew; he had heard a *crack* which had come from the wheelhouse; he could feel that something had gone very wrong up there. The little trawler was changing direction and had stopped challenging the high waves; it was wallowing and slewing around into the deepening troughs and allowing the sea to hit it amidships. What on Earth was his father doing up there? He looked up, shielding his eyes from the water battering the deck viciously, searching for Jorge's familiar figure. There was no one there; why would his father allow the vessel to change course? If he had wanted to go below, he would have shouted to Jeronimo or one of the crew to take over. Jeronimo started running, slipping and stumbling across an increasingly slick and treacherously heaving deck to the streaming metal rungs of the steps up to the wheelhouse. He hauled himself up there, chest heaving from the effort of battling the wind and the waves and tried to open the storm door; it wouldn't budge. He wiped rivulets of salt water away from the Perspex window and peered in; no one there, at first glance. He tried the door again; something was obstructing it. He stood on tiptoe and angled his gaze down; he saw his father's body on the floor, head hard against the door. He let out a shout of panic and tried frantically to open the door. By pushing slowly, he was able to open it far enough to put one foot in the opening, while he bent down and tried to wriggle his shoulder and arm in, to push the man's body out of the way, so he could get to the abandoned wheel. Noises behind him alerted him that the other crew members had arrived; there was a lot of confusion as men tried to shout over the top of each other, and the wind and the waves provided their own contribution to the mayhem. Finally, Jeronimo managed to reach in far enough to grab the freely spinning wheel and held on tightly.

"Get help!" he yelled to the men still on the deck, looking up at the unfolding drama above.

"Any help we can get is in there!" they screamed back. "Get the door open!"

"What's the matter with your papa?" one cried.

"I don't know! Grab a grappling hook or something I can push him out of the way with!" Jeronimo yelled back. "If we don't get control of the wheel, we'll go under!"

Three sodden men slipped and scrambled their way across the streaming deck to grab something that would get the injured man out of harm's way while they opened the wheelhouse door. The slapping noises of their wet footsteps were muffled by the rising wind, but their shouts reached Jeronimo's ears as he stood, wedged in the tiny opening, twisted at an almost impossible angle to try and maintain some control over the wheel; he felt his wrist would snap any moment if they could not get his father's stocky body out of the way. They were all in deep trouble, and no one knew where they were; the sea was tossing their vessel around like a child's bath toy, and they were in grave danger of the mast snapping or the machinery giving way and killing someone. Jeronimo suddenly and illogically felt a pang of conscience and guilt for confronting his father. What had happened, to make Jorge pass out on the floor?

A sudden jab at his shoulder jerked Jeronimo back to reality, as a sharp-bladed hook on a long pole was thrust into his free hand; how he was going to manoeuvre it through the door, he didn't know.

"Santiago!" he yelled to the man behind him. "Take this and see if you can get an end through this gap and push Papa's body out of the way, but gently! Don't want to injure him more than necessary." Jeronimo wriggled his body off to one side, as far away from the base of the door as possible, to insert the pole through the gap. The heaving seas did not make his situation any easier; the little trawler was yawing badly, pushed this way and that by the powerful waves; if he slipped, he would be badly injured or tossed overboard from this height. He shuddered at the thought; what made him shiver almost uncontrollably was not the biting cold of soaked clothes and skin, but the memory of what he and his father had done, in consigning a dead man to the depths without even a prayer for the lost one's soul. Was this judgement sent upon him and his parent? He couldn't even let go for an instant to cross himself; he had never felt quite so helpless in his life.

Grunting, his father's lifelong friend and *compadre*, Santiago poked at the inert body with the blunt end of the pole.

"It's no good, young one," he growled at Jeronimo, "I'll have to reverse the pole and try to hook his trousers and push him out of the way. Stand aside if you can." So saying, the older man carefully withdrew the pole, reversed it, and inserted the wicked-looking hook through the gap and felt around like a blind man until it met some resistance. "Got 'im!" he panted, and pushed with all his might.

Suddenly, the resistance was gone from the door and Jeronimo literally fell into the tiny space.

"Oy, careful, lad! You'll end up stuck like a fish on the business end of that hook!" Hands grabbed his icy wet clothes and hauled him upright on the sill of the room; together they looked in at Jorge. The old man's lips were blue; there was no rising or falling of the powerful chest. He looked dead, as dead as the man on the deck, Jeronimo realised; the young man's teeth were chattering, and he was now trembling all over with shock, freezing wet clothes and the cold coils of fear which had turned his belly to ice. Suddenly, work-roughened hands were manhandling him down the few steps to the deck, and he was bundled below, to be stripped, towelled and redressed like a small child. Yet he could not stop shaking, and he needed to be with his father. He was sure his *papa* was dead, but somewhere deep within him was a tiny, flickering candle flame of hope that he was wrong. His lips moved constantly in silent prayer.

He struggled back up to the deck in time to see the familiar faces of Santiago and Edgardo struggling Jorge's body across the deck towards the cabin below. Jeronimo leapt out to help; he looked up at the wheelhouse; Alejo was in charge. The ship had ceased slewing around in the troughs, a plaything for the sea, and had begun meeting the crashing waves head on once more. A small trail of blood mingled with the sea water and was soon washed away, back into the ocean.

As soon as they had Jorge stretched out on a bunk, Santiago and Edgardo piled blankets on top of the inert body, and Jeronimo began chafing the man's hands to warm them up; Jorge was like ice. Edgardo put his ear to Jorge's chest; nothing. There was no heartbeat, no tell-tale rise and fall of the chest. Edgardo looked meaningfully at Santiago; they exchanged an imperceptible nod and a look. Edgardo coughed tellingly and looked at Jeronimo, sorrow in his eyes. "I'm sorry, Jerri," he began, "but your father is no more." The three men swiftly crossed themselves, then Santiago leant forward and gently closed Jorge's eyes. "Goodbye my old friend. Go with God," he whispered. "I'll look after your boy."

Jeronimo was speechless. He slumped down onto the bunk next to his father's body, lowered his lips to the cold lifeless forehead and kissed it gently. Shudders wracked his body, and he buried his face into his father's wet jersey and cried like a baby. Santiago put a weather-beaten hand on the young man's back, patted it gently and rested it there for a second or two before he and Edgardo left the youngster to grieve. The two crewmen looked at each other but were silent until they had the privacy of the wind-swept deck once more.

***

"We'll have to put him on ice, unless Jeronimo wants him buried at sea," Edgardo observed.

"Yes," Santiago replied thoughtfully. "The lad blames himself, you know. They had a terrible row about that body that showed up in the nets—I heard them while we were hustling that young

Colombian idiot below. Speaking of Colombian idiots, where's the other one, that Hernan? I haven't seen him since we locked up his buddy. Crazy, the pair of them. I'd love to know why Jorge gave them a berth for this trip – there's something not quite right about either of them. Edgardo my old friend, you, Alejo, Diego and I will have to keep a careful eye on everything if we're to get home safely. I have a bad feeling, a bad feeling this is not over yet."

***

Jeronimo finally managed to control his sobbing and wiped his eyes with the back of his hand; his nose was running, and his wet sleeve had to be a handkerchief for now. He kissed his father's forehead once more, whispered, *"Papá, I'm so sorry,"* and rose wearily to his feet. The trawler had stopped pitching and tossing all over the ocean, and he could at least stand without falling over. Like an old man he made his way to the deck, and smiled wanly at the crew, *his* crew now as they went about the business of pumping out the water that had slopped in while they had been struggling with the wheelhouse door and getting Jorge's body to relative safety. He squinted up and saw Alejo's familiar form at the wheel, and walked across a steadier deck to talk to him.

Jeronimo climbed the few steps up to the wheelhouse and opened the door. Alejo was humming tunelessly to himself as he steered a course for home. Jeronimo looked around and noticed the *blip* on the radar screen.

"Alejo, how long has that blip been there?" he asked the older man.

Alejo shrugged his shoulders expressively. "Dunno, Jerri, just been battling to get the old girl back on course so we can go home. Sorry about your papá."

"Thanks. Life won't be the same without him. Do you want a spell?" Jeronimo asked. "I'm fine to take over now, if you want to go get a coffee from Diego. I thought I smelt some brewing below."

"Thanks, kid. Then I must get back to tidying the lines away. That was quite a blow we had. We shipped some water below decks too."

Jeronimo gave a watery chuckle. "Santiago's already got the pumps working; we should be fine now." He crossed himself superstitiously to ward off more ill luck. He took over the wheel and gave Alejo an absent-minded wave as the older man left the cramped space.

He checked their course; ENE. Ah, so they were going to slip away between New Zealand's South Island and Macquarie Island, out into the South Pacific and then almost due east for South America until they had to turn south to run down the Chilean coast. If they needed to, they could land in Chile and pick up fresh supplies. They would have to negotiate their way around Cape Horn, but at least they would get home. He knew they had enough fuel, but the time it took to reach Argentina would depend on the weather out in the Pacific.

Jeronimo sighed. He wouldn't have wanted it to be this way, not at all; but in a way it felt *good* to be in charge for a change. His father could be a very stubborn man at times. He pondered what to do about his father's body; should they try to store it on whatever ice they could spare from their meagre haul of fish, or should they commit it to the deep, in the time-honoured tradition of seamen.

He pondered about the Colombian they had locked up below, and what to do about the other one too. Ernesto, the hot-headed one, the one who had started this whole debacle, had threatened him. Normally, Jeronimo would have laughed it off, or fought the thug, but a small fishing trawler is a bad place to be at war with another; too many things could be used as weapons, and there was always the danger of going overboard "accidentally" in the middle of the night.

Jeronimo peered at the radar screen; the blip was closer than before. He wondered if it might be another ship searching for the *anglo* they had tossed back into the sea; it would be simple enough to lie, if asked. As long as everyone kept their mouths shut tight. The Colombians were the only unknown quantity, he reflected. The others, Santiago, Alejo, Edgardo and Diego — they were all good men, and loyal to his father.

He reached across and turned up the volume on the radio. The Pan message was still being broadcast. He was about to turn the volume down again when he heard snatches of a crackly conversation. He froze; he had heard the words *Sea Guardian* mentioned. He turned the volume up a little more and tried to comprehend what was being said, but his command of English was limited, and anyway, the transmission was very staticky. He peered again at the radar screen; the vessel was definitely getting closer. He prayed it wasn't the *Sea Guardian* ship he had heard on the radio, but he had a sinking feeling in his guts that it probably was. Ah well, he and his crew would have to tough it out.

A shout from the deck brought Jeronimo out of his reverie; Santiago was shouting and pointing at the horizon off the port side. He had found a battered old pair of binoculars and was concentrating on something Jeronimo couldn't see far in the distance. He glanced at the radar; there it was, coming steadily closer across the screen, a spot lit up in green whenever the needle swept across it. The spot and Santiago's mystery sighting had to be one and the same thing. Jeronimo called down to Diego.

"How fast can we go, Diego? Can we outrun whatever's coming?"

"Fully laden we could do around ten knots, Jerri, but we don't have a big catch on, so we could probably push it up to fifteen. If we run much faster, we'll go through the fuel more quickly and we don't want to run out of gas in the middle of the Pacific."

"Fine. Set the speed to fifteen knots and we'll try to outrun them."

"Okay, Jerri, you're the boss."

Jeronimo wondered if he was doing the right thing, trying to outrun the other vessel; they hadn't really sighted it clearly yet, and already they were acting as if they had something to hide. Perhaps they could just amble along, pretending to be fishing; that gave him an idea.

"Diego, can we run at around eight knots please? I'm going to try to outsmart whoever it is."

"No problems."

Jeronimo called down to Santiago who was intent on the horizon.

"Can you ask Alejo and Edgardo to put out some small nets please, Santiago? If this ship is looking for us, we can pretend we're just simple fishermen trawling for southern blue whiting. Ask Diego to hide the toothfish we have on board, under a heap of ice. And perhaps you could get that other good-for-nothing Colombian bum to help move my father's body onto the ice, to deter any casual snoops."

"Good thinking, Jerri. You're your father's son, all right. If we can't outrun them, we can try to fool them. I still can't see any flags yet, they're too far away, but it won't be long before we sight their colours. I'll keep watch."

"Thanks, *amigo*. I knew I could rely on you."

The older man grunted as he swung his binoculars back to the horizon off the port side.

Jeronimo closed the storm door to keep out the biting cold and kept a watchful eye on the radar screen. He noted their bearing and speed; looking through the rear window he could see the two crew members playing out the shorter nets, one to port and the other to starboard. He smiled; that should deflect any nosiness from the approaching vessel. He turned up the volume on the radio and kept watch.

He didn't have to wait long before Santiago shouted up to him. He opened the door to hear the older man more clearly. "I can see their flags, Jerri. It's those *Sea Guardian* bastards and they're heading straight for us."

"Stay cool, Santiago my friend, stay cool."

He closed the door and concentrated on their course, while listening intently to the radio. He picked up a message which squawked out into the wheelhouse.

"Ahoy, this is *Sea Guardian*, this is *Sea Guardian*. Heave to and prepare to come about."

"*Qué? No entiendo. Lo siento.*"

"*Santa Teresa, Santa Teresa,* this is *Sea Guardian*. Prepare to heave to and come about. Does anyone speak English?"

Jeronimo answered again in Spanish, "I'm sorry. I don't understand."

A disembodied voice came through the static in Spanish, "*Santa Teresa, Santa Teresa,* this is *Sea Guardian. This is Sea Guardian.* Prepare to heave to and come about."

Damnation! They were tricky, these people. He had no option but to shout down the order to Diego to reduce the speed, and prepared to come about, as ordered. He thought it might be better to cooperate; perhaps they would not see through his ruse and leave them to go home.

The seas were churning, and the little trawler bucked and bobbed sickeningly as the speed which had driven it forward was dramatically reduced; they were barely crawling along now, and any further reduction in speed would be dangerous to their safety. The *Sea Guardian* vessel came to within hailing distance and the officer on duty announced his intention to board them. Damn! They were going to have to brazen it out after all.

The next few minutes were a flurry of activity as the other vessel lowered a fast dinghy which sped across the choppy water to them. Uniformed men swarmed up onto the deck, and Jeronimo found himself in the middle of a heated argument. Unfortunately, the Spanish speaker had come across and was demanding to see the captain. This was Jeronimo's big chance to bamboozle them.

"This is my father's boat. He died this morning. I'm captain now."

"Oh, I'm sorry. What's your name?" The man's accent was American, but his Spanish was good enough.

"I'm Jeronimo Gonzalez. And you are?"

"Roddy Griffiths."

"Pleased to meet you, Roddy. How can I help you?"

"Papers? Fishing licence?"

Jeronimo hastened to get the necessary papers and fishing licence from his father's logbook in the wheelhouse, while the newcomers quizzed the crew.

The *Sea Guardian* officer was very interested in what they were doing out here, so far from anywhere. He asked, "Have any of the crew had seen a body? A man fell overboard from a large vessel heading towards Macquarie Island, and there was a general alert in the area. Did any of you hear the distress call?"

"No," Jeronimo explained, "neither I nor my father speak English."

Officer Roddy listened to Jeronimo's story about how Jorge, his father and captain, had suffered a fatal cardiac arrest that morning, and how they were now heading for home in Argentina with the body on ice. His eyebrows lifted in disbelief, and Jeronimo hastened to invite the man down to the hold to see where his father's body was being stored on the ice.

"Why are you carrying ice?"

"Well," Jeronimo explained with many shrugs and gestures, "we came out to fish for Southern Blue Whiting but have not had much luck, so we are heading for our home port, Rio Gallegos, to bear the sad tidings of my father's death to my mother and siblings."

"So," the American persisted, "if you're heading for home in haste, why are you idling along at a slow speed with the nets out?"

"Ah," Jeronimo explained with more gesturing and shrugging, "our holds were empty; we were hoping to catch at least a little to feed our families."

"And," the officer enquired, "how big is the crew?"

"Eight in total," Jeronimo explained, "but my father has died, one is unwell and has been confined to his bunk below, so that leaves six to take the trawler home. Perhaps if you would care to see him?"

Oh yes, the officers were very interested to see both the corpse on ice, and the sick man, in case they could render some medical assistance. Jeronimo hastened to assure them he was not injured—he was unwell with seasickness, as this was his first voyage.

Alejo, Edgardo and Santiago stood by and listened intently to this conversation; they exchanged some meaningful looks and directed warning glances at Jeronimo from time to time; the lad was becoming a little cocky in his attitude.

The American and his bulky blond Scandinavian assistant indicated to Jeronimo that they would now like to go below decks to check out his story; Jeronimo shot a worried glance at the three older men, but they stood still, watched intently by the other, armed officers. It was an international crew; a quick glance at them confirmed that one was a slim, watchful Asian, the other a tall, well-developed but sun-burnt northerner. It was not obvious that either of them spoke Spanish, but he warned his crew anyway.

"Stay here. Say nothing in case they speak Spanish!" The older men nodded.

Jeronimo led the way with reluctance to the hold, where the American and his assistant indifferently inspected Jorge's body, then lifted it out of the way to conduct a thorough search of the packed ice. Traces of congealed blood flecked the ice where Jorge's body had lain. Eyebrows were raised; questions asked, and the corpse was turned over. There, in the middle of the old man's back was a wound that had oozed blood through his shirt and jacket onto the ice. Suddenly the whole deal turned very serious, and the *Sea Guardian's* crew was on high alert. Jeronimo let out an anguished scream at the sight. He was sure his father had suffered a fatal heart attack, but no! Someone had murdered him in cold blood! Although the older men had piled plenty of ice on top of the meagre catch of toothfish, the illicit haul was also soon discovered, and Jeronimo knew he was in a lot of trouble. The only thing that would save them now was the fact that, due to the seal-man's untimely appearance in the nets that morning, they had suspended their fishing in those waters before they had amassed a larger haul of their illegal booty. The American explained to Jeronimo in his accented Spanish that he and the crew would be fined on the spot, and that their licence to fish would be revoked; the crew could also be prosecuted for illegal, unreported and unregulated fishing under the United Nations Convention on the Law of the Sea.

Jeronimo protested, claiming that their catch had been accidental, that they had been fishing for southern blue whiting all along, that surely such a small quantity of toothfish was nothing… The *Sea Guardian* officer was adamant; the crew would be fined and lose their licence. Their gill nets would be confiscated. Their paperwork would be taken back to *Sea Guardian*. Any trouble and the crew could be placed under arrest.

Right about now, Hernan, the elusive Colombian, and Ernesto, whom Jeronimo blamed fully for his father's death through the slaughter of the seal man, made their appearance, Ernesto being brought by crew members from his makeshift prison. They were innocent, they claimed; they had signed on to catch whiting, they protested; it was all Jeronimo and his father's fault if there was illicit fish in the hold! They had nothing to do with anything!

At this point, Jeronimo, who had kept his temper under control throughout the whole proceedings, turned on the pair, screaming at them that it was all *their* fault, and especially Ernesto's, that his father had died, after the stress of finding a seal that Ernesto had shot with a high-powered rifle in their nets, and how the Colombian had brought bad luck to the ship in more ways than one. Ernesto's temper flared; he had not forgotten or forgiven the humiliation dealt to him by Jeronimo earlier in the day. He started screaming back, threatening Jeronimo with pain beyond belief for daring to speak to him in that way. Hernan stayed silent. Roddy and his companions, unarmed and alarmed by the potential for violence, now suggested calmly but firmly that perhaps everyone should simmer down and that the whole crew should reassemble on the deck.

Ernesto did his best to implicate Jeronimo and Jorge as the masterminds of the illegal fishing operation; Jeronimo shouted that if it hadn't been for Ernesto shooting and killing a seal, they wouldn't be in this mess. Listening to the rancorous exchange, the Spanish-speaking *Sea Guardian* officer quietly ordered his companion to search for weapons; a high-powered rifle was quickly unearthed beneath Hernan's bunk along with a quantity of knives.

Jeronimo thought quickly; he could rid himself of these useless Colombians and perhaps curry some favour with the *Sea Guardian* officers at the same time. He motioned Roddy aside, and spoke to him very quietly; with much gesturing and shrugging of shoulders, he told him what Jorge had revealed to him shortly before his unexpected death, about the Colombians' presence on the boat, how they were certainly no sailors, let alone fishermen, how they had bullied his father on behalf of a larger syndicate of illegal fishing fleets and how Jorge had resisted their threats.

He spoke of how Ernesto in particular had threatened him, Jeronimo, in the presence of the other crew members and had attacked him with a filleting knife over the shooting death of a seal. About the seal's other-worldly transformation into a man, he said not one word; the officer would think he was totally crazy! And about his father's and his action in throwing the dead man back into the sea, he could never confess such a deed, either.

Roddy offered to remove Jorge's body for an autopsy ashore, but Jeronimo stubbornly refused; he had to take his father home for a proper burial, or his mother would never forgive him. The officer also suggested that Jeronimo lock up both Colombians and contact the Coast Guard when they were closer to land, if Jeronimo felt there was a case to answer against the two foreigners. He apologised for not being able to arrest and remove the Colombians, along with their weapons. He could and did confiscate all the gill nets and the trawler's papers and departed, after issuing Jeronimo with a large fine to pay, and taking photos of the illegal toothfish haul.

As soon as the motor launch had left them, Jeronimo barked out orders to imprison Ernesto and Herman and lock up the weapons; to pull up the smaller nets and get under way at the best possible speed; they had been out here long enough. He was not able to go back for more fish; they would have to make do with what they had. Their families wouldn't go hungry, and the greedy middlemen could go to hell. He just wanted to get his father home for burial, if it was at all possible. The men looked at each other and shrugged. Sometimes the sea treated them well; sometimes it did not. Such was life.

Chapter seven

Thousands of kilometres to the north-west, someone was, in fact, listening. While he waited for his mate, Jacko, to swing by to pick him up for their weekly game of golf that morning, Andy Grey decided it was useless going down to the shed to tinker with his engines before going out for a long walk and a few desultory swings at a silly little white ball.

Andy's wife had strongly encouraged him to take up the game as a way of staying fit once he retired after thirty years of active employment. Andy really didn't know what he thought about the whole idea, but was inclined to agree with Mark Twain's opinion of golf as being "a waste of a good walk". He made himself a coffee and wandered through the living room to his "office". That way he would know when his mate arrived to collect him and the golf clubs.

He sat down on his rolling chair, and slid into the cramped little cubby that was his personal radio domain. Built into an alcove off the living room, this area was chock-full of equipment, all housed on shelves which started just above desk level and just kept mounting up the wall behind. On either side of the built-in desk was a small table, each supporting an open and active laptop. On the desk itself stood transceivers of all kinds, UHF, VHF, HF and shortwave, a keyboard and mouse, and two scanners. On the first shelf stood a large flat-screen monitor, a rear-vision mirror, a tiny TV screen, speakers and more receivers. Attached to the walls were handpieces and a large map of Victoria.

Andy was a radio buff.

He loved nothing more than listening in to the emergency services, monitoring fire reports during the scorching summer months when the threat of bushfires was ever-present in regional Victoria, or to the police's activities out and about. One laptop monitor was dedicated to ambulance activity, the other to the police.

Andy was a very community-minded man; if he heard

something happening, quite often he would phone one of his contacts in the local media and give them the tip-off.

He had only just sat down, mug of coffee in his hand, when the HF radio began receiving on the 8 MHz band. That meant there was something happening at sea. Andy quickly put down the coffee mug and hit the Record button on the tape recorder his high-tech cubby-hole also featured. He picked up his mug again, and sipped thoughtfully while he listened.

It was a Pan message—that meant something nasty was happening. He raised the volume and leant in closer so he could hear the chatter more easily. HF radio broadcasts messages from all around the globe, so he had to listen intently, to pick out which ocean, and which hemisphere was involved in this drama. Sighing, he relinquished the mug once more and picked up a pen. Better if he could write notes to support the taped message.

He heard the radio operator speaking to another ship.

"Pan pan, I have emergency traffic, over." Andy knew this meant the satellite phone was not functioning because of heavy seas or low cloud cover, otherwise the radio operator would have been using it to call.

Another voice came through. "*Aurora Australis, Aurora Australis,* this is *Sea Guardian.* Can we be of assistance, over?"

"*Sea Guardian,* this is *Aurora Australis.* We have Man Overboard, we have Man Overboard. Our coordinates are Latitude 51oS, Longitude 156oE. Over."

Sea Guardian came back through the airwaves. "*Aurora Australis,* we are twenty hours away, over."

"*Sea Guardian,* thank you. I understand. We're turning back now to search along the run. Good hunting. Out."

Andy sat back in his chair. Man overboard. Not good. He quickly accessed his atlas and searched up the coordinates he had jotted on the paper. Shit! The poor bastard had gone overboard into the Southern Ocean; he would stand no chance, not at those latitudes. The water would be freezing.

He tapped his teeth thoughtfully with his pencil. Taking a mouthful of his coffee and grimacing—it had gone cold—he picked up his mobile and speed-dialled his contact at the local newsroom.

"G'day, Stevo, it's Andy Grey. … Yeah, good thanks, and yourself? … Listen, mate, have you heard anything about a flap on out at sea today? The Southern Ocean. … What? Okay, mate, I've just been listening in— … yeah, as usual, and I've heard some chatter on the HF band. Apparently, some poor sod's gone overboard from the *Aurora Australis*. … Yeah, I know, it would be its last trip before winter to Macca and the Antarctic base. … Here are the coordinates. Oh, you will? Good on you mate. … Right, Stevo, talk to you later. Bye for now." And he hung up.

Andy was ruminating on this when the front doorbell chimed; he reluctantly scooted his chair out of the tiny space, took his mug to the kitchen, rinsed it dutifully, picked up his golfing gear and went out to meet his mate.

***

In the local ABC radio newsroom, the journalist, Steve, quickly took the information that had fallen into his hands and knocked at the manager's office door. Fred was on the phone, but motioned the younger man in, and indicated he should sit down. He finished his call, then smiled at Steve.

"G'day, young Steven, what can I do for you?"

"Fred, I've had a call from a mate of mine, who's just given me some information about a man overboard in the Southern Ocean, from the icebreaker *Aurora Australis*. He's given me the Lat. and Long. coordinates, and he's usually a pretty reliable source of information. What do you think we should do about it?"

"Get onto AMSA in Canberra straight away and ask their Media Office if they know anything about it. Good work, Steven. If it's kosher, it'll be breaking news."

"Thanks, Fred, I'll get onto it right away." Steve left the manager's office, sat down at his desk and dialled the necessary number in Canberra.

"Good morning, Deidre," he said, when the voice on the other end had identified herself, "this is Steve Black from the Central Victorian ABC newsroom. I wonder if you can help me? Or perhaps I can help you…"

Steve then outlined the tip-off he had received from Andy, included the Lat. and Long. coordinates, vouched for Andy's reliability as an amateur newshound and asked if AMSA's Media Office could confirm this.

The Media Officer at AMSA said no, she couldn't help him at this minute, but she would investigate the story through the appropriate channels, and get back to Steve as soon as possible, if there was a media release to be made.

Steve returned to his work; he was realistic enough to know it could take hours before he heard anything from the Australian Marine Safety Authority. It would depend on what they already knew…

He busied himself with his work, sorting and sifting information, chasing up other, more immediate news leads. He mentally shelved the story of the man overboard, as various local news items took up his time and attention.

***

At the far southern end of New Zealand's South Island in Invercargill, Kevin Gillespie, another ham radio operator, was also listening in. He intercepted the same message and immediately contacted the local police station, to report what he had heard. He was on good terms with the officers there and also had a good reputation as being a reliable source of information. The officers had no reason to doubt him, and they soon put in calls to the Australian Marine Safety Authority in Canberra, to pass the message along.

***

Far away in Chile, Vicente Rojas was listening in on his HF radio, twiddling the dials to tune in the 8MHz band; he was the son of a fisherman, and took a keen interest in the chatter that went on between ships of different nations. Vicente was confined to a wheelchair, the legacy of a childhood disease which had left him with limited mobility; he spent much of his time in his bedroom, headphones clamped to his ears as he accessed the outside world through his equipment. Vicente prided himself on his ability with languages; in addition to his native Chilean Spanish, he spoke Brazilian Portuguese and passable English, with smatterings of Russian, Japanese, Korean, and Chinese. All these he had acquired through the long sleepless hours of the nights following his illness, when pain and depression deprived him of rest; his body may have been impaired, but his mind was sharp and keen to learn. His radio set had been the gateway to the world, and he made the most of it. Although it was only 3:00 a.m., Vicente was wide awake; he heard the *Aurora Australis*'s Pan call and wrote down the message. He also heard the conversation between *Aurora Australis* and the *Sea Guardian* ship which responded but could not assist in a search. Vicente's ears pricked up; a man lost at sea! This was big news! He took off his headphones and reached for his mobile phone; there was an announcer on the late-night radio show to whom Vicente spoke regularly when he couldn't sleep. Perhaps the radio station would be interested in a news story…

***

Much later the same day in Central Victoria, Steve Black was on his way out of the office to follow another lead when his mobile rang in his pocket. He stopped and pulled it out, checking the number. His heart started to race, while his breathing accelerated.

It was Deidre, in the AMSA media office. She told him that the Authority had been receiving calls from other radio operators across the country and from police stations that had been contacted with the story, one as far away as New Zealand's South Island; the story had been verified by the ship concerned and emails would be sent to all radio stations and the relevant authorities with a press release shortly. She stressed that obviously the name of the deceased, or suspected deceased would remain confidential until the police in Hobart had made the necessary visit to the man's family. Steve quickly assured her that he was aware of the protocols and wished her a good day.

Steve Black hummed happily to himself as he drove out of the car park to pick up the local news story.

***

When he returned to his desk early that evening, Steve opened his emails to check for any new information. There it was! True, he was only one journalist on an enormous list of recipients, but he was happy. Deidre in Canberra had been true to her word; there was the statement concerning the disappearance his contact had tipped him off about earlier that morning.

"The Australian Maritime Safety Authority has confirmed this afternoon that a passenger from the ice-breaker *Aurora Australis* has disappeared, believed drowned, en route to Macquarie Island. The passenger is believed to be a sixty-year-old scientist travelling to Macquarie Island to take up a posting at the permanent station. He is believed to be an expert in pinniped populations."

Pinniped? Steve made a note to look up that word later.

"The captain of the *Aurora Australis* confirmed that an exhaustive search was made of the ship as soon as the passenger, whose name cannot be released at present, was reported missing early this morning. *Aurora Australis* retraced its route, in conjunction with the Search and Rescue wing of this organisation this morning, but the search had to be called off early this afternoon in heavy seas due to worsening weather and an approaching storm front.

Grave fears are held for the passenger's life. Captain of *Aurora Australis*, Peter Gallagher, has voiced his opinion that any further search would be strictly a recovery, rather than a rescue mission. He cited the condition of the seas and the ambient water temperature as 'not conducive to the maintenance of human life.' *Aurora Australis* has resumed its voyage towards Macquarie Island, where its cargo and passengers are due to be landed for the coming winter's expedition."

Andy had been spot-on with his information; Steve made a mental note to buy the man a pint when they next met. He picked up his phone and dialled Andy's number.

"G'day, Andy, it's Steve. How's it going? … Yeah, good thanks. … Listen, mate, I've just had an email from AMSA in Canberra. … What was that? … Yup, it's all true. Apparently some boffin's gone overboard. … Yeah, no worries, mate. … Just rang to say thanks and I owe you one. … Okay, Andy, catch you later. Ciao."

Steve pressed End on the call, thought about it for a couple of seconds then dialled his girlfriend's number.

"Hi, sweetie, it's me. Look, something big's happened at work and I won't be able to get away for a while. … Yes, I know I always say that— … Yes, I know we're supposed to be going to your mum's for dinner tonight, but— … No, love, this is— … Listen, Verity, this is a really important story— … Yes, I know I say that every time, but this time it's *big*. … Tell your mum I'm sorry, and I'll see her next week. … Okay, love, sorry. … What? … No, I don't know what time I'll be home. … Okay, 'bye. Love you."

He ended the call and turned back to his computer. He knew he wouldn't be going home any time soon and that he wasn't going to be very popular when he did. However, right now there was a breaking-news story to write.

Steve flexed his shoulders to ease the cramped muscles, cracked his knuckles, and began typing. His story would be on the early morning news.

Chapter eight

Wireless Hill Base Station
Macquarie Island

That same fateful Thursday morning, the radio operator burst through the door to the main office in the hut which served as the headquarters of the scientific mission on Macquarie Island.

"Boss, boss, I've just received a Pan message from the *Aurora Australis*. They've lost one of their passengers overboard and they've had to turn back to join the search and rescue effort. By the sounds of it, everyone has been involved — AMSA and all their mob. Goodness knows when they'll get here!"

"Steady on, Pat, and slow down!" Marcus Devlin, the station head growled. "Now, start again, and this time take it slowly. You know I can't understand a word when you gabble like that!"

Patrick O'Reilly took a steadying breath and recounted the message he had just heard across the satellite phone, ticking the items off on his fingers.

"*Aurora Australis* has lost a passenger overboard, one of the scientists coming here for the winter, sometime over last night or early this morning. They've sent out the international 'man overboard' signal, and they have now reversed their course to join in a search and rescue effort, so they won't be here on time. The captain wanted to know if we'll have enough supplies to get us through for a few extra days – they're not sure when they'll be able to get here. I guess it all depends on whether they find their man as to how delayed they'll be. Captain Gallagher is hoping to be here by Saturday or Sunday at the latest."

Marcus Devlin, a veteran at running this station, took the news in his stride, but was already doing some very serious mental calculations. Two or three extra days before the ship could arrive for reprovisioning the station was no crisis; they had plenty of fuel oil and food to see them through until the weekend, but if the ship were to be delayed for another week or more, then they may possibly begin to experience some shortages. But Devlin was confident it would not come to that; all the same, his inner demon nagged — it might be wise to institute a ban on some unnecessary fuel usage and to ask the cook to ease up on his excellent and bountiful meals in the meantime, just until the ship arrived.

Some of the scientists and tradespeople might complain, but he was sure they would understand the necessity of a little belt-tightening in the interim. The ship would eventually arrive.

"Okay, thanks, Pat. I reckon we'll be okay for another couple of days. Grim news, but. Wonder who the poor bastard was. No mention of a name?"

"No, boss, no names at present, but I'll keep my ears on the radio for any updates."

"Okay, best not to mention this to anyone at present, eh? Get back to your radio and let them know we're okay, for now. Oh, and wish them good luck, eh?"

"No worries, boss, my lips are sealed!" Patrick promised.

With that, Pat left the room to return to his domain, the radio room, where he spent most of his waking hours.

Marcus Devlin walked briskly down to the galley and had a chat with the cook about the possible necessity of some mild rationing for the next few days, then shrugged into his heavy outer gear and went to the supply sheds where the fuel oil was housed.

After he had satisfied himself that they were not going to starve or freeze, he returned to his office and continued his duties; in the back of his mind was this unwelcome news, and he wondered what on earth could have happened. Captain Peter Gallagher was one of the most experienced ship's masters anyone could hope to meet, but even someone with all the man's years of experience couldn't factor in human stupidity.

***

"Weather's blowing up a beauty!" gasped Kieran, one of the scientists, after he had been virtually hurled through the outer door by the wind, later in the day. "Don't think we'll be able to get out to do our stuff in it for hours. I'm going to check the Met forecasts, see what they're saying."

He shrugged out of his heavy waterproof coat in the wet room and disappeared down the corridor into the depths of the main hut to the radio room.

The lights were on in the room where Patrick was seated, seemingly glued to the headphones, and the equipment, all showing various signs of activity in the outside world, was ranged around the walls. The man could hear the keening of the wind outside the heavily insulated metal skin of the hut; it was really starting to sound as if they were in for a big blow, all right.

After greeting Patrick and finding him preoccupied, Kieran went to the console to update the meteorological forecast for the next twelve hours, then the long-range weather forecast. The news was severely disheartening; a larger than normal storm was brewing, with high seas and tides forecast, accompanied by gale-force winds.

He grimaced; no one was going to be out and about for the next twenty-four hours at least. There was an abnormally nasty weather front approaching the island; they would have to literally batten down all the machinery and bring in anything at all which could become a projectile. No sense in anyone being injured by flying debris.

He took his readings, then exited the radio room, carefully closing the door behind him as he took the grim weather news to the boss.

Patrick barely acknowledged the other man's presence; he was too busy listening to further developments on the life-or-death search taking place in the inhospitable Southern Ocean, but he had nodded a vague greeting and deliberately concentrated on his equipment while the younger man was present so that he would not have been tempted to share the grim news.

In the mess at lunchtime, Marcus took the opportunity of having most of the station members there to inform them of the day's happenings, the forecast gale, and the fact that the resupply ship would be late in arriving. There were a few good-natured groans from some of the scientists and tradespeople who were approaching the end of their year's posting on Macca, but they were all very conscious of the reason for the delay, and they confined their jibes to a few joking remarks like, "What? Got to put up with this cooking for much longer? Argh!" or "But I've got a hot date planned for when we get back!" which would be answered with "Hope she likes scratchy beards, then, Red!" and other silly remarks. The reason for the delay was too appalling to contemplate. Scientists may be a jealous lot amongst themselves, as competitive and spiteful as school children at times, but they would band together in sympathy for one of their own, any day.

After their meal, the company disbanded. The gale-force winds were screeching and wailing outside, blowing up flurries of early sleet and freezing water. There was no way any of the work force would want to risk their necks out in the imminent tempest unless it was absolutely necessary. Those who couldn't avoid going outside to secure heavy machinery and lock down all smaller, potentially lethal objects were already on their way, slipping and sliding across the treacherous terrain to their workplaces. They would stay in constant contact with the radio room and each other by walkie-talkie, until they had everything secure and could return to the relative warmth and safety of the station buildings. Possibly the most perilous task for the day was to release the weather balloon into the teeth of a Furious Fifties gale, taking with it the precious radio sonde which would record fluctuations and anomalies in the Earth's stratosphere, and send the data back to the waiting meteorologists.

Some personnel went off to enjoy some unscheduled leisure time: watching DVDs, writing letters home for the ship to take back to the real world if they were staying on for the winter, or playing games in the recreation room. Some went back to work in the many laboratories as usual after lunch, checking on their experiments and recording their results; there was afternoon surgery as usual for the station doctor, Jenny Jones, and calls to make home, weather permitting. The radio operators had changed shift, and the new man, Ken, had just put on his headphones when an incoming message caught and held his attention. What he heard made his blood run cold. He could feel the icy prickles down his spine as the staticky message came through.

"... missing man ... *Aurora Australis* ... believed ... Dougal Ferguson ... *Sea Guardian* ... AMSA ... search and rescue ... called off ... IUU fishers ... high seas ... rough weather ... force ten ..."

The transmission was becoming scratchier due to the increasing velocity and ferocity of the wind, but he could put enough information together to send him racing to find Marcus, who was still on duty in his office, contemplating the next few days.

"Boss, boss, think we've got a name for the man overboard," Ken panted, bursting through the doorway. "I think they said Dougal Ferguson."

"Bloody hell!" Marcus swore sharply. "Keep your voice down, man!" Ken stared at him, open-mouthed. "Shut the bloody door, for God's sake! Doug Ferguson? Never!"

Ken closed the door and swiftly walked to Marcus's desk. His face was easy to read; doubtful, hesitant, young.

"Sorry, boss. Might have misheard, but I'm sure that was the name."

"Okay," Marcus growled, "but keep it under your hat for now. Don't want anyone getting the wrong end of the stick until we know for sure. Any clues as to when they'll be here?"

"Not at this moment, no."

"Is *Aurora Australis* still in the search zone?"

"No. From what I could pick up from the transmission, which was pretty scratchy and patchy, they've called off the search because the weather's going to hell out there. Even the spotter plane has quit."

"Poor bastards, getting stuck in that. Pete'll be in a fine lather when he gets here." Marcus scratched his head, then smoothed down his ruffled fair hair. "You know this's his last supply run out to Macca and the Antarctic base, don't you? He's due to retire. What a shitty way to end your career. I feel sorry for him. Pete's a good bloke."

"Yeah," agreed Ken. "He skippered when I came down here last year. He's one of the best blokes I've met!" He hesitated, pulling on his lower lip. "I'd best be getting back to the radio. I'll be back as soon as I know anything more."

Marcus smiled sympathetically at the departing man and went back to his calculations.

Chapter
nine

Hobart – Office of the *Hobart Examiner*
Thursday evening

"Yes!" Twenty-three-year-old Stacey O'Connor leapt to his feet, pumping his fist in the air and sending his chair careening backwards across the crowded little office he shared with two other junior reporters. It crashed into a pile of archive boxes, causing an avalanche of newspaper clippings and computer printouts. Stacey, normally known as a neat freak around the office, barely gave the chaos a backward glance.

The Gods of Journalism had finally smiled on him. He went racing into the boss's office with a message he had just received on his mobile.

"Mr Milligan, excuse me, sir, but… get a load of this! Like wow!" Stacey was almost incoherent; wildly excited, he thrust the phone under his editor's nose.

"Whoa! Slow down, Stacey, you'll burst a valve if you keep this up! What's up?"

Niles Milligan, editor on duty that Thursday evening, put on his reading glasses and studied the message.

What he saw stunned and galvanised him into action.

"How the hell did you get this?"

"Got a mate who's on Macca, er Macquarie Island, in the radio shack. Thought I might like a scoop story."

The editor in chief looked at the lad through narrowed eyes. Scoop story, at his age? Get real. He smiled calculatingly.

"Thanks, Stace. I'll get on this right away." He looked up at the youngster standing in front of his desk, flushed and eager as a puppy.

"You can go, I'll deal with this. This needs to be in the early edition in the morning." He looked up again. Stacey was still standing there.

"What do you want, Stacey? Do *you* want to write the headline?" When the lad nodded, a nervous smile playing around his lips, Niles Milligan laughed aloud.

"Oh laddie, laddie. This is a big story, or at least it *will* be tomorrow. Better let one of the senior journos do the story, eh? You go on back to your local stories. There'll be others, don't you worry." His tone was dismissive; the lad was white as a ghost.

"No. Mr Milligan, sir. My mate sent *me* the SMS! I *know* I can write just as well as one of those overweight old codgers…" His voice trailed away. Milligan *was* one of those overweight old codgers. He tried again, more diplomatically this time. "Give me an hour, boss, and I'll have something for you…"

Stacey could almost see the wheels turning in his boss's head; the cub reporter hated wheedling and pleading, but he was thoroughly bored with the copy they gave him to write in that over-crowded and over-heated little cubby-hole they called an office. No wonder a lot of journos worked from home these days; with crappy conditions like this, who could blame them for rarely coming near the place. Milligan's eyes narrowed, then widened as he smiled at the cub reporter.

"Okay, Stacey, you have an hour to come up with the headline and a by-line. Now, close the door on your way out, there's a good lad."

Niles Milligan opened his email screen and found the official statement sitting in his inbox. He clicked the mouse and there it was, a scoop if ever he saw one, *if* he could find out the identity of the poor bastard who had gone for a long cold swim. There must be an exclusive for the newspaper with the grieving widow in this, somewhere. This would boost falling circulation numbers.

Milligan read through the official press statement and hit Print, then listened to the photocopier whir. *What the fuck is a pinniped, anyway? I'll google it when I get a chance.*

While he was waiting for the statement to emerge from the machine, he picked up the phone and punched in an extension.

"Trinity Trinling here. Can I help you?" A young, well-enunciated but rather breathless voice answered on the second ring.

"Ah, young Trinity, it's Mr Milligan here. I may have a job for you. Could you step into my office for five minutes?"

"Oh, of course, Mr Milligan, I'll be right there," her voice trilled through the phone. Niles ended the call and replaced the receiver.

He smiled widely, picked up the printout and sat down, smoothing his thinning hair back and leaning back in his leather armchair. If they still allowed smoking on the premises, he would have lit a cigar in celebration. He settled for drumming his fingers quietly on the desk.

A soft rap on the door announced the arrival of Trinity a few minutes later. Milligan sat up straight.; he was all business-like smiles and welcome.

"Come in, come in. How are you, Trinity? Well, I hope? Good, good. Close the door, there's a good girl. Come in, sit yourself down."

"You said you had a story for me, Mr Milligan?" Trinity breathed at him, brushing back the long, straightened blonde hair which was her absolute vanity, then blinked freshly-mascaraed eyes at him. As she breathed in, her soft, pale blue cashmere top strained above two beautifully augmented breasts. Niles found it hard to meet her eyes. He was fixated on those glorious mounds and could feel himself hardening beneath his boxer shorts. Fuck, she was a tease! She smiled sultrily at him with parted lips and wagged one finger at him; he finally lifted his eyes to hers.

"Ah yes, Trinity dear, I most certainly have. I've just received this from Canberra, from the Australian Maritime Safety Authority. Could be a really big story. I wondered if you would like the opportunity to write the by-line? We'll get it into tomorrow's early edition. It'll mean we'll have to work late tonight."

"No worries, Mr Milligan, I didn't have anything special planned. I can stay as late as you like." She smiled breathlessly at him, her glossed, rather pouty lips parting in anticipation.

"Excellent, excellent. Good girl. It may be an all-nighter. Now, come here and check this out."

As she moved silkily around to his side of the desk, he vacated it, walking softly but quickly to the window. After a quick but thorough glance through to see who was in the office space beyond, he closed the venetian blinds, and quietly thumbed the lock on the door. He returned to his desk and stood next to Trinity as she leant over the desk, elbows resting on the tooled leather as she read the press statement from AMSA. A knowing smile curved her lips as she waited for the next move in their game.

He knocked a pen off the desk and bent down to retrieve it. Straightening up, his left hand *accidently* brushed Trinity's backside, pertly thrust out in trousers tightened by firm butt muscles as she continued to lean over the desk.

She made a small noise and wriggled; he patted the luscious arse, then smacked it, quite hard.

He was rewarded with a little giggling squeak; as he bent over to point out the salient points of the story, his hand continued to caress her backside, each stroke downwards reaching further until he reached her crotch as she continued to wriggle and thrust out at him. He rubbed his hand back and forth against her, while she moaned softly. He could hear her breathing accelerate with each caress.

Finally he sighed, pointed out a really important part of the story with one hand, and wriggled his other down inside her trousers. This time he was rewarded by a sharp intake of breath. As she stopped moving, and stood straighter, her trousers loosened; it was his turn to make the moves. His fingers undid her zipper then wriggled the fabric aside before creeping downwards under her panties where they found the sweet spot they were searching for.

Oh, you dirty little bitch, you're wearing those silky French crotchless camiknickers again! His erection was already almost at bursting point as he fondled her silky underwear. He could feel the increasing pressure against his boxer shorts; he'd have to do something about that damp spot before he went home. She was driving him wild.

He played with her clitoris until she moaned; she was heating up, and the whole area became very damp and slick. Using her natural juices as lubrication, he slipped his fingers just inside her vagina, and began thrusting them in and out. She moaned more and started arching against the pressure. Lifting his other hand from the desk, he pushed her trousers and panties out of the way. The way was clear. He rubbed his thumb against her clitoris while slipping his slick, increasingly slippery fingers in and out of her wet hole, until she bit her arm to prevent herself from crying out.

As she reached her orgasm, she arched and squeezed her thighs together; he quickly withdrew his hand, flipped a small shiny package onto the desk in front of her, and unbuckled his belt, allowing his trousers to drop to the floor. He had already unzipped his fly, so that his excited penis could be ready for action. One quick, practised flick of the hand sent the boxer shorts after the trousers, leaving his member free and standing to attention. With his garments pooled around his ankles, he bent her over the desk once more, admiring her backside lifting invitingly towards him. He grasped her hips as her hands glided through her legs to expertly assist him roll on the condom and guide his penis into her warmth, all in one smooth manoeuvre. This was a well-choreographed dance they enjoyed. Aaaah, it was so *hot! She's so tight!* It was always good.

He placed one hand on her back, flattening her down onto the desktop and squashing her large breasts onto the tooled leather; he could see her face in profile, pink tongue flicking over wet pouting lips parted in breathless enjoyment, eyes closed in ecstasy, long blonde hair partially obscuring her face. She had moved her arms to grasp the opposite side of the desk, and lay quite flat across it, opening herself to his attentions. He held her hips, and, steadying himself, slowly started thrusting.

He imagined himself riding a bucking bronco and thrust hard. Her body pressed into the desk with every lunge. He wanted to shout for the sheer physical joy of fucking her but knew that one of them would probably be sacked if their indiscretions were discovered. Well, *she* would be, and that could be a problem. Who knew what she might be capable of, if she suddenly found herself out of a job for screwing the (very married) boss. Women's liberation and equality only went so far. He couldn't take that chance, but she was a real little cockteaser and she loved every minute of the game they played.

Besides, he was having too good a time. She had a tight little pussy, and those boobs! He just wished he could bury his dick in between them and fuck them too. These thoughts whirling around made him even hungrier for her assets, and he accelerated his stroke rate. The sweat was pouring out of him now, and he grunted with every lunge. Fuck, she was good! She certainly was an active little playmate, thrusting backwards to meet and ride him; her low-pitched moans drove him wild. And those muscles! Squeezing and massaging his penis from the *inside*. She was definitely a good fuck, and she knew it.

He knew she usually didn't like it so fast, but he was too aroused, and frustrated; he hadn't been able to wheedle sex out of his wife for at least a couple of weeks, and he had a load on that he was anxious to get rid of.

He could never really see the point in masturbation, not when there were pretty little things around the office who would welcome both his attentions and the news scoops he might drop into their deserving laps. His thrusts were becoming jerkier and more insistent. Anyway, it was *his* turn! Faster and faster, breaths shorter and shorter until he shuddered under the intensity of his own climax. He collapsed, purple-faced and sweating profusely, onto Trinity's back as they lay spreadeagled across the top of Niles's desk momentarily.

Grabbing and holding the condom carefully in place, he withdrew his rapidly shrinking penis from her hot vagina, then shuffled off to his private restroom, which he had insisted of having installed when he had arrived from Sydney to become editor in chief.

Trinity laughed quietly to herself as she redressed herself; he had been in such a hurry today, he hadn't even tried to rip her bra off, or maul her breasts as he usually did. *Wilma must be keeping him on short rations, the silly bitch*, Trinity thought. So much the better for Trinity, who was all about Trinity and no-one else.

Trinity was used to having her own way; she had a reputation on the newspaper as a ball-buster; *if only they knew, the poor suckers, just how true that saying is, in this instance!* She quietly chuckled. She tidied her hair, fished in her trouser pocket for a small pocket mirror to check for make-up damage, gave herself the once-over for tidiness, peeled the cashmere sweater away from her back where the boss had sweated all over it and picked up the slightly crumpled printout from Milligan's desk. She unlocked the door and sailed out into the general office, calling "I'll get right onto it, sir" as she closed the door behind her. She managed to look hard done by and imposed upon, in case anyone should be there to see, and wafted the printout around as if it were contagious.

Trinity marched back to her desk in the cramped office and started work on the headline and by-line for the morning's paper. Milligan was right; it probably would take most of the night, checking facts and calling up favours from contacts, to write a scoop headline for the morning papers.

She smiled and hummed to herself as she started work.

"You sound pleased with yourself, Trin," came an unexpected voice from behind a computer monitor on the other side of their workspace. She jumped.

"Oh Stace, you gave me such a fright!" Her hand automatically flew to her prominent breasts in their strained cashmere prison, and she opened her eyes very wide, fluttering her eyelids to show her distress.

"Yeah, right, sorry," came the mumbled reply. "Whatcha working on, anyway?" he asked.

"Oh, just some research Mr Milligan asked me to do for a possible suicide off a ship. Nothing very interesting, really."

"*Fucking what*!?" screeched Stacey, jumping up and knocking his chair over again. He pointed a shaking finger at her. "That was *my* lead. *I* got it from a contact. How the fuck did *you* get it?" He looked over at her smug, slightly smudged expression. "Oh, *I get it!* You've been shagging the boss for a story again. You are truly pathetic, you know that? You are *such* a slag!"

Stacey picked his chair up, slammed it down and walked to the door, snagging his jacket off the coat hook.

"I need some coffee," he muttered, "anything to get a bad taste out of my mouth and the bad smell of you out of my nose. Fucking whore!" he jeered, and left the room, slamming the door so hard it bounced open again.

"Whatever you say, sweet pea," she murmured carelessly as she lifted the phone and started dialling, "and whatever it takes."

Trinity wondered who this big-wig was, and how he had gone overboard. Suicide, obviously. Loser. Ah well, she'd find out soon enough. There wasn't a member of the public who was proof against Trinity Trinling's charms when she wanted to find out something. And she knew it.

She set to work; deadlines were deadlines, and she was going to make sure *her* name was on that by-line in the morning's edition of the paper.

In the outer office, near the water cooler, Stacey encountered Sam, social pages reporter and third occupant of their cramped quarters.

"'Sup, Stace?" she enquired. "You look like you just sucked a lemon."

"TT" — he made the initials sound like titty — "is up to her usual tricks, the bitch. She's just fucked my scoop out of the boss, I'm sure of it. I mean, she's no better a journo than I am. In fact, I'm a better fucking journo than she is, any day! She makes me sick! She thinks her shit doesn't stink!"

"Yeah, I know what you mean. She can't be very good at her job if she has to let the boss screw her in order to get a story. Some of us—" She sniffed derisively, flicking her fingers through her short black hair. "—are good enough to get by without having to prostitute ourselves to do it."

She patted him sympathetically on the back as she turned to cross the space to their shared office. "Cheer up, Stace. You're obviously not pretty enough for him," she joked as she walked away.

"Bitches!" Stacey growled, and promptly choked on his water.

Chapter ten

Hobart
Thursday night to Friday morning

The same bleak email came through to the office of the Hobart Police around the same time Thursday evening as Steven Black at ABC Radio in Central Victoria and the Hobart newspaper received theirs.

Nathan Truscott in the police media centre uttered a low whistle as he read the AMSA press release.

He hit the Print button on his computer and went to retrieve the hard copy. He continued into the main office, where the evening shift was holding its daily handover briefing before the assembled personnel dispersed to their various duties ahead of whatever the night offered in the way of emergencies.

Carrie Harkaway and her colleagues were in their usual seats, listening intently to the duty sergeant outlining the cases on their books.

Nathan walked over to the officer and silently handed him the press release from AMSA. The older man's bushy eyebrows rose in surprise as he read the despatch.

"Ahem, people, before you go, there's one last thing." He read the despatch aloud, pausing at the end for comments.

"What the hell is a pinniped?" asked Constable Grey.

"No idea. Look it up in Google," suggested the sergeant.

"Oh, right-o, Sarge."

"Any idea who the missing man is?" asked Gavan Hopper, the Detective Inspector on duty that night.

"No names are mentioned, but I'm sure there'll be another release, before too long. In the meantime, people, we have work to do. Yes, Carrie?" the duty sergeant asked as the young detective constable raised her hand. She had turned quite white when he had read the fateful news.

"Pinnipeds are seals and sea lions, that sort of thing." There were a few murmurs of "smarty-bum" at her apparent knowledge. She continued, "My fiancé, Jeremy, is studying them. He's on that ship, Sarge. He was travelling with his professor. He's about sixty, I believe—his professor, that is, not Jeremy," she said, blushing as a ripple of laughter broke out around her.

"Do you know the family, Carrie?" Gavan asked.

"Well, yes, I've been to their house with Jeremy a few times, and his wife and I had supper together Monday night after the ship sailed. Do we have a passenger manifest from *Aurora Australis,* boss? I could go through it to check against the names."

"Good thinking, Carrie; the job's yours. You'll probably have to contact the Port of Hobart authorities. Get onto it. There's sure to be an after-hours number."

"Righto, boss, I'm on it."

"Okay, Jonesy," Gavan said to the duty sergeant, "sorry to interrupt. Was there anything else?"

"No, sir, we'd just about wrapped up when this arrived."

"Thanks, Jonesy. Okay, people, let's get busy, and stay alert. Have a good shift, everyone."

As they all shuffled out, some back to their desks, some out to follow up leads or off to the patrol cars, Gavan caught Carrie by the arm. Her face was pale.

"Are you all right?" he asked.

"Yeah, it was just a bit of a shock to hear the news. If it's who I think it is, his wife'll be devastated. She's a good person." She looked at him with anguished eyes. "If it *is* her husband, could I break the news to her, please? I think she'd prefer it came from someone she knows, rather than from a stranger."

"If we can get a name before you end your shift, then of course you can go to her. No one will ever fight you for *that* duty, that's for sure. Job's all yours, girl."

"Thanks, boss. I appreciate it. Jeremy would like it that way, too. I'm okay now. I'll get to work right away."

"Good hunting. Hope you get a name soon."

"Me too. Have a good shift, boss."

"You too. See you." He turned on his heel, pulling his mobile out of his pocket as it rang. "Hopper," he barked into it as he walked away.

Carrie returned to her desk in the space she shared with other officers and opened her computer to begin her search.

She rang the Port of Hobart Authority, got their after-hours number and started her enquiries.

The duty officer promised her an email of the passenger manifest from Monday's departure within the hour.

She tried Jeremy's mobile number, but he was obviously too far away.

Next, she tried to contact the ship by satellite phone, without success.

Tapping her teeth with a pencil, she sat for a few minutes, thinking about Jeremy and Dougal. She wasn't sure if they were the only two scientists going to Macquarie Island for the seals and sea lions, but she had a horrible suspicion that they would be.

Dear God, what will Beth do? She'll be devastated if it's Dougal. So will Jeremy; he looks on him as a dad. When are they going to send that bloody email? Have the papers got wind of this? I'll have to go to see Beth in the morning, confirmation or not. Poor lady, she deserves to know before the bloody media starts camping on her doorstep. I wonder what happened... did he fall overboard... surely to God he wouldn't have jumped... would he?

Realising that all these musings wouldn't get her anywhere, Carrie gave herself a mental shake and opened her email page.

Nothing. She got up and went over to make herself a coffee from the machine. She sipped it thoughtfully as she returned to her computer. There was nothing to do about this but wait. In the meantime, there were other cases awaiting her attention. She put down her coffee mug, and set to work.

Friday morning's headlines were bold.

"MAN OVERBOARD!" they proclaimed to the early morning commuters, as they raced for buses or scurried along the windy streets of Hobart.

The radio stations had been featuring the story since the early newscasts started at 6:00 a.m., and the television breakfast shows were full of speculation.

The hunt was on for the passenger's identity.

By the end of her shift, Carrie had received a copy of the passenger manifest for *Aurora Australis*, which had confirmed her gravest fears.

There were eight scientists due to engage in marine mammal monitoring and research, four on Macquarie Island and four at the Antarctic base. In each group, two were pinniped specialists, and two were studying whale migration patterns and herd numbers.

The communication from *Aurora Australis* by marine-band radio had confirmed that all but one of those passengers were alive and as well as could be expected in the circumstances.

That left Dougal Ferguson, sixty-year-old professor of pinniped research at Hobart University unaccounted for.

Wearily, she switched off the computer, and prepared to make an unhappy visit.

***

Ms Trinity Trinling, after working all evening on the story, had just woken to a windy morning. From her apartment up the slopes of Mount Wellington, she could see the trees bowing and swaying in the wind. Shafts of early sunlight dappled the thrashing leaves.

She was well pleased; her enquiries had elicited some interesting information of the possible identity of the missing man, but she knew it would be more than her job was worth to speculate openly in the morning news. One of her contacts, an earnest, pimply, bespectacled young man whose sole hobby was ham radio operation, had come up with this information late last night. He kept her informed of all sorts of interesting newsworthy titbits, mainly in the hope she would eventually come through with her seductive promises.

Fool! she thought scornfully as she dressed for the day ahead, *like I want to play with spotty little boys. Over my dead body!* But she always kept these thoughts carefully hidden when dealing with her adoring minions.

Makeup completed and a light overcoat slung across her shoulders, Trinity locked up the apartment and went to retrieve her car. She had been given an address in Rose Bay, and on the way she was to pick up Gus, the news photographer, who would capture any action on film. He would also drop his pants for her at the crooking of her little finger, she was sure. She laughed. She loved her job! Manipulation of the opposite sex was such fun!

Thanks, Daddy, I learnt it all from you.

***

Carrie arrived in her own car at Dougal and Beth's house in Rose

94

Bay a little after 7:30 a.m. She had already phoned Beth on her mobile, to make sure she hadn't yet left for work, but hadn't mentioned the reason for her visit.

Beth's curiosity had been aroused, but she had not asked questions, agreeing to wait at home until Carrie could get there.

She walked up the path, past the neatly maintained rose bushes, and the last of the summer flowers growing in profusion in the garden beds. Beth must have been waiting for her, because, before she put her finger to the doorbell, the front door opened and Beth stood there, dressed for work, with a quizzical smile on her face.

"Good morning, honey, come on in." Beth took Carrie's arm and looked closely at the weary face. "You look done in. Coffee?"

"Morning, Beth. Yes please, I'd love one."

"Come on down to the kitchen, girl, and make yourself comfortable. I'll just get the machine going again."

The slim little figure bustled away. Carrie always felt like a giant next to this woman; sure, she was much taller than Beth, but it was the woman's sheer *energy*, like an inner fire, which made her movements so quick and decisive. Carrie was reminded of the fairy tales from her childhood about pixies and elves. That was it! Beth reminded her of a pixie.

She smiled, despite the heavy news she was carrying, and found a bar stool to prop on while Beth produced mugs of steaming black coffee, the sugar bowl, a jug of milk, and a plate of lavishly buttered raisin toast.

She sat down with Carrie and patted her softly on the arm, saying, "Eat, girl, before you fall over. You look exhausted. Bad night at the coalface, huh?"

Carrie grimaced as she munched her way through a thick piece of toast. She nodded, chewing and swallowing, before clearing her throat and speaking.

"Beth," she began hesitantly, turning to face her.

"Carrie, honey, what's wrong? Has something happened? Are you okay?" Concern was written so clearly across the older woman's face, Carrie could have cried. Beth never seemed to think of herself, only the welfare of others. She really would have been a wonderful mother. Carrie found her voice.

"Beth, it was a long, tough shift. There has been an accident out at sea, and the authorities have let us know that someone went overboard."

"Oh, honey, that's just awful. Poor person. I hope they find him or her. Where did it happen?"

"Out in the Southern Ocean. Oh Beth, I'm so sorry, but we think it was Dougal."

The colour drained from Beth's face; she was ghost-white and staring at Carrie as if she had suddenly started speaking Martian. Her knuckles turned white as she gripped the back of the bar stool for support.

"Wha.... What?"

"Beth, come and sit down in one of your armchairs. Here, let me help you…"

"I'm fine, hon. Bring the coffee, there's a good girl."

Beth moved across into the family room, and sat down in her usual chair. Carrie followed her with the mugs, coffee pot, and the remains of the toast. She put them down on the glass-topped table, within Beth's reach.

"Now, start again," Beth demanded. "Slowly. Someone has gone missing from a ship, and the police think it's Dougal. That's just insane!"

"Beth, I've been working all night on passenger manifests from *Aurora Australis*. That's who reported the man overboard situation. All their other personnel and crew are present and accounted for, just not Dougal." Carrie sighed wearily, a heavy weight on her shoulders. Her eyes started filling with tears; she quickly blinked them away.

"No! I don't believe it could be him. He *promised* me!" Beth's head slumped forward onto her chest, her body sagging under the impact of the news. She started speaking again, but as her voice was absorbed by her clothing, Carrie had to bend forward to hear the words. "… he *promised* me this would be his last winter away. He *promised* me he wouldn't go away again without me after this trip."

Beth lowered her head into the palms of her hands and sobbed. After a few moments of silence, she lifted her head, sniffed, and looked directly at Carrie. "Well, if it *is* him who's disappeared, I guess he'll be keeping his promise, eh? I guess he'll never go away again, ever."

She sat back, rested her head on the cushioned chair back, and closed her streaming eyes. Carrie could see her mouth moving silently.

The doorbell ringing broke the silence. Carrie glanced at Beth, who still hadn't moved a muscle. She stood up and walked through the house to the front door. Peeping through the spy-hole set into the door, she could see a face framed by long blonde hair. Opening the door a little, Carrie asked, "May I help you?"

"Oh *hi!* I'm Trinity Trinling from the *Hobart Examiner*. Are you Mrs Ferguson? The wife of Dougal Ferguson?"

"No, sorry, I'm not." Carrie made to close the door, but the pushy young woman held her hand firmly against it.

"But the address we have is this one. Now, are you Mrs Ferguson, or is that your mother?"

Trinity batted patently false eyelashes at Carrie, who stood, completely unmoved.

"Neither, I'm afraid. Good day." And closed the door on the surprised reporter.

Trinity's photographer, standing back a little for better focus, was smiling wryly to himself, when she rounded on him.

"What are you snickering about, Gus? That's his wife, or his mistress, I'm bloody sure of it."

She pushed the button of the doorbell again, and held her finger there until the tall, willowy woman stood in front of her once more.

"Who is it, honey?" came a call from the back of the house.

"No one important, dear. Finish your breakfast. I'll get rid of them," Carrie called over her shoulder.

Trinity tried to dodge around Carrie to see into the house. For the first time in ages, Carrie was very happy she was as tall as she was, and very agile through her sporting interests. She blocked the reporter's efforts to snoop. Trinity was doomed to disappointment.

"Who was that?" asked Trinity, thrusting a directional microphone into Carrie's face.

Carrie batted the offending thing away, and held up her hand, palm out, in a warning gesture.

"My friend, with whom I was enjoying a late and up until now, quite leisurely breakfast. Now, *if* you don't mind, I would like to go back and finish mine, before the toast is cold. I *do* so *hate* cold toast. Don't you? Now please go away and leave us to enjoy our meal together. Thank you."

Carrie closed the door again, paused and removed the battery from the doorbell. She placed it on the hall table and went back to Beth.

Trinity stood outside and pushed on the doorbell repeatedly; there was no noise from inside.

"The smart bitch has taken out the battery. Hmm, that means they have something to hide. After all, why wouldn't they want to talk to *me*?" She turned to Gus, who was gazing away into the distance. She was positive he was laughing at her again, and Trinity Trinling hated to be laughed at.

"Come on then, Useless, let's go. We'll think of something else."

She stormed off down the path, sparks erupting where her three-inch heels struck the flagstones. Gus grinned to himself. He must remember her hissy fit for the boys at the pub after work — they'd love a laugh at Trinity's expense. Everyone around the office knew what a slag the woman was, and how she got her assignments from the Editor-in-Chief; they'd really enjoy the joke.

***

Carrie went back and flopped down wearily onto the couch. Beth was there, gazing out the huge windows at the river, nursing a coffee. She had her mobile on her lap. She seemed quite calm and self-contained again.

Carrie could only wonder at the woman's composure; she was sure she would be a nervous wreck, were she to be in the same situation. Just having to ascertain all the information she had trawled for overnight had left her wrung out and close to tears.

She sipped her coffee thoughtfully, looked across at Beth, who hadn't moved a muscle, put her cup down, and closed her eyes. She wanted to rest them, just for a minute. Her eyes stung, gritty after a night spent staring at a computer screen, or trawling through ships' manifests.

Carrie woke up four hours later, covered with a brightly coloured blanket. She fingered the exquisite softness of the weave, before putting it carefully to one side and standing up. God, but she was stiff and sore in the hips. She walked over to the kitchen area. Everything had been cleared away and there was a note on the breakfast bar.

Carrie,

You looked so peaceful, I didn't have the heart to waken you.

Stay until I get back – I've just run to the store to get some supplies for lunch.

I'm okay. Don't fret about me. I haven't lost my marbles or anything.

Beth

PS: Towels are in the linen press in the front hall. Feel free to use the guest bathroom if you want to take a shower. Second door on the left past the kitchen if you're approaching from the back room.

B.

Carrie shook her head in amazement. Actually, it wasn't such a silly idea, to take a shower, but she'd have to put her slept-in clothes back on. Still, it would be better than that grimy feeling she got when she had been working all night.

"Okay, Mumma Bear," she muttered. "I'll go and get clean."

As she emerged from the shower, she heard the back door open, and light, quick footsteps on the slate floor.

"Hi, honey, I'm home…" shouted Beth from the rear of the house.

Carrie opened the bathroom door a tiny way so she could be heard in the kitchen. "Oh, hi, Beth, I took you up on your offer of a shower."

"Good! We always operate more functionally when we are clean, I'm sure of it. I'm fixing lunch. Stay and have a sandwich, then I'm sending you home. You should be safe to drive now."

"Beth, you really are a gem!" came the reply from the bathroom.

***

Friday night, the television news led with a bulletin about Dougal.

"The circumstances leading to a man going overboard remain unclear, but Tasmanian police will speak with passengers and crew upon the ship's arrival in Hobart. Sergeant Jones said the man's family has been notified, and his name will be released in the next few hours. *Aurora Australis* was withdrawn from the search on Thursday afternoon due to foul weather and heavy seas. Tasmania Police will assist with the investigation, but the death is not being treated as suspicious at this stage. Police will prepare a report for the coroner."

Beth curled up in her favourite chair and turned the television off. She couldn't bear to hear any more. She was exhausted and inconsolable. She leant her head against the back of the chair and closed her eyes.

Chapter eleven

Macquarie Island
Friday p.m. to Saturday a.m.

There had been one hell of a storm Thursday night. Anything not secured or locked away would have suffered major damage, or been blown into the sea. Fortunately for the occupants of the station, the maintenance people had done their jobs thoroughly, and there was little debris lying around when the tempest finally screamed away on its destructive path across the miles of ocean towards the east. Campbell Island, off the southern tip of New Zealand, and further east still, the rugged outcrop of land of Tierra del Fuego, would be in for a pounding in a few hours' time.

Aurora Australis had radioed in, giving its coordinates, and advising the station that they would be delayed by the howling fury of the Furious Fifties Force Ten gale.

The radio operator had replied that there would be nowhere to moor safely anyway, as the same filthy weather had hit the island.

It was agreed by all parties to wait; those on Macca would huddle in their reinforced dwellings and listen to the banshee winds, hoping and praying that the tempest would not dislodge them from their rocky quarters, while those at sea would have to ride it out, in huge seas and screaming gales.

The climate scientists and meteorologists, branded as prophets of doom by some cynics and climate change deniers, were in their element; they had warned the Australian government and anyone else who would listen, repeatedly, that the weather events would just continue to worsen around the planet due to global warming. The response from the government had been a collective "fingers in the ears" response. The scientists had been studying climate science for years now on Macquarie Island and in the Antarctic, and had published the conclusions of their tests and computer models. They had kept lobbying and quoting their findings; they said these "once in one hundred years" storms were occurring far more frequently and violently than ever.

"If something isn't done soon," one heavily bearded man predicted, "then the Earth is doomed to rising sea levels, global poverty, displacement of millions of people in low-lying countries and areas, and an increase in the Earth's temperature. The science is in," he continued to expound to anyone who would listen. "We're able to prove, through our computer modelling programs that average temperatures are rising, or in some places, falling. The weather patterns are close to being out of control."

Another, intense young woman added, "These are all clear indications of the climate being irrevocably changed. Earth is near a tipping point, beyond which global weather patterns will spin out of control, and there will be consequences of catastrophic proportions. This storm is an example of the increasing violence of the natural world, all exacerbated by the pollutants which are being spewed hourly into the Earth's atmosphere from huge power stations and the burning of fossil fuels." She sat back, apparently exhausted by the passion of her rhetoric.

Marcus Devlin had heard all these arguments before; he agreed with the scientists. After all, that was why there was a base here, and its transient population.

"Sounds like you're preaching to the choir, guys. I'll leave you with it. I've got work to do." He retired to his office, away from the lively debate going on in the dining room, glad to distance himself from the noise and hubbub for a while. He settled to his work, logging the events of the previous night and the damage done. Fortunately, he had an excellent crew, and there had been little loss of equipment; no lives lost, he recorded, and few injuries to the personnel. They would ride this one out as they had done countless times previously. No one would be permitted to leave the huts until the all clear was sounded inside the station.

***

Out at sea on Thursday night, Peter Gallagher and his crew were really struggling to keep *Aurora Australis* on a steady course for Macquarie Island. The majority of the passengers had kept to their cabins since the hunt for the professor's body had been called off; unused to such conditions, most were unbearably ill. Even the cook

102

and his assistants had closed the galley after securing as much as they could. There had been damage there and elsewhere on the ship. The ice breaker was being tossed about like a toy, swooping down into the huge troughs, and soaring back up the other side of enormous waves. Peter Gallagher was just very thankful they no longer had to carry sled dogs on the decks; the poor creatures would have been drowned or swept overboard into the maelstrom.

Stabilised though it was, *Aurora Australis* was no match for mountainous seas like this; the best they could hope for was to try to ride it out without going to the bottom. Peter Gallagher had passed an anxious and sleepless night in his chair on the bridge. The constant buffeting of the wind and waves, and the vicious thwacking of greenish sleety water onto the glass of the bridge, made visibility impossible; his officers were running solely on their instruments to navigate and keep the ship steady.

The communications officer listened for hour after weary hour, reporting to his captain any changes in the meteorological forecasts. He was also listening out for transmissions from Macquarie Island; the station there would be able to report when it was safe to approach the island, to offload both passengers and equipment.

Peter Gallagher reflected that it had been a more hazardous voyage than usual at this time of year; the weather patterns had certainly been bizarre during the previous Tasmanian summer. He had been on duty now for more than twenty-four hours and was feeling his eyelids starting to close. He shook himself awake, and tried to concentrate. He knew he would need to sleep soon, but not until this bitch of a storm had blown itself away, and they could begin to make progress. He forced himself to get up and walk around, to check on instruments and his officers; they, too, were exhausted. He checked the ship's chronometer; this watch would be relieved soon, and the other officers would take their places on the bridge. He checked it again. The figures blurred and shifted before his eyes. He squinted to see clearly. Five in the morning local time; it would be daylight soon, and they would be able to assess what damage had been sustained during the hours of darkness. His eyelids began to close… just a few seconds' relief from the glare of the screens; that was all he needed…

"Er, Pete," called George, the comms officer on duty, jerking him out of his daydream. "Macca has just radioed. The storm's mostly gone from there, and it should be clear to dock later in the day."

"Thanks, George. All we have to do is get there, now. Any change in the met forecast?"

"Weather should be improving after daybreak, but no guarantees. Anything to send back to Macca?"

"Let them know we'll be on our way as soon as these swells ease up a bit. No telling when that might be; this shit could go on for hours yet."

"Right you are. Transmitting now." George started transmitting to the radio operator on Macquarie Island, to apprise the station of their location, current situation, and the course they were steering.

***

By midmorning, Peter Gallagher had finally left the bridge and retired to his cabin for some rest. The seas and winds had abated sufficiently for the ship to be making progress at last. A fresh complement of officers, including the first mate, had taken the watch on the bridge, and he could leave the ship to them, at least for an hour or so. He ran his hand through his hair; he was absolutely exhausted, and in that moment, knew he had made the right decision when he had announced his intention to the ship's owners to retire after this voyage.

He slipped off his shoes, lay down on his bunk fully clothed, and was asleep almost before he could pull the top cover over himself.

***

By late Friday afternoon, *Aurora Australis* was almost to Macquarie Island. The seas had subsided considerably, and most of the passengers had emerged from their cabins; they looked very seedy, and still quite green around the gills.

Peter Gallagher was back on the bridge, refreshed by several hours' sleep, during which time the gods of the sea had apparently smiled on them. Nursing a freshly brewed coffee in a lidded mug, he was able to see the damage the previous night's storm had caused. The decks were washed clear of debris, and it appeared that the lashings had held, despite everything the fury of the gale had hurled at them. One or two containers had been slightly dented, but everything was still in place. Peter was profoundly thankful; the stations on Macquarie Island and on the Antarctic ice shelf needed every bit of equipment and supplies the ship carried.

A ragged cheer went up from passengers and crew alike as the ship finally approached their mooring near the island. There was no port, no wharf; the ship would anchor offshore, and the containers and fuel oil drums would be lifted from their deck mountings and shuttled onto the shore by the helicopters. Other supplies, and the passengers would be landed by inflatable rubber boats, or IRBs.

On the island itself, a crowd had gathered to greet the incoming ship; there was relief amongst the departing expeditioners that their ride home had finally arrived. Some expeditioners had signed on for an entire year's research and work on the base, and would be staying on to show new personnel the ropes. Although it was late in the day, unloading of the supplies took top priority; the helicopters would ply back and forth between ship and shore until every container had been safely offloaded. The provisioning crew were rested and keen to begin. At this time of the year, the days of almost endless sunlight had gone. They were on the cusp of the southern winter when there would be little daylight for the next six months.

Peter Gallagher was in the last IRB to leave *Aurora Australis* for the island that afternoon. Conditions aboard were dire; the crew of twenty-four had stayed aboard and had a gargantuan task ahead of them. It was their duty to clean the stinking cabins, to prepare the ship for tomorrow morning's departure and to ensure that everything was ready for the passengers continuing on to Antarctica and those returning home to Tasmania. Peter's weary face was grim as he stepped onto the shore. A sardonic drawl broke into his gloomy musings.

"Well, would ya just lookit what the tide washed up! How're ya doin', Pete?"

"Marcus! That was just about the worst John Wayne impersonation I've ever heard. How are you, mate?"

Marcus clapped Peter heartily on the shoulder.

"Better than you, old man! Good to see you! Helluva trip, was it? Look, sorry to hear about what happened out there. No luck finding him, then? Come on up to the office. You look done in."

Talking non-stop, Marcus led the way from the shore to the welcoming shelter of the base station. When they were seated in Marcus's office, the exhausted captain accepted a mug of strong black coffee, and the two men were able to discuss matters in private.

"Bad business, this," remarked Marcus, looking directly at his friend. "What the hell happened?"

"That's the $64,000 question. Nobody knows, apart from the fact that an intelligent, well-balanced, and lively man seems to have jumped overboard in the middle of the night. Of course, we turned around to go look for him, and the AMSA people sent out their whizz-bang recon plane to join in the search, but the weather turned to shit and we had to abandon the search. The poor bastard couldn't have survived in the conditions, not unless he turned into a merman."

Both men laughed at the absurdity of that particular hypothesis. They drank more coffee and chatted about conditions on Macca, then Peter left Marcus to tidy up his last pile of paperwork so he could hand over to the incoming station manager. He promised to catch up again after the evening meal, and wandered back to check on the offloading and reloading of his ship. The daylight was almost gone. The dark days of winter would descend on this part of the world very soon.

As night fell, the loading zones were illuminated by enormous floodlights, driven by the powerful generators which ran every source of electricity on the island. Load after load of provisions were safely brought ashore, and the sealed containers of Macquarie Island's waste had been lifted out to the ship and securely lashed to the decks. Only then would the helicopters be returned to the ship and secured in their hangars. The passengers had come ashore hours earlier, and were finding their land legs again; after three horrendous days at sea, they found it somewhat difficult to adjust to a surface which did not pitch and toss every step of the way. Some of them staggered around as if they were drunk; their sense of balance had been seriously compromised. Those who were leaving Macquarie Island assured the newcomers that they would be fine in a day or two; they had all been through the same bizarre sensation of the solid earth moving up and down beneath their feet.

Friday night's dinner was a festive occasion for those who could face food; the incoming expeditioners were thankful to have arrived, and most of the homeward bound personnel were thankful to be leaving this remote outpost. Toasts were made to the incoming and outgoing personnel, with a friendly reminder from Peter Gallagher that the "big yellow taxi" would be leaving at 0930, for those joining it. Passengers and their gear were to be ready to embark, via helicopter by 0830.

After dinner, Marcus Devlin sat down in his office with Roger MacDougal, the incoming head of station and Peter Gallagher. Roger produced a bottle of whisky which he had brought along, and the three men toasted each other's good health, a safe voyage back to Hobart, and a successful mission for Roger. Peter gently refused Marcus's offer to have a bed at the station for the night, saying that he slept best in his own bunk, and he still had paperwork to complete before they sailed in the morning. He bade the two men good night and walked steadily to the shore, where an IRB was waiting to take him back to his ship.

Marcus and Roger still had the official handover/takeover procedure to work through before either of them could retire for the night.

Conditions were cramped; the incoming expeditioners did not normally move into their new quarters until the homeward-bound personnel had vacated them, but these were exceptional circumstances. No one could be expected to live aboard until the hard-working crew had completed their daunting task of cleaning up the mess caused by the effects of the storm. There were bodies in sleeping bags on every available horizontal surface at the base station that night.

True to his word, Captain Peter Gallagher sent the first of the IRBs to land promptly at 0830 Saturday. The expeditioners continuing on to Antarctica, and those returning home to Tasmania were all assembled, with their gear, as he had directed the previous evening. The IRBs worked a shuttle service; as one took its complement of personnel and their gear aboard, and started out for *Aurora Australis*, another took its place.

By 0930, all the passengers were aboard; the ship's engines were already growling to be on the way, and the crowd of seasoned hands and newcomers were on the shore this morning to wave farewell to the "big yellow taxi" which they wouldn't see for months to come. *Aurora Australis*'s horn sounded a long, echoing farewell to the island as it got under way for the run down to the Antarctic continent to complete its mission. It was late in the season now for the ship to be going on to Antarctica, and it would only stop in at Casey Base before making for home in Hobart. Sea ice, "growlers," and freshly calved bergs would become a major threat to shipping from now until the next voyage at the end of the year. The ship's company had another four days' voyage before they reached Casey Base, the closest Antarctic base to Macquarie Island. The passengers found their sea legs quite quickly. For the crew it was business as usual: cooking, cleaning, maintaining the ship and making sure that everything ran as smoothly as possible. Life aboard *Aurora Australis* resumed its own rhythm.

Chapter twelve

Macquarie Island
Sunday

After *Aurora Australis* departed on Saturday morning, the new expeditioners were given their initial briefings, and had settled into their winter quarters. The unusually high tides and vicious storm had left a certain amount of debris around the base, and all hands were expected to help clean up. Later, experienced hands would show the new chums around the station. Rosters for duties were drawn up, as every person was expected to volunteer for extra chores regularly. Saturday night, there was a small celebration to welcome the rookies.

By Sunday morning, life had returned to normal, and the new scientists and rangers were able to venture out with the seasoned staff, carrying their sample pots and paraphernalia, to meet the wildlife and start their work.

Giles Ferrant, a fellow pinniped expert, staying on for another winter to monitor the seal and sea lion populations, was out with Jeremy Munroe. Giles was aware that Jeremy's supervisor, Dougal Ferguson, had disappeared from *Aurora Australis* en route to Macquarie Island, but Jeremy seemed reconciled to carrying on his studies alone for now, until a new supervisor could be found. Giles had sought him out the previous evening at the welcoming party, expressed his condolences, and offered to have Jeremy tag along with him on his rounds. He was keen to show Jeremy his area of interest.

As they slogged their muddy way through the heavily vegetated and waterlogged peat bog, known locally as featherbed, towards the shoreline, they spoke little. The midges were still very active, and the act of speaking involved getting mouthfuls of the nuisance insects. Once they were down by the shore, the men were able to chat about Giles's current project, and he in turn quizzed Jeremy about his doctoral research. Both men were a similar age, and they found conversation relatively easy as they went.

Giles said he wanted Jeremy to see a particular colony of seals, which gathered on a stretch of the pebbly shore; they scrambled across lichen-encrusted rocks, still slick and treacherous from the pounding surf spray. As they approached the boulders, Giles stopped abruptly and squinted.

"Can you see that over there, Jeremy?"

"Where? Oh there," Jeremy replied, following the direction of Giles's pointing finger. "Looks like a casualty of the storm. I guess that happens often?"

"Sometimes. Occasionally, but not usually. The seals stay well out to sea when there's a big blow on; it seems to be safer out there, under the waves, but sometimes a predator will get them, or they die of old age. Let's take a look, shall we? We'd better go age and sex the creature anyway; it could be a female; if she has a pup, it'll starve."

Giles scrambled away towards the dark body. Jeremy followed more cautiously; he didn't want his first day to be his last because of a broken leg.

Giles reached the body and let out a sudden yell that brought Jeremy clambering over the remaining rocks at top speed. He stopped so abruptly when he saw what the other man was yelling about, he slipped between two boulders, wrenching his ankle. He yelped in pain, but Giles didn't turn around; he was staring at a corpse. Jeremy couldn't believe what was in front of his eyes either; it was not a seal at all.

A man lay, flung carelessly across a wave-cut platform, limbs awry, clad in a long dark coat; he was not a pretty sight. Jeremy looked at the face, then turned and vomited violently; he wore some on his clothes as it sprayed back on him in the wind. The dead man's face was lacerated and purple with bruises, but the worst of it was that the eyes were missing. Jeremy had never seen anything quite so hideous in his life. His face went white as his brain started to whir; there was something familiar about that coat.

Meanwhile, Giles had also lost his breakfast, but he wiped his mouth on one sleeve as he fumbled around in his jacket for his two-way radio. He was pressing the button, shouting at the radio operator at the base to pick up his call.

"C'mon, c'mon, pick up! C'mon, damn you! Oh, there *must* be someone there! Pick up!" he screamed into the two-way. In frustration, he dropped the device, which squawked into life; he'd forgotten to release the button in his panic. He scooped it up quickly and started gabbling into the radio.

He shouted to Jeremy, "They're on their way with a sled. We have to wait here for them."

Jeremy nodded mutely; he sat down heavily on the slippery rock, rubbing at his ankle and pulled his padded anorak tightly across his chest. He didn't want to look at the battered corpse; he was suddenly very cold, and his foot was on fire. He looked across at Giles, who shook his head and huddled into his own warm clothing. There was nothing to do but wait. The man was beyond help.

***

Eventually two people bearing a stretcher between them came clambering over the rocks towards the shocked men. They shouted something but their words were snatched away by the whistling wind. Giles picked his way over to them, shouted and gestured, then led the way to the body. Jeremy got up painfully to offer help, but Giles waved him to sit down again.

Between them the three men manhandled the body onto the stretcher, and made their way cautiously across the rocks. Jeremy joined them and took a corner of the stretcher. It was a long, slow walk back to the base; Jeremy limped along, his ankle throbbing.

When they arrived at the base station, they were directed to the doctor's surgery where Dr Jenny Jones was waiting for them. She had already organised a trolley for the corpse, and the men put their burden down gently but with obvious relief. As she went to cover the body with a sheet, she brushed its long greying hair aside and had a quick preliminary look at its face. Jeremy was watching her, fascinated; suddenly the penny dropped, and he *knew* why the coat had niggled at his brain. He gasped loudly and grabbed hold of the trolley so he wouldn't fall. Jenny looked at Jeremy; his face had turned green and he was sweating profusely. She ordered him to sit down at once and asked one of the station hands to bring a cup of tea for him; he was in shock. While she was waiting for the tea, Jenny told him to take off his boot; she had noticed him limping when the men had arrived.

"No, it's okay, I'll be fine, Doc."

"I'll decide that, thanks!" she said with a twinkle in her eye. "That's what they pay me for, you know. How did you twist your ankle?"

"I slipped on a rock and got caught between two large ones when we found the body. Sorry if I stink, but I forgot about the wind when I was sick."

The doctor laughed. "Well, you won't do that again, will you! Now hold still while I take off this boot and look at your foot." She eased Jeremy's heavy hiking boot off and the ankle began to swell immediately.

"Hmm, can't feel any broken bones. I think it's just sprained. I'll bandage it for you and you'll have to keep off it for the rest of the day. Doctor's orders!" she added as he started to protest.

Giles brought the tea and Jenny made Jeremy sip it; it was sweet, hot, and black, and when he started to revive a little, some colour came back into his face.

"Jeremy, is it?" He nodded. "Now, Jeremy, how are you feeling? You are very pale, and you're a bit clammy. Is the ankle paining you a lot?"

Jeremy shook his head. "No," he replied miserably, "no. But I recognise, or at least I *think* I recognise the dead man. I think it's my professor. He went missing a few nights ago when we were at sea. Sorry, I think I'm going to be sick again."

The doctor moved with amazing speed as she grabbed and thrust a steel bowl into his hands so he could vomit without fouling the floor.

"Giles," she said quietly as she applied a compression bandage to Jeremy's foot and ankle, "can you please ring Roger? I think he needs to get here now. He'll want to talk to young Jeremy here, and then will you show him back to his cabin and make sure he stays off that foot at least for today please? I don't think it's broken, but he'll need to keep it elevated and iced to bring the swelling down."

She looked at Jeremy. "Okay, so you heard all that, and you're going to do it, okay?"

"Okay, Doc, and thanks. And thank you for the tea. It was real nice."

Giles rang Roger in his office; he was there within two minutes.

"Now, young man, you think you know this man under the sheet?"

"Yes, sir, I believe it's my professor, Dougal Ferguson. He went missing Thursday morning. I know he's a mess, sir, but I think it's him. I recognise his coat; I've seen it hanging up in our cabin, and it always hangs in the front hall at his house. And he had long grey hair and blue eyes. And he was tall and leanly built."

"Thank you. I remember seeing the professor at mealtimes on the ship, and Peter Gallagher and Marcus were talking about the incident when the ship arrived Friday. I also remember helping to keep watch for the professor on Thursday morning."

Roger lifted a corner of the pale green sheet and looked at the corpse's face; he managed not to recoil, but it was revolting. The crabs had made a feast of the poor bastard's eyes. No wonder the lad had puked!

"Okay, I believe the doctor would like you to go and rest that foot for the rest of today. I'll be in my office if anyone needs me." Roger left the room abruptly; the sight of the professor's face had shaken him. He headed into the mess and poured himself a strong black coffee and took it with him to his office. He called the radio operator, explained the situation and asked him to put through a call to *Aurora Australis*. Peter Gallagher needed to know his lost scientist had been found. The problem of getting the man's body back to Hobart was something he would have to talk to Peter about; it would be at least another week before *Aurora Australis* could swing by and pick it up. He picked up his coffee and wandered along to his office.

With Giles helping him, Jeremy hobbled out of the doctor's room and back to his own cabin, where he dutifully elevated his foot with pillows and took out a book to while away some time until lunch. The book lay untouched; Jeremy was thinking.

***

When the lunch gong sounded throughout the building, Jeremy was dozing. He groggily opened one eye, and winced as he moved his foot. His stomach growled; he had lost his breakfast and it was demanding food. He swung his legs carefully over the side of the bunk and gingerly put his foot to the floor. The sprained ankle wouldn't bear his weight without pain, but he was hungry and wanted to eat. He sat for a couple of moments, then grabbed the chair and used it as a walking frame, hopping along behind. His progress was slow, but steady, and he reached the dining room door. There was a certain satisfaction on his face as he wrestled the door open, and shuffled through. His unorthodox entrance earned him a round of ragged applause. He dropped into a seat, sweating, but triumphant. Giles was at a far table, but he came over and helped Jeremy to hobble to the self-service cafeteria; Jeremy was able to snag a tray, and, hopping along, could select his meal from the range of foods available. Only at the end of the line did he relinquish the tray to Giles, who carried it back to the table for him.

"Thanks, I owe you one," he said.

"Not at all. Enjoy. I'll catch up with you after lunch."

"Okay. Thank you."

Giles returned to his own meal, leaving Jeremy to eat in peace. The others at the table were unsure whether to mention the grisly discovery the two men had made that morning, so they enquired about his ankle, and then started talking about the weather, always a safe topic. The Aussies were in a heated discussion about their favourite AFL teams back home; names were bandied about with a casually knowledgeable air. Jeremy didn't follow the Australian football scene; he'd been brought up on baseball, gridiron, and ice hockey. He was just starting on his main course when one of the general hands who had come to the rescue earlier in the day leaned across from his table and asked him about the body.

Jeremy froze, fork halfway to his mouth. He looked at the man, then deliberately returned his food to the plate.

"He's in the doctor's surgery as far as I know. What of it?"

"Someone said you knew who it was. How's that, then? You've only just arrived."

Others at the table pricked up their ears; this was news to them.

"I recognised him. He was on the same ship I came on, like a lot of the people here."

"Yeah, but..." persisted the man. "Someone said..."

"Shut up, Frankie! Let the man eat in peace. He looks half starved!" There was a trickle of amiable laughter around the table. Frankie reddened, but shut his mouth, and concentrated on the mound of food on his plate. Jeremy felt the man's discomfort and resentment at being taken to task; he decided to settle the matter. He spoke quietly but firmly.

"It was my professor who went missing on Thursday morning from *Aurora Australis* on our way here. They think he fell overboard. I recognised his hair and his coat." He glanced at Frankie, whose face was still flushed with embarrassment, and asked, "Anything else you'd like to know? Or can I have my meal in peace!"

"Sure, sorry, mate. We were just wondering, seeing as how we came down and helped you back with him."

"It's okay, I guess. I'd just rather not talk about it at the moment, if you wouldn't mind—I've already lost one meal today. I'd rather not lose another. It was just a hell of a shock."

"Yeah," butted in another man, "Giles was as sick as a dog too."

"Okay, fellas," said a red-headed woman, "I'm eating, here. Subject's closed."

They all resumed eating, until Jeremy felt a tap on his shoulder and saw Roger McDougal standing there.

"Jeremy, when you've finished eating, could you come and see me in my office please?"

"Sure, Mr McDougal."

"It's just Roger, Jeremy. We don't stand on ceremony here."

"Oh, okay, Roger, I'll be there."

The station head patted Jeremy on the shoulder and returned to his own table. He was sitting with Giles and a few other, older scientists. Jeremy returned to his meal, and was interrupted again, this time by Jenny Jones, who was holding out a crutch to him.

"Someone told me you'd improvised, but this might be handier, until you can put the weight on your foot again."

Jeremy blushed; his table companions laughed light-heartedly at him.

"Thanks," he laughed. "This'll be much easier than the chair."

"Full marks for ingenuity, young man," she said, and returned to her workplace.

"Think you've won a fan, young Jezz!" quipped one of the 'wags'.

"Uh, you think so?" he asked.

"Yep!"

Jeremy managed to eat the remainder of his meal without further interruption, and, hefting the crutch under his arm, did a few practice steps before turning towards the station head's office.

Roger was already back behind his desk as Jeremy knocked at the door.

"Ah, you wanted a word, sir?"

"Jeremy! Come in, close the door and sit down. Take a load off..."

Jeremy hopped to close the door, then sat down in an upholstered chair. He waited politely for the older man to say what was on his mind.

"Jeremy, I just want to bring you up to speed with what's happening with the authorities. I've asked Ken to radio *Aurora Australis* to let them know we've found a body. Now," —he looked Jeremy in the eye—"we're going to have to contact the police in Hobart and bring them up to speed. They'll have to contact his next-of-kin, and the coroner. I need to know… how sure are you that this is your missing professor? I mean, really sure…"

Jeremy sighed, and rubbed his face wearily with his hands. "I'm as sure as anyone can be, given that he's been battered around. Look, let me put it this way, as I told you earlier, I recognise his coat, his hair, his height and build. I'm *positive* it's him."

"Okay, thanks. Sorry to put you through this. You were friends with the professor, I believe?"

"Yeah, he was my prof, and my mentor and my friend. We did field trips together, and I went to his house a bunch of times. He is, *was*, a really cool guy, you know. Not like some stuffy old man, more like someone who was genuinely *interested* in what I had to say, and was happy to discuss stuff, and argue about stuff, and he and his wife welcomed me into their home. I mean, that's *massive*!" Jeremy sat back, suddenly exhausted by feelings which bubbled up within him.

"Thank you, Jeremy," said Roger McDougal. "I know it must be difficult for you, but we have to have our facts straight before we ask the police to contact his family."

"Oh God, no!" Jeremy exclaimed, "that would *kill* Beth! No, Roger, I'm positive it's Dougal Ferguson. Do you want me to put my name to it?"

"No, no, nothing like that. Thanks for coming in. Glad we could sort it out."

"So, what happens now?" Jeremy wanted to know.

Roger sighed. "Now I prepare a statement for the police in Hobart, stating that the body has been found and identified, and let them know how he will be sent home. There's no other way than by ship—a helicopter doesn't have the range, and a plane can't land here. Even a seaplane would be tricky. No, he'll have to stay cold somewhere until we can get Peter and his band of merry men to swing by and pick him up. In the meantime…" He looked meaningfully at Jeremy's bandaged ankle and foot. "In the meantime, I'll have a word with Giles to find you some light duties in the lab until that ankle's better. Can't have you out in the field — there'd be all kinds of OH&S issues, so you'll stay indoors until further notice. Okay?"

Jeremy sighed heavily. "Okay," he agreed. "Thanks. I feel kind of lost without the boss anyway. And I can't stay in my cabin all day; I'll go stir-crazy!"

"Exactly! Now, off you go, and if you see Giles, send him to see me, will you? Thanks."

Jeremy quietly hobbled out of the room as Roger set down to compose the statement for the police, but popped his head back around it.

"Ah, Roger, do you have a contact at the police? Get the radio guy to ask for Carrie Harkaway — she's a DC and my fiancée." And disappeared again, closing the door behind him. He hobbled off to look for Giles and the prospect of some lab work.

Roger gave his statement and instructions to contact DC Harkaway in Hobart to Ken in the radio room, and sat back to wait for Giles.

An hour later, Jeremy was summoned back to the radio room, to take a call from Carrie. Just hearing her voice made him feel better already, but he realised he had some serious thinking to do, regarding his future

***

Jeremy would have ample time to mull over events in the next few days while he mourned his friend and mentor. On Monday he was given enough work in the station laboratory to keep his hands and his brain busy for at least some of the time. The swelling in his ankle reduced, along with the sharp pain, and by the end of the week, he had taken the crutch back to Jenny Jones in the station's surgery. She had examined the ankle and declared it fit for work. She did warn him, however, not to injure it again, if he could help it.

After some heavy reflection, Jeremy couldn't see the point of staying on without his professor's guidance and their joint tasks, even though the crew had made him welcome. By the following weekend, he had, announced his intention to both Giles and Roger that he wished to return home, and requested a berth on *Aurora Australis* if one could be found.

Roger was sorry to see the young man relinquish his research work, but had come to understand that the bond between Jeremy and his professor had been very strong, and that Jeremy would more than likely need some grief counselling in the months ahead.

He voiced his disappointment that they would lose Jeremy so soon, but approved his loyalty and decision to return home. *Aurora Australis,* would, in all likelihood, be back to Macquarie Island by Monday morning and would take Dougal's body off by helicopter; Jeremy would accompany him.

Chapter thirteen

In the meantime, the call from Macquarie Island came to the South Hobart Police station via satellite phone on the Sunday afternoon that the professor's body was found. Carrie Harkaway had just started her shift when the switchboard put the call through to her desk.

"Hi, this is Carrie Harkaway, how can I help you?"

"This is Ken Sutton, radio operator on Macquarie Island. I have an urgent message from Roger MacDougal, station head. It reads: 'This morning a body was discovered on the rocks of Macquarie Island; it has been tentatively identified as that of Dougal Ferguson, missing from *Aurora Australis* since Thursday morning. Initial identification has been made by a colleague. *Aurora Australis* has been contacted and will collect the body en route to Hobart from Casey Base.' Message ends."

Carrie was shaken; Beth would be devastated. She answered calmly, "Thank you, Ken, I have your message. Could you send through a hard copy please?"

"Can do, right away. Any message for the boss?"

"Yes, tell him thanks for the information; we'll get onto it straight away. Ken, is Jeremy okay?"

"He had a bit of an accident out on the rocks when they found the body, but he's okay and resting up. He's just sprained his ankle. He'll be fine. I believe you know him?"

Carrie laughed in relief.

"Yeah, he's my fiancé. Can you send him my love please?"

"Will do."

"Thanks. Bye."

"Bye."

She hung up and tapped her fingers on the desk. A hard copy of the report would appear sooner or later; meanwhile, she had to find her DI and tell him the news. Then they would have to contact Beth Ferguson and break the bad news to her. Carrie had already volunteered to be the family liaison officer, even though it was usually a job for uniformed police.

She got up from her desk and went through to the DI's office. She knocked, entered, and gave him the news.

"Initial identification, eh? Okay, Carrie. You know this fella of yours—no chance he could be clutching at straws?"

"I don't think so, Gavan. I don't think Jeremy would be that desperate. But who knows?"

"Well, it's important, Carrie. We may have to go tell the man's wife she's a widow—we need something substantial to go on. Can you ring your bloke?"

"They rang by Sat phone, so I guess I could try that way. Leave it with me." She left his office and returned to her desk in the squad room. She picked up the phone and asked the switchboard for assistance. She was soon through to Macquarie Island station.

"Hello, Ken is it? This is Detective Constable Carrie Harkaway from the South Hobart Police. Yes," she laughed, "we just spoke. Is Jeremy available to answer a few questions please?"

"I'll have to get someone to get him. Can I call you back in, say, ten minutes?"

"Sure," Carrie answered. "Thanks."

"Cheers."

She had nothing to do but wait for the phone to ring. She had made herself a coffee and brought it back to her desk. While she waited, she opened her laptop and created a new Word document for the case. She typed in some notes. When the phone rang eight minutes later, she snatched it up. It was the switchboard again, redirecting the call she was waiting for.

"Hello?" she asked.

"Hi, it's Ken here from Macquarie Island. I have Jeremy Munroe to speak to you. One moment please." There was muted mutterings in the background, then Jeremy's voice came on the line.

"Hey, Carrie. How are you?" He sounded older, drained of emotion.

"Better than you, by the sounds of it, Jezz. Wonderful to hear your voice, honey!"

"Same here, babe. Roger said it was urgent I speak to you. This is about Dougal, isn't it?"

"Yeah, sorry. My DI wants to know how certain you are that the body is Dougal's. It's just that we don't want to go to see Beth if it isn't him after all. It would just distress her unnecessarily. Are there any clues as to why it could be him, apart from your gut feeling?"

"His hair is the same, it's his height and build, I couldn't tell by his eyes, because they're, well, missing…" Jeremy heard Carrie's sharp intake of breath and paused to gulp as well, suppressing a renewed urge to vomit. He continued quietly, "He's pretty battered around, Caz, but please don't tell Beth that. I guess the give-away is that the body's wearing a long dark fur coat, just like the one the professor kept hanging in the front hall, and took with him on this trip. It was the only thing missing from the cabin when he disappeared. Close enough?"

"Sounds close enough to me, sweetheart. Gavan, my DI, just wanted to make sure you weren't mistaken, I guess."

"No, honey, as far as anyone can tell, it's him."

"Are you okay, though? The radio guy said you'd been injured."

"Sure, honey, I'm fine. I just slipped and twisted my ankle between some rocks. Nothing serious, I promise. I'll live!" he joked.

"Okay, you'd better!" she ordered. "Catch you soon."

"You bet! Love you!"

"Love you too. Bye."

"Bye." And the phone went dead.

Carrie went back to Gavan's office and knocked on the door again. "It's him, boss. I've just spoken to Jeremy and he confirms that it's Dougal Ferguson all right."

"Shit!"

"Yep."

"Well, are you still willing to be the FLO? I know you know the family, so I'd appreciate it. I'll clear it with the super, and with uniform section. Let's get the paperwork prepared then we'll go around to see her. Do you think she'll be home?"

"No idea, but I can phone her first. She won't have gone far if she's out."

***

Stacey, the reporter who had his lost his scoop to the ambitious and mercenary Trinity, got a tip-off from an informant about the call from Macquarie Island. Miss Trinity was not at work that day; Stacey was at home too, but dropped everything to contact the police for confirmation of what he'd been told. The police were cagey about it;

the widow had not been informed, but they could confirm that a body had been found, washed up on the rocky shores of Macquarie Island the previous day. He set about checking the *Aurora Australis*'s passenger manifests, and came up with a name. Miss Trinity was not about to get *this* plum delivered into her scheming little hands. He lifted the phone and punched in a number.

"G'day, Gus, what're you up to? … Nothing? Excellent! Listen! I just got a tip-off from my friend on the switch at the cop shop. You know that bloke who went overboard a few days back? … Uh-uh, that's the one … Yeah, the slut got the by-line … Yeah, I know … Anyway, they've got an ID on him. Want to come with me? Excellent! I'll swing by and pick you up … Oh, you'll meet me there? Of course, you've already been there with TT. See you in half an hour. Bye."

He picked up his car keys and let himself out of his apartment, smiling and whistling. Miss Bitchface Trinity was not getting his scoop again!

***

Beth decided she needed to get back into her routine, and was going swimming at the local gym. Just as she was about to leave, the front doorbell rang through the house. Irritated, she went swiftly along the central corridor and was about to open the front door to greet this unexpected visitor, when she heard loud male voices. Through the living room curtains, she was dismayed to see a man with a camera and microphone boom advancing up the front path. She hurriedly dropped the curtain and reached for her mobile phone. The doorbell pealed again, and as the chimes died away, it was activated once more. She was seriously annoyed now. Her fingers were shaking with frustration as she found Carrie's mobile number, and hit the Call button.

Carrie answered, "Hobart Police, DC Harkaway speaking."

"Carrie," Beth said urgently, "thank goodness! Look, I know you're at work, but I wondered, can you come over?"

"Beth, are you okay? You sound distressed. Has something happened?"

Little did the girl know, Beth thought, but took a deep calming breath and answered, "There appears to be two reporters at my front door, and I think there's a TV van parked in the street. The doorbell is ringing non-stop. It's driving me crazy just now. I just wondered if you could pop over if you had time, or perhaps advise me what to do…" Beth let the thought die away. What was the use? She was going to have to face these people, and she was going to have to get used to dealing with them and their ilk. Dougal's disappearance had been headline news in the local daily papers for a day or two, but she thought the excitement might have died down by now. Apparently, she was wrong.

Carrie's voice arrested her attention. "Beth, stay where you are, if you can. I'm on my way."

"Thanks, you're a sweetie. I'll put some coffee on."

"Give me twenty minutes?"

"Cool, see you then."

She pressed End and put the phone back into her pocket. With a despairing sigh, she dropped her handbag onto the hall table, and retreated to the kitchen. She closed the connecting door, so the insistent jangle of the doorbell was partially muffled, and busied herself, preparing coffee for her and Carrie. She wondered fleetingly about how the girl would get through the press, then chuckled. They'd be fools to tangle with *her*; she was a tall, well-built young woman, with a confident and commanding air when needed. Beth thought about sending her a text message, advising the lass to come in through the back gate, where hopefully the journalists would not have camped yet.

As she picked up the mobile, it rang; Beth was exasperated. She looked at the caller ID—an unknown number. She pressed Reject and went back to sending Carrie a message. The phone rang again, then the house phone started ringing. She didn't bother answering it; she suspected it would be the press. Not content with hounding her on her doorstep, they were harassing her on the phone now. Perhaps it would be better if she went and faced them, if only to make them stop.

She carefully lifted the receiver from the house phone, so it couldn't ring again, then crept through to the front hall, taking a stepstool so she could access the doorbell control panel. Lifting the panel, she removed the batteries, and hid them in the hall table drawer. The clamour of the doorbell ceased immediately, and for a moment there was peace; then the knocking started. *These people are worse than sharks scenting blood,* she thought. She picked up the stepstool, and tiptoed away.

Suddenly, there was a furious pounding on the back door; Beth jumped, clapping one hand to her chest. Her heart was knocking almost as loudly as the noise at the door.

"Beth! Beth, are you there? It's Carrie." As she hurried to unlock the door, she heard "Go away, or I'll have you done for disturbing the peace. Leave the poor woman alone — she hasn't heard the news herself yet. Back off!" She heard Carrie sigh in exasperation at the reporters. "Beth, it's Carrie. Can you let me in, please?"

As Beth opened the door to admit her friend, camera flashes blinded her, and there was a clamour of demanding voices. "Mrs Ferguson, can you give us a statement please, love? Is it true your husband's been found? Ah, come on, love, give us a statement."

"I told you to BACK OFF!" shouted Carrie as she, a tall greying man, and a uniformed female police officer pushed their way through the door and shut it firmly in the faces of the people yelling on the back doorstep. She caught Beth gently by the shoulders and guided the older woman back into the kitchen. The jug had boiled. Carrie took charge, making coffee for them all.

"Carrie, thank goodness you could come, love. Oh! I'm sorry, I only put out two mugs — I'll get more..." Beth turned to find two more mugs, and a plate for some biscuits. As she lifted out a plate for some biscuits, she registered the significance of not one but three police officers. The plate slipped through her suddenly nerveless fingers, to shatter on the slate floor. She turned anguished eyes to her friend, who was looking very solemn.

"Sorry, my nerves are a bit jangled this afternoon — all this palaver going on outside. I'll just clean this mess up, won't be a moment." As she turned to leave the room, Carrie caught her gently by the shoulders and sat her down on one of the barstools.

"Danielle will do that for you, won't you, Danielle?" Carrie asked the WPC quietly. "You just sit down, and I'll pour the coffee, okay?"

The young female officer did as she was bid, disappearing and reappearing with a dustpan and brush; she cleaned the debris from the floor, depositing it into the kitchen tidy. Beth sat, stunned. What had the reporter said?

"Carrie," she faltered, face drained of colour. "Thanks for coming over. I can't imagine why those reporters were here. I'm so glad you could take time out from work to come and rescue me. I feel so silly..." Her voice faded, and her heart faltered as she saw the look in the girl's eyes.

Carrie sat down near Beth, and gently took her closest hand. "Beth, we were coming to see you because…" The young detective looked up at the other officers. "Gavan, let me do this, okay? Thanks." Carrie returned her attention to Beth.

"Beth, this is Detective Inspector Gavan Hopper and WPC Danielle Smyth." Both police officers nodded to Beth. Carrie continued, "We received news early this afternoon from Macquarie Island; a body has been found on the rocks. Apparently, they found it after a particularly bad storm; it had been washed up onto the shingle and two of the scientists discovered it early this morning." She looked at the older woman, whose face had turned ash-white under her light tan. She quietly ordered the DI, "Put plenty of sugar into Beth's mug, please. Hers is the blue one. Thanks, Gav." Her DI meekly did as he was asked; Carrie was on a mission.

Hot sweet coffee was put on the island bench in front of Beth, and Carrie continued gently but inexorably, "The medico on Macca had a look at the body —" She paused, chafing Beth's hand while the older woman moaned "No!"

" — and she has taken photographs which were sent to the station around lunchtime. Jeremy's identified him. As far as he can tell, it's Dougal. Oh Beth!"

Carrie caught Beth as she fainted and slipped from the stool; she lifted the small woman bodily into the family room, where she placed her softly on the couch, and wrapped the Indian rug around her. Beth had gone into shock. "Dani, could you phone for an ambulance, please? Mrs Ferguson's in shock and may need medical attention."

"Beth love, try to take a sip of this, please." Carrie sat down on the edge of the couch, cradled Beth with one arm, and lifted a mug to Beth's lips. Beth moaned and her eyelids fluttered, but her lips sought the sweet hot liquid, and she drank it like a child, slurping greedily while Carrie held the mug for her.

Carrie was distraught, for both of these beautiful people. Beth she loved like a mother, and the professor was such a lovely old man, fatherly in an absent-minded way, who always had a kind word for her, and took such an interest in her Jeremy, and his work. She was a professional, though, and couldn't afford to allow her own feelings to get in the way.

She pushed down her emotions and took a deep, calming breath.

Still cradling Beth in her arm, Carrie talked soothingly to her, "I'm so sorry, Beth. I hated being the one who had to tell you, but I felt it would be better coming from me, than from a stranger. They're going to bring Dougal's body back to Hobart on *Aurora Australis* when it returns from Antarctica. They will want you to go to the mortuary to identify him. Shh, I'll take you there; you won't have to do it alone."

Beth had started shaking violently inside the rug.

"Where's that bloody ambulance?" Carrie demanded. "Why isn't it here by now?"

The female officer peered through the window. "It's coming down the street now. Those bloody press vultures are taking photos of it; they're having a bloody field day!"

"Right, Danielle, get out there and order the mongrels off the property and out of the street. And if they refuse to disperse, arrest the bloody lot of them!"

The WPC gave her and the DI a strange look; she knew Carrie had recognised the photos of the man who had been found out on Macquarie Island, but she hadn't realised the depth of the bond between the older couple and herself. She let herself out and began issuing orders. Carrie could hear the young woman's voice through the closed door.

"Look. Just let the ambulance through, will you? You need to leave, and you need to leave NOW!" she barked.

"Ah, give us a break, sweetheart, we're only doing our jobs, just like you. All we want is a statement from the lady, and a photo or two. It's not every day a prominent person gets killed around here."

"Get lost, all of you! The lady needs medical attention, and right now, you are all obstructing the authorities in their rightful duties. Do I need to arrest you for disturbing the peace?"

"Geez, you buggers are a pack of killjoys! Come on, fellas, let's go, or we'll all be languishing in the cells. Talk about freedom of the press—not!" And with much muttering and grumbling, the group moved away down the street and into their waiting cars. Finally, the ambulance was able to park outside Beth's garage, and Danielle escorted the paramedics inside to where Carrie was holding Beth.

"She's had a shock. We've given her a hot sweet drink, but she's icy cold."

"What's her name?"

"Elizabeth, but she prefers Beth."

"Elizabeth! Beth! Can you hear me? I'm Joe and this is Simone; we're here to look after you."

Beth's eyelids fluttered; she slowly opened her eyes and looked around, slightly bewildered.

"Carrie? Did I faint? I'm so sorry, honey."

She struggled to sit up, and smiled wanly at the ambulance officers.

"I'm so sorry. There was no need to call you here, I'm fine, really I am!"

"We'll just check to see you're okay, Beth, then we'll leave you in peace."

***

After checking blood pressure and other vital signs, the ambulance officers decided that Beth was suffering shock, but was otherwise strong and healthy. They left, accepting Carrie's assurance that she would stay with Beth for the next few hours.

Carrie made more coffee, and they all sat in the comfortable chairs while they watched Beth's colour improve; she seemed calm now. Gavan Hopper cleared his throat and spoke softly to Beth.

"Hello, Beth, I'm DI Hopper, er, Gavan. I was wondering if you feel up to answering some questions now? Otherwise we could do this tomorrow morning."

He intercepted a warning glare from Carrie, but kept speaking. His voice was soothing and Beth started to relax, despite the occasional shudder which ran through her small frame.

"No," she answered wearily. "No, let's do it now. I don't think I could stand it, to have to wonder all night about Dougal. Tell me the worst. Tell me what happened to my husband."

Gavan sat down in a chair opposite Beth, and said, "Carrie has told you already that your husband's body has been found on Macquarie Island. At the moment, they're keeping him safe at the station there, until *Aurora Australis* steams back from the Antarctic to collect him. According to the doctor on Macquarie Island, he drowned."

He stopped at a warning signal from Carrie. Beth had buried her face in her hands, leaning forward as if warding off blows. Carrie placed a gently restraining hand on Beth's shoulder as the woman curled into a foetal position, rocking to and fro.

"My daddy drowned…" she whispered into her hands.

There was a profound silence in the large room for several minutes.

Beth gave a deep shuddering sigh, swooped in a lungful of air and sat up. She brushed her hair back from her face, and turned a grief-stricken but stoic face to the detective.

"Well, at least my Dougal's not missing any more. At least he'll come home to me… he promised me this was to be his last trip." She gave a loud hiccupping sob, and added in a smothered voice, "I guess he kept his promise, after all." At this, she burst into heart-broken tears.

Gavan looked meaningfully at Carrie and Danielle; he wasn't really comfortable around weeping women, but he had a job to do, no matter how unpleasant.

Beth gave a loud sniff, fished around in her pocket for a tissue or hankie, and blew her nose thoroughly. She wiped her eyes, was silent for a moment then added, "Jeremy found him? Oh, the poor boy! How horrible for him. He has such a good heart, your young man, Carrie. I know Dougal was extremely fond of him."

"It went both ways, Beth," said Carrie. "Jeremy idolised the professor."

Beth finished with her hankie, took a deep breath, and faced the Detective Inspector.

"So, Inspector, what did you want to ask me?"

Gavan Hopper was amazed at the woman's strength; she had processed the news with a surprising calm, almost as if she had been waiting for it.

"Mrs Ferguson, Beth, ah, did you and your husband have any problems in your marriage?"

Beth turned an astonished face to him, eyes wide with shock.

"Problems? No! No! No, we were very happy. He promised me he wouldn't be going on any more long assignments after this posting. He wanted to spend more time at home, here, with me…"

Her voice trailed off into a whisper.

Gavan was gentle, but relentless. "I'm really, really sorry to have ask you—did the professor have any money worries? A gambling problem? Any physical or mental health issues you knew about?"

Beth thought fleetingly of sums of money which had disappeared regularly from their account over the years; she was sure her face would betray her with a sudden rush of colour to her cheeks, but no one seemed to have noticed.

"Not as far as I am aware, Inspector," she answered stiffly. "He was not a gambler, to my knowledge, and as far as I know, he doesn't have any mental or physical health problems. He just loved doing his job and spending time with his seals, and giving lectures at the university when they invited him to speak. He wasn't ambitious or greedy. He was a *good* man and I think I resent these questions! Dougal's not coming back—he must have perished in those frigid waters, although why he would have done something so foolhardy, I'll never know. He couldn't even swim! But why in God's name would he jump overboard in the middle of the bloody Southern Ocean? I will never, *ever* believe he committed suicide, as the press is insinuating." Beth's voice had risen; by now she was shouting at the officers. She stopped, appalled by her behaviour; it wasn't their fault Dougal had died.

She pulled herself together and spoke in a calmer fashion. "Sorry, I know it's not your fault."

She clamped her lips together, and folded her arms defensively across her breast. The looks she shot at Gavan Hopper would have intimidated a lesser man.

"Beth, er, ah, I am not in the least impugning your husband's good name. Please understand that these are routine questions we need to ask. We're just trying to understand why he would have jumped off a moving ship in the middle of the ocean, especially if you say he couldn't swim. We're just trying to ascertain whether it was a tragic accident, or foul play. We're hoping it was a tragic accident, but we have to ask questions in order to rule out any underlying motive he might have had to commit suicide."

The word hung in the air; a dangling sword.

"My husband would *never kill himself!*" Beth hissed at him. "How *dare* you even *imply* it?"

Reproached, DI Gavan Hopper asked, "Did your husband own a long dark coat, by any chance?"

Beth exploded out of her chair with such force it nearly tipped over.

"That bloody coat! That bloody coat!"

Gavan Hopper looked stunned as Beth raged at him, "Do you know how many times I wanted to send it to the thrift shop? Do you know how many times he said *No*? How could you... Yes, he owned a long dark coat—it was sealskin, I believe. Dougie's had it forever, I think. Don't tell me they found his coat, too?"

The police exchanged meaningful glances, which Beth intercepted.

"He had it with him? Oh, that's just *too much!*"

She paced angrily around the room, took several shuddering breaths in order to calm herself and said with icy dignity, "If you've finished asking your *routine* questions, Detective Inspector, I'd like you to leave now. Carrie will see you out!"

A chastened Detective Inspector, and a mystified WPC, at a smouldering look from Carrie, stood up to leave. Gavan Hopper was all apologies, and not only to Beth; Carrie looked fit to kill.

"I'll stay with Beth tonight, Gavan," she said politely, coldly. "We'll be fine. I'll see you in the morning."

She escorted both of her colleagues to the back door, saw them out and locked the door.

"Beth, I'm so sorry… That Gavan, he's a bit persistent at times."

Beth sighed wearily. "No, honey, he was just doing his job, I guess. Sorry I got carried away… that blasted old coat… Please apologise to that nice little Danielle for me, will you? I was very rude." Beth's voice was heavy, and now that Gavan had gone, her shoulders slumped and she sat down and snuggled into her rug; she was icy to the bone and very, very tired.

"Carrie honey, you don't need to stay here all night. I'll be fine, really."

"No deal, Beth. You've got me for tonight at least." She stopped in front of Beth, and asked, "Is there anything to eat, apart from biscuits? It's just that it seems like a long time since lunch and I'm getting a bit hungry."

As she had hoped, this childlike appeal worked on Beth, who sat up, flipped off the rug and stood up slowly.

"Oh sweetie, I'm so sorry, I should have cooked something. I can't even remember what's in the larder right now." She swayed on rubbery legs and sat down abruptly. "Guess you'll have to forage for yourself, kid. Don't think I can stand up right now."

Carrie rearranged the rug around Beth's shoulders, gave her hand a pat, and went across the large room to the kitchen to prepare a meal.

They shared an omelette, some toast, and more coffee. When

Beth suggested a Scotch, Carrie found the tumblers and poured each of them a drink.

Beth curled up on the couch, and dropped off to sleep in exhaustion.

Carrie quietly covered her with the beautiful rug, turned out the lights and settled down on the window seat to watch the flickering lights across the river. It would be a long night.

Chapter
fourteen

75oS Latitude
As far south as a ship could go.

For those returning for another Antarctic winter, the colonies of penguins and fur seals scattered along the icy coastline were a welcome sight; the newcomers were rendered speechless, utterly dumbfounded by the sheer *enormity* of the place. They appreciated being able to disembark straight onto the ice shelf that the ship nuzzled up against; no need to moor offshore and be ferried across as they had needed to be, to get to Macquarie Island's rocky shores.

Aurora Australis arrived in the early morning, and by mid-morning had offloaded all the supplies necessary to sustain life on the Antarctic ice shelf, plus the sixty-odd expeditioners and service personnel arriving to replace those who had spent the summer or an entire year at the base. Glaciologists, meteorologists, climate change scientists, chefs, medical staff, and the trades people vital to the maintenance and smooth running of the base; they were keen to disembark and get busy in their new home for the next six months at least. Those who had finished their year of research and observation were looking forward to processing their valuable data, and to being reunited with family and friends back in Tasmania and beyond. They were already aboard, with their duffel bags and precious statistics. The ship's three helicopters had been busy since *Aurora Australis's* arrival, transferring supplies to and waste containers from the base. The constant pulsing of the rotor blades echoed across the frozen landscape; they would not stop until everything and everyone was where it should be. Part of the Australian Antarctic charter decreed that all waste would be removed, ensuring that the Antarctic remained the most pristine environment on Earth.

The crew was kept busy during this time; the daylight was receding day by day; soon there would be months of almost total darkness. Even in the morning and middle of the day, the floodlights were switched on for working safety. The ship would only remain at Casey as long as it took to ensure that all was in order, then Peter Gallagher and his navigator would have to set the ship's course basically north-east, back to Macquarie Island; time was of the essence now, as the usual seven-day voyage would have to be lengthened due to having a body to collect. Even retracing their route, it would still be a seven- or eight-day voyage, and there was always the risk of encountering the ever-present ice floes and bergs. Peter had only the time to exchange the briefest of pleasantries with the station leader before the cargo and passenger reloading was completed.

"Bad business, this!" remarked Gareth Lumley, station leader, who was staying on for another winter. "Bad business indeed! I've never met this bloke, but what a hell of a way to die."

"Yeah," replied Peter. "Now we have to backtrack to Macca to pick up his body instead of going straight home. That's going to be fun, I don't think!"

"Well, it's too far for a chopper to fly from anywhere to pick him up. What is it? Over 1100 kilometres from Hobart to Macca? Doubt there'd be a chopper capable of a round trip. Anyway, mate, good to see you again. Guess I won't be seeing you when I go home in October; didn't you say you were retiring?"

"Yeah, that's right. Don't know what I'll do with myself, but it comes to us all, my friend, it comes to us all."

"Shame this shit had to go down on your last voyage, though," Gareth echoed Peter's thoughts.

"Yeah, but you know the old saying 'Shit happens!' Well, everyone's aboard, you've got enough supplies for 300 days, so we'll make a move. Take care of yourself, and look after the greenhorns, eh? Don't let them go falling into a crevasse!" With a chuckle, the two men did an awkward, one-armed, back-slapping ritual, and Gareth descended the gangway to the shelf ice. He shouted up at Peter.

"So long, mate, and thanks for everything. Safe journey!"

"Thanks!" Peter shouted down to the man. "See you in Hobart some time. We'll go and have a pint."

"You're on! See you!" And with that, Gareth started towards his motorised sled for the brief bumpy ride across the ice shelf back to the station.

The gangway was hauled up, and the ship got under way. It was a long way home.

***

Peter stood at his place on the bridge as the ship nosed its way away from the ice shelf; he kept a keen eye on the screens, always watchful for any floes. "Set course for Macca, mate," he said to Bob, his navigator. "We've got a body to collect." He sighed. Going back to Macquarie Island was the last thing Peter wanted to do. Meanwhile, there was the problem of where to stow a body for the return trip to Hobart; he would have to speak to the crew. No one was going to be happy about having a corpse aboard, let alone the sheer bloody inconvenience it would cause.

"Jack," he called out to his second-in-command, "see what you can do about finding some cold storage for the professor's body once we have it aboard.

"Glenn, when you can get through, call the Macca base station to let them know we're on our way back, please? Tell the new station boss, what's-his-name again… Roger… tell Roger we won't be putting ashore. We'll send a chopper in to lift the prof's body out on a stretcher, so they'll need to have it ready for us when we arrive."

"No worries, boss," Glenn replied. "Do you want me to make contact with AMSA or Hobart to let them know we're on our way?"

"Yeah, probably wise. Thanks, mate."

Glenn got busy with his various radio sets, to alert Macquarie Island that they were at sea and headed back. With a favourable reply, he pushed back his rolling chair, flipped his headphones down onto his neck, and grinned at his captain. "All done, boss, they'll be expecting us in four days or so. We'll be in touch again once we have the island in sight."

"Thanks, Glenn. That's one problem taken care of. Now we have to work out where to store the professor's body. Jack!" he called again, "get the crew to prepare a secure space on the cargo deck for the body please."

"Will do. On my way."

Jack left the bridge; Peter watched the man pick his way carefully across the deck. Although the vicious winds had abated, there was still the risk of slipping on the wet decks. Harnesses were still necessary out there. Peter returned to his watch for ice; with his binoculars, he scanned the horizon and closer to the ship's bow. So

134

far, so good.

"Bob," he spoke quietly to the navigator, "keep an eye out, eh? . I'm going down to the mess to speak to the crew and passengers; they deserve to know we're diverting to Macca. They won't be happy, but tough luck."

***

Peter made his announcement in the mess, and took some questions. Most were to do with time frames for reaching Hobart, a couple were about the professor's demise; these questions came from the expeditioners returning home after their stint in Antarctica. Peter dealt with these, then left the mess with a plate of food and some coffee. He spoke to Jason's assistant, who agreed to have more coffee and sandwiches brought up to the bridge for his officers, who couldn't spare the time at present to get a decent meal.

Having organised all of this, Peter returned to the bridge. They were making good time now; the waves, while larger than the average vessel would find comfortable, were no match for the stabilised icebreaker. She ploughed through them with ease. Very few passengers had retired to their cabins with seasickness.

***

Four days later, they were within helicopter distance of Macquarie Island. Peter asked Glenn to raise the Wireless Hill Station, with an ETA of noon, Sunday. The station radio operator confirmed this, and assured Glenn that they would be at the shore with the professor's body.

Two hours later, the radio operator received another call, to say that all was in readiness; the professor's body had been securely sealed in a body bag and strapped to a stretcher. The station head, a couple of general hands and the medic would meet the helicopter at noon. Glenn took a message, which he then relayed to his captain.

"Pete, we'll be picking up the prof's body, he's been put into a body bag and is ready for transport on the stretcher. There's another thing – that young Canadian bloke is coming home with the body. Apparently, he was the one to identify what was left of the prof, and he's insisting on returning home. They want to know if we'll pick him up too."

"Of course! Jeremy, wasn't it? We'll find him a berth somewhere. Guess he didn't want to be left behind. He was pretty close to the old man."

"Were they related, do you think? They looked pretty similar, from what I can remember."

"No, I believe the lad was his student, nothing more. Okay, Glenn, thanks for that. I'll find the youngster a berth."

***

It was a very subdued and quiet greeting the helicopter pilot got when he shuttled the craft across to the island just after midday. He landed on the helipad, rotors kicking up the odd flake of snow, and dust from the rocky ground. It took very little time for the small welcoming party, including Jeremy, to carry the stretcher across to the chopper, whose rotors were still whirling lazily above their heads. Between them, they transferred the dark body bag onto the chopper's sled, secured it with straps, and stood back. Jeremy waited for the pilot's signal to get aboard, duffel bag in his hand; there was an awkward moment of handshakes, "goodbye and thank you" to Roger — the new station head, Jenny — the doctor, and the two general hands — Brett and Lee — who had helped carry the laden stretcher from the cold storage to the shore for its melancholy journey home.

Jeremy hopped aboard the helicopter, fastened his harness, donned the headphones, and waved to those on the shore. Then he sat back in his seat and closed his eyes. James, the pilot, eyed him surreptitiously; the Canadian was a mess. James spoke into his mike, gave the others a whirling gesture with his finger, to warn them to stand well clear, and carefully lifted off. Roger, Jenny, and the others held their arms across their faces to protect themselves from the downdraft as the chopper lifted into the air.

The sled bearing Dougal's body came clear of the ground, and swung a little in mid-air beneath the craft. James radioed in to Glenn, who could see they were on their way; Peter gave Dave the chief engineer the order, "All Ahead, Full Speed," sounded two long blasts from the horns in farewell and the ship began to move out into open water while the chopper was flying towards it.

Those on shore raised their hands in farewell and watched the ship steam away. James put the helicopter down perfectly on *Aurora Australis*'s tossing helipad deck, and several crew members came running. They secured the chopper to the deck with chains, then removed the sled containing Dougal's remains; they manhandled it to a secure, sheltered cold storage point on the forward deck, and chained the capsule down. Jeremy hadn't uttered a word until the helicopter touched down; he sat motionless until everything was off, and the safety checks were complete. James looked directly at Jeremy and motioned him to remove his headphones and unbuckle himself, and gave him a thumbs up gesture.

Jeremy turned to James and simply said, "Thank you!"

The pilot spoke into his microphone. "Roger that, boss, out." He turned to Jeremy.

"Um, Jezza, the boss wants to see you on the bridge, pronto."

James then removed his headphones and unbuckled his harness. Jeremy repeated his thanks to the young pilot, who smiled deprecatingly, and slapped him on the shoulder. "Get going, sport, the old man is waiting for you. Best not keep him waiting, eh?"

"Thanks again, for bringing Dougal and me back."

James smiled sadly and growled softly "Go on mate, get out of here."

Jeremy clambered down from the cockpit and took a few tottering steps across the deck before he found his rhythm, and made his way up to the bridge. He was very glad his sprained ankle had healed in the time he had waited for the ship to return.

"Well, Jeremy, we meet again! The boys have the professor's body stowed safely away, and we'll find you a bunk somewhere." Peter looked closely at Jeremy. "Lad, you look like shit! When did you last sleep or eat?" Jeremy caught a glimpse of himself in the bridge's windshield; the captain was right, he looked absolutely haggard. His face was gaunt from shock and lack of sleep; he was looking wretched.

"Got a girlfriend in Hobart, Jeremy?" Peter asked.

"Carrie, my fiancée. She's an Aussie, from Sydney originally. She's a detective."

"Well, I suggest you get some grub into you, and get some decent sleep before you get anywhere near Hobart. Otherwise, she'll take one look at you and run screaming! Now go and rest up. That's an order!"

"Just tell me where to go, please, and I'll go stow my gear. Oh, and thanks for taking me home too. I just couldn't stay there on the island and leave Dougal's wife to cope alone. She's been like a mom to me, and to Carrie as well. Besides, I have to see her and explain— I feel so guilty. I should have stopped him."

"I'm told you were the one to identify his body, is that correct?"

Peter asked.

Jeremy gulped; it was not a pleasant memory. "Yeah, it sure wasn't nice. He'd been a bit munched up by a whole bunch of crabs and stuff." He shuddered.

"Okay, lad, off you go. Go and see the steward in the mess. He's expecting you, and he'll show you to your berth. He'll also rustle you up some grub, and then you need to go and get some serious beauty sleep."

"Thanks. I feel pretty done-in."

***

Jeremy settled into his accommodation and spent the following three days either staying in the cabin he was sharing with a couple of seasoned expeditioners returning from Casey, sitting alone on the deck with Dougal's body in its capsule, or eating quietly in the mess. He didn't feel like making small talk, and avoided others when he could. He spent a lot of time in introspection. He was looking forward to seeing his girl again, but he was apprehensive about his reception from Beth; he was grieving for the loss of his mentor, and for the opportunity he had relinquished on Macquarie Island. He wasn't sure what his future held; all these thoughts and worries made him a virtual recluse.

He would be relieved when it was all over. But life would never be the same again.

***

Peter Gallagher asked his comms officer to radio ahead to Hobart Port Authority, to give an ETA, and request a berth at the dock. He also had him request an ambulance to meet the ship when it docked, to collect the body for the mortuary. He had been in touch with the coroner's office, to advise them about Dougal's return, and had contacted the police in Hobart. The families of the returning expeditioners had already been notified about the delay. Peter also contacted a certain young female detective, to ask her to come to the dock.

***

Thursday morning, *Aurora Australis* steamed slowly up the Derwent to Macquarie Wharf. There was a crowd of smiling faces awaiting her; she had brought their family members home safely after months or a year away. The expeditioners themselves were lined up along the rails, and as the ship pulled in, enormous cheers went up, uniting sea and land. An ambulance had pulled up, close to the gangway. This caused a ripple of curiosity and unease amongst the crowd on the quay, but they were mostly focussed on seeing their loved ones again. There was a certain amount of excited jostling amongst the crowds as the passengers disembarked. They were quickly swallowed up in welcoming embraces, and led away by their families, all talking at once and asking rapid-fire questions. Once the crowd had dispersed, a capsule was carried carefully down the gangway by four crew members to the waiting ambulance, followed by a pale-faced Jeremy. The ambulance officers got out and went to open the rear doors for the capsule. A smartly dressed Carrie approached the capsule.

"Jeremy!" Carrie called quietly.

"Carrie? Carrie! How? What? What are you doing here?"

"'Hi' would be good, sweetheart," she laughed as he rushed forward to embrace her.

"Hi, honey, I'm home!" They hugged and kissed hungrily, as if he had been away for years. She pulled away from him slightly, laughing.

"Yep, I can see that, sweetie. Come on, the car's waiting. I'll take you home then I must get back to work."

"Okay. Thanks for this. We'll talk tonight, yeah?"

"Okay, darling. Let's get you home. Then you can rest."

"I must go and see Beth, Carrie. I can't rest until I've seen her; I need to explain to her about Dougal. I feel real bad about the whole miserable situation."

"When did you last sleep, Jezz? You look like a ghost."

Jeremy chuckled. "The captain said if I didn't get some sleep and some food, you'd run for cover when you saw me!"

Carrie laughed as she opened the car and stowed his duffel bag in the boot. "Well, I did consider it, for about a split second..." She found herself locked in his arms again as he whispered against her hair.

"God, Carrie, what am I going to do?" With that, his lean frame started to shake, and she felt his tears on her head. She tightened her grip and held him tight until he had cried himself out.

"C'mon, hon, let's get you home. Get some sleep and then you can phone Beth to let her know you're back. She's not angry with you, Jezz, but she's really angry with her husband for going overboard, when he couldn't swim. She doesn't blame anyone but him. She blew up at my boss the other night when he suggested Dougal may have committed suicide. God, I've never seen her so angry." She stopped; he was staring at her in a disbelieving way. "Why are you looking at me like that, Jezz?"

"Dougal could swim! We often went swimming when we were on field trips. Didn't Beth know that?"

They got into Carrie's car; she looked across at him. "Curiouser and curiouser, said Alice…" she quoted. "Home. Now. And that's an order!" She put the car into gear and away they went.

Chapter fifteen

Thursday

Beth was in her cubby at the museum, recording Australian Aboriginal artefacts when her mobile phone vibrated on the desk.

"Hi, Beth, it's Carrie."

"Oh hi, honey! How are you?"

"I'm fine, thanks. Listen, I have some news. *Aurora Australis* came in this morning with Dougal's body aboard. The coroner's office sent an ambulance and he's at the mortuary."

"Oh. Okay. Thank you for letting me know."

"Jeremy has come home too. I picked him up at the dock and took him home. He's feeling pretty low at the moment. He's blaming himself for what happened, and he wants to come to see you."

Beth was surprised; she hadn't imagined Jeremy would tear himself away from his research work on Macquarie Island. His loyalty to her husband she found touching.

"Of course I'll see him! Did he think I'd be angry with him?"

"Well, actually, yes. He was a mess at the dock, but he calmed down and we've talked. Could you give him a call? I think he's scared to phone you."

"Silly boy! Sure, I'll call him in a while. Thanks for letting me know, honey. You two young ones must come and have a meal with me, real soon."

"Thanks, Beth. That would be great. Talk to you soon. Gotta go. Bye."

Beth hung up and returned to her cataloguing; her thoughts wandered towards Jeremy though. She'd finish what she was doing and give him a call. He was probably asleep right now.

Her mobile vibrated on the desk again; she put down her work and sighed heavily.

"Elizabeth Bouchier."

"May I speak with Mrs Ferguson please?" a slightly nasal female voice enquired.

"Speaking," she replied.

"Good morning, Mrs Ferguson. This is Annette from the coroner's office. Your husband's body was delivered to us this morning, and I wondered if you would be free at four this afternoon? We need you to come in to do a formal identification." Beth inhaled sharply at this terminology, but said nothing. The telephone voice continued, "It was initially identified as that of your late husband, Dougal Ferguson, on Macquarie Island, but we need his next-of-kin to identify him formally. Is there someone who could accompany you?"

"Not really," Beth sighed, then added, as a sudden thought hit her, "Perhaps his student could come in with me. He accompanied my husband's body back to Hobart. Perhaps I could ask him."

"That would probably be wise, Mrs Ferguson. It's never pleasant to have to go through this sort of thing alone..." The woman's voice sounded so overly solicitous that Beth felt the stirrings of anger.

"Fine. And where is your office?" Beth interrupted tersely.

"We'll have him ready for you. Thank you for your time."

It was obvious that the woman was about to end the call.

"Just a moment!" Beth said. "Would you be so kind as to give me the *address* please? I'm not locally born and bred."

"Oh, I'm so sorry. It's 48 Liverpool Street, in the Royal Hobart Hospital. Do you need directions?"

"No, thank you," Beth replied rather acidly, "I'm sure I can locate it. Thank you for your call."

"I'm sorry for your loss, Mrs Ferguson. Thank you. See you this afternoon at four. Goodbye."

Beth looked at the phone after the woman had terminated the call. She started to feel queasy, but she knew this was just the beginning of a roller coaster ride of emotions. She would have to get through it, somehow.

She sighed and called Jeremy.

He sounds more terrible than I feel, she thought as the young man answered the phone groggily.

"Jeremy, my dear boy, I'm so sorry. Did I wake you up?"

"Beth? Oh Beth, I'm so sorry... I should have rung you already. I feel so gutted by all of this. I feel guilty."

"Jeremy!" she spoke sharply to shake him out of his self-pity. "Jeremy, could you do me a huge favour, please? I need you to come to the morgue this afternoon at four, if you feel up to it. The coroner's office just rang. I have to go identify Dougal formally." Her voice caught on the enormity of what she was saying.

Jeremy was suddenly awake and alert. "Of course I'll come with you, Beth! What time and where?" he asked.

"Four o'clock, they said, at the morgue here in the city. It's a formality and they suggested I might want someone with me. Could you meet me there, please?"

"Where are you now? Are you at home? I could swing by and pick you up…"

"No, thank you, dear, I'm at work. I have to stay busy; that way I don't have to think about what has happened. Could you come by at, say, 3:50 p.m., to the museum? According to their directions, I don't think it's far. Hobart's not that big a place, is it?"

He chuckled a little. "Not compared with Vancouver or Ottawa, no. Okay, Beth. I'll be there at 3:50."

"Thank you, Jeremy. I just didn't know who else to call."

"No need for thanks. It would be a privilege to help you. Bye now. See you outside the museum."

"Thanks again, Jeremy. See you then."

She ended the call and tried to marshal her thoughts to the job at hand. She remembered to put the time into her phone calendar so she couldn't miss their appointment, and resumed her collating.

At 3:45 p.m., the mobile phone buzzed her five-minute alert. She downed tools, called to her colleague in the next office that she was leaving for the day, and went out into the late autumnal weather. There was a watery sun, which gave a little warmth, but the wind was turning cooler each day. Beth was glad she had remembered her jacket that morning.

Jeremy was prompt, and jumped out of his car to run around to open the door for her. She was gratified by this old-fashioned courtesy, and gave him a warm smile. He returned hers with a pale imitation. He was a ghastly colour, she reflected, and realised that he'd had almost as huge a shock as she had. Her warm, motherly heart went out to him. She leaned across the gear stick and kissed him gently on the cheek.

"Let's get this over with, shall we? You look terrible, and I don't want to even think about it."

"Beth, I—"

"No!" There was a vehemence bordering on panic in her tone, and her hand went up in a warding-off gesture. "No. I can't talk about this right now, Jeremy. We'll speak later, okay? Right now, I have to do something I think we all hope we'll never have to; identify a loved one's remains. He's at the Royal Hobart Hospital, in their morgue. Annette, I think her name was… Annette will meet us. I know I could have walked, but I just needed some company."

***

Although they were a little early for their appointment with the dead, Beth and Jeremy didn't have long to wait. A *tack-tack* of high heels on the linoleum floor announced the arrival of the coroner's assistant.

"Good afternoon. Mrs Ferguson? And this is…?" the same nasal voice enquired. Grey eyes looked appraisingly at Jeremy.

"Good afternoon. Annette, is it?" Beth asked. The woman smiled sympathetically and nodded, bouncing a very full head of long, tousled sun-bleached hair in their direction.

"This is Jeremy."

The woman's eyes widened in appreciation, and one of her perfectly drawn eyebrows raised slightly.

"Hello, Jeremy. Thank you for coming in. Who will be identifying the body?"

"I will" said Beth crisply.

"I wonder, Mrs Ferguson, if you could give me his details please?" she produced a black clipboard and a silver pen. "Name of deceased?"

"Dougal James Kenneth Ferguson."

"Date of birth?"

"20th April, 1955."

"Address?"

"Maranoa Avenue, Rose Bay."

"Marital status?"

"Married, to me."

"Children?"

"None living."

Beth felt Jeremy flash a glance in her direction.

"Children deceased?"

"Look! What is this all about? Why do you need to know about dead children?"

"It's routine, Mrs Ferguson. Children deceased?"

"One. Male. Age 3 years 2 months at time of death."

"Name?"

"Malcolm Dougal James Ferguson. Date of birth 27th June, 1990."

Beth was angry; how dare this officious young woman open old wounds like this? What possible use could they have for knowing this information?

"And your late husband's parents?"

Beth sighed; this was ridiculous.

"James and Morag Ferguson, both now deceased, and no, I don't know their dates of birth or death. Anything else?" She was icily polite now; her face was white with fury. She breathed deeply to calm herself.

Annette, unconcerned by any distress she might be causing, consulted her list.

"No, that would appear to be all, thank you. Would you both like to come through now? Follow me, please."

Without waiting for a reply from either of them, Annette turned on her heel and walked off, business-like in her crisp dark suit and four-inch heels. Beth and Jeremy exchanged a brief look and followed the woman quickly. Obviously it was a very busy place, with little time for pleasantries.

Annette led them into a small, darkened alcove with a padded bench seat, but both Beth and Jeremy remained standing. There was a plate glass window, with a maroon curtain drawn discreetly across the glass. Annette pressed a button located to one side of the window. An attendant peered through a corner of the curtain on the other side of the glass, looked enquiringly at Annette, gave a thumbs-up sign, and opened the curtain with a slightly theatrical flourish.

Beth's hand flew to her mouth as she tried to smother an anguished cry; her legs felt weak. Jeremy grabbed her sleeve to prevent her falling, then put a comforting arm around her shoulders to support her. Together they slowly went closer to the window.

Beyond the glass, on a trolley, body decorously covered by a white sheet, lay her late husband. Only his face had been exposed for identification purposes. Jeremy relaxed a little. Dougal was not as severely battered around the face as Jeremy remembered from his initial ID on Macquarie Island, for which he was *very* grateful. The skin had relaxed and most of the bloating had gone; the multiple lacerations had been cleaned. The mortuary assistants had closed Dougal's eyelids over the empty eye sockets. Jeremy shuddered involuntarily. Dougal's face now looked as if he had had a challenging time shaving one morning. Lighting in the room gave a more life-like appearance to the corpse's face, too. The attendant looked enquiringly at Beth; she looked at him, ashen-faced, and nodded. She mouthed the word "Yes."

Annette, who had been standing to one side, waiting with a clipboard and pen, now asked Beth formally, "Do you identify this person as Dougal James Kenneth Ferguson, your late husband?"

"Yes," Beth whispered. She cleared her throat. "Yes," she answered more definitely. "Yes, this is the body of my late husband Dougal James Kenneth Ferguson." She looked up at the attendant waiting on the other side.

"Thank you," she mouthed. He nodded in acknowledgement and covered the corpse's face.

Annette produced her clipboard.

"Can you sign here, please?" Annette asked, holding out the clipboard and the pen for Beth's signature. Beth obediently signed her name, handing back the clipboard; it was suddenly *real*.

She stuffed her knuckles into her mouth to keep from crying aloud in that quiet, sombre place.

Beth found herself crushed into Jeremy's jacket; the young man's arms went around her and held her close as he wept bitterly. She made soothing noises to him, patting him gently on the back like a baby. *They should have been Malcolm's arms*, she thought suddenly, and mourned afresh for the little son she had lost so many years ago. She could not cry. She was numb, numb to the very depths of her being.

***

Jeremy stood in that darkened room, weeping for his friend as the man's widow patted him on the back, comforting *him*, losing herself in a maternal moment. He sobbed to her of how Dougal had thought the world of her, how much he had spoken of her when he and Jeremy were working together. He gradually calmed down, as she continued to pat him on the back and croon to him in an unknown yet vaguely familiar language as one would, to soothe a distressed infant. Her words filtered into his consciousness, and slowly he came back into himself. Jeremy loosened his hold on her; she stood alone, then scrabbled around in her handbag for a handkerchief, which she offered him.

He wiped his nose and then impulsively bent to plant a kiss of thanks on Beth's cheek and whispered, "Sorry about that." She managed a ghostly smile.

"Thank you, lad. Are you okay? Shall we get out of here?" He nodded and opened the door. The foyer was empty; Annette had disappeared into the maze of corridors. Beth didn't know if she needed to complete more paperwork, but she had had enough, and decided to leave anyway. Annette could contact her again if she needed to. The atmosphere in here was altogether too depressing to stay a moment longer than necessary.

The autumn afternoon air was fresh, pure, and clean, and a balm to the spirits after the gloom of the hospital mortuary.

They walked slowly back to the car in the watery sunshine. Jeremy opened the door for her again, made sure she was settled comfortably before starting the engine and pulling away from the kerb.

"Do you want to go back to work, Beth, or shall I take you home? I can ask Carrie to pick me up later, and we'll bring your car home for you. Okay?"

Beth sighed. She was suddenly too exhausted by grief to return to the museum.

"Home, I think," she murmured. "Yes. That would be nice. I don't think I could face going back to work today. I think I need to be alone for a while."

"Okay, sounds like a plan."

They drove to Beth's house in silence; Jeremy concentrating; Beth already contemplating the task ahead.

When they reached the house, Jeremy took out his phone and dialled Carrie's number. He briefly explained what had happened, where he was, and what he proposed to do about getting Beth's vehicle back to her.

Carrie obviously agreed with this plan, judging by the smile of relief on Jeremy's face.

He accompanied Beth into the house, but instead of taking him through to the large area at the back, Beth stopped in the front hall, and gave him her spare car keys from the bowl on the hall table. She then gently but firmly propelled Jeremy out the front door, gave him a brief hug, reassured him she would be fine, and closed the door on the outside world. It was 4:30 p.m.

***

After Jeremy departed to collect her car, Beth wandered aimlessly around her living room. She closed her hand around the framed photograph of Dougal and held it to her lips momentarily, before replacing it tenderly on the mantelpiece. She frowned at the light patina of dust which had accumulated on the surfaces in the formal lounge room in the past three days; she must dust again, very soon. She moved across the room to the liquor cabinet, and leant down to extract a bottle of Tamdhu and a crystal tumbler. She loved this single malt whisky which came from a small boutique distillery in the Scottish Highlands, not far from Culloden; it had been Dougal's all-time favourite.

With shaking fingers, she poured a modest quantity into the glass, raised the glass silently to his photograph and sipped thoughtfully. She could feel a prickling at her eyes; she blinked tears away, looked lovingly at the photograph once more and left the room, glass in hand. She glanced at the hall clock as she passed; 5:00 p.m. What time would it be in Scotland? Were they already on British Summer time, or not? She couldn't decide—best to leave it for another hour.

She went to the kitchen and fixed herself a sandwich, and a mug of coffee. The house was silent, and she was glad to embrace that silence while she ate and drank. She automatically put her crockery and utensils into the dishwasher, and consulted her wristwatch. 5:30 p.m. Still too early. She marched to her bedroom, collected up her dirty clothes and went to the laundry. She fed the clothes into the front-loading machine and started a load of washing going.

At 5:40 p.m. she went out to the letterbox to check on the post; there was the usual jumble of junk mail and windowed envelopes. The junk mail was quickly disposed of into the paper recycling bag; the windowed envelopes she placed on her desk in the large, modern, airy "Great Room" as Dougal had laughingly described it when they had renovated the house. She checked her watch again. 5:45 p.m. She put her wrist to her ear, to listen for the faint ticking; yes, the watch was still functioning, but the time was slouching past on leaden feet, for sure. Returning to the lounge room, she topped up her glass with a splash more Tamdhu and took it with her.

She was having trouble calculating the time difference between Australia and Scotland; her brain seemed to be very sluggish. At six o'clock she decided she would not be dragging anyone from bed in the middle of the night, and could wait no longer. She walked to her desk and rummaged around in the top drawer, finally locating the address book she sought.

Picking it, the Scotch, and the cordless phone up from its cradle, she walked to her favourite chair overlooking the river, put her glass on the side table, and sat down. She pinched the bridge of her nose very hard between thumb and index finger, leaned her head back against the padded chair cushion for a long moment, took a very deep breath then opened her eyes and flipped open the book.

Finding the number she needed, she dialled, and listened to the ring tone on the other end of the line. She had a sudden attack of nerves.

"Halloo?" a female voice answered, on the other side of the world.

"Oh hello, Shona… it's Beth, Dougal's wife." *Your sister-in-law.*

"Oh hello, Elizabeth." The woman paused. "How are you?"

"I've been better, thanks. How are you?"

"Och, not so bad, lassie, not so bad. How's my wee brother?"

Beth took a very deep, steadying breath. "Shona, that's why I'm calling. I'm so sorry to be the bearer of bad news, but Dougal's dead."

There was an ominous silence on the other end of the line. Beth was breathing rapidly; she took another sip of Scotch. *This is so wrong! Sad news is better delivered in person, but I can't see any other way to do this. I don't think my sister-in-law has discovered Skype yet.*

"Hello, Shona, are you there?"

"Aye, lass, I'm here, but I canna believe what you're saying. What? How? When? Where?" With each question, Shona's voice rose in pitch across thousands of miles.

"Oh, Shona!" and Beth's voice cracked. "Oh, my dear, I'm so sorry. He went overboard from a ship, and the police think it was suicide, and I just don't believe it. I *can't* believe it!" She stopped, took a hasty sip of her drink, and choked, coughing as the spirit burned its way down her throat.

"Anyway," she resumed, clearing her throat, "they've brought him back from Macquarie Island, and I've just been in this afternoon to identify him, and it *is* him. And he's all battered, like he's been in a terrible fight, and…"

Beth was breathless, gasping for air, chest heaving. She felt as if she had just run a marathon.

"Elizabeth! Elizabeth! Are you there? What happened? He would never do such a wicked thing, not my wee brother! There must be some terrible mistake…. Are you sure?" Shona's voice was trembling.

"Shona, I'm not sure about the suicide angle; *I* don't believe he would commit suicide, either. But the fact remains that he is dead. He's at the morgue, the mortuary I think you call it; I've just seen him. They've scheduled the post-mortem for tomorrow morning apparently; it's all in the hands of the coroner."

"Yes, thank you, dear, I ken right well what a morgue is. We do have the telly here in Scotland, you know!" Shona's tone was sharp. "But when did this all happen? And why was his face battered? And why didn't you tell me sooner?"

Beth took a very deep, calming breath. She should have known that Dougal's older sister would be full of questions; *she* was full of some fairly awkward questions herself!

"Apparently he went overboard in the early hours of Thursday two weeks ago."

"Two *weeks*? But what was he doing on a ship, anyway?"

"He was on his way to Macquarie Island, down near Antarctica, to spend the winter there, studying his beloved seals. He had a student with him, who reported him missing the next morning, and who has now come back with his body. Jeremy, his student, did the initial identification at the base on the island after his body was discovered, based on the tatty old fur coat he was apparently wearing when they found him. He had this mangy old coat which he would never let me send to the thrift shop, you know; it was his favourite, he said. Insisted on taking it whenever he went away. I really can't understand what he saw in it. But he could have afforded at least a new one…"

Beth knew she was babbling now, filling in the silence so she wouldn't have to answer more unanswerable questions.

There was a sharp intake of breath on the other end of the line, but she didn't notice. Shona remained silent.

"The police," Beth continued, "have been asking me all kinds of questions about him; whether he was depressed, if we had money worries, that sort of thing. They haven't entirely ruled out foul play, but I think they'll be inclined to treat his death as a suicide. Anyway, they'll know, one way or the other, I guess. They're pretty thorough here."

"I'll get on a flight and come out to you straight away, Elizabeth," Shona exclaimed.

"No! I mean, not yet, please, Shona, if you wouldn't mind. They can't tell me when his body will be released, so I can't even organise a funeral… No! Please wait until I know something more."

By now she was fighting tears. She carefully took another sip of her drink, sniffed, and recovered herself.

"Sorry, it's been a bit of a nightmare, and I know this is the worst possible way for you to find out, but I couldn't think of any other way to let you know, and I knew you'd *want* to know, that you *needed* to know and… and the damned press have been trying to dig up our lives. He hasn't done anything wrong, and neither have I, but they won't leave us alone. Better for you stay out of it, until I know what's happening. *Okay*?" The last word came out as a high-pitched cry.

"Dinna fash, lassie," came the calm, sad reply, "I can hear it in your voice that you've been through a deal of woe. I can pack a bag and be on a plane in twenty-four hours if you need me."

"Thank you so much, Shona, and I'll hold you to that promise, but at present there's nothing that can be done, except to wait."

"Do you at least have some friends down there in Hobart?"

"Sure, I have work colleagues, and a couple of university wives. Plus, Dougal and I are close to his student and the lad's fiancée. Jeremy looked on Dougal as a father-figure a bit; I suspect there was a bit of hero-worship going on there," she chuckled weakly, despite herself, "and his fiancée is the nicest lassie. She's a detective here. She's been appointed my Family Liaison Officer, even though she's in CID, so she'll be here a fair bit. I suspect she volunteered for the job, because it's usually given to the uniformed police. Jeremy arrived back in Hobart on the ship only this morning with Dougal's body — do you know he's given up his year's PhD research to bring Dougal home? He blames himself, I think; feels it's his fault somehow.

"Dougal was well liked and respected here… no one can believe he would kill himself, and neither do *I*! I mean, *what was he thinking, going off a ship in the middle of a cold bloody ocean in the middle of the bloody night!*" Beth's voice had risen to a shout, anger overpowering sorrow. She sucked in a huge, shuddering, ragged breath, then breathed it out slowly.

"Sorry, Shona. Not your fault. Listen, I have to go now. There's someone at the front door. I'll ring you again when I have definite news. Sorry. Just can't talk any more right now. Look after yourself. Bye!"

She pressed End on the call, cutting off an anxious question from her sister-in-law mid-sentence. She threw the phone gently onto the couch, drained the last drops of her drink, placed the tumbler onto the glass-topped side table, and closed her overflowing eyes.

Chapter
sixteen

Friday morning

Beth had already been at work for two or three hours that morning, recording artefacts of the long unknown dead, when a stainless steel trolley bearing her own, recent dead was wheeled into the main autopsy suite of the Royal Hobart Hospital Mortuary two city blocks away.

Dougal's cadaver had been stripped of the long dark coat which had all but shrouded it since it was discovered on the rocky ledges of Macquarie Island. The coat had been placed into a large Ziplok plastic bag, awaiting further examination, and ultimately, disposal.

The harsh artificial lighting in the autopsy suite had not been designed to show off a person's best features. It was relentless in its intensity; it showed up every bruise, laceration, and injury consistent with a body being torn up by rocks, opportunistic crabs, and other scavengers. The face had suffered the worst ravages; after the bloating from drowning, the skin was now putty-grey and slack. Something had enjoyed a feast on its eyes, and the empty sockets were unsettling.

Dr. Julius Macfarlin, the pathologist from the coroner's office appeared, gowned, masked, and gloved. His attendant was similarly clad; they both wore long rubberised boots.

It was achingly cold in the chilled room, and their breath puffed out in little clouds from their masks.

The pathologist picked up a clipboard on which had been written an initial identification by Jeremy Munroe and cursory examination by Doctor Jenny Jones, station doctor on Macquarie Island. He nodded while reading the report; the initial assessment was death by drowning, due to where the body had been discovered.

He picked up a tiny recorder and clipped it to his lapel; through this he would record all his findings and the procedure of the autopsy.

"Right to go, Fred?" he asked his assistant.

"Yes, Doc, he's ready for you."

"Okay, then, sir," he spoke softly to the cadaver. "Let's see what you have to tell us about how you died."

"Judging by the look of him, Doc, he drowned," Fred chipped in.

"Yeah, thanks for that, Fred. It does look just *slightly* obvious, doesn't it? Anyway, let's have him open and see what surprises, if any, he has in store for us."

He moved around to the toe tag, and read, "Dougal Ferguson, aged 60 years. So, what's your story then, Dougal Ferguson?" he asked as he looked at the man on the trolley.

He retraced his steps to the side of the body and picked up his scalpel, switching on his voice recorder before he made the first cut.

He waited for Fred to take some post-mortem photographs as a further record of their investigations.

"The body is that of a well-nourished sixty-year-old male, who has been identified as Dougal James Kenneth Ferguson, of Rose Bay. Initial external examination of the body indicates death by drowning, due to the slippage of the skin, and other signs… body appears to have been in a good state of health and fitness prior to death… he appears to have his own teeth, in good condition… eyes are missing, presumed eaten by crabs or other shoreline scavengers."

The pathologist kept speaking softly into his lapel recorder as he performed his task meticulously and methodically; creating the familiar Y incision to reveal the internal organs. These were skilfully and gently removed, weighed, and examined for disease or any pathological reason why a man would throw himself overboard. He asked his assistant to take blood for toxicity screening. The coroner might be looking at an alcohol-related accidental death.

"Fluid in both lungs indicate that death was caused by drowning. Fred, take a sample of the fluid please for analysis? Thanks."

He continued his narrative. "Liver and kidneys do not appear to be enlarged or diseased. There is, however, evidence of some internal bleeding, from causes unknown. I can find no trace of tumours. Heart appears normal, with not much fatty tissue around the heart muscle itself. Stomach contents are minimal, indicating that he had not eaten within several hours before he jumped, or was pushed from the vessel, although there appears to be the remains of a beverage."

After completing a thorough examination of the body, he called for his assistant, who was busy taking and labelling tissue and blood samples for despatch to the pathology laboratories.

"Fred, can you give me a hand to turn him over, please? Thanks."

Together they flipped the body so it lay prostrate on the steel tray. Dr Macfarlin started at the corpse's extremities, closely examining them. Hands and feet were relatively unscathed, except for lacerations and evidence of nibbling. Peering in and probing with his forceps, he found minute amounts of rock grit in the lacerations, and commented on it to his voice recorder. He continued this way for each section of the body, recording his findings, or lack of them. He made a comment on how relatively untouched the entire torso, legs and arms were, clear of animal attack or lacerations, except for some regular, diamond-shaped patterning in light pre- and post-mortem bruising across the chest and upper thighs. Fred duly photographed these in some detail; they were a puzzle.

"Fred," he asked quietly, "Can you go and get his coat from that box over there please?"

Fred finished sealing and labelling tubes of tissue for the Path Lab, and retrieved the bag. He brought it back to the side bench so the pathologist could have a better look.

"So, what do we have here?" he mused as he lifted the long dark skin coat out of the large plastic bag. "Could you clear me a space on that other trolley please? I'd like to take a better look at this." Between them, the men carried the coat, draped it onto a sterile trolley covered in butcher's paper and switched on the powerful overhead lights.

There were minute particles of rock grit which the pathologist teased out from the fur, all of which were collected and sealed into containers by Fred, while the doctor kept working, searching and recording. Small samples of the fur coat were removed for analysis. Dr Macfarlin worked his way methodically up the coat; Fred heard the doctor give a low whistle, and say, "Look at this!"

Fred took the two steps necessary to look closer, and peered at something near the doctor's pointing index finger. It was a hole, almost circular, featuring slight fraying at the edges, but it was not a hole Fred had ever seen occur in nature.

"Are you thinking what I'm thinking, Doc?" he asked. "It doesn't look like a tear from a rock to me."

"I'm thinking it looks suspiciously like a bullet hole, Fred. Measure and photograph it, please. Now then, let's have another look at your back, Dougal."

The pathologist returned to the first trolley, and started measuring with his hands up the back and along the spine. "How far from the shoulder seam, Fred?" he asked quietly.

"Thirty-five centimetres down, towards the middle."

"Thanks. Aha!" Dr Macfarlin measured this distance with a stainless steel tape, and whistled softly to himself again. Fred looked up; he knew that his boss had found something quite interesting, as he would put it.

"Well, this is quite interesting, Fred."

Fred smiled; right on cue. "What have you found, Doc?"

"There appears to be a wound site on his back, in line with his spine. Now, if I just have a look in here…" The pathologist dug around, located something hard beneath his tweezers, positioned them and pulled. Out popped a rather mangled bullet. The doctor gave another low whistle, louder this time. He addressed his remarks to the voice recorder, "… a bullet, extracted from the spinal cord of the deceased."

He held his hand above the mouthpiece of the recorder, and turned to his assistant.

"Probably lucky the poor bastard drowned, Fred, he would have been a paraplegic, or worse, had he survived."

Macfarlin removed his hand from the sensitive microphone and continued recording his observations.

"I am now moving the deceased's coat to lay over his back, in order to establish a correlation between the bullet in the deceased's body and the coat. Give us a hand here please, Fred? Thanks."

Between them they manoeuvred the coat into position, and Fred photographed from every angle.

Macfarlin produced a long steel skewer and inserted it through the hole in the coat into the body.

"Happy snaps, please? Thanks." Into the recorder, he said, "The bullet hole in the deceased's garment is consistent with the entry point of the wound in the deceased's upper back. That may explain the internal bleeding already observed. Thanks, Fred, give me a hand

and we'll put this back in the bag. One, two, three, hey-up!"

With the coat safely returned to and sealed in the bag, the two men turned the body onto its back once more, and the assistant started sewing up the Y incision.

Fred paused, needle in his hand, as the doors opened, and a young assistant entered the room.

"What is it, Alfie?" he asked, looking across to the newcomer.

"Ah, er, um, I just came to pick up some test tubes for the lab, Fred."

"Okay. They're on the side bench," Fred said dismissively as he returned to his task, stitching up the scalpel wound. He didn't notice the young man hovering close by, listening to the pathologist summing up his investigation on his voice-activated recorder.

"Immersion in water of extreme temperatures, such as the Southern Ocean, for any length of time, would lead to hypothermia and death within hours, if not minutes, depending on the ambient temperature of the water. Without a buoyancy vest or some other flotation device, drowning would follow. However, with a bullet lodged in his spine, this man would have been unable to move his lower body. Hence, drowning would have occurred very quickly. Some light pre- and post-mortem bruising across the chest and front of the upper thighs is indicative of contact with a net or cage ante-mortem. In my opinion, death was caused by drowning, exacerbated by a period of captivity and a gunshot to the victim's back which lodged in his spine, caused bleeding in the internal organs, and rendered him helpless."

Fred finished his grisly job, tying off the sutures with a neat knot. Alfie was still hovering nearby.

"Neat job, Fred," he commented.

"Thanks, Alfie. Did you find what you were looking for?"

"Yep, thanks. So, this wasn't a simple drowning, then?"

"No, poor bastard was shot in the back. Miserable way to die…"

"Hmm, yeah, you're right there," Alfie commented, glancing at the name on the toe tag, and sauntered off, calling, "See ya, Fred."

"Yeah, see ya."

Alfie's soft soles made no noise on the polished linoleum tiles as he walked away.

The pathologist switched off the recorder; he walked to the sink and cleansed himself thoroughly with antibacterial liquid and a scrubbing brush, then walked over to the pedal-operated bin; plastic gown, gloves and paper mask were dumped inside for collection and disposal.

His green boots he had already hosed down; he stepped out of them, left them on a steel grid to dry and padded to his office, calling back, "You nearly finished there, Fred? It's lunch time, and I'm starved! I'll process the post-mortem report when I get back. Right now, I could eat a horse! I'm off for a nice juicy steak." The pathologist locked the voice recorder into the top drawer, picked up his sports jacket, slipped on his shoes and sauntered out. He reappeared ten seconds later. "Send that bullet off to forensics, will you, Fred? And get those tissue samples and bloods over to the lab for analysis as soon as possible. See you later." The doctor left, whistling happily as his shoes squeaked their way down the highly polished floor.

Fred grimaced; these pathologists were quite eccentric. Blood and gore in the morning, followed by a rare steak for lunch? He shook his head.

He covered Dougal's body with a clean pale green sheet, wheeled the trolley across the room and into the freezer bays. Opening a locker door, he slid the body on its tray smoothly off the trolley straight into the chiller.

Fred closed the door, and went to do his ablutions; he hosed down his boots and left them on the steel grid to dry, removed and disposed of his outer protective wear, picked up his jacket and shoes, and went out in search of a salad.

In an adjoining alcove, Alfie waited until Fred's footsteps had receded in the distance, then took a mobile phone from the pocket of his scrubs and dialled.

"G'day, Trin, it's me…. Yeah, you were right… and it wasn't suicide. He's been murdered… Yeah, you owe me big time. I could get the sack for this." And he ended the call.

On Friday evening, commuters were treated to the screaming headlines from the newsstands as they made their way home for the weekend.

"PROFESSOR MURDERED AT SEA."

The by-line carried Trinity Trinling's name. Annoyed by Beth's lack of cooperation in speaking to the media, the reporter had wreaked her revenge. The newspaper report carried information about the cause of the professor's death, the fact that he had been shot, and speculated about on-board grievances which may have led to murder. While the article stopped short of actual accusations, it insinuated that animosity had led to cold-blooded murder.

The ABC TV news led its nightly bulletin with the report in a far less sensational way.

"The ABC can reveal that the man reported missing from the icebreaker *Aurora Australis* fifteen days ago is believed to have been murdered. Professor Dougal Ferguson, a leading researcher into pinniped populations at the University of Tasmania, disappeared from the icebreaker in the early hours of Thursday 27th April. An extensive search of the supply ship failed to establish his whereabouts. It is not known if Professor Ferguson fell or was pushed overboard. Professor Ferguson's body was later discovered by scientists on Macquarie Island. There was no explanation as to how the body came to be there. Professor Ferguson's body was transported back to Hobart aboard *Aurora Australis*, which made an unscheduled detour to collect the deceased from Macquarie Island. Police are continuing their investigations into Professor Ferguson's demise. Professor Ferguson's widow, Dr Elizabeth Bouchier Ferguson, has been assisting the police with their enquiries into the professor's finances and possible mental state at the time of his disappearance. No motive has been established for either suicide or murder at this point in time."

The news broadcast failed to reach Beth, who was busily occupied in her kitchen, baking biscuits.

Chapter
seventeen

Friday Night

Beth welcomed Carrie and Jeremy at the front door and ushered them in. She led them past the formal lounge and Dougal's study, along the central corridor, to the rear of the house, where the large room elicited a low whistle from Jeremy. Beth smiled at him; he was obviously as impressed as his fiancée had been a bare two weeks past.

"Wow!" he breathed. "What a fabulous view you have!"

"Thank you, Jeremy," Beth acknowledged with a small nod. "Now, would you kids like a coffee? I have the machine ready to start. Go in, make yourselves comfortable."

"Would you like a hand, Beth?" asked Carrie.

"No, no, sweetheart. I have it all under control. If you want to come talk to me while I put out the cookies, sugar, and milk, that'd be cool."

Carrie sat down on one of the bar stools, and planted her elbows on the bench. She felt so comfortable, sitting and chatting with the older woman; it was homely and somehow comforting; she felt as though she had come home. She swivelled around to smile lovingly at Jeremy, who was wandering the room, apparently fascinated by Beth's collection.

"You okay in there, lad?" called Beth.

"Oh sure, Beth, I'm just admiring your great collection of stuff," Jeremy replied absent-mindedly.

Built into the window embrasure ran the continuous padded seat, upholstered in navy blue, where Carrie had spent a sleepless night; white filmy curtains were tethered off to the far sides of the windows with blue tiebacks; there was a decidedly nautical theme to this room. A circular scrubbed pine table with four chairs jauntily dressed in navy-and-white-striped canvas sat off to one side of the large space, whilst a wicker chair, obviously Beth's, facing the huge windows, was also upholstered in the same style and colouring. The only splash of contrasting colour was a beautiful blanket, woven in a tribal design predominantly red and black, with purple and white stripes, draped over the back of that chair. As Jeremy looked around him, he could see that this was also a work space.

Against the wall opposite the dining setting, was a white desk, crowded but neatly arranged with a computer and all its accoutrements, folders neatly filed into purpose-built pigeon-holes at the rear of the desk, and along the adjoining wall. Almost stretching to the ceiling, above and on either side of the desk along the pine-clad wall, were drawings, sketches, framed prints, masks, and carved animals on glass shelves — mostly Inuit and Pacific Northwest First Nation art and artefacts. This was most definitely *Beth's* domain. It really summed the woman up, Jeremy thought, looking at the scene through a scientist's eye — neat, businesslike, ordered, but with compassion, respect for the culture of others, and a love of wildness and savage beauty.

He was physically drawn to the display of artefacts, drawings and the totem pole on its own shelf above Beth's desk. He moved across to the wall to examine them more closely; stylised orcas, seals, dolphins, and all manner of sea creatures were featured in the art of the Northwest Pacific coast. Beth had obviously been collecting them for years. He turned to say something, and caught sight of Beth's face in profile, the planes of her face emphasized by the kitchen downlights. Something from his childhood tickled at his memory, but dissolved as quickly as it had formed, a butterfly of thought that flitted away, uncaptured. He returned to his examination of the artworks; he was drawn particularly to the totem pole, and its mysterious, carved creatures and faces.

His thought was broken with the arrival of Beth, Carrie, and the laden tray. He opened his mouth to speak, but something in Beth's meaningful look stopped him; *coffee and comfort first, time for serious talk later*. He managed a sheepish smile; she could obviously read his mind, or his face.

She smiled wryly back at him and handed him a mug of coffee.

"Help yourself to milk and sugar if you want it, Jeremy."

"Thanks, Beth, this is fine as it is."

"Sit down, sit down, lad. Be comfortable. Here!" And she patted the padded cushion on the couch.

"Come sit here and relax with your girl. You're like a cat on hot bricks!"

"Beth, I…"

"Not now, lad. Drink your coffee and let's enjoy the dying of the day. Be calm, lad; be still."

Jeremy and Carrie exchanged looks; Carrie was smiling lovingly at him. He smiled and shrugged, settled back into the comfortable cushions, and sipped his coffee, gazing across the river to the lights beginning to twinkle on the other side. Beth was right; it *was* calming, sitting here and looking out onto the evening landscape.

He could feel his body begin to relax; he hadn't been able to unwind since that dreadful day on Macquarie Island when they had found Dougal's body on the shoreline after the storm. He had been almost afraid to close his eyes at night since then; he could see the man's face, battered and bloated in his nightmares. He was profoundly thankful that the technicians at the mortuary had at least been able to tidy up a few of the ravages the crabs and other hungry little sea creatures had exacted on it, before Beth had had to see it.

He shuddered involuntarily, and a little hot coffee spilt onto his trouser legs.

"Sorry! Ouch! That was hot!" he exclaimed.

"Are you okay?" both women chorused.

"Fine, just being a bit clumsy."

Beth looked at him sideways, disbelieving.

"I'll go get a damp cloth for your pants. Stay there." And was gone and back in seconds, holding out a clean, dampened tea towel to him.

He accepted it wordlessly, and cleaned his clothing as best he could. The washing machine would sort out the worst of the stains. He felt slightly silly, spilling stuff on himself like a small child.

Beth watched him scrub at his trousers, and then as he got up to return the cloth to the kitchen. He really was a dear young man, and had obviously been well brought up. His mother would have been proud of him. She thought she remembered Carrie saying that his mother was no longer living.

She offered the coffee pot.

"More?" she asked.

He laughed, embarrassed. "Please."

They all laughed, then a peaceful and companiable silence fell over the room once more. They drank coffee and munched Beth's home-baked biscuits as the night gently swept an indigo mantle across the landscape; they watched as the fire-fly lights of the traffic on the opposite shore flitted here and there, and the streetlights outlined the ribbon of streets and roads that wound up into the hills.

Beth brought out a bottle of Scotch and three glasses. She opened it and held it poised, an enquiring look in her eyes and an eyebrow arched in their direction.

Carrie shook her head. "Best not, Beth, I'm driving tonight. The coffee'll do me fine."

"Jeremy?" Beth asked.

"Please."

She poured a generous measure into two tumblers, handed him one and took the other. She moved her chair around so she was facing more into the room, and sat down again.

"*Slàinte mhath, gille.*" She laughed aloud at his bemused expression. "It means 'Good health, lad.'" She raised her glass to him.

He laughed and drank, savouring the smooth velvety single malt in his mouth before swallowing very slowly. He could feel it warm him and lend him strength. He could feel Beth's eyes on him; he frowned slightly; he was sure she reminded him of someone, but again the thought escaped, unfettered.

"Okay, Jeremy, talk to me! It's been trying to burst out of you like a fried sausage out of its skin."

To his utter surprise and shame, he burst into tears for the second time in two days.

"Beth," he sobbed and hiccupped, "Beth, I'm so sorry… I should have woken up when he left the cabin… I should have stopped him… I don't know what to do… I'm just so very, very sorry… I feel so guilty… why *him*?"

Beth was suddenly by his side; he was sandwiched between her and Carrie. His fiancée ran her hand gently up and down his back, soothing, reassuring; Beth put her arms around him and rocked him like a baby. He turned into her embrace and laid his head on her shoulder.

"Hush, laddie, hush now," she murmured, and started singing a lullaby softly into his ear; it was in a different language, but somehow Jeremy recognised it as the tune she had crooned to him the previous day at the mortuary.

He sat up and stared at her in amazement. He stopped his sobbing, gave a very loud sniff, and dived a hand into his pocket for a handkerchief. Beth let go, and patted him firmly and reassuringly on the knee and returned to her chair; she folded her hands together, sat back and gazed out the window at the lights, allowing him time to regain his dignity.

Jeremy blew his nose, wiped his eyes, and looked at Beth searchingly.

"That song, Beth, where did you learn it?"

"Oh, it's an old cradle song my mother sang to me when I was a baby. She learnt it when her mother sang it to *her*. And *her* mother sang it to my grandmother before that. You know how these things get handed down through the generations." Beth took a deep, steadying breath and said softly, "I used to sing it to my son when *he* was a baby, too. Why?"

"This is going to sound really crazy, but I'm sure I've heard it before, somewhere."

She looked at him. "Well, as my people are from the Northwest coast, and you're from over East, I believe, I don't know how you *could* have heard it before. It's in *Sm'algyax*, the Tsimshian native tongue. That cradle song is all I can remember of the language; it's pretty much died out now, like a lot of indigenous languages. Happens all over." She shrugged. "Perhaps you heard it on a recording or a radio program somewhere."

He shook his head. "I just can't remember… maybe you're right. It's just that it sounded *familiar*, somehow."

Carrie's hand found his, and the young couple sat quietly with Beth, each lost in their own ponderings, watching the lights stain the dark satin of the river.

Jeremy's eyes once more returned to the wall of line drawings, sketches, and the totem pole on its shelf. Again a thought flitted into his mind, but skittered away before his conscious brain could capture it. He was sure he had seen something similar.

He shook his head to clear his confusion. "That totem pole on the shelf, Beth. Where did you find it?"

"My grandmother's people. We didn't always live on Vancouver Island; my great-grandmother Tilly was full-blood Tsimshian; her clan was the *Gispwudwada*, the Killer Whale Clan. She came from Prince Rupert, Kaien Island, up the Northwest coast. My mom was given that totem pole to take with her when she moved to Nanaimo to live with my father."

Jeremy squeezed Carrie's hand, placed a soft kiss on her hair and stood up. He had spotted something on another shelf. He carefully put down his glass, walked over to the object, and looked closer. It would be easier to see in stronger light. A strange prickling sensation like ants crawling over him ran down his arms.

"May I?" he asked, hand hovering near a small, slightly browning photograph.

"Sure, lad."

He picked it up, brought it into the better light of the room, and looked closely at it. His face suddenly paled, and the hairs on the back of his neck stood up as he turned and looked at his professor's widow. He was suddenly very cold.

"Beth, ah… what are you doing with a picture of my granma Maddy and great-granma Bibi?"

***

There was an absolute stillness in the room, broken by the sharp thud of something hitting the table as Beth almost dropped her empty glass. She jumped up and stared at him.

"That's me with my mom, Jeremy," she said flatly. The simple statement fell into a pit of shocked silence. He looked from the picture to her, stunned.

She walked over to him, took his arm, and slowly turned him around to face her. She looked deep into his eyes and spoke very quietly and deliberately.

"That was taken in Nanaimo, Jeremy, ten years ago. That's me with my mom," she repeated. "We went to visit with her back in Canada before we moved here. That was the last time I saw her alive, and the last photo we ever had taken together. She died two years later."

Jeremy shook his head in disbelief. "I'm so sorry, Beth, I really thought… I could have sworn…she looks so much like my granma. I guess I'm a little more screwed up than I thought…" His voice trailed off, and the hand holding the framed photograph started to droop. Beth retrieved the precious item from him, and carefully replaced it on its shelf. She led him back to the couch, where Carrie sat, looking from one to the other of them with incredulity.

Jeremy sat down and looked at his fiancée searchingly.

"I'm really losing it, honey," he mumbled. "Sorry."

Carrie hugged him and held him close. "You've had a very long and emotional couple of weeks, sweetheart." She looked at Beth, who was still standing, motionless in front of them.

"Look, Beth, we'll go if you like. You look pretty tired yourself. It's been a long, hard time for you, too."

"No!" Beth exclaimed, then hastened to soften the command. "No, it's fine, really it is, Carrie. Please don't run away just yet." She focussed her attention on Jeremy, whose face had finally regained some colour.

"Jeremy, why would you think that it was your grandmother and her mom?"

He shook his head. "I could have sworn it was her! I have photos that belonged to my mom, of her granma and my granma and me in Ottawa, back before they all died. I have an album at Carrie's place. I brought all my precious stuff with me. I'll see if I can find it."

Beth smiled. "That would be lovely, dear. I would love to see your family photos, if it won't cause you too much pain. Can you bring them over next time you and Carrie come to visit?"

"Sure thing, Beth. I'm pretty sure I know where they are. They're in a box of mementoes. Somehow I couldn't bear to leave them behind. Granma Maddy and Gramps kept them for me after Mom died, while I was still at school and college; Granma kept them until she herself died last year."

"Oh Jeremy! I'm so sorry to hear your mother is no longer living, and to lose your grandmother as well. Is your grandfather still alive?"

"No, Gramps had a massive heart attack back in 2002, while he was out fishing one day with some buddies. They brought him home. That broke Granma Maddy's heart. She was never really the same after that."

Beth knelt down in front of him and gently put her hands on his shoulders.

"And now you've brought my man home to me." She leant forward and kissed him softly on the top of his head. "Thank you, lad," she whispered. "Thank you from the bottom of my heart. That must have been extra hard for you. It must have dredged up all kinds of sad memories." She released his shoulders, and sat back on her heels, looking at him.

Jeremy nodded numbly; he was suddenly exhausted. "I would really like to go home and get some sleep now, if you don't mind, Beth. I'm feeling pretty done-in right now."

Beth rocked back on her heels and stood up effortlessly. She extended her hands to him and he took them, then levered himself up out of the comfortable seat. He stood in front of her, still holding her hands, then impulsively gave her a hug.

"Thank you, Beth. Thank you for not blaming me."

Beth stared at him in utter amazement. "How could you even *think* such a thing, Jeremy?" she demanded. "It was *not* your fault! Stop torturing yourself. Whatever my silly man did, he did *all by himself,* for *whatever crazy reason. So, stop it!"*

She turned to Carrie, who had also risen. "Take him home and put him to bed, Carrie dear, he's overtired and talking nonsense!"

She hugged Carrie, gave her an encouraging smile, and ushered them back to the front door.

"Drive safely, you two!" she called as they walked away to their car.

"Okay, Beth, talk to you soon!" came the reply on the evening breeze.

Beth went back into the house, poured herself another Scotch, and sat down in her favourite chair. As she held the side of the cool glass against her cheek, she looked anew at the photo which had sparked so much emotion from Jeremy.

"Now, I wonder what brought that on?" she murmured, as she sipped her drink.

She sat facing out into the deepening night, not really seeing the flicker of lights across the river as she sank into deep thought.

Something Jeremy had said had triggered an elusive train of thought. If she tried to capture it, it slid away sideways out of her grasp, but hovered tantalisingly close on the periphery of her conscious mind.

She thoughtfully took another sip of her whisky, then walked across the room to pick up the controversial photo. She looked at it, and held it while she sat down. Taking another mouthful, she looked again at the women in the photo; she looked really hard at the images of herself and her mother, Selena, laughing into the camera. Dougal had taken the shot; he had made some really silly comment and had made them laugh in delight as he had caught them, open-mouthed, forever on film.

Why would Jeremy think that she would own a photograph of his grandmothers?

Something did not add up…

Reaching backwards for her soft rug and draping it around her shoulders, she raised her eyes once more to the moving tapestry of light across the river and let her mind wander. It was a technique she had learned years ago, to calm and soothe her thoughts; it also had the benefit of allowing her often chaotic mind-chatter to resolve and distil itself into coherent trains of thought.

"Bibi," she murmured. "Bibi. I had a great-aunt *Biba*, but she disappeared long before I was born…. Why did Jeremy react in a such a strange way? How did he recognise that silly old cradle song? Why did he think my mom was his great-grandmother? Hmm…. Curious…."

She sat motionless, gazing out. Occasionally she would take a tiny sip of the distilled spirit, and allow the smoky velvety liquid to trickle over her tongue before slowly swallowing it. She could feel it running gently down her throat, and the slight, pleasant after-burn it left. She felt warm and slightly drunk; she started humming the cradle song aloud to herself. Her grandmother had not only sung the song to her mother, she had also sung it to Beth as a baby.

Her eyes had closed and she was drifting into sleep, still cradling her glass, when the synapses finally fired.

She jumped up, exclaiming as a few drops of whisky splashed onto her hand. She hurriedly put down the tumbler, licked her hand and scurried across the room to her desk. Locked away in a battered old tin box inside her desk cupboard was what she was looking for.

Her excitement was mounting; she fumbled around in the top drawer, searching for the tiny key she knew she had stored away in there.

"Ha!" she exclaimed as her fingertips located the key.

She carefully brought out the box, and placed it lovingly on the table. She pulled out a chair and sat down. Cautiously, she inserted the key into the aperture and turned it. With a soft click, the lock was released and she could open the container.

Nestled inside were papers, photographs, a lock of fine baby hair in a frame, and a scroll of paper. She extracted the scroll, and painstakingly unrolled it; it was very old, and she did not want to tear it due to her impatience.

"Patience brings its own rewards," she murmured as she manoeuvred the fragile paper, placing weights along its length until the whole document was at last revealed.

She sat back, flexing her shoulders. She squeezed the bridge of her nose between forefinger and thumb before opening her eyes and starting her search. If she *knew* what it was she was hunting for, it would be so much easier.

Basing her search on nothing more than a hunch, she put on her reading glasses and peered at the faded, browning ink scrawl.

There was her name, and Dougal's... and Malcolm's at the bottom.

She slipped on a white cotton glove she had taken from the drawer, and traced her finger along the entries.

As she puzzled her way back through the generations, she said aloud her parents' names — Selena and Jacques Bouchier — their dates of birth and death. Moving purposefully back through time, she registered her grandmother's name — Hannah. Hannah's birth and death dates were recorded. No husband mentioned, but Beth already knew that amongst her grandmother's people, descent was matrilineal, and that no shame attached to any unmarried girl who became pregnant. There, at the top of the family tree were her great-grandparents' names — Tilly, full-blood Tsimshian woman and Jean LaRoque, her husband.

Beth finally found what her subconscious mind had unlocked; Tilly and Jean had had two daughters, Hannah and Biba. Yes, Biba was seven years younger than Hannah, but she had disappeared several years before Selena, Beth's mother, had been born. When Selena had taken Beth to visit her extended family in Prince Rupert as a child, Beth would often overhear the older women talking late into night, when Tilly would weep and talk about how their lovely Biba had been taken away by the State, not long after Tilly's husband had been tragically killed in a logging accident, and Tilly was left to bring up two young children. Hannah would remind her mother that she, Hannah, was a teenager at the time, and already out working, but the old lady had re-invented history as her memories shifted and blurred with age. Great-grandmother Tilly may have mourned Biba as dead, but Hannah had been just as sure that her sister hadn't died; she just had no way of finding her. Sometimes the late-night conversations could get quite heated between the two older women.

Beth sighed, removed her glasses, then pinched the bridge of her nose and rubbed it between thumb and forefinger. She leant back in her chair, suddenly drained and exhausted. Biba; the trail had gone cold long ago. There was no other information in the family tree about her great-aunt except her birthdate in 1920.

Slightly frustrated at this dead end, Beth gently lifted the weights and allowed the ageing document to curl in upon itself. Opening the tin once more, she carefully replaced the scroll and relocked the container.

She would see what the internet had to offer, in the morning.

The tin was reverently put away in the cupboard. Beth took the glasses to the kitchen, turned out the lights and went to bed.

That mystery would have to wait.

Chapter eighteen

Saturday

Beth woke up early and was seized with a burst of energy she hadn't felt for at least two weeks. She couldn't stand the sight of empty rooms any longer, and the housework could wait. She dressed in comfortable running gear; securing her keys and mobile phone in the zip-up pocket of her hooded sweatshirt, she let herself out of the house and went down to the river's edge. The morning mist still hung over the water; the playground near the riverbank was deserted at this hour, and the equipment hung inert and damp in the still, chill air.

She walked along the misty path and through the nature reserve the local council had planted in the pleasant, tree-lined street. There were few people outdoors, and she felt she had the world to herself for once. The past two weeks had been hard; she had been overwhelmed by the tumult of unwelcome news and events in her life. She had felt smothered and stifled; now she had the opportunity to breathe and be alone for a precious hour. She was not expecting any news or company today; the realisation pleased her, and she felt her lips curve into a smile.

As she power-walked along the riverbank, her thigh muscles started their familiar burning. She almost welcomed the pain; it made her feel alive again. She strode on, relishing the cool May morning, scuffing her feet in the autumn leaves now carpeting the walking tracks in red, amber, and brown. As she walked, her mind began ticking once again over the strange revelations of the previous evening and how strongly Jeremy had reacted to her photograph; it would be interesting to find out how much he remembered, or had tucked away in his effects, about his mysterious grandmother, no, *great*-grandmother. She had to admit she was *curious*; there weren't many Canadian First Nations people living in Australia, let alone in

Tasmania. Seriously, what were the odds of meeting someone who had a background similar to hers, so far across the world? She broke into a slow jog and reached her designated end point, turned, and started heading for home, still hugging the bank as she went. When she reached the playground, she walked briskly up the slope, and across the children's play area, treading almost silently through the pine bark spread beneath and around the play equipment, until she reached the street. As she crossed into her tree-lined avenue, she could see an unfamiliar car outside her house.

She flipped her sweatshirt hood over her dark hair and started jogging slowly towards the house, noticing two people, one young man with a piece of heavy equipment balanced on one shoulder, the other a bosomy long-haired blonde holding a mobile phone; they were knocking at her front door. Beth continued her leisurely pace, breathing evenly and jogging straight past them. The blonde turned hastily around and called out in a shrill tone, "Excuse me, do you know if the Fergusons live here? We've been trying to rouse someone."

"Sorry, no English," Beth mumbled as she put some distance between herself and the pair. She was fairly sure they were from the media; it was too early for religious callers, and she was in no mood to speak to anyone, anyway. She could hear the blonde speak sharply to the young man, and soon heard the squeak of the gate as they left the property. She kept jogging along, slower and slower, until she heard the roar of a motor, and watched as the strangers' car went down the street and turned right. Beth jogged on the spot for a couple of seconds, turned and jogged back casually the way she had come. When she reached her house, she walked calmly up the path, let herself in with her key, and closed the door before the unwanted visitors could return.

Kicking off her jogging shoes, Beth padded through to the kitchen and started a pot of coffee. While the machine was burbling away, she found the biscuits, and her favourite mug. She went into the family room, booted up her laptop, then returned to the kitchen. When the coffee was ready she took it and her snack to the scrubbed pine table in the family room, sat down with her laptop and started a search. As she surfed the internet, she sipped the hot coffee and munched on a biscuit; there was so much information to be had at the touch of a fingertip.

She typed in a question and scrolled down through the list of sites, choosing which might be the logical one for the information she was seeking. Her enquiries took her to a popular genealogical website; it required name, date of birth, date of death (if known), country of origin, and many other questions. Beth hopped up and found her credit card to create an account, then grabbed the tin she had opened the previous night. She unrolled the scroll again and weighted it down, then read through the dates. As she read off the dates and names, she typed the information into the site's ready-made family tree templates. She wasn't expecting an instant answer, so she wasn't disappointed. But at least she had made a start.

Beth returned to the main menu on the Web, and went on a hunt. She was looking for anything which would fill in some gaps; she was looking for a ghost named Biba. After Beth had looked at her family tree the previous evening, her mind had been working overtime to make sense of what might have happened. All she had were some forty-five-year-old memories of her grandmother and great-grandmother's late-night stories of loss. She knew Biba had been removed from Tilly's care around the age of ten; she knew that her own grandmother Hannah had escaped because she was too old to be 'retrained,' at seventeen or eighteen years of age. That would make the era the thirties, Beth worked out.

She searched for information on the removal of half-caste children from their full-blood mothers in the early part of the 20th century. What she found broke her heart; the forcible removal of small children, their institutionalisation far away from their families and homes, the abuses they had had to suffer, the denial of their native heritage, the prohibition on speaking their own languages, even the denial of their own names. They had been taken as far away as was humanly possible, to be "integrated" into white society. An article she found on the *creativespirits* website summed it up.

"Canada apologised on 11 June, 2008, to its Indigenous peoples for its past actions that eroded 'the political, economic and social systems of Aboriginal people and nations' … The government acted on a report which had been tabled two years earlier … From the 19th century until the 1970s—dates very similar to Australia's own history—more than 150,000 Canadian Aboriginal children were required to attend state-funded schools in an attempt to assimilate them into Canadian society… and the purpose of "killing the Indian in the child" … They were forbidden from speaking their native languages or participating in cultural practices. There were an estimated 130 Residential Schools across Canada. An estimated 90,000 survivors fight to have their stories recorded … The last Residential School closed in 1996 … In May 2006 the Canadian government reached a CDN$1.9-billion settlement to compensate survivors … *We Were Children* (directed by Tim Wolochatiuk, 2011, 83 min) chronicles the profound impact of the Canadian government's residential school system through the eyes of two children who were forced to face hardships beyond their years … As young children, Lyna and Glen were taken from their homes and placed in church-run boarding schools, where they suffered years of physical, sexual, and emotional abuse, the effects of which persist in their adult lives."

Beth stared at the article, tears running down her face. The late-night stories suddenly made sense. She remembered her mother telling her, when she complained as a child about not being allowed out alone, that Grandma Hannah had been almost paranoid about her own, Selena's, safety, when *she* was young, because Hannah was not married, and she lived in fear of Selena being taken, like her own sister had been, years before. Grandma Hannah had been very distrustful of many white folks, especially government officials.

Beth dried her eyes and started a search; she put the names of the children mentioned in the documentary into Google and explored; she googled the director of the documentary. She wrote down as much information as she could find; she hunted for some of the institutions which had been named and shamed in the extensive investigation which had lifted the lid on a veritable "Pandora's box" of systematic abuse and mistreatment of native Canadian children.

Beth spent most of the day at the computer; she got up only for bathroom breaks, or to make more coffee. She eventually tore herself away from her research around three for lunch, but took it back to the computer and ate while she continued to trawl the Web.

By 5:00 p.m., she had gone back into the genealogy site, and reviewed what she had written. On an impulse, she clicked on the icon advertising DNA testing; she sat there a moment, reading the information and requirements. After some deliberating, she chose 2 as the quantity of kits she needed. She completed all the required fields and clicked Pay.

She started printing out a lot of the information she had gathered over the course of the day. These pages she collected into a document wallet, which she carefully labelled and slotted into one of the cubby holes at the back of her desk.

Glancing at the clock on the wall, she decided to give herself another thirty minutes of research, before calling it quits for the day. Her head ached slightly from the computer screen, and her shoulders were tight. She called up another link, and started searching for clues there. Eventually, she bookmarked some pages and closed down the program. Her eyes were gritty and sore, and she needed food.

Beth fed herself, tidied up, made another coffee and curled up in her favourite chair. She found the remote control and switched on the television; she channel-surfed for a while, finding nothing worth watching, nothing that caught and held her attention for more than a couple of minutes. She just wasn't in the right frame of mind; she dimmed the overhead lights and sat, wrapped in her blanket, watching the lights reflecting across the rumpled flowing river. Eventually she fell asleep and didn't wake until the morning light streamed in through the bay windows.

***

Sunday morning, Beth was slightly stiff and cramped from sleeping curled up; she took a long, hot shower and did some stretches, then made her favourite Canadian breakfast—toast, scrambled eggs, bacon, and maple syrup. She couldn't remember when she had last indulged, but she felt better for the comforting familiarity of the meal.

After such a large breakfast, Beth decided that she had better go for a brisk walk. She took much the same route as she had the previous day, but this time she stopped in the playground facing the river, and sat on one of the swings, gently pushing back and forth with her feet, until she had gained some momentum. Her short, dark hair and her clothes streamed behind her as she held tight, leaned her body back and swung higher; she felt ridiculously liberated, pumping her legs to maintain the momentum, hands curled tightly around the uprights.

For a few precious minutes she was a child again; playful and carefree; she loved every second! She was brought back to reality by a small piping voice asking, "Mummy, why is that old lady on the swings?"

"I imagine she's having a swing, just like you like to do, sweetie!" came the mother's reply.

Beth stopped pumping her legs, and gradually the swing lost its momentum. She put one foot down to stop it completely, and turned to the young woman and the small child.

"Hi there!" she said brightly to the child, "do you like playing on the swings?"

The child was suddenly struck shy, but the mother laughed. "Yes, she loves all the play equipment here, but the swings are her favourite. It's such a lovely park, isn't it?"

"Yes," Beth agreed, "I walk past it frequently at the weekends. It just looked so *inviting* this morning, I couldn't resist." She stood up, smiled, and said to the child, "There you go, honey, it's all yours. You have fun now!"

"Mummy, why does the lady talk like an American?"

Beth smiled. "Why, sweetie, that's because I'm Canadian. My name's Beth. What's yours?"

The little girl hid her face behind her mother's flowered Happi pants, and curled her fists into the fabric. The young woman extended her hand. "Hello, I'm Anna and this is Amity. Come and say hello, Amity." There was a shake of the small blonde head. "Do you live around here?" Anna asked.

"Yes, I live just up that street and around the corner. Yourself?"

"We just moved here from Melbourne, four months ago. My husband got a teaching job here in Hobart; we felt like a change of scenery. Have you been here long?"

"We've lived here around ten years, I guess."

"What are the neighbours like, around here?" Anna asked.

"Truthfully, I couldn't say, for other streets. My husband and I work pretty much full time, and we're only really home at weekends. But the neighbours I've met are nice. Has the little one started kindergarten yet?"

"No, no, she's just three. We like to go to the playground, and we like going into town and looking around the shops. They have good story-time sessions at the library too, but there aren't a lot of children in this neighbourhood, so we spend a lot of time together." Beth thought that Anna sounded a little wistful and homesick.

"Do you have a pen, or a phone? I'll give you my number. I'm in and out to work a fair bit, but if I'm home, you're welcome to come over for a coffee. Do you like milk and cookies, Amity?" she asked the child. A tiny face peeped out from behind her mother's clothing, and the blonde curls bounced as the child nodded solemnly.

"Done deal, then. Here's my number." The two women exchanged mobile numbers and Beth left them in charge of the playground.

Beth walked home with a lighter heart, and a spring in her step that had been absent for weeks. What was even nicer, was that there were no unfamiliar cars or strangers out on the street near her house.

Next item on the day's agenda: coffee, a snack, and back to the hunt for her great-aunt.

She fired up the computer once more and resumed her search. On a whim, she picked up the phone and dialled Jeremy's number. The call went through to his message bank; she could hang up or leave a message, so she chose the latter option. "Hi, Jeremy, this is Beth. I wonder if you would call me when you have a chance? I have a favour to ask of you."

Chapter Nineteen

Hobart

The following Thursday, Beth was seated opposite her husband's solicitor, in his comfortably appointed office overlooking the Derwent River. She had met him once or twice in the ten years they had lived in Hobart, but they had never mixed socially. She considered him an unctuous sort of character, a little too slick and glib for her liking. However, he seemed concerned to carry out his client's wishes, and after the necessary preliminary small talk which often precedes important business dealings, came to the real reason for their meeting.

"My dear Mrs Ferguson, er, Doctor Bouchier," he began, gazing at her earnestly over the half-moon of his glasses, "please allow me to extend my condolences to you on the untimely death of your husband. It must have come as quite a shock." He looked across the wide desk at her; she nodded her acknowledgment of his statement. Her face did not betray her thoughts as she sat motionless and silent, steeling herself against the bitterness of his pity, and the indignity of having to be there at all. She pursed her lips together tightly and stared blandly back at the solicitor.

"Thank you, Mr Finn," she answered, tonelessly. "I believe you called me here to discuss Dougal's will?" She was all icy resolve. This man disquieted her; she did not like the way he looked at her. She found it unwelcome, but she had dealt with tougher people than this legal man. She found his gaze almost calculating or speculative; it made her uncomfortable, and she was wishing this interview was already over.

The solicitor droned through the terms and conditions of Dougal's last will and testament, which Beth already knew, as the couple had never held secrets from each other.

Yes, it had been her husband's wishes to be buried in Scotland or cremated and to have his ashes returned to his native land if possible.

Yes, naturally, possession of their house and land and all his money would flow to her, as his widow and next-of-kin, except for a small monetary bequest to his PhD student, Jeremy Munroe, plus a sum of money to be disbursed to the Marine Biology department of the university, for research into the seal populations of the Antarctic.

Their house was completely freehold, and her car was modern. She would not be forced to sell up and move elsewhere if she elected to stay in Hobart.

She was not surprised about the two small bequests; they had discussed the matter, as they always did.

Beth realised with a jolt that a significant part of her life had now ended with an abruptness which was brutal. She did not begrudge young Jeremy his windfall; he was a nice lad, and he had found the love of his life right here in Hobart; Carrie was an independent young woman who would cope very well with extended periods of separation, if he chose to go back to his research on Macquarie Island, or further afield.

Beth had liked Carrie immediately, and the two women had become firm friends in the short time they had known each other. Carrie was becoming like a daughter to Beth; with the girl being far enough away from her own family in Sydney to appreciate the counsel of a mother-figure, Beth filled the role instinctively. She loved young people; their energy and zest in turn energised her and kept her young at heart.

She realised she had been gathering moonbeams far away, as these thoughts flowed effortlessly through her mind, when she was jolted out of her reverie by Kenneth Finn asking quite loudly from across the desk, "Doctor Bouchier, dear lady, are you quite well?" in solicitous tones.

"What?" She looked at him, startled. Her eyes refocussed to the present moment. "Oh yes, thank you, I was just reminiscing about those odd little things we tend to forget about until we are reminded again." She did not elaborate.

"So," and here she looked directly at the man, "is that all, Mr Finn?"

"Almost, dear lady. There's just one other thing." He busied his hands, shuffling papers and stacking them neatly into their folders.

He extracted a large bulky buff envelope from a folder, then tied the bundle up with a coloured ribbon, and placed it on his desk.

Beth smiled to herself; he was such a pedantic old person. Just watching his precise and methodical movements, made her want to laugh. He reminded Beth of her grandmother; a fuss-budget if ever one existed.

She coughed politely to cover her mirth, straightened her suit skirt, stood up with her bag over her shoulder, and extended her hand. "Thank you, Mr Finn, for all your assistance. You have been incredibly kind and understanding. Good day."

With this she turned to leave, but Kenneth Finn's long fingers plucked at her sleeve; the pressure on her clothing forced her to stop. She turned around to face him, an enquiring look on her face. He was clutching the envelope, holding it out to her.

"Professor Ferguson entrusted me with this, for you, should the need ever arise."

Wordlessly, Beth took the proffered envelope from his hand and tucked it under her arm. She prepared to leave.

"You are very welcome to stay and read it, my dear. Ah, would you like a cup of coffee or tea?"

Beth looked at the handwritten salutation on the front of the envelope. As she smoothed her fingers across her darling's writing, she felt the crackle of paper and a hard, smooth flatness inside. It felt like a plastic case. She felt emotions rising as she took a step back and felt her calves meet the chair.

"No. Thank you all the same, Mr Finn, I won't have tea or coffee, but I'll leaf through the contents before I go, in case there are other legal points to clarify."

"A splendid idea, Mrs Ferguson, excuse me, Doctor Bouchier. Please, take all the time you need. I have no other appointments scheduled for this afternoon. I am at your disposal." He bustled away in search of his own refreshment, and Beth sat down.

She checked that the man had gone, then opened the package.

Tipping it up, she extracted two items; one was a sealed envelope and the other, a CD. How curious, Beth thought, examining the title of the disc, that of all the things Dougal would have left her, it would be a CD of folksongs sung by Joan Baez. How very odd…

She opened the envelope, smiled fondly at Dougal's familiar, precise handwriting, and unfolded his last letter to her.

"My Dearest and Only Love,
There is so much to tell you. If you are reading this, then you will know
that I am dead."

Beth let out an anguished sob and buried her face in her hands, still clutching the precious missive, while her frame shook with suppressed grief. She scrunched her eyes shut to stop the tears, swiped at her eyes surreptitiously with the back of her sleeve, and continued reading, though the words blurred in front of her eyes.

"I left this with my solicitor, hoping that you would never have to read this, but the worst has obviously happened, and you need to know the truth."

What was this all about? Beth straightened, took a deep breath, and bent to her reading once more.

"I am so sorry we have never had any more children, my love; but I have a confession to make to you. I once loved another…"

What? What lies had he told her for the past twenty-nine years? A startled gasp now escaped Beth's tight lips; this was bizarre…

She could feel a worrying pounding just behind her temporal lobe; she wondered if she was having a seizure of some sort, or a stroke. By now Mr Finn had appeared again, carrying his cup of tea and a plate of biscuits on a tray; she asked the solicitor in a strangled voice if she could have a glass of water. He looked at her sharply, put down his own refreshment and brought a full glass to her; her hands shook so much that some of the water slopped onto the carpet. When she had finally managed to drink the remainder, she returned to the letter, eyes blurring and hands shaking so much now she could hardly make out the words.

"…but that was many years ago, before we met. It was while I was in Canada in the autumn and winter of '82, monitoring seal populations in the North, and joining in the protests over the seal pup cull. Cathy was on one of the protests, and we just clicked, I suppose. We were young, and passionate about the cause; one thing led to another, and before we knew it, we were lovers. We became almost inseparable for a few wonderful months. They were heady days, even in the heightened emotion and anger of the protests on both sides, up in the North. Do you remember going up there, darling? You went there with me in later years, when I was doing more research. In fact, when I met you, you reminded me so much of her."

With an audible gasp, Beth let the letter drop into her lap, almost flinching, while her mind whirled and raced. *The bastard! How could he!* Fascinated despite herself, she picked up the letter and resumed reading. It was like a car crash; she could neither bear to look at the precise script flowing across the page, nor could she bear to look away. She knew there was more, and she had to discover the repugnant truth for herself; and she was no coward.

Squaring her shoulders unconsciously, she sat more erect in her chair, clamped her knees tightly together, and resumed reading her husband's confession.

"What I didn't know at the time, and wouldn't know for years, was that Cathy had fallen pregnant during our time together and had borne me a son. I had to leave the protest early to return home to Scotland – my father had fallen gravely ill and wasn't expected to live. We both know the old rascal made a complete recovery, but I didn't return to Canada that year – the hunting season had ended by the time my father was well enough for me to leave again. Cathy must only just have been pregnant when I left. She didn't contact me, never wrote or rang. So, for years I had no idea at all. How could I tell you, anyway, Beth?

You, who were such a wonderful mother, who could never have more children after the trauma of our own wee Malcolm's death. How could I tell you I had fathered another, healthy, son?"

Beth drained the dregs of water from the glass, steeling herself to be calm. How *dare* he!

"Anyhow, Cathy eventually managed to find me in 1994, the year after our own wee boy drowned; she wrote to me care of the research facility I was working at. I couldn't bring myself to break your heart even further than Malcolm's death had done.

I wasn't sure I believed her story in the beginning, so I organised for DNA testing to be done for them both and sent to me. I had mine done, too – you'll find those results in the envelope along with the CD, but the others I destroyed, as I promised Cathy I would."

Beth felt inside the envelope; her hands were shaking, and she found it difficult to grasp the stapled pages. She withdrew her fingers and continued reading; his bloody DNA test could wait until later.

"The long and the short of it is that, after I was certain he was my son, I started sending money to her, only for the lad's education and upkeep, you must understand. Apparently she had never married and was finding it hard to make ends meet, but I promise you, darling, we never met again. I never thought I would ever meet my son either, but I felt it was the honourable thing to do, at least, to support him through his high school education.

She died some years back, when the lad was in his early teens. The only reason I found out was because her bank contacted my bank to ask what I wanted to do about the contributions I had been making, because she was deceased, and the account had to be closed. I eventually tracked him down and paid his school directly each quarter; he was living with his grandparents, and I couldn't approach them, not after so many years. Anyway, I had never met them. What could I have said to them? I kept a discreet eye on the lad's progress, while he finished high school and entered university. I transferred funds for his tertiary education, too. He's a very bright young man.

His mother had left him little, but with my bequest disguised as anonymous bursaries and scholarships, he sailed through his university degree and Honours year at the University in Nova Scotia, where he majored in Marine Biology. No surprises there, I suppose. I have never revealed our relationship but have continued to support and mentor him through his education into doctoral studies.

More recently, he moved to Australia, here to Hobart, in fact, to begin his thesis. He came to our university, where he is researching pinniped population decline and sustainability. Naturally, we met through his work and we became close friends as well as colleagues. He's been a frequent visitor to our home, occasionally with his delightful young lady, and you have become fond of him too. He doesn't suspect he is my child, and I will never tell him. I beg you not to reveal our relationship to him either, but please keep a watchful and motherly eye on him for me.

I'm not proud of what I've done, dearest love, in keeping such a huge secret from you, but seeing Jeremy at last, I am fiercely proud of the fine young man he has become. He will make good use of the bequest I have provided for him; of that I am certain. His childhood probably wasn't all it could have been, but then, my darling, whose is?"

Shudders wracked Beth's shoulders, but no noise escaped her tightly clamped lips; her hands shook so badly she could no longer see the words while her thoughts flew furiously.

And our wee Malcolm's childhood was far too short, and you blamed me for that! Is this my punishment then, Dougal?

She sniffed and reached into her pocket for her handkerchief. Blowing her nose vigorously, she looked up to see Dougal's solicitor gawping at her, concern and curiosity writ large across his face. He looked as if he were about to jump up to come to her aid.

"I'll be all right, Mr Finn, just give me a minute please", she said, holding up a hand as if to ward him off.

Finn eased himself back into his chair. "Take all the time you need, Mrs Ferguson. Professor Ferguson did warn me you may need some assistance or comfort, if and when you ever had to read this letter."

"When did he update this?" she asked abruptly, shaking the letter at him.

"Two months ago, if my memory serves me correctly. He was adamant that I was never to burden you with this if he passed away naturally; it was only to be given to you if he died due to some misadventure, which is what appears to have happened. I'm so sorry, Mrs Ferguson." He gazed at her sympathetically across the top of his half-moon glasses. "Is there anything I can do for you? Anything at all?"

"No," she whispered, "no, thank you. I must finish reading this, this …"

Suddenly the letter was crumpled into a ball between her fingers, and she sat very still, ramrod straight, while her thoughts whirled, jarring and raging against each other. He had betrayed her. He had betrayed their love, and the trust she had always reposed in him. Why?

She looked down; the letter was in danger of being shredded by agitated fingers. She consciously smoothed out the pages, sniffed loudly, and returned to Dougal's letter.

Bastard! How could you do this to me? Poor man, she relented in an about-face of emotion, *you must have hated having to keep such a terrible secret from me all those years.*

The letter continued, *"There are some other truths I must reveal to you, which I could never do when I was alive."*

She was stunned afresh; what now? She acknowledged with a grudging pride, that her husband had always had a defined sense of honour; it was one of the many fine things she loved about him, and he wouldn't have consciously shirked a duty, especially one this serious.

Suddenly it made sense about the money that had disappeared from their bank account from time to time; the police had even asked if he had had financial problems, a gambling addiction or outstanding debts.

She *had* wondered, years ago, if he had a gambling habit which he was concealing from her, or a mistress. Somehow, she was relieved to learn that her suspicions had been unfounded, but a *son?* Her mind was still skittering away from the facts.

And then it hit her… he had mentioned a name. Jeremy… Jeremy was Canadian… Jeremy had always reminded her of someone… Carrie had even commented on it… finally, the truth hit her like the proverbial sledgehammer… Jeremy was Dougal's *son*! And unexpectedly she was laughing hysterically, laughing at the sheer *irony* of it all! She laughed until she could no longer breathe; she was literally gasping for air, and physically buckled over from the strain.

Rapidly, Kenneth Finn, the solicitor, was kneeling beside her chair, his short, corpulent frame bending over her slumped body, his arm firmly around her shoulders, squeezing her arm in an entirely unwelcome way, whilst patting her hand with firmer and firmer taps and calling her name while she struggled to make sense of it all. She must have passed out for a second or two. Did he think he could take advantage?

"Mrs Ferguson! Mrs Ferguson! My dear! Is there someone I can call? A doctor, perhaps?"

Beth struggled to sit up; she had canted off to the left a little and the solicitor's concern was touching but overbearing and uncomfortably intimate; she found it distasteful. He assisted her to sit straight but did not remove his arm from her shoulder. She eased her hand from his grasp, opened her eyes and looked directly at him.

"Would you please remove your hand from my shoulder, Mr Finn?" she asked coldly.

The solicitor hastily withdrew his hand as if he had touched hot coals. "My apologies, dear lady. Are you feeling better?"

"I'll be fine, thank you. The past few weeks have been particularly hard. It's been a little much to take in, all at once." She smiled weakly at him. "Do you think I could have another glass of water, please?"

"Would you like something stronger, perhaps?" Finn asked.

"A Scotch would be nice, if you have any…"

"Of course, Mrs Ferguson, your husband always enjoyed a Scotch with me when he came to see me…" Hearing her sudden intake of breath and seeing the pallor of her already ashen face, the solicitor hastened away to the liquor cabinet, conscious of having made a *faux pas*, mentioning a deceased husband to his grieving widow in such a banal way.

Mr Finn was more than slightly rattled this afternoon; he would never have imagined that his gentle and courteous client could have willingly inflicted such distress or such unseemly outbursts of hysteria on such a loyal and loving wife, a woman whom he personally found very attractive. He was extremely curious about the revelations Dougal Ferguson had included in his final letter to Elizabeth; but he held his peace and wisely said nothing. There was nothing to be gained by appearing nosy at this juncture; the lady may wish to speak of it in the future, or not…

Kenneth Finn poured a generous amount of the amber liquid into two glasses, and carried them carefully across the room, handing one to Beth, who sipped hers thoughtfully.

"*Slàinte, Dùghall dubh, bha thua a 'grad duine!*" she toasted her husband in her limited Gaelic, lifting her glass towards the ceiling, and drank deeply, then translated for the startled solicitor, "Cheers, black Dougal." She didn't bother to tell him she had just called her husband a rotten man as well.

"Ah, just so!" Kenneth Finn exclaimed with relief. "Feeling any better now, Mrs Ferguson?"

"Much, thank you," came the short reply. She was in control once more and spoke quite abruptly.

"I can see there's nothing in here with regards to legal matters, Mr Finn, so I shall finish reading this letter at home."

"Of course, of course! It's entirely up to you, Mrs Ferguson. The letter is yours. It obviously contains distressing news… if there's anything I can help you with…?"

If the solicitor was hoping she would confide in him, he was doomed to be disappointed and remain unenlightened.

"No more upsetting than many other letters I've had to read in my life," came the crisp reply.

Beth stood up, replaced the letter in the envelope, then folded it neatly and stowed in her handbag, which she had picked up off the carpet.

"I really mustn't take up any more of your valuable time, Mr Finn. Thank you for your kindness this afternoon." She extended her hand to the solicitor, shook his hand calmly but firmly, and turned to take her leave.

Kenneth Finn stared at her retreating back; he was filled with admiration for her… such a shame she had decided not to confide in him.

As his eyes roved across the floor, he spotted the CD which had slid from her lap. He raced after Beth, calling her name until she stopped abruptly, standing stiff-backed by the front door; apologising profusely, he handed her the item, which she accepted silently, with a gracious nod and a hint of a smile.

The portly little solicitor watched her walk resolutely towards her car.

Chapter
twenty

Beth sat in her car a long time before she could trust herself to drive safely. Her mind was still in chaos, and her hands shook badly, now that she was away from the solicitor, but the shot of whisky eventually steadied her nerves sufficiently for her to concentrate on the road. All she had to pray was that she wouldn't be breathalysed on her way home. That would just cap off a really disagreeable and painful afternoon.

She drove home sedately. No-one challenged or stopped her on the way; once home, she went through the motions of normality — park the car, check the letter box, and let herself in. She went straight through to the huge family room at the rear of the house, to the shelving unit near the dining table, and picked up a framed photograph of her husband with Jeremy, taken when they had been out together on a field trip.

Walking with it to the window, she held the picture up to the late autumn afternoon light which streamed in exuberantly; she scrutinised the image of two men standing side by side, laughing at some silly joke. There *was* a resemblance that she had never consciously noticed; the high cheekbones, the slant of the eyes; the signs were all there. Their colouring was different though; Dougal was dark-haired, but greying and weather-beaten and ruddy in complexion, while Jeremy was sun-bleached light brown and slightly olive-skinned. His mother must have been a dark-haired beauty, by the looks of it. She recalled Dougal's words in the letter about how Beth had reminded him of his other love, when he and Beth first met.

Beth laughed derisively at herself when she recalled what she had said to Carrie not too many weeks ago; this revelation made a total mockery of Beth's so-called superior powers of observation. What a fraud she felt. *Some expert you are on recognising tell-tale signs between original and fake artefacts, Elizabeth!* Her laughter felt hollow, too loud. *She* felt hollow. She felt like screaming and was almost tempted, just for a split second, to hurl the photo at the wall.

Controlling her unexpected fury, she returned it with exaggerated care to its customary place on the shelf, and went and made coffee. Mug in hand, she made herself comfortable in her armchair near the combustion stove, and extracted the letter, the official-looking white envelope containing Dougal's DNA results, and the CD from her handbag. She placed the CD and the white envelope on the coffee table, unfolded the letter once more and started reading. She skimmed the page until she reached the part where she had been forced to stop due to her overwhelming surge of emotion, sick realisation and uncontrollable laughter.

"In the package Kenneth Finn will have given you there is a CD, which I would ask you to play. It may help to explain what is not easily explicable..." She looked across at the CD; she returned to the letter. *"... if you have not listened yet, then please don't read any further until you have."* Beth re-read the words, confused. What difference would a collection of music make to this puzzle? She ignored this advice and read on.

"My love, please believe me when I say that I have never loved anyone the way I love you... my love for you is as deep as the ocean, and as high as the stars. Cliché and trite, I know, but so true. You have fulfilled my life and stood by me for many years, and without you I would have been lost, many times over, and in ways you could never even begin to imagine. Thank you for being such an understanding and forgiving woman; I truly do not deserve to have been so loved, the way you have loved me. And now I fear I may turn your love into hate and anger, but I feel impelled to confess all and throw myself on your mercy, if that's what it takes. I just beg you, darling, please try not to hate me or my memory.

As you know, I came from Orkney, from a long line of fisher-folk; we have all been involved with the sea in one way or another for generations, and ours has always been a deeply entrenched culture of folklore and superstition. You may have noticed this when we lived there a while, when I was away researching the seals and their cousins. I do not know if you ever really listened to the songs the old folk used to sing at the ceilidhs we attended, but they held my secret even then.

How can I tell you that at times in my life I haven't been quite human? Did you never guess there was something amiss?"

Beth thrust the pages away from her, stuffed her fist into her mouth, and stared at the letter lying on the floor as if it were poisonous. She really couldn't stand much more of this; she would go quite insane if she didn't find some answers, and soon! This had to be a sick joke!

She stood up abruptly, paced around the familiar room, then sat again, unable to reach a decision on what to do. If only she had someone she could talk to, but the knowledge that he had been unfaithful… no, that was not strictly true… the knowledge that he had fathered a child and had held on to that secret for so many years… that was unbearable! She wouldn't even be able to talk to Jeremy or Carrie about this! Her tears broke out afresh.

She was so restless; she paced like a caged animal through the house. She marched into the garden, hoping that the late afternoon sunshine would soothe her spirits, but even that didn't work. Her thoughts and emotions were too raw, too turbulent for her to find any peace at present. She re-entered the house, changed her clothes, and with cleaning materials set about scrubbing everything she could lay her hands on. She went to their bedroom and pulled all of Dougal's clothes out of drawers and wardrobes, piling them onto the floor. If she couldn't solve this problem, she could keep herself busy, and hopefully exhaust herself in the process.

Two hours later, the house was sparkling clean; it was always kept in a neat and tidy manner, but now it positively shone! The fact that the bedroom was like a tip, with clothes strewn in untidy heaps all over the floor, was irrelevant. She could close the door on the chaos for now. The rest of the house was done. Beth was exhausted physically; her muscles ached and her feet hurt, but her mind was only marginally less frantic. She heated some soup, made toast, and attempted to eat, but any appetite had disappeared.

After two mouthfuls, her stomach roiled; she dropped her spoon and raced to the bathroom, where she vomited repeatedly until there was nothing left. Sour dregs of whisky burned her throat as she regurgitated everything she had consumed that day. Even after the food and drink had gone, she could not stop heaving and retching. Finally she slid, exhausted, into an untidy heap on the bathroom floor, head touching the cold tiles, while her heart broke into splinters and she cried herself into oblivion.

***

Hours later, she came to her senses, cold, stiff, and aching all over her body. She wearily lifted her throbbing head, and struggled to her feet, leaning heavily on the toilet seat to lever herself up. She felt dreadful; she was desperately in need of a drink, and her eyes were so puffed-up she could hardly open them. She staggered into the kitchen, where she drank glass after glass of cold water from the tap. She couldn't believe how thirsty she was. Refilling the glass one last time, she took it through to the bedroom, not bothering with lights, and tripped over the jumbled mess of clothing, spilling the water.

She fell onto their bed, too tired even to undress apart from kicking off her shoes. She wrapped their quilt around herself and tried to breathe deeply, willing herself to sleep. Although she was desperately tired and emotionally drained, she could not sleep; all she could do was cry. The words of the letter returned to haunt her; she tried to make some sense of the whole weird thing, but she had an almost uncontrollable urge to scream.

Towards morning, as the late autumn dawn began to tint the sky, suffering from total exhaustion, she fell into a deep yet uneasy sleep, which was haunted by dreams of dark-skinned monsters emerging from the sea before metamorphosing into pale humans; dreams she hoped never to experience again.

***

Friday morning, Beth phoned the museum, and took the day off, pleading a terrible headache. She was in no fit state, she decided, to face the expressions of kindly concern and embarrassment she had been encountering since Dougal's death, and she certainly couldn't face them today.

Beth took her coffee to the master bedroom and set to work to sort out her late husband's clothing. Being a neat, methodical person, she sorted the items into several piles; one for the thrift shop, one for the bin, one for the rag bag she kept in the laundry, and one she didn't know what to do with. This last pile was the largest, by far.

Dougal had kept a heap of raggedy old clothes he liked to wear on field trips; these could go into the rag bag in the laundry, or, if they were too far gone, into the rubbish bin. His good clothes were suitable for donation to one of the local charity shops. These two piles were bagged up separately. The bag of would-be rags she bowled down the passageway towards the kitchen. The thrift shop bags she stacked neatly inside the front door. The items which were not even fit for polishing cloths, she stacked into the en-suite rubbish bin. When this overflowed, she grabbed the kitchen tidy. Old pens, bus tickets, parking permits, and a horde of "treasures" came out of his top drawers; the day-to-day detritus that gets emptied out of pockets, and promptly forgotten. Most of these went into the rubbish bin. Some, Beth kept by to sift through later.

The largest pile of clothing, she really had to think about; there was his hat, which she really couldn't bring herself to part with, and a couple of long scarves she had knitted for him. There were other items of clothing she would have to decide about. As she sat there, mechanically sorting through the garments, it suddenly occurred to her; she would have to provide a suit and a shirt and tie at least, to the undertakers, when Dougal's body was eventually released from the mortuary. She had to go and retrieve the bags from the front hall, and go through them all again. Damnation! Why hadn't she thought of it earlier?

Beth selected Dougal's best suit, one that still fit him, and a white shirt. She teamed this outfit with a plain black tie; these she carefully hung back up in the wardrobe in a suit bag, for a later date. There was really no telling when his body would be released; would he need underpants, socks, and shoes?

She would have to ask the undertaker when she got around to contacting one. Just in case, she rescued a pair of underpants, socks, and his dress shoes, and stored them with the other items.

Sighing, she retied the bag and took it back to the front door.

Stretching to unknot her shoulder muscles, Beth retraced her steps to the back of the house, collecting the bag of rags along the way. She shoved them into the laundry and shut the door; she'd deal with them another day.

After lunch, she sat down in her comfortable chair and reopened the envelope. In her cleaning frenzy the previous day, the letter had been thrust back inside; she took it out, along with the CD. No sense in prolonging the inevitable. She put the disc in the stereo and searched for the track Dougal had nominated in his letter. Track six.

As the haunting voice of Joan Baez filled the light-filled room, Beth closed her eyes and listened to the track he had requested.

"An earthly nurse sits and sings,
And aye she sings by lily wean –
'Little ken I my bairn's father,
Far less the land where he dwells in.'
For he's come one night to her bed's foot

And a grumbly guest I'm sure he'd be.
Saying, 'here am I, thy bairn's father,
Although I be not comely.'
'I am a man upon the land,
I am a silkie in the sea,
And when I'm far and far frae land,
My home it is in Sule Skerrie.'"

Beth's eyes flew open. She listened intently to the remainder of the song and scanned the CD for notes on the song. She read aloud:

"An ancient Scottish ballad from Northern Scotland and the Orkneys, concerning a half man, half seal. The man in the ballad begets a child on an earthly woman, then returns to claim and pay for his Silkie son, and foretells both his and his son's death at the hands of the woman's future husband."

Beth turned off the CD, picked up the letter and smoothed out the pages she had mangled the previous night. Dougal's confession continued.

*"If you have listened to the song, you will have uncovered my greatest secret, my love. I was lucky, or unlucky enough to have been born with this gene; I don't know if Jeremy carries it, but I wouldn't be surprised. You may, by now, have guessed the significance of my old coat, the one you have been so keen to dispose of to the thrift shop for so many years, and the one reason I have resisted all your loving attempts to modernise my appearance. It was my means of transformation, love; without it I could never return to the form of a seal. I know I told you I couldn't swim, but that was to protect myself from exposure to prying minds and unanswerable questions. I did **not** want to become a specimen to be 'studied'. Mine was a secret life, and one I was unable to share with anyone apart from my kinfolk.*

In my will, I have requested that my body be cremated; it would have been impractical for you to transport my earthly remains to the far north of Scotland. Awkward questions might have been asked. So, cremation is the only other way. If you can forgive me for the deception I have practised on you for all these years, please grant me this favour, darling; go to Orkney if you can, and scatter my ashes on the ebb tide. That way they will be carried back to my ancestral home, to the sea stacks of Sule Skerry. Yes, darling, the place really exists.

Ask my sister Shona to help you; she lives in Scotland and has always had her suspicions about me and my coat. She was always watching me when I was young; I suspect she guessed long ago. Speaking of the coat, please send it to the flames with me; it must go with me to my final rest."

Beth closed her eyes, clenched her fists until the knuckles were white, and breathed evenly through her nose. She was almost afraid to open her mouth in case she should scream or burst into more hysterical laughter. She opened her eyes and scanned through the body of the letter once more. She lifted her gaze to the river; something niggled at her memory. Worrying would only frighten away the intangible thread of thought, so she deliberately and calmly put the letter down on the table and went to her library of folders.

She searched through the Canadian native folktales she had collected over the years she had lived on Vancouver Island; the particular anecdote she wanted was a Tsimshian story of transformation. She leafed through the pages of closely written notes until, with an exclamation of triumph, she found the story she wanted.

She took the folder back to her chair, and read it through; yes, there it was, a tale of transformation from her own People, but this time it was the *wife* who metamorphosed into another creature. It was about the Beaver Woman, and a story she had loved as a youngster; it had always captured her imagination.

"*... first beaver was a woman who had a husband who constantly nagged her about her housework. In order to get away from him, she dammed up a stream and spent her days swimming. The more he nagged her, the more time she spent in the water. Eventually fur grew over her body, and her leather apron turned into a flat beaver tail that slapped the surface when she dived. After that, she never returned to her nagging husband, and lived happily as a beaver, inside her dammed-up stream...*"

Beth laughed aloud at the apparent absurdity of the story, but it was like so many of the Australian Aboriginal Dreamtime legends of how the world and its creatures were made; an attempt to explain the inexplicable.

Like a bolt out of the blue, Beth realised what had been niggling at her thoughts, the phone call to Shona. She remembered the sharp intake of breath on the other end of the line when she had mentioned something about Dougal's old coat being missing along with him. So, Dougal had been right about his sister.

A sharp rapping at the front door brought Beth sharply out of her thoughts. She crept through the house and peeped through the spyhole in the front door. She breathed a sigh of relief; it was only the postman, and he was turning away to walk back down the path. She quickly opened the door and called out to him; he turned and smiled at her, holding out two large packages, and a device for an electronic signature. She smiled and took delivery of the packages; they bore the logo of the genealogical site she had accessed the previous weekend.

Beth hurried indoors to open one package. Inside was a numbered letter from the society she had contacted, along with a flat white box. She opened it and looked inside; she read the instructions and decided to do her DNA sample immediately. No, wait! When had she last eaten or drunk anything? The instructions specified a waiting period at least one hour, to prevent the risk of cross-contamination. She remembered having lunch and a coffee, but how long ago was that? She decided to wait another fifteen minutes, just to be on the safe side. But she could just have a look, while she waited. From the box she extracted two zigzag-edged cotton swabs on long sticks, encased in sterile wrapping, and two plastic capped vials containing a liquid of some sort.

Following the instructions, she scraped the cotton swab against the inside of her cheek for the prescribed sixty seconds, then carefully inserted it head-first into the plastic vial. She let it stand for a couple of seconds, then grasped the whole thing firmly and pushed down on the centre tube, which released the long stick, leaving behind the head of the swab in the vial. She closed the vial and ensured it was sealed securely; next step was to invert the vial a few times to coat the swab thoroughly. She then placed the vial into the bag provided and repeated the process on the inside of the other cheek. Once she had completed all the steps, Beth put the second vial in with the first, sealed the bag and placed it in the padded envelope she found in the bottom of the box. There was a consent form to complete, which she did, placing it in the envelope. She had just finished putting the sealed envelope on the kitchen bench, ready for posting, when her mobile phone rang. She checked the caller ID; it was Jeremy.

"Hi, Beth, sorry it's taken me so long to get back to you, but I've been kind of busy at the lab. There's been a lot to do, to finish writing up all of the professor's reports and hand them over to a new guy here. I didn't get your message until yesterday, and when I called you, your phone was off. Are you okay?"

"Oh hi, Jeremy, thanks for getting back to me. I kind of figured you'd be busy, and it wasn't urgent at the time, but I have a favour to ask of you."

"Okay. How can I help?"

"Look, it's going to sound kind of weird, but I wondered if you would be willing to take a DNA test for me? I can't tell you what it's about at present, because I'm working on a hunch, but would you be a sweetie and do it for me?"

"Hey, you've made me real curious, now! I'm always up for a challenge. When did you want to do this?"

"Are you and Carrie free tomorrow evening? I know it's short notice and all, but I wondered if you two would like to come over and have an evening meal with me?"

"Well, *I'm* free, and I'd *love* to come eat with you, Beth, but Carrie's working tomorrow evening. Should we wait until we're both free?"

"No, no! That'll be fine. You come by yourself, lad; we'll have dinner together, just the two of us… as long as Carrie doesn't mind?"

"She won't mind me coming to dinner — she'll just be wild that she missed out on some of your home cooking!" He laughed, and Beth laughed with him.

They arranged a time and ended the call.

Beth looked at the envelope on the kitchen bench and hugged herself with excitement. She'd have Jeremy all to herself for a couple of hours; she was certain she wanted him to do the DNA test, to check out the theory which had been humming around in her brain since the previous weekend.

What Beth hadn't quite decided, was whether to share at least some of the contents of Dougal's letter with the young man; she would decide *that* when they had had a long conversation. Jeremy had a story to tell.

Oh! She must send him a text to remind him to bring over his family photos, if he could find them!

Chapter
twenty-one

"Let's eat out here; it's our favourite part of the house. Dougie and I usually ate here, except in the worst of the summer heat. Come on, I'll show you where the placemats and napkins are kept. You can set the table, while I go fix the meal. It's a little late in the year for the twilight, but we can still watch the mist rise on the water, and the lights on the other side. I've always loved twilight; it's my favourite time of the day, I must admit. Dougie always said they made him melancholic; he preferred sunrises. Did you know that in the tropics they don't really have twilight? The sun is up, and then, boom, it's gone. Twilight lasts about thirty seconds, or so it seems. Not long enough for me, I prefer a slow, gentle ending to the day as the world settles itself down for sleep. How was your day?"

Beth chattered non-stop as she led Jeremy through the house. She had spent an industrious day, disposing of Dougal's clothes at the thrift shop, supermarketing, preparing the evening meal; plus tidying up the rest of Dougal's immediate belongings. His treasures and knick-knacks still required attention, but she had postponed that job until a 'rainy day'. She was brimming with energy and a new-found burst of enthusiasm. Jeremy was somewhat relieved by her apparent return to normality.

"Beth, slow down!" Jeremy laughed. He had arrived promptly at seven, carefully carrying a paper bakery bag, and a folder. Beth relieved him of the bag, and peeked inside; bless him, he'd brought along a rich gateau for dessert. She put it on the breakfast bar and reached to kiss Jeremy on the cheek.

"Thank you!" she exclaimed. "What a thoughtful young man you are! I hope you like stew… it seems a little ordinary after seeing this gorgeous cake. Oh, and there's home-baked bread, as well."

"I don't care what you feed me, Beth," laughed Jeremy. "It all smells so good! Carrie said your food is wonderful!"

"Flatterer!" Beth twinkled. "Now come put your stuff down, and

I'll serve dinner. Hungry?"

"As a hunter!" he replied.

She laughed aloud and brought the hot pot to the table. The bread, still warm and yeastily aromatic, sat on a wooden serving board, with a knife and a tub of butter alongside. The stew was placed on a heat-proof mat, and Beth gave Jeremy a ladle; he was to serve himself.

They ate in companiable silence. Jeremy went back for a second helping of stew, which made Beth smile broadly, and finally she cleared the table and went to make coffee. Jeremy asked if he could help with the dishes; no, apparently he couldn't but *was* dispatched to the cupboard and cutlery drawer for the dessert plates and forks. Like Carrie before him, Jeremy felt *at home* here; it was strangely as if he belonged, somehow. He decided it was to do with the woman who lived here.

"Jeremy dear, would you put this wonderful confection on a plate, please, and take it to the table? There's a fresh cake knife hiding somewhere in the second drawer down... I'll just finish making this coffee and bring it in. Go ahead, don't stand on ceremony."

Yes, it was *definitely* the woman who lived here who made this house a home.

Beth cut the cake into thin wedges.

"Coffee and cake, a perfect end to a wonderful meal." Jeremy sat back, replete. "You're a fantastic cook, Beth. It's a wonder the professor stayed so slim!" He patted his stomach, then realised what he had said. He looked sharply up at Beth; she was sitting quite still, regarding him thoughtfully, while he reddened furiously.

"Jeremy. Let's get one thing very clear, right now, shall we? Dougal's body has died, but his soul and his spirit is still here in this house. It's okay to talk about him—you won't upset me. He was a large part of my life; no, he *was* my life for many years. If I have to put up with people tippy-toeing around the subject or measuring their words so Dougie's name is never mentioned for fear of upsetting me, well that's just going to upset me further. And yes, he did manage to stay slim despite my cooking! He exercised a lot, and he burnt a lot off in excess energy."

Beth looked Jeremy in the eye, challenging him to argue with her, but he was a sensible young man. He smiled apologetically.

"Sorry, Beth, it won't happen again. We got to be really good friends over the past year and a bit. It would hurt me not to be able to talk about him, too."

"Good!" Beth exclaimed. "Now, let's get these things cleared away, so we can have a look at your stuff. I was quite intrigued by what you said last weekend when you were here."

"Sure thing! And did you want me to do this DNA test tonight?"

Beth's hand flew to her mouth as she gasped; her eyes went wide, then she started laughing.

"Oh dear! That's right! I was going to get you to do that before dinner, but I quite forgot! And we've just eaten! Silly me! Ah well," and she patted his hand, "you'll just have to stay an extra hour or so, won't you! You can't do it until at least an hour after you've eaten. Come on, let's see your family photos while we wait. I'm intrigued!"

Jeremy brought out his mementoes and spread them out on the table; he and Beth were soon totally absorbed in his memories. There was the picture he had mentioned, of three generations of women, and him as a young child. Beth had resolved to approach this hunch-driven quest in a professional manner, treating each item as an artefact; but she wasn't prepared for the beautiful young woman whose dark eyes gazed at her from the photograph, hands resting protectively on a young Jeremy's shoulders.

"Is this your mom?" she asked almost in a reverent whisper. "She's beautiful."

"Yeah, I guess she was. She was just Mom, you know?" he shrugged. "She's been gone a long time. Over twenty years. I was seven years old when that was taken. Guess that makes it twenty-five years ago."

"And this is your grandmother and great-grandmother?" Beth persisted. She could feel her heart-rate elevating; she fought to keep a rising excitement in check.

"Yeah. This," he indicated an older woman, "was Granma Maddie, and this," he pointed out, "was my great-granma Bibi."

Beth stared at the women's faces. "Wait here!" she commanded and jumped up to fetch the photo which had started all this discussion the previous weekend.

"There!" she whispered. "This is me and my mom, like I told you. Look at them!"

Jeremy looked closely, comparing the two photographs.

"Wow!" he whistled softly. "I see why I made the mistake. They could be sisters--you and my granma Maddie could be sisters. How can that be, then?" he asked, tearing his eyes away from the photos to stare at Beth.

"I don't know, laddie," she said softly, patting his shoulder, "but I got this crazy idea last weekend, after you and Carrie had been here, and I've been doing some digging. That's why I ordered those do-it-yourself DNA kits. I've already done mine. I couldn't wait. Now you just have to do yours. If you're still willing, that is…"

"Sure, I'm willing. I just can't see what it will prove, that's all."

"It may prove nothing, but it *may* answer some questions I've had for a very long time. Wait here, while I show you something…" Beth got up again and went to her desk. From it, she extracted the small box and an old album. She unlocked the box and produced the scroll she had scrutinised the previous weekend. Clearing space at the other end of the table, she carefully unfurled the document, weighted it down, and found her cotton gloves.

"Come look at this, Jeremy. This is my family tree. Tell me what you see?"

Jeremy walked to the other end of the table, and leant over. "Okay," he said, scanning across the document. "Oh!" he exclaimed. "Oh!" He had seen the name Biba up near the top, daughter of Tilly and Jean-Pierre LaRoque. He looked up, questioningly, at Beth. "How? What? Tell me!"

"This is a really, really long shot, Jeremy. But here goes. My great-grandparents are here," — she indicated with the gloved finger — "and they had two daughters. One," — pointing at Hannah's name — "is my Grandma Hannah. The other," — her finger skated across the page — "is their younger daughter, Biba. Now, Biba disappeared from their lives in 1930, okay? My great-grandfather Jean-Pierre was killed in a logging accident in 1929, leaving my great-grandmother to bring up two daughters. She didn't work, if the family stories are correct. Hannah was sixteen years old when her father died, and Biba was nine. About a year after Jean-Pierre's death, Biba just didn't come home from elementary school one day; we heard later that there had a been like a raid, if you want to put it that way, by a church organisation, aided and abetted by the government of the day, to round up half-breed kids who were fatherless, and take them to live in 'schools' over East. I learned a lot about this when I was researching on the Net last weekend. They wanted to 'beat the

Indian out of the kid', to use their words, and these kids were institutionalised, so they could be 'assimilated' into white society. They were abused, in many ways, and punished for speaking their own languages, using their tribal names, or practising their own beliefs. Based on what I've read, some didn't make it, and others have committed suicide in the years since. It broke my heart to read this, believe me."

Beth heard Jeremy's rapid intake of breath, but she continued.

"Anyway, that was the last they ever saw or heard of Biba. My great-grandmother mourned her younger child till the day she died, and my grandmother was paranoid about my mother as a small child. Grandma Hannah never married, so she was really scared the same thing would happen to her daughter. When I was young, my Mom, Selena,"—Beth pointed to the names in turn—"was really anxious about my safety too, even though she was married, and my dad was still alive. But Dad was away at sea a lot, so Mom was left alone with me for weeks on end."

Jeremy's eyes were like saucers. He glanced up at Beth, who was standing, looking out at the river. She remained motionless until he spoke.

"So, you're wondering if there's a *connection* between us? Is that right? Are you thinking that your, what, great-aunt Biba might be my great-granma *Bibi*? Oh man, that's insane!"

Beth turned slowly; she levelled a steely gaze at him. "You think so? Even though Biba's not a common name, Jeremy? Take the test, then," she challenged, "and let's see who's *insane!*"

Jeremy stood up, abashed. He had never heard Beth so earnest since he'd met her.

"So," she challenged. "Are you game?"

"Hell, yes! Oh, sorry! Heck, yes! Bring it on! Has it been an hour since dinner yet? Let's do it!"

Beth laughed, and let out a sigh of relief; she hadn't realised she was so tense about this.

"Yes, lad, I think we'll be safe now. Let's check the time, and I'll get the kit ready."

The tension had gone out of the air; they were able to laugh and share a joke while they opened the second box. Jeremy was taller than Beth, so he sat down and meekly held his mouth open while Beth administered the cheek swabs and stowed them safely into their plastic vials. She presented him with the consent form and a pen, with a small flourish, and then it was all over. Two large, sealed envelopes lay side by side on the kitchen counter.

"Okay, Jeremy, you deserve another piece of cake and a coffee, as a reward."

He laughed aloud. "Oh Beth. This means a lot to you, doesn't it?"

You don't know the half of it, my lad.

"It will just prove whether my crazy, insane hunch is right, that's all. The tests will take about six to eight weeks to process, apparently, and then we'll get an email. Could be fun comparing them when we get the results. Now, I'll make more coffee, and get you your cake. Then I want you to tell me about your family, if you wouldn't mind. I'm interested to know the story behind these photographs."

"Sure! Bring on that cake!"

"Ah, every man has his price," she laughed as she went to the kitchen.

While Jeremy was demolishing a second generous slice, Beth dug out some old family photographs of her own, so she could show him Dougal as a young man. She still hadn't decided if she was going to abide by Dougal's wishes and keep Jeremy's parentage from him, or whether she was going to disclose the truth, but she was swinging towards the latter. Jeremy deserved to know the truth, she decided, and the letter would make many things clear.

Jeremy had eaten his cake and rinsed his plate; he sipped his coffee thoughtfully as he wondered where to begin.

"I never knew my dad, Beth. My mom would never tell me."

"Carrie mentioned a little about that, after you guys had sailed for Macquarie Island. We got talking, and she was happy, talking about you; she missed you a bunch, you know."

"Yeah, I know. Anyway, I was born in Ottawa, where my folks had lived all their lives. I don't have a family tree, but I guess I could sketch one for you. My mother was Catherine Munroe, only daughter of Madeleine and Andrew." He stopped, tracing an imaginary chart in the air with a finger as he was thinking. "Okay. Andrew was from Scottish forebears, and Madeleine was a part-breed. Her mom's name was Bibi. Bibi was brought up in a church residential school, so my granma Maddie told me. Bibi never talked about it to me. She was real old when I was born — she must have been sixty-three years old or so. This photo of the four of us was the last one taken of her — she died soon afterwards."

Beth rested her hand lightly on Jeremy's shoulder for a moment, then asked, "When was your grandmother born, Jeremy? Do you know?"

He closed his eyes and scrunched up his face as he tried to remember. "I think it was before World War Two, but I'm not sure."

Beth looked at him in shock; if the two women were one and the same, Biba would have been less than nineteen years old when her daughter was born.

"I remember my mom telling me, after Great-Granma Bibi died, that she had worked as a domestic servant in some big house in Ottawa, after she left the school where she lived. Mom never knew who her grandpa was…

"Anyway, I never knew who *my* dad was, either. Guess it must run in the family, huh!"

That statement, said with such cynical resignation, was what finally tipped the scales for Beth.

"How would you feel, Jeremy, if you could find out about your dad?"

"I really don't know, Beth. I guess I'd have a lot of questions to ask him. I'd want to know why he abandoned my mom and me. Mom always said she had *me*, and that's all that mattered, it was all she needed. I don't remember her ever having any serious boyfriends when I was a kid, and I'm pretty sure she never mentioned knowing who my dad was, or even crying over him. But I guess I'd be pretty pissed off with him, all the same. It was real tough, being a kid with no dad.

"Mom put herself through college at night to finish her studies, and got a job teaching science at a local high school, so we were okay for a while. When she started to get sick, and had to take a heap of time off, the money kind of dried up, and we did it hard for a while, but my grandparents helped us out, until I got a scholarship for school. Mom would never spend any of the money on herself — she said it was for me, for my education, you know, books, and stuff."

"How old were you when your mom died, Jeremy?"

"I was twelve years old. When Mom got sick for the last time, the house had to be sold, and we went to live with Granma Maddie and Gramps. The money she made from the sale of the house pretty much went on medicines and hospital costs. When she died, I stayed on with Granma Maddie and Gramps, living with them through high school, until I left to go to university in Halifax. Gramps died the first year I was in university. I didn't know whether to stay at university or go home to Granma Maddie, but she was adamant that I was to stay where I was. I used to go home to visit her as often as I could, and I spent my long vacations at home in Ottawa with her. We got on so well. It really hurt me *bad* when she died. She was my last living relative."

"Jeremy, dear. That's so sad. I'm so sorry to drag up painful memories for you."

"Sure. It's okay, Beth. I guess it's good to talk about them once in a while. But I still miss them a bunch."

Beth patted him gently on the shoulder, got up and went to her desk, where she had stowed Dougal's letter of confession. As her hands closed on the envelope she took a deep breath.

Sorry, Dougal, but he needs to know. She picked up the letter and returned to the table.

"Jeremy, it's been a pretty torrid time for us both, in the past few weeks. I had to see Dougal's solicitor yesterday, no, Thursday. He wanted to go through the terms of Dougal's will, and he had some paperwork for me. The good news is that Dougal has left you a small bequest, money to allow you to live while you continue your research and get through your doctorate, if that's what you still want to do.

"No." She held up her hand to stop him from butting in. "Let me finish, please? There's also a sum of money for the university so the marine biology research can go on. Plus—" She paused, knowing that she was betraying Dougal's plea for anonymity. "—he left me a letter. And a couple of other things." She sighed. "Thing is—" She closed her eyes momentarily, then looked at him. "I'd like you to read it, or at least *part* of it. He mentions you."

Saying no more, Beth passed the first page of the letter to Jeremy, and closed her eyes again.

There was a hush in the room, broken only by the rustle of paper.

"Why have you given me this letter?" Jeremy's sudden outburst made Beth jump. She opened her eyes, and looked at him. He looked upset and bewildered. She was asking herself the same question at that moment.

"Ah, Beth? Why did you give this to me? It's terribly personal. I feel kind of uncomfortable about doing this. I don't think I want to read any more, thank you." Jeremy's voice died away until it was little more than a husky whisper into the silence. His outstretched hand proffered the page to her.

She accepted the sheet of paper and waited.

Jeremy turned anguished eyes on her; Beth had a sudden pang of guilt. His face looked so *forlorn,* she felt so sorry for him. She put her arm around his shaking shoulder. "Where did you get to?" she asked quietly.

"He was talking about your little boy. Sorry, I couldn't go on. It's too sad and personal."

"Would you prefer it if I read it to you, lad?"

"Only if you really want to."

"Well, to be honest, I don't really want to, but I feel I owe it to you. I think you need to know what he wrote. Okay, here goes."

Chapter
twenty-two

Beth cleared her throat, and started reading the letter aloud at the point where Cathy had contacted Dougal.

She read the letter clearly, slowly, glancing at Jeremy from time to time. He looked slightly perplexed, but nodded whenever their eyes met. When Beth reached the parts about the DNA test, the bequests of money, the death of the boy's mother, and even the mention of a particular university, she looked across at him; he was staring back at her in sheer disbelief. He was ashen-faced and had started shaking. He opened his mouth to speak, but Beth held up a warning hand.

"Just let me finish this before my courage fails me, Jeremy." She knew that she had just opened Pandora's Box; she could never put the lid back. Taking a deep breath, Beth continued reading to him.

When she reached the part about Jeremy's arrival in Hobart, she faltered and looked up. The expression on his face told her that he had put the final pieces of the jigsaw together, and was looking at the picture of his life. He jumped up and was pacing the room; his distress was palpable.

"The *professor* was my *father*? I can't believe it! No! That can't be right! Why would he abandon my mom and me? I had a father all those years, and I never *knew*?" he shouted.

Beth sat in grim silence and watched, powerless as Jeremy paced like a caged animal around the room, trying to make sense of the unbelievable facts. He sat down abruptly, covered his face with his hands and began to weep bitterly. Beth, understanding some of his mental anguish, moved towards him, put an arm around him, and let him cry; he turned towards her and buried his face in her shoulder. She understood his distress only too well; the letter had reduced her, too, to tears, as well as hysterical laughter, only a couple of days before. She patted him soothingly on the back.

"There, there," she crooned to him, "there, there, lad. It's a lot to take in right now. Dougal asked me not to reveal his relationship to you, and I've betrayed his trust. I'm so sorry, honey!"

"Yes, no, yes, oh, I don't know! I don't know *what* to think any more. This is too much!"

Beth calmly smoothed out the page; keeping Jeremy held close to her, she read the final part of that page of the letter to him, in which Dougal apologised for keeping Jeremy's existence a secret but stating his fierce pride in the fine young man his son had become. When she had finished reading, she put down the page and hugged him wordlessly.

Eventually, Jeremy sniffed, sat back, and fished around for a handkerchief; he blew his nose, wiped his streaming eyes, and muttered, "Yeah, I vaguely remember Mom making me get a blood test, but she would never tell me why. She did one too. But I still don't get why Mom would never tell me, or why he never contacted me! That's just *cruel*!"

Beth squeezed his shoulder gently and let him go. He was like a coiled spring; he jumped up again and started pacing while he processed everything. Beth let him; he would have to sort his feelings out for himself. She sat, helpless, impotent, while he paced. Finally, Jeremy turned an angry, tear-stained face to her.

"I didn't even win those scholarships for myself! I'm a complete *fraud*! How could he have *done* that to me?" He had raised his voice and was now shouting.

"Don't be ridiculous, Jeremy!" Beth snapped at him. "You were obviously a smart child; you *are* a smart young man. Does it really matter *how* the money was found?"

He stopped in mid stride and glared at her.

"It matters to *me*! It matters a *lot* to *me*!" he shouted. And in that instant, if Beth had never noticed it before, she could see the similarity between father and son.

"I understand, lad, I really do," she apologised. "You're more like your father than you could know! It's about your honour, *your* feelings of worth and integrity, isn't it!" The young man nodded, red-faced, swollen-eyed, and mute with shame; at least he had stopped pacing.

Beth persisted, hoping he would listen. She raised her voice.

"Well, I guess that's why Dougal provided for your education, Jeremy — *that* was about *his* honour, and caring for his son, albeit at a distance. If you want to blame anyone, Jeremy, blame *me*! Dougal provided for you, but never told me, because I suffered a nervous breakdown after our little boy drowned. He says so, here in his letter!

"And would I have welcomed you, a *stranger*, another woman's child, into my life, so soon after our own wee boy had died? I *doubt* it, to be honest. But *I'm* not very happy to only be finding out all of this now, either! Do you think it's been a walk in the park for me, too?" Her voice had risen almost to a shout.

Jeremy looked at her in surprise and sat down abruptly in the closest chair. He stared at her as if he were only *seeing* her for the first time. He reached across and took her hand.

"I'm so sorry, Beth, it's just hit me, *hard*. I don't blame *you*. I don't blame you for a second! Please, never think that!" He stood up. "Would you excuse me, please? I think I'd like to be alone for a while. I don't think I feel very well." He squeezed her hand. "Can I come back a little later? I don't think I want to go home just now. I'm not up to talking to Carrie about this, not yet."

"Sure, honey. Do you want me to make up the spare bed?"

"No thanks, but I'd like to take a walk in the fresh air. My stomach is all churned up."

"I can imagine! You didn't see me the other night, when I got this bombshell dropped on me, either. I was quite a mess. Go for a walk, go for a run. There's a playground down by the river's edge. Go have some time — it's a lot to absorb. And if it's any consolation, I feel very guilty for going against Dougal's wishes, but I felt you deserved to know whose son you are. Go on! Off you go. Take a key from the basket on the hall table so you can let yourself back in. I guess I'll still be awake." Beth stood on tiptoe and kissed him gently on the cheek.

***

When he returned an hour later, calling "Hello?" Beth was curled up in her favourite chair, with her Indian rug wrapped around her. She was staring out at the lights dancing on the ripples of the wind-ruffled river.

"I'm out back, lad. Would you like a hot drink?" she called.

Jeremy walked into the room and sat down in a nearby chair. "That would be good, thanks, it's getting quite cold out there. No, wait," he said, reaching for Beth's hand before she could get up, "first, I want to apologise for getting upset with you. I was out of order. I had no right to take out my frustration on you. It just hit me blindside, I guess." He lifted Beth's hand to his lips and kissed it reverently. "Thank you for being there. I know it's not your fault, and I know you only acted with the best intentions."

"Ah yes, good intentions, laddie. The road to Hell is supposed to be paved with them! Let me make you a hot chocolate, or would you prefer coffee?"

"A hot chocolate sounds just wonderful, thanks. Can I help?"

"No, honey, unless you want another piece of cake. Just help yourself, it's in the cake tin, or there are home-baked cookies in the blue container, if you prefer."

Beth got up and draped her blanket across the chair back. Jeremy helped himself to a couple of ginger biscuits and munched them while he watched her prepare their drinks. He sat down on a bar stool, and she lifted one mug over to him.

"Hey!" he exclaimed, suddenly grinning at her. "I realised something while I was out walking. I guess I'm not an orphan anymore!" He jumped up, strode around the island bench, and pulled Beth to him. She found herself crushed in a huge bear hug.

"Can't. Breathe. Jeremy. Let. Go. Please?"

"Oh, sorry!" He released his vice-like grip and allowed Beth to step back a little. She was sucking in air and looking at him strangely.

He returned her look, and they both burst out laughing. He seized her hand, and they did an impromptu jig around the room.

"I've got a mom, I've got a mom," he sang.

"Jeremy, honey, stop! I'm getting a stitch!" she gasped.

Jeremy's mobile interrupted his mad capering.

"Hello?" he answered breathlessly. "Oh, hi, honey. Yeah, I'm still at Beth's … no, just talking heaps and drinking hot chocolate … is it really that late? Well, I guess I should be getting home, then. I'll just finish my drink. Oh, okay, I'll tell her. See you soon, honey, love you a bunch."

"I take it Carrie's finished work then?" asked Beth.

"Guess so." He sipped, then drained his mug.

"Look, I'd better go. Can I come back soon, so we can talk some more?"

"Of course! Let me give you a hand to pack up your stuff."

"Can I come by and pick it up tomorrow?"

"Of course you can. And thank you for bringing the great cake.

You'll have to come back to finish it off. Bring Carrie if she's not busy. Actually —" She thought a moment. "I wondered if you would have some free time in the next few days. Dougal's study will need to be sorted out, and I really don't know where to start. I figured you'd be the right man for the job."

"Will do. It'd be an honour. *Thank you so much!*"

Beth gave Jeremy a huge hug and kissed him on the cheek. "Drive safely, please, my boy. Don't want to lose you, now I've only just found you!"

She saw him to the door.

"Night, Beth." Jeremy got into his car, buckled up and drove away into the night.

Beth felt like she'd gone a dozen rounds in the boxing ring — she was exhausted, but for the first time in weeks, she was cautiously optimistic and almost *happy.*

*****

Sunday afternoon, both Jeremy and Carrie came to visit. Beth set Carrie to making a pot of coffee, while she took Jeremy into Dougal's study. There was so much material in there; research papers, lecture notes, and a stack of scientific paraphernalia to be sorted through; there would be enough to keep the young man gainfully occupied for days, if not weeks. Beth left him in the middle of the mess; he looked happy there. She wandered back down to the kitchen and family room, to talk with Carrie, who was curious to know what had transpired the previous evening; apparently Jeremy had been too tired to discuss it when he got home.

Beth told her about the conversation she and Jeremy had had, the photos they had looked at, and the family trees they had compared. Carrie's sharp eyes spotted the two large white padded envelopes on the kitchen bench; following the line of the young woman's gaze, Beth found herself telling her about her own crazy theory and the DIY DNA tests she and Jeremy had done.

Beth was unsure if Jeremy had dropped his biggest piece of news on Carrie, so she waited for the other woman to bring up the topic. Together, they cut the remains of the cake, made coffee and afternoon tea. They sat quietly; Beth brought out some family photos and they looked through them, Carrie commenting from time to time on one or another of the early photos of Dougal. She once more pointed out the resemblances between Dougal and her fiancé; Beth squeezed her arm gently and called Jeremy to join them for refreshments.

He came via the bathroom; there had been a lot of dusty stuff to sort out, and he had needed to wash his hands.

"Don't be silly, lad! You don't have to ask! Make yourself at home!" and gave him a very meaningful look. He shook his head slightly and sat down at the table.

"Cake! My favourite!" he exclaimed. Beth rapped him softly on the knuckles.

"Don't be too cocky, mister!" she chided, laughing.

Carrie was watching this interaction between them; she was curious. Beth looked very happy, and Jeremy seemed more relaxed than he had been since he had brought the professor's body back on the ship.

"Okay, you two, what's going on? And should I be worried? Or jealous?" she demanded, laughing.

"Over to you, Jeremy, my boy!" Beth encouraged.

"Well, it's like this!" Jeremy began. "Last night Beth showed me a letter, which changes *everything!* It turns out I've had a dad all along; I just didn't know it. And I'm not an orphan anymore either. I've got a stepmom! And she's sitting in front of you!" he exclaimed with obvious delight, gesturing grandly at Beth.

Carrie looked from him to Beth, who nodded, and back to Jeremy, who was beaming with delight.

"Okay…. How?" she asked.

Jeremy looked at Beth, who produced the first page of the letter once more. Beth handed it to Carrie, who read through it, without looking up, or asking questions. At the finish of the page, she quietly handed the paper back to Beth, and smiled hugely, almost smugly at her.

"I *told* you they looked alike, didn't I?" Carrie declared quietly.

"Yes, honey. Yes, you did. It took me a while longer to see the resemblance, but it's there, all right, and not just in looks. Jeremy behaved just like his father would have, when he got all huffy over something last night, didn't you?" She aimed the last, smiling comment at her newly found stepson, who reddened slightly.

"Yeah," he admitted sheepishly.

"So," Carrie observed, "you've gained a stepson, and Jeremy's finally found a stepmother. I think that's fantastic!" She jumped up and hugged Beth, laughing delightedly.

"I just *knew* you were the kind of mum *I* would want!" Carrie kissed Beth on both cheeks and sat down, reaching for Jeremy's hand. "And," Carrie continued, "that means you'll be my stepmother-in-law when Jezz and I get married!"

"Oh!" exclaimed Beth. "That sounds ominous! 'Beth' will do just nicely, thanks!"

The three of them laughed, finished the cake, drank more coffee, and Jeremy went back to Dougal's study. He wouldn't complete the clean-up today, but he had made a start. He begged some garbage bags from Beth, for storage until he could come back.

An hour later, the young couple left, with promises to return to visit soon. Carrie had to work, and Jeremy would need a shower after ploughing through reams of dusty notes and research data. Beth was relieved; she had been very happy with their company, but she felt they needed some space, to talk and help Jeremy adjust to his new knowledge. And Beth could do with a little solitude, after the emotional upheavals of the last twenty-four hours.

twenty-three

Monday

On her way to the Museum that morning, Beth stopped at the post office, and sent the envelopes on their way. The police called to say Dougal's body was due for release the following day, and she could go ahead and make the arrangements for his funeral. She thanked them, and assured them that she would come in later to collect his effects. The police were still holding all of Dougal's gear from his cabin on *Aurora Australis,* along with his coat. The forensic pathologist and coroner had finished with it.

Beth had to turn on a heater when she got to work; it was cold in the basement where she often worked, and she blew on her fingers to warm them. She made coffee and cradled it, appreciating the warmth of the cup, while she started on her tasks. She had spent so much time away from the museum in the past month, her enquiries and cataloguing had been piling up; she groaned softly when she saw Post-it notes, and scrawled messages littering her desk. At least she had been able to do a little at home, by email.

Dougal's gear to clear up at home, tasks at work, and now a funeral to organise. She didn't really know where to begin, how to organise a funeral; she had only been twelve years old when her father had drowned off the coast of Vancouver Island, and she had already been living in Australia with Dougal for two years when her mother died. Dougal had organised wee Malcolm's funeral all those years ago; she had been too shattered, and later sedated, to contribute or even remember much of the planning process. Consequently, she had no idea about how to begin, apart from the Yellow Pages.

So that's where Beth started. She piled up the Post-its and the hand-scrawled requests into one corner of her desk; and searched Funeral Directors and Funeral Homes. She leafed through the advertisements, undecided, then picked up the phone. The closest to her home was on the opposite side of the river, but easily accessible to the CBD. She spoke to the receptionist, Vanessa, and was asked to hold the line while she was put through to Mr Vincent Holden, chief funeral director.

"Good morning, Mr Holden, is it? My name is Elizabeth Bouchier Ferguson. I need to organise a funeral for my late husband. My husband's body is currently at the city mortuary, and is due for release now. I wonder if your company would be prepared to handle the funeral arrangements, please?"

"Mrs Ferguson, was it? Just let me jot down some details while we talk. Now, name, age, address, and date of birth of the deceased?"

Beth gave him Dougal's details; she was a little hazy on the date of death, but thought it would probably have been the night he disappeared from the ship.

"Ah, yes. I recall hearing the tragic news on the television, Mrs Ferguson. You have my sincere condolences for your loss. Of course we would be honoured to handle Professor Ferguson's funeral service. We would normally need his doctor's details, and the death certificate if possible, but if the matter is being handled by the coroner's office, they will be able to supply the relevant details when we contact them. This *is* a coroner's case, I take it?"

"Yes. We met a young woman, Annette, when we went to identify Dougal's body." Beth's voice wavered momentarily, but she cleared her throat. "Perhaps she could help you with all those details?"

"Just so, just so. Now, Mrs Ferguson, if you'll bear with me, I'd like to go through some options for you, to ensure the service is what you and your husband would want, and also to ensure that it runs smoothly. Would you have time to come in, say, this afternoon? Or tomorrow morning?"

Beth grimaced at the heap of search requests stacked at the corner of her desk and rubbed her forehead; another few hours wasn't going to make much difference, somehow.

"I can come in this afternoon, Mr Holden. What time would be convenient for you?"

"Excellent, dear lady, excellent! Say, around four? Would that suit?"

"Fine, thank you. I have the address. I'll be there at four. Goodbye for now."

"Goodbye, Mrs Ferguson, until this afternoon."

Beth ended the call and stared around her in dismay; her life had descended into chaos in the blink of an eye. She was just thankful that she was reasonably autonomous in her line of work, and the museum hierarchy had been more than understanding and sympathetic about her situation. She glanced at her wristwatch, set an alarm on her mobile phone for 3:30 p.m., and started work; she would see how many of the Post-it note requests she could work through or redirect before she had to leave for North Hobart. Fortunately, it wasn't far out of town.

***

Beth arrived at the funeral home just before four, having caught a lucky break with the afternoon traffic. She walked into the front foyer of the lovely old building and introduced herself to the receptionist, Vanessa. She was ushered to a chair, while Vanessa called the funeral director on the intercom.

"Mr Holden will be right out, Mrs Ferguson," Vanessa informed her in a light, pleasant voice.

"Thank you."

A door opened to one side of the receptionist's desk, and a tall man in a dark grey suit entered the foyer and called her name. He extended his hand and invited Beth into his office.

"Mrs Ferguson, again, allow me to offer my sincere condolences. Thank you for coming in so promptly. Please! Sit down."

"It was mutually convenient, Mr Holden," replied Beth, sitting down. "Thank you for seeing me without delay. I believe there were some details we need to discuss?"

"Just so, just so. Now, may I offer you a tea, or a coffee while we chat?"

"Coffee, black, no sugar, thank you. That would be nice."

Vincent Holden buzzed through to Vanessa's desk and placed their orders. Beth observed him while he was busy; he was in his mid-sixties, tall, slightly corpulent, and almost completely bald. Business was obviously good; the man was wearing a discreet, but superbly cut charcoal cashmere suit. His desk displayed the obligatory family photos, but few other personal effects.

Vanessa delivered two cups of coffee and a plate of small, sweet biscuits. She smiled kind-heartedly at Beth, and left, gently closing the door behind her. Vincent Holden took a sip of coffee, placed his cup on its saucer, and opened a glossy brochure.

"Now, Mrs Ferguson, let's discuss how you envisage your husband's memorial service. I have here"—he turned the brochure around so Beth could see the contents—"our range of standard caskets and coffins, but we also offer our clients the opportunity to choose a personalised casket if they desire one."

Beth gazed at the extensive array on offer.

"Thank you, Mr Holden, but I think Dougal would have preferred something very simple. He was not a man for extravagance, or unnecessary expense; I think, this one," she said, pointing to a neat, relatively unadorned box, "would suit our purposes just fine."

Mr Holden had opened a book, into which he now wrote a note. "Ah yes, the Econo Slumber model. A wise choice, Mrs Ferguson, it's a very popular casket. Now, what about flowers, music, and the like?"

"Roses, if possible, please, Mr Holden. And some heather, if that can be arranged?"

"Certainly, certainly." He jotted down her request. "Music? Most families prefer to choose three pieces."

Beth thought for a moment; an imp of an idea had leapt into her mind, and she suppressed a quiet giggle. "Perhaps a Scottish folk-song my husband was particularly fond of, perhaps the 23rd Psalm, and some bagpipes. Dougal was Scottish, and he loved his pipes. I think 'Highland Cathedral' would be appropriate, or perhaps the 'Skye Boat Song'? Although, perhaps not the 'Skye Boat Song' – Dougal was from Orkney, not the Western Isles. No, 'Highland Cathedral' would be better."

Holden nodded, made more notes and looked up. "And the particular folk song?"

"'The Great Silkie' sung by Joan Baez. If you don't have it, I have it at home; I'd be happy to provide it for the occasion."

"Excellent, excellent. And the version of the 23rd Psalm?"

"Any."

"Very well." More notes. "Any specific theme for the ceremony, Mrs Ferguson? We do appear to have a Scottish flavour developing here—heather, bagpipes."

Beth blinked in surprise at the man; of course! She would ask Shona to bring a saltire to drape across Dougal's coffin.

She smiled. "Yes! Yes, you're right! I'll ask my sister-in-law to bring a Scottish flag with her, to drape over his coffin. That's brilliant! Thank you!"

Vincent Holden was impressed by Beth's sudden burst of enthusiasm; her face appeared lit from within. He smiled, and made the necessary notes.

"Now, what about the eulogy, Mrs Ferguson?"

The smile vanished just as abruptly from Beth's face; who could she ask to speak about her beloved man? *She* did not want to speak; after the revelations of his letter, she didn't feel she knew him as well as she had thought. Who else was there? Jeremy? No. Jeremy had only known Dougal for just over a year. One of Dougal's colleagues at the university? No. They had been colleagues but not friends; for a moment she was stumped.

"Mrs Ferguson, if you care to give me some details of your husband's life and achievements, we would be honoured to speak about him, if you can't think of anyone who could give a more personal, intimate account of his life?"

"That would be just fine, Mr Holden. I'll email them to you," Beth said, "and I'll ask his sister if she would be willing to say a few personal words about her younger brother. She'll be coming for the funeral, from Scotland, as soon as I have a date to give her."

"Excellent thought, dear lady. Now, media. Have you given any thought to a slideshow display of photographs or a video of your husband?"

"I guess I could go through some photos and choose some for you. Do I have to put them together, or does your firm do it?"

Vincent Holden steepled his fingers together thoughtfully. "We usually recommend that the family does any pictorial presentation, Mrs Ferguson. It seems to be a way of helping family members to come to terms with the loss of their loved one. However, if you prefer, you could just provide us with the photographs, and we could arrange a suitable slideshow presentation for you."

"Okay, I'll think about that one, Mr Holden. Was there anything else? Oh, what about refreshments?"

"Just so, just so, Mrs Ferguson. That was the final item on my agenda. We can offer a selection of sandwiches, finger food, cakes etc., along with tea and coffee. Again, if you prefer to organise this yourself, you are most welcome. Otherwise, our company is happy to provide a fully catered after-ceremony function."

"Thank you. I'll give that some thought. At the moment, the important thing is to bring Dougal's body here from the mortuary. Once that's done, we can talk further about a possible date for the funeral. Does your company organise the death and funeral notices for the papers, and how long would you estimate before we can hold the funeral? It's just that I must give my sister-in-law time to organise international flights."

"Once we have your husband's body, Mrs Ferguson, we will prepare him. There is no rush to hold the service, he'll be safe with us. Oh, one more thing, dear lady, is there to be a viewing?"

"No!" she exclaimed, remembering the shambles of poor Dougal's battered face and the missing eyes, then corrected herself. "Not a general viewing, thank you, but I dare say his sister would appreciate being able to say her goodbyes when she arrives."

Vincent Holden stood up, and extended his hand to Beth. "Of course, Mrs Ferguson. I fully understand. We'll have him presentable for your family members. Thank you for coming in. I feel we have dealt with most of the organisational details now. If you have any questions, please don't hesitate to call. Vanessa will help you, or I will."

Beth shook his hand. "Likewise, Mr Holden. Thank you for your time and assistance. If you have any queries, please don't hesitate to call me, either. Goodbye for now."

"Goodbye. Vanessa will see you out."

Vanessa appeared at the door and escorted Beth from the office. She gave Beth a business card and wished her a good day.

***

Beth sat in her car and made some notes of her own, while she could remember them. They hadn't discussed the cost of it all, but she wasn't worried about that; both she and Dougal had taken out funeral insurance when they had settled in Australia. It was just a matter of making a phone call, and the money would be released.

She drove home, back across the bridge. She realised she must live almost opposite. She went to the bay windows at the rear of the house and looked across at the green of the Botanical Gardens, and, if she squinted a little, there was the chimney of the crematorium attached to the funeral home. Huh! She'd never noticed it before!

Beth trawled through photographs of Dougal and selected

several which spanned his life from childhood to the last photograph taken on his final field trip of the previous summer. These she put carefully into an envelope, which she sealed, labelled, and set aside; she also found and set aside the Joan Baez CD after attaching a note detailing which track number it was to be. Apart from herself and perhaps his sister, no one would ever know the true significance of the song; she was not sure if she would ever share that knowledge with Jeremy, either. Some things are not meant for exposure, in the end. She found a CD of pipe music, and set it aside with the folk songs, placing them into another, larger envelope together with the packet of photos. She made a note to ask Vincent Holden or Vanessa about the musical arrangement of the 23rd Psalm.

Beth found the list she had scribbled in the car; she could now begin to cross the items off as she dealt with each one.

<u>Refreshments.</u> Beth decided to cater for the event herself. Dougal had always loved her baking, and Jeremy certainly liked her cakes and cookies; he'd proven that! Creating another list, she leafed through a couple of cookbooks and chose Dougal's favourites, as well as some general crowd-pleasers, both sweet and savoury.

<u>Flowers.</u> The funeral home could deal with those, even though Beth loved gardening. She made a note to ask Mr Holden for sprigs of heather to be distributed to the mourners at the funeral.

She made another note to remind herself to ask Shona to bring a Scottish flag with her when she came from Scotland, as well as to ask her sister-in-law to give a personal eulogy for Dougal.

After an hour, Beth was fairly sure she had covered all bases. She sat down and composed an email outlining her requests to Vincent Holden, and attaching a biography of Dougal's life for him. She hit Send and closed the computer. She was tired and hungry. Enough for one day, she decided. She needed to feed herself, and to think.

***

Later that evening, Beth phoned Shona again as she had promised. She gave Shona the details of what was about to occur, and asked her sister-in-law how much time she would need to catch flights, etc. She explained that no date had been set for the funeral until Shona could book a flight, but that Dougal's body had now been released from the mortuary to the funeral home.

Shona assured her that she could be on a plane within forty-eight hours, and to go ahead with setting a date for the service.

Beth asked if Shona could bring a saltire to drape across Dougal's coffin and whether the older woman would be willing to speak about her brother. Shona immediately accepted the invitation to speak, and promised to bring the flag with her. They spoke for a few more minutes, while Beth filled Shona in on what had been happening since they had last spoken. Shona promised to phone Beth with her flight details from Edinburgh, and a couple of minutes later, Beth ended the conversation, assuring Shona that she would meet her at the airport on her arrival. She also suggested that her sister-in-law stay with her for at least a week, so she could show her around, and spend some time getting to know Jeremy. Shona's reaction to the news of Jeremy's existence had initially been one of shock, but when the older woman had been reassured that Beth was delighted to have found a stepson, she amended her view to one of cautious optimism, and said she would look forward to meeting her nephew.

Beth smiled as she hung up; it would all be okay. Her final task before going to bed was to compose another email to Vincent Holden, giving him permission to set the date for Dougal's funeral service and cremation early the following week. She had already explained that Dougal's family had to fly from Scotland; she asked if that would give the funeral directors sufficient time to place the relevant notices in the daily newspapers. She also included her proposals for the floral tributes, and catering. She promised to take the music, photos, and a short biography of Dougal's life to the funeral home the following day, and leave them with Vanessa. She requested an answer as soon as possible, so she, too, could begin to make her own arrangements.

Chapter
twenty-four

Tuesday

Late in the morning, Beth received a phone call from Vanessa at the funeral home, asking for Dougal's clothes. Beth asked about undergarments; apparently, underwear was optional, as were socks and shoes, but Beth could bring them in, if she wished. Also, Vanessa added, Mr Holden wondered if Beth had had an opportunity to find photos and the music she wanted played at the service; Beth confirmed she had put them aside and would bring them in, along with Dougal's clothes and a summary of his life for the celebrant on the following day. She also mentioned that she had already said all of this in an email written and sent late the previous night. Vanessa laughed and gave Beth her email address.

"Best to cc me into any emails, Mrs Ferguson. That way they'll get to me first thing."

Vanessa took the opportunity to tell Beth that heather could be provided and asked if Beth had any idea how many people might attend. Beth said no, she had no idea at all, then remembered about the funeral notices for the papers. Vanessa assured her they had already organised these, and both the death notice and funeral notice would be placed in the local newspapers the next day if Mrs Ferguson agreed with the wording. She read the content of the notices to Beth, who approved them. Beth made a mental note to send Vanessa a personal "thank you" after the funeral; she had been more than efficient and friendly — she had been compassionate.

"Would 11:00 a.m. next Monday be convenient for your husband's funeral, Mrs Ferguson? Would that be sufficient time for any overseas attendees to reach Hobart?"

"Yes, thank you, dear. My sister-in-law is the only person who will be coming from overseas, as far as I know, and she should be here by Friday or Saturday at the latest. She'll also be bringing the saltire, the Scottish flag, for Dougal's coffin. I know she'd like the opportunity to say goodbye to her brother; would that be possible? It's just that his face was a bit of a mess, when I last saw him."

"Of course, Mrs Ferguson, just ring us a little ahead of when you would like to do a viewing. We'll have him ready for you. Was there anything else?"

"Flowers. I asked Mr Holden to organise flowers for the chapel."

Vanessa laughed. "That would be me, Mrs Ferguson. I organise all those details for my father. I've ordered red roses, baby's breath, some native flowers and greenery, and of course, the heather. We'll do two urns, one for either side of the casket."

Beth was impressed. "Oh! I'm so sorry! I didn't realise that Mr Holden and you were related. Thank you so much, Vanessa. That sounds lovely."

The girl laughed. "That's quite okay, Mrs Ferguson, it's a family business. Thank you! One other thing," she added. "Dad mentioned that you would be doing your own catering. When would you like to deliver the bakery items to us?"

"Probably Saturday morning, if that's okay. It'll be mainly cookies, er sorry, biscuits, and I'll put them into airtight containers, so that they'll still be fresh on Monday. I'll also make some cocktail-sized savoury nibbles. Oh, and I was wondering about tea and coffee. Do we have to supply those?"

Vanessa laughed. "Not at all, Mrs Ferguson. We'll provide those, along with milk and sugar, the crockery, and any cutlery. Don't worry about any of that."

"Oh, Vanessa, do you have a recording of the 23rd Psalm? I don't own such a thing. I wondered if your company would have one, as it seems to be very popular at funerals."

"Yes, we do. Has my father told you that you'll need to come in ahead of time, say Saturday morning, just to check the order of service and to vet the celebrant's eulogy for your husband?"

"No, he hasn't, but can we discuss that tomorrow when I bring in all the other stuff, if that's okay? Won't Mr Holden be delivering the eulogy himself?"

"Of course we can, Mrs Ferguson. Didn't my father mention that we employ a celebrant, unless you would prefer a priest to conduct the service?"

"No. No, he did not. And yes, a celebrant will be fine. We aren't religious people. Will I be able to meet with him prior to the service?"

"Of course, Mrs Ferguson. I'll ask him to be here tomorrow when you come in. His name is Barry Wray. He works with us regularly. You'll like him, trust me. See you tomorrow. Say, 4:00 p.m.?"

"Fine. See you then."

Beth returned to her work, but her mind wasn't really on it; she sighed, gave up trying to concentrate on something that had become very arduous, and went in search of her supervisor. She would need more time off. The museum's bosses had been more than generous with all the leave she had had to take, and she felt a little bad about asking for a week more, but when she found the supervisor in her small office on the first floor, the woman readily agreed to Beth taking as much time as she needed.

Beth rang Jeremy's mobile; there was a heap of work to be done at home; he would need to come over to finish sorting and clearing Dougal's study before Shona arrived. He agreed to come over that afternoon. Beth was ticking off her mental list when the phone rang again. It was an unknown number.

"Mrs Ferguson? This is Desk Sergeant Jones at the Central Hobart police station. We have your husband's effects here. Would it be possible for you to come and collect them?"

"Oh, good morning, Sergeant. I could come in this afternoon if that would be convenient?"

"That would be good. Just ask for me at the front desk. I'll be on duty until four."

"Okay, thank you. I'll be in as soon as I can get away from work."

"Thank you, goodbye."

"Goodbye."

Beth pressed End and sighed. It was probably a good thing she was going to take some time off; this week was shaping up to be hectic. She buzzed her supervisor and told her that she had some errands to run. The supervisor wished her well.

"Hope it all goes well, Beth. Take as much time as you need, my dear. We'll see you back here when you can make it. Any news on your husband's funeral service?'

"Monday at 11:00 a.m., at Tunstall Family Funerals in North Hobart. Thanks so much for giving me this time off—it's shaping up to be a really chaotic week."

"Yes, these things have a habit of snowballing, don't they? If there's anything we can do…?"

"Yes, it appears so. Thank you, I'll let you know. 'Bye."

***

Beth scurried out of the building. She dumped her stuff in the boot, and stood there for a couple of minutes, looking at her ever-growing list of things to do. First stop, the police station, to collect Dougal's effects; she wasn't looking forward to it, but it was one more thing to check off her list. She drove the few minutes to the station. Desk Sergeant Jones was on duty, and true to his word, he had three large bin liner bags containing Dougal's belongings ready for her, plus his duffel bag. The sergeant expressed his condolences to her and offered to carry the bags to her car; she thanked him and led the way out.

Returning home, she carried the bags in, one by one. These, she put into his study; Jeremy could deal with the paperwork, and she would sort out the contents of the duffel bag. She figured she could deal with those later. On impulse, Beth decided to get the delivery of Dougal's clothes, photos, and music out of the way; she dialled the funeral home's number and spoke with Vanessa. The young woman assured her that she would be there, although the celebrant wouldn't be available until the following day.

Beth loaded the package and a suit bag with Dougal's funeral clothes into the car and set off. She was out in North Hobart in a matter of minutes and delivered everything to Vanessa. She and the young woman held a brief conversation about the music, and Beth read and approved the wording of the funeral notices while she was there. Beth remembered Dougal's instructions about the disposal of his coat; she stressed to the young woman that her husband's coat was to go into the coffin with him.

When she got home, loaded with supermarket bags, Jeremy's car was parked outside. Beth garaged and locked the car, grabbed the bags, and greeted him at the front door.

"Hi, honey, how are you? Have you been waiting long?" She reached up and kissed Jeremy's cheek.

"Hi, Beth, no, I've only been here a little while. I tried your cell phone, but it went to message bank, so I phoned the museum and they said you'd gone to run some errands. Anything I can do to help?"

"Thanks, if you'd like to take one of these bags for me while I unlock the door. I had to take Dougal's clothes to the funeral home, along with photos they'll use for a media display for the service, and the music I chose. They're doing the flowers, and they'll provide the tea and coffee, etcetera, but I said I'd prefer to cater for the refreshments myself. Dougal always loved my cooking. It's the least I could do, and it'll keep me busy. Coffee?"

"Please! What can I do to help you?"

"Well, Dougal's study is the top priority for now, lad, so you could start in there. I spoke with my sister-in-law, Shona, last night to let her know about the funeral, and she reckons she'll be arriving Friday or Saturday morning, so I offered to meet her at the airport. It's been a terrible shock for her."

"It's been a terrible shock for you, too, Beth."

"I know, lad, but I'm trying to stay busy, so I don't have to think too much about it all. Have you already had lunch? I've been running all over town this morning, and I'm starved!"

"Well, I had a late breakfast, but I guess a sandwich would be cool."

Beth laughed aloud. "Boys and their stomachs!"

He grinned sheepishly. "Guess we never stop growing. But if you're too busy…."

"Nonsense! How much more effort is it to create two sandwiches, instead of one?"

"Fair enough, I guess. Let me help! What can I do?"

"Well, you can start by putting the cold stuff into the fridge for me and grabbing out some bread and butter. There should be packets of cold chicken and ham in the green bag, and some salad vegetables in the blue bag. I'll put the coffee on."

Jeremy blinked and grinned; he hadn't been ordered around in such a motherly way since he was living with his granma Maddie. He liked it.

After lunch, Jeremy went to Dougal's study to continue his sorting, and Beth sat down with her list, and made notes. A companiable silence fell over the house, punctuated only by the occasional rustle of papers from Jeremy's labours at the front of the house, and the sound of pages turning in the family room, as Beth leafed through recipe books. Around 5:00 p.m., Jeremy left to return home to greet Carrie at the end of her shift, promising Beth to return next day to continue his sorting.

The remainder of the week fell into a curiously steady rhythm; Beth would bake and clean house while Jeremy faithfully appeared on her doorstep late each morning and worked through the professor's clutter until around five or six each afternoon, stopping only for lunch.

By Thursday afternoon, the study was noticeably cleaner and more organised than it had been for months; Jeremy had removed piles of papers and specimens in cartons to the university and had even cleaned down the almost empty shelving unit. Beth had washed, cleaned, dusted, and polished until the house sparkled; she had prepared the spare bedroom and guest bathroom for Shona, and had baked and boxed up dozens of sweet biscuits, and bite-sized savoury snacks for the post-funeral refreshments.

Shona had phoned Beth late Wednesday evening with her flight details from Edinburgh; she would be leaving Edinburgh that afternoon, *her* time, she said, and would be arriving on a Qantas domestic flight from Melbourne late Friday morning, Beth's time. Beth wrote down the flight numbers and promised to meet her sister-in-law at the airport.

Thursday evening, after Jeremy had gone home, Beth sighed and swept a weary hand through her messed-up hair. Everything that could be done, *had* been.

***

Friday morning Jeremy phoned to ask Beth if she needed moral support at the airport; she laughed and told him not to be so silly. Beth set off for Hobart International Airport at Cambridge in plenty of time to meet Shona's flight. She had no problems; traffic was light at that time of the morning, and the Tasman Highway was a clear run. Beth was into the domestic terminal in plenty of time; she purchased a coffee and sat down in the arrivals lounge to wait. The flight was on time, and soon the passengers were streaming through the door from the sky bridge. Some were met by friends or family, others, carrying briefcases, strolled through and disappeared to claim their baggage. Beth had had a few qualms whether she would recognise Shona after all these years, but the minute the woman stepped through the doorway, Beth *knew* she couldn't have mistaken her, ever! She was tall, lean built, and had cropped white hair, but the familial resemblance was striking even now; Beth almost caught her breath as she looked at the woman. She smiled and went to greet her sister-in-law, and the two embraced.

"Good flight, Shona?" Beth asked.

"Och, I'm certainly glad it's over for now, lassie. It will be good to breathe some clean air, after hours of stale, recycled stuff. And it will be good to walk a wee bit after being cooped up in those seats. Not a lot of leg room for tall people, really."

The two women made their way down to the arrivals hall and waited their turn at the carousels for Shona's luggage to make its entrance. As they waited, other people darted in and out like hummingbirds, searching for and retrieving precious belongings; the hall echoed to people's chatter and the clatter of trolleys and baggage being hefted and wheeled away. Beth was happy to wait for the thrum to die down a little; obviously, Shona felt the same way. They spoke of inconsequential things, like airline food, cabin crews and the service aboard, and the heat in Dubai; they avoided the elephant in the room, the reason for Shona's precipitous visit.

Once Shona had retrieved her suitcase, Beth led the way across to the car park and they left the airport precinct. It was a quiet drive back along the Tasman Highway, but the late autumn sunshine had peeped out from behind pendulous clouds to greet its international visitor, and Shona professed herself delighted with both the landscape and city, sun-kissed in the distance. Beth chattered about Hobart and suggested that while Shona was in Tasmania, they would do some sightseeing in and around the city; perhaps as far as Port Arthur or places beyond, weather permitting.

Once home, Beth showed Shona her bedroom and the guest bathroom, and left the older woman to shower and freshen up. Beth knew what it was like to sit on a plane for over twenty-four hours without the opportunity for anything more than a "cat-lick" wash and a change of clothes. She started preparing lunch; Shona had assured her that she had had a snack and a hot drink on the flight from Melbourne, but Beth was hungry, and she hoped her sister-in-law would find an appetite after her ablutions.

By the time Beth had prepared a platter to share, Shona had showered, changed her clothes, and professed herself a new woman. Shona picked at the food on the platter; she had eaten quite enough on the various flights to feed a small army for a week, she declared, but she was happy to have arrived, and thanked Beth for the food.

They ate in silence; Beth's appetite had been strangely diminished by the presence of a stranger in her house, but between them, they managed to finish most of the platter. After lunch, Beth showed Shona where to put her dirty laundry, and promised to have the washing done by the next day; the older woman immediately offered to help, and insisted she was *family*, not a guest. She would do her share of the chores! If Beth was taken aback by Shona's vehemence, she was careful not to show it. Otherwise, it would prove to be a very long week ahead.

"Shona, be welcome in our home. And *of course* you're family! But I'm sure Dougal wouldn't have wanted you slaving away over washing machines and the like, though, so I'm happy to put your clothes through with mine, if you don't object? Now, let me show you where things are kept—that way you can help yourself to drinks and food any time you want. You already know where your bathroom and bedroom are, so let me show you the rest of the house. This is where I mostly live and work. Dougal and I had the place remodelled when we arrived here ten years ago. We loved to sit out here in the evenings, and we used this room more than any other, I guess. Come through, and I'll give you the guided tour."

Beth showed Shona the house, stopping to admire Dougal's newly cleaned and tidied study, then continuing to the formal lounge and the master bedroom. They went out into the garden, where Shona was able to admire late-blooming roses and the native flowers which were still in evidence throughout the front garden beds. Beth pointed out the river at the end of the street and offered to take Shona on a walk down to the river's edge later in the afternoon when the sun was about to set. Shona seemed amenable to a diversion, and the exercise would be welcome after the long flight across the world.

Back in the house, Shona went to unpack, and hang her clothes in the wardrobe, in readiness for the funeral the following Monday morning. Beth busied herself preparing a slow-cooking meal for dinner; she was somewhat at a loss to find topics of conversation. She knew they were both avoiding the unpleasant topic of Dougal's death, but she couldn't come straight out and say anything until the older woman seemed ready. Cooking had always soothed Beth at times of crisis, and she became absorbed in her task; she didn't hear her sister-in-law enter the space until Shona's Scottish accent broke the silence.

"All right, lassie, tell me everything that's been happening. No need to stop what you're doing, girl, but we need to talk." The older woman sat down at the breakfast bar and watched Beth.

Beth turned and exhaled, a loud sigh of relief escaping her lips.

"Oh Shona, *thank you*! I have wanted to talk to you, but I didn't know if you would be ready to talk about Dougal just yet!"

"Och, lassie, he was always a headstrong wee lad. Always in and out of scrapes as a *bairn*, but he had a smile that would charm the birds out of the trees. He could get away with anything!"

"I always loved his smile, Shona, and he was a good man. I loved him very dearly!" Beth's voice wobbled on the last statement, but she was determined not to cry, not yet.

"I know you did, lass, and so did he," came the gentle response. "He always called you his soul mate, in the truest sense of the word. Which is why I was so taken aback when you told me he had fathered another child!"

"Jeremy was conceived long before we met, Shona, and I guess Dougal kept his existence secret for his own good reasons. Dougal left me a letter, and in it he explained a lot of stuff. I'll show it to you later if you want to read it. He mentioned you in it, too. And Jeremy is a fine young man. I'm very fond of him, and I feel blessed to have found him. He's coming over this evening to meet you. He's really very nervous about the thought of having an aunt. He's never had one of those in his life before."

"None? No relatives? How sad for the poor laddie. Well, I promise I won't eat him!" Shona smiled as she said this, and Beth laughed in relief.

"Well, that's good! Because I've become very fond of the lad, and his fiancée is a honey. You'll meet her too, but perhaps not this evening. She's a detective with the local police, you know, and a very bright young thing. I have a feeling she'll go far in her profession. I don't know if she is working tonight, but I think Jeremy might want to come alone anyway."

"Good. It will be grand to meet my nephew — the word feels so strange, after all these years. Oh, Elizabeth!" Shona stopped, glancing at Beth's suddenly stricken face. "I'm so sorry, my dear, I'm so sorry! I didn't mean to drag up unhappy memories of wee Malcolm! Forgive me?"

Shona jumped up and hugged Beth awkwardly; she realised the

impact her words had had on her sister-in-law. Beth disentangled herself and gave a watery chuckle.

"It's okay, Shona. Malcolm's been in my thoughts a lot just recently, too. I look at Jeremy and wonder if Malcolm would have resembled him, had he had the chance to grow up." She sat down opposite her sister-in-law and looked her straight in the eye. "Shona, I was *furious*, absolutely *furious* with Dougal after he disappeared and left me that letter. I felt so *betrayed*! I thought we had had no secrets between us, in years of marriage, and he was harbouring two *huge* ones! And I felt such a fool because I never had an inkling of any of it! First the existence of his other son—I must admit that rocked me to the core, Shona, but Jeremy was born long before we even met. But his *other* secret was *shattering*, until I remembered that there is a similar type of folklore among *my* people too. Suddenly I was able to put it into perspective. Mind you, Shona, I have to admit they were a pretty torrid few days for me. Part of me still doesn't want to believe anything so *fantastic*, but who am *I* to question what goes on in the world we can't see?"

Shona reached across the breakfast bar and took Beth's hand. "Lassie, you're talking riddles," she said gently.

"Wait, I'll get you the letter." Beth slipped her hand free and jumped up to retrieve the letter from the drawer in the bureau. She handed the whole thing to Shona and busied herself while the older woman silently read her late brother's words. When the pages stopped rustling, she looked up to find a pair of sharp blue eyes staring at her across the room.

Chapter
twenty-five

"So, you know now, lass," Shona nodded at Beth. "I always knew he was different. Our mam used to worry about him, whenever he was out and about, but he *was* her only son, after all. Now," she asked meaningfully, "has young Jeremy inherited this gene from his father?"

"I really don't know, Shona. I wouldn't know how to ask him."

"Hmm," said the older woman, "there has to be a way to find out. Where is Dougal's seal-skin coat, Elizabeth?"

"It's in a bag that I collected from the police station the other day. The coroner has finished with it, so it's at the funeral home. Dougal insisted that it be cremated along with his body. You read his instructions, didn't you?"

"Aye, lass, I did. Has it crossed your mind to ask young Jeremy to try it on?"

Beth looked at Shona, shocked. "No! I have never thought such a thing! Do you think I should?"

"Probably not, lass. I suspect Dougal may have been one of the last of his line. Did you ever notice anything unusual when you took wee Malcolm into the water at the beach?"

Beth looked at her, amazed. She had never even considered that, for an instant. "No, he was just a normal wee boy. He loved splashing in the waves when the weather was warm enough, and he got very wet, plenty of times, but he stayed as he was, a *normal wee boy*."

Shona steepled her fingers together in front of her and looked thoughtful. "I wonder," she mused, "if the gene only kicks in at puberty, or some such…. What do you think, Elizabeth?"

Beth was startled. "Well, that would explain why Malcolm could go for a dip in the sea without turning *furry*, but how would one even begin to find out? I mean, if I asked someone about such a theory, I'd be locked up and they'd throw away the key!" She laughed, but Shona and she knew that Beth was not joking.

"Aye, lass, you're probably right. Still, I'd be curious, just the same. Now, I fancy a nice walk down to the river, if you've finished all the supper preparations. And when we come back, I've a few things for you. Remind me!"

***

The two women took a leisurely stroll down the street and along the river's edge. Shona exclaimed at this and that, the tangy freshness of the air, the vibrant colours of the landscape, the mixture of European and native foliage, the lack of traffic, and the gentle gift of afternoon sunshine. They spent a happy hour or so, just ambling along, stopping here and there, while Shona admired the wildflowers that still clung to their stalks ahead of the inevitable winter winds. They stood a long time, just breathing in the peace and quiet, until the peal of a school bell across the river, echoed by its fellow close by, signalled an end to their solitude. Cars started, children poured like water from school gates, excited chattering filled the air; it was Friday, and the children were free for two glorious days again.

"Time to go?" Beth asked.

"Aye, lass, before the wee things overrun us, like mice!"

Beth laughed aloud at the analogy and the two women headed for home.

Shona had gifts for Beth; a duty-free bag containing a bottle of whisky and a heavily embroidered table runner, from Dubai, and a small, soft package containing the flag Beth had requested for Dougal's coffin. Beth thanked her, and left it wrapped, ready to take to the funeral home the next day. The whisky she extracted from the bag, and impulsively gave Shona a kiss on the cheek.

"Thank you, Shona! This is lovely. We'll have to have a dram after dinner!" She delved once more into the bag and gently drew out the table runner, which she unfolded and draped over her arm, to admire the richness of the colours: blues, golds, and deep mulberry. "Thank you so much! This is beautiful!" Beth went straight to the scrubbed pine table and threw the runner across its diameter, standing back to admire the splashes of colour against the light wood. She smiled, nodded, and thanked her sister-in-law again.

"Oh, that's just perfect for this room. Thank you so much!" Beth was slightly embarrassed by this largesse and felt awkward for a second. "Coffee, Shona?" she asked.

"No, thank you lass, but a cup of tea would be lovely. May I make it?"

Smiling, Beth directed Shona to the tea caddy, and the biscuit tin, and tried not to watch overtly as the older woman made herself at home in *her* kitchen. They were like a pair of cats, really, circling around each other warily, neither of them willing to upset the other, or give offence, but neither of them willing to concede their place in the scheme of things, either. She went to the laundry, where she hauled out the load of washing she had started before going to the airport. She called out to Shona and took the washing to hang in the afternoon sunshine. Judging by the heavy pewter grey of the clouds, there would be rain before morning, she guessed, but the clothes would benefit from some sunshine now, nonetheless.

***

Jeremy arrived in time for dinner, bearing a bunch of carnations for Shona. Beth met him at the front door with a reassuring smile and a hug.

She nodded at the flowers. "Nice touch, lad. She'll be impressed. Now come on in and meet your new aunt Shona, honey. It's all good. She's read your dad's letter and she understands the situation now."

Jeremy's breath came out in a loud whoosh; he hadn't realised he'd been holding it in. He was sweating slightly, a bundle of nerves, but he gave Beth a wry grin, and extended his elbow to her; she tucked her hand into the crook of his arm and squeezed it gently.

"Okay, Beth, I'm as ready as I'll ever be. But," he whispered, "I don't think I've ever been this worried, not even when I had to face a panel of examiners!"

Beth laughed aloud, and they walked together down the passage and into the family room.

"Shona, my dear, allow me to introduce your nephew Jeremy Munroe, Dougal's son from Canada."

Shona was standing by the window, looking out at the lights beginning to twinkle across the river; she turned, and her hand flew to her breast.

"Laddie, you could have been your father standing there! I'd know you anywhere. Come and let me look at you!" Shona crossed the room and held him at arm's length, to scrutinise him closely. She smiled and hugged him. "Och, but it's good to meet you, laddie. You're just like my brother!"

Beth smiled fondly and gratefully as Jeremy offered the older woman her floral gift; the two embraced and started talking. She had been more concerned about Shona's acceptance of Jeremy than she had realised. Beth found a vase and filled it with water, then started hauling out dinnerware.

"Come on, you two," she called, "dinner is ready. Let's eat while it's hot. You can chat over dinner. If you give me the flowers, Shona, I'll deal with them." The bouquet was hastily arranged into the vase, which was then placed on the dining table, and they went to eat.

Jeremy held out a chair for Shona; her surprise at his obvious good manners showed only in the upwards quirk of an eyebrow and a brief smile. They served themselves from the hot pot.

***

After dinner, Jeremy insisted on washing the dishes, while Shona offered to dry them. Beth put them away, made coffee for herself and Jeremy, and offered Shona a pot of tea.

They sat in the family room and drank their beverages; Shona and Jeremy hadn't stopped talking since they had met. Beth was grateful for the instant liking they had taken to each other but felt a little tinge of wistfulness; just by looking at the two sitting there, she could tell they *belonged*. She wasn't jealous, but she felt a pang of utter loneliness in her soul. She was genuinely happy for aunt and nephew, but her own solitary status suddenly weighed heavily on her.

Shona regaled Jeremy with stories of Dougal's childhood, and Jeremy told his aunt about his own early life. At a lull, Beth was able to steer the conversation towards the following morning and asked if Jeremy wished to come with the two women to the funeral home.

"Of course I'll be there, Beth! Do you want me to swing by and pick you both up? Or shall we meet there?"

"What are your plans for tomorrow after we've been there, Jeremy?" Beth asked.

"Nothing planned, really. Carrie is working in the evening, but we've the whole day free, if you wanted to do something."

Beth glanced at Shona, then back to Jeremy. "Well, lad, I wondered if we could do a spot of sightseeing after we've been out to North Hobart. The Salamanca market might be open, and there's the view from the top of Mount Wellington, if Shona would like to go up there." Beth looked at Shona and added, "It's not as high as the mountains in Scotland, I know, but the view of Hobart is quite pretty from up there. Was there anything you particularly wanted to see and do while you're here, Shona?"

The older woman replied, "Och, lassie, I'm happy to see everything you want to show me. I believe Tasmania, and Hobart in particular, has an interesting convict history? I'd like to see some of the buildings from the early days of settlement. It's a very young country, after all, isn't it?"

"Only European settlement is young, Shona," Beth replied. "The indigenous culture goes back at least 40,000 years or more. That's part of what I do at the museum."

"Could we go to the museum, d'you think? I've a mind to see as much as possible while I'm here."

"Sure!" Beth agreed. "Perhaps we could do that during the week."

"I could show you where the professor, um, I mean my father worked at the university, if you like, Aunt Shona," Jeremy added. "He was very highly thought-of there."

"Tell you what, Jeremy" — Beth had had an idea — "why don't you pop into the tourist office on your way through in the morning, and pick up some brochures on what's to see around Hobart and beyond?"

"Hey, that'd be a plan!" The young man grinned at the two women. He stood up. "I'd best be on my way, Beth. Carrie will be finishing her shift soon, and I'd like to tell her what's going on tomorrow and ask her if she'll meet us after we've been to see… my father."

Beth stood up and hugged him; she loved this youngster more every time she saw him.

"Good idea, lad, I'll see you out."

"Goodnight, Aunt Shona. It really has been great meeting you, great to actually have an auntie of my own. See you tomorrow, yeah?" Jeremy went to Shona's chair and planted a light kiss on the top of her head. "Night."

"Och, good night to you, laddie. It's wonderful to meet you too! Away with you now!"

Beth walked Jeremy to the door and smiled at him.

"See?" she challenged him with a laugh. "I told you it would be okay! Love to Carrie now. See you in the morning, around ten thirty?"

"Ten thirty it is, cap'n!" Jeremy gave her a mock salute and ambled off into the night.

***

Saturday morning, the two women were up and ready for Jeremy when they heard the familiar note of his car. Juggling the parcel, containers of food, and the bag containing Dougal's seal-skin coat, Beth accompanied Shona to the front door, checked that she had keys, and locked up.

It wasn't far from Beth's house to the funeral home, and the Saturday morning traffic was reasonable across the bridge. Beth directed Jeremy to carry the food containers then picked up the package and the bag, and led the way into the front foyer. Vanessa was at the front desk, and she greeted Beth with a smile.

"Good morning, Mrs Ferguson. How are you? Ah, I see your son has the refreshments for Monday? Here," Vanessa spoke warmly to Jeremy, smiling and opening her arms for the plastic containers, "let me take those from you. I'll make sure they are kept safe and cool, although the way the weather seems to be turning, it won't be a heatwave on Monday, that's for sure. I'll be right back!" Scooping up the containers from Jeremy, she disappeared into the kitchen. She was only gone a couple of minutes, then she was back, all smiles and efficiency.

"So, Mrs Ferguson, let me buzz through and see if your husband is ready to view." She made a brief call, then came around the desk to take them through to the viewing room. "He's ready for you all, now. Take as long as you like, I'll just be back through that doorway."

Vanessa left them in a well-lit room, with benches and a stand containing Dougal's coffin. Shona gave a strangled cry and stuffed her hand into her mouth. She went to her brother's coffin and gazed at his face. "Oh laddie, sweet laddie, what did they *do* to you?" she murmured, tears trailing down wrinkled cheeks. She reached out and touched his body, then leant in and kissed his forehead lightly. "Oh, my wee boy!" she kept murmuring. Jeremy went and stood next to his new aunt, and gripped her elbow quite firmly, as he, too, gazed into the coffin.

Beth went and stood on the other side of Shona, putting a hand on her sister-in-law's back in sympathy. She forced herself to look; Dougal's face was still marked, but the cosmeticians had done an excellent job, smoothing out most of the lacerations, and someone

236

had filled in the hollows of the missing eyes, so he almost looked normal again. She breathed a sigh of relief as she and Jeremy exchanged a meaningful look and a rueful smile. She was sure he was as relieved as she, to see the man's face at least partially restored; Shona should never know how mutilated her brother's face had been before his body had been discovered on Macquarie Island. Beth leant in and kissed Dougal's icy lips and forehead. "Goodbye, my own dear heart. I love you and forgive you," she whispered to his closed ears. She placed her free hand lightly on Dougal's forehead in a silent benediction and straightened up. She took a step backward and sat down, to allow Shona some private time. Jeremy stood with his aunt and looked down at the man he had known as a mentor and friend but had never known as a father. Beth watched his face reflected in the window behind the coffin; she could almost read his mind by the expressions flitting across it.

They had been there probably ten or fifteen minutes before Vanessa silently slipped into the room and sat down beside Beth.

"Mrs Ferguson, Mr Wray the celebrant has arrived and will see you when you are ready," she whispered.

Beth patted the young woman's arm. "Thank you, my dear, if you'll wait a moment?" She got up and whispered to Jeremy, "Take as long as you need, honey. I'm going to meet with the celebrant. Vanessa will direct you to me when you're ready." Jeremy nodded his acknowledgement, and Beth left the room with the young assistant.

Barry Wray, the celebrant, was a short, stocky little man with faded red hair and an open, friendly face. Beth chatted with him for a few moments, then he walked her through the proposed order of service for the Monday morning. Together, they checked over the notes on Dougal's life Beth had provided, and she was touched by the way in which the man had put together a eulogy. They shook hands and arranged to meet at 10:30 a.m. on Monday, there at the funeral home. He saw her out to the front office, where Shona and Jeremy were waiting with Vanessa. Beth suddenly remembered she was still carrying the bag containing Dougal's coat, and the package Shona had brought from Scotland.

"Vanessa, this is my husband's old coat. He was most insistent that it go with him and be cremated along with his body." She handed the bag to the young woman. "And this is the flag my sister-in-law, Shona," Beth indicated the older woman sitting there, "brought from Scotland to drape on my husband's coffin. Could you look after those things please?"

"Of course, Mrs Ferguson. The coat will go in with your husband, and the flag will be draped on his coffin. Leave it with me. Now, was there anything else I can help you with today?"

Beth looked at Shona, then Jeremy; both shook their heads. "No, thank you, Vanessa, I think we have all the bases covered now. See you Monday."

Vanessa and Beth shook hands. "I'll be here, Mrs Ferguson. See you then."

***

The weather had turned for the worse; it was sprinkling raindrops as they emerged under the canopy outside the main entrance. Jeremy dashed to the car and brought it around so the two women wouldn't get wet.

"Och, this is nothing!" scoffed Shona as she settled herself proprietorially in the front seat next to Jeremy. "It's nothing more than a *smirr*, as we call it at home. Now, laddie, where to next?" She half-turned to Beth, tucked away in the back seat. "What did you have a mind to do, Elizabeth?"

Beth ground her teeth slightly, but answered affably enough, "Jeremy dear, aren't we collecting Carrie for an afternoon out?"

"On our way, Beth. Carrie said she'd be ready." He put the car into gear and drove back to the unit he and Carrie shared.

Carrie came out and climbed into the back with Beth. Brief introductions were done as Jeremy started driving. Salamanca Place was the first port of call for the sightseers. "Not much of a day for sightseeing, is it, Beth?" Carrie commented as Jeremy wound his way through the one-way streets of Hobart.

"No, honey, I'm thinking we might have to rethink our plans. Coffee first. Shall we go back to that little café bakery we visited earlier?"

"That's a splendid idea, Beth." She spoke to her fiancé around the driver's seatback, "Jeremy, do you know where Peppino's Bakehouse is, on Salamanca Place?"

"Sure, hon! Do you think we'll be able to find parking there on a Saturday? It's pretty popular, as a general rule," he replied, "but we can go look. Is that okay with you, Beth?"

"Sure thing, honey. You can always drop us off outside the café and go find a parking spot, if it's still raining."

"Okay, Beth, you're the boss!" he laughed, as he swung around into the busy street and stopped the car. The three women got out and he scooted away, to find a park. Luckily, the café wasn't too crowded, despite being a Saturday lunchtime, and they were able to find a table for four with a pleasant view of the market area and street scene.

"I don't know about anyone else," Beth said, picking up a menu from the counter, "but I'm hungry. I'm going to order something to eat with my coffee. Shona? What would you like, dear? Would you like to see the menu? Carrie, honey, I guess you've only just had breakfast..."

"Yes, I have eaten, but I would *love* one of those yummy lemon tarts we had last time, to go with my coffee. I don't know what Jeremy will want, but he's sure to be hungry!" The three women shared a joke against the absent member of the group, who turned up, and declared himself ravenous. This sent the women, especially Beth and Carrie, off into peals of renewed laughter. Jeremy looked from face to face, then said with a smile, "Okay, I guess you were taking bets on whether I'd be hungry?"

"Absolutely, lad, absolutely!" gasped Beth. "Let's order!"

There was silence as they consulted menus and made decisions. When Shona offered to pay, she was told, gently but firmly by Jeremy, that this was *his* treat to them all. Beth cocked an eyebrow at him, but he smiled blandly and ignored any protests.

Beverages and food were delivered, and a companiable silence fell over the table as they concentrated on their meals.

"That's better!" declared Jeremy as he pushed his empty plate away and drained the last of his coffee. "I hadn't realised I was so hungry! Well, it's been a long time since breakfast!" he protested, in answer to Carrie's raised eyebrows. Everyone laughed.

"What would you like to do, Shona?" asked Beth. "The museum is open and so is the art gallery, if you've a mind to go there."

"Wait a moment," said Jeremy, fishing in his jacket pocket, "I collected one of these for us to look at, on my way through the market." With a flourish, he produced a tourist information guide, and they all tried to look at once.

"Jeremy, honey," said Beth, "you've got the guide. Read it out to us, and then we can decide. The weather looks as though it may clear — I can see a few patches of blue in the sky."

Jeremy cleared his throat and began. "Well, let's see. There's the Museum of Old and Modern Art, Salamanca Market but it's only open on Saturday mornings, the Tasmanian Museum and Art Gallery, as Beth has already suggested, the Maritime Museum, the Zoo and there's 'Zoodoo,' a wildlife park, and the Botanical Gardens and the Queen's Domain for walking in, let's see, there's Mawson's Hut Replica Museum, the Army Museum, the Tench, the Female Factory or Franklin Square."

"What's the Tench, laddie?" Shona demanded.

"It was a penitentiary chapel from the early days of the colony."

Shona shuddered. "No thank you, laddie, I think not. What was the Female Factory, then?"

"It was a women's prison from the early days of Hobart, when Van Diemen's Land was established as a penal colony. It was made famous in *The Potato Factory* by Bryce Courtenay, the famous author." Carrie looked enquiringly at Shona, who shook her head.

"No thank you to that one too. I'd like to look at something a bit cheerful if that's possible today."

"Or," continued Jeremy, looking at the guide book, "we could take a cruise out on the Derwent to Ironpot Lighthouse, or around the bay, or we could drive up to Risdon Cove, where the first British settlement was supposed to be, before they discovered that Hobart was a better location. No?" The women shook their heads.

"Well," he ploughed on, undeterred, "there's always Port Arthur, but that's pretty grim, and it's really a day trip, anyway. How about Mount Wellington, to look at the views? I'm at your disposal, ladies."

They sat, discussing their options, until Jeremy got up to pay the bill, and they all trooped outside to wait while he collected the car. By the time he returned, they had decided on the Maritime Museum.

***

By 4:30 p.m. they had had enough sightseeing for one day, and Carrie gently reminded Jeremy she had to start work in less than an hour and a half. He dropped Beth and Shona off at Beth's house, and took Carrie home. Beth and Shona had a simple supper, and prepared to curl up with the television or a book for a few hours before bed.

"I guess we could have gone to the movies," Beth admitted, "but I'm a little weary now."

"So am I, lassie, so am I! They're an energetic pair, aren't they?"

"They sure are. But they seem very happy together, and they make a nice couple."

"Indeed they do, lass. When are they thinking of getting married? I'd like to send them a wee something from Scotland for their nuptials. What's Carrie's story, lass?"

Beth had to admit she had no idea when the intended marriage was to take place, but was able to tell Shona a little of Carrie's background, and about her current profession.

"And what will young Jeremy do about finishing his doctorate now, d'you think?"

"I have absolutely no idea, Shona. I think he's having a hard enough time coping with all of this, without having to think to the future, just now. I guess he'll find another supervisor, and complete his studies, but whether he stays here or moves elsewhere, is an unknown." Beth shrugged. "Shona, would you like to join me in a wee dram? I have an open bottle of Tamdhu. It was Dougal's favourite."

"Thank you, Elizabeth, that would be lovely. We could drink a toast to the man himself."

Beth found and poured out two glasses of the exquisite Scotch, they clinked glasses and toasted the departed man in Gaelic. "*Slàinte mhath, Dùghall, mo bhràthair*," Shona intoned, adding in English for Beth's limited Gaelic, "Good health, Dougal, my brother" and Beth added her own toast, "*Slàinte mhath, Dùghall, mo ghràidh.*" Shona echoed her sentiments, "Good health, Dougal, my dear."

They finished their drink, and curled up to watch the lights across the river. Shona started falling asleep; Beth realised with a guilty start that the woman was probably suffering from jet lag, and must be exhausted. Beth gently woke the older woman, and suggested that an early night might be in order for them both. Shona agreed, and took herself off to bed. Beth sat, curled up in her chair for an hour more, wrapped in her favourite blanket, gazing at nothing through the darkened glass, before falling asleep.

Chapter
twenty-six

Sunday morning, Jeremy and Carrie collected Beth and Shona for a day in the country. Carrie had already taken the front seat, so the two older women sat in the back.

"Where are we going today, Jeremy?" asked Shona.

"It's a surprise, Aunt Shona, but we have a picnic packed, so all you have to do is sit back and enjoy the scenery."

They cleared the city and suburbs, heading north, away from the coast. They turned off the main road at the town of Brighton and went out to visit a native wildlife sanctuary, where they were able to show Shona wombats and Tasmanian devils. Winding their way along, they drove to Shene, to admire the Georgian convict-built architecture from early colonial times. In Oatlands, their next stop, they visited the Callington Mill, third oldest windmill in Australia, more sandstone convict-built buildings, and the church. Finally, they stopped for lunch, then visited a woollen mill, where Shona purchased a fine, soft merino sweater for herself, declaring herself delighted to have found such a good bargain.

Taking time to stop and admire the scenery, they returned to Hobart. Once there, they headed to the Botanical Gardens, where they wandered for an hour before high tea, Beth's treat. Jeremy and Carrie took the older ladies home, promising to be at the funeral home by ten thirty the next morning, to lend their support.

After revisiting the highlights of their day, Beth and Shona went to bed early. Tomorrow they would say goodbye to Dougal for the last time.

***

The morning of the funeral, Beth arose early, and went for a brisk walk. She breathed in the heavy morning air like a fine wine, but was glad to return to the house for a hot shower and breakfast. Shona was already up; she was in the kitchen, cooking breakfast for them both.

"I didn't like to wake you, my dear, but I was sure the aromas of toast and eggs would rouse you," said Shona.

"Thank you, that was very kind, Shona dear. I've been out for a long walk and now I'm hungry!"

The two women ate together, watching a watery sun struggling to break through the clouds which were hanging menacingly low over Mount Wellington. The river's surface was soon dented by rain drops, then a downpour obliterated the view totally.

"I suspect the sky is mirroring my feelings this morning, Shona."

"Yes, it's a mourning sky, indeed."

After tidying up, Beth fetched the car. Shona waited under the shelter of the front porch, before dashing through the downpour under an umbrella. She was wearing a severely cut wool suit of deepest grey, while Beth wore navy blue, with a white blouse and a blue and white scarf. They arrived at the funeral home at 10:30 a.m. on the dot, and were met at the door by Vincent Holden and Barry Wray.

"Thank you for coming in a little early, Mrs Ferguson," said Vincent Holden. "You will need to stand near the door, to welcome the mourners. In the meantime, may I offer you both a hot beverage? It's very inclement this morning. I fear our Indian summer has deserted us at last."

"Thank you, no, Mr Holden. Although a glass of water would be welcome," Beth answered. She looked at her sister-in-law. "Shona? A hot drink?"

"A dram would be more welcome, dear, but I'll settle for some water, too, thank you."

Beth smiled. "Yes, a dram would be warming, for sure. But I'd best stay with the water for now."

A jug of water and two glasses were placed on a small table behind them, and Barry Wray poured for them.

"I believe you will be speaking about your brother, Miss Ferguson?"

"It's Mrs Wallace, thank you, and yes, I would like to say a few words about him."

"Oh, I do beg your pardon, Mrs Wallace. Would you like to speak first, or after I have delivered my words?"

"Oh, afterwards, I think. I believe you are delivering a short biography of my brother's life? Good. Mine is more a personal account of Dougal, you understand."

"Of course, Mrs Wallace. Please excuse me. I'll just go and see that all is in readiness." He excused himself and disappeared through the doors into the room set up as a funeral chapel.

Beth and Shona stood together at the front door, and sipped their water quietly. Vanessa arrived with two wide, shallow baskets containing sprigs of heather, and printed leaflets. When Jeremy and Carrie arrived a few minutes later, they greeted both women with a kiss and a brief hug; emotions would begin to run high, and neither of the youngsters wanted to precipitate a flood of tears with awkward words. They had intended to go straight into the chapel, but Beth had a job for them both.

"Jeremy, honey, and Carrie, dear, would you stand with us, and hand out a sprig of heather and an order of service to anyone who comes today, please?" Beth lifted the baskets and handed one each to the youngsters.

Jeremy's voice caught as he answered. "Sure, of course, Beth. That okay with you, Carrie?"

"Of course! I'd be honoured to help."

Jeremy and Carrie were kept very busy; in one and twos, people began to arrive, then the trickle turned to a small flood. Beth's colleagues from the museum had come in a minibus, and Dougal's colleagues from the university arrived in groups. Several people unknown to Beth arrived and shook hands awkwardly, eyes not daring to meet hers as they murmured condolences, accepted their sprigs of heather and escaped into the chapel.

Too soon, the celebrant came and whispered that it was time for all of them to go in; Beth looked at her sister-in-law, then her stepson and his fiancée, and they moved together into the chapel. There were chairs reserved for them at the front; seeing Dougal's coffin on the raised dais at the front of the chapel, draped in the flag with the blue and white diagonal cross of St Andrew, and the urns of flowers in silent tribute on either side, brought a huge lump to Beth's throat. She swallowed with effort; it was so *surreal*, being here at all. She ushered the others ahead of her; she wanted to sit on the aisle.

The celebrant greeted the assembled throng in a respectful and subdued tone, thanked everyone for attending, and went through the necessary formalities. The first musical offering began to play, and the soulful voice of Joan Baez filled the lofty room. There was a rustle of handkerchiefs being extracted from handbags and pockets; Beth sat, rock-still, dry-eyed, her eyes riveted on the elevated, draped coffin. She was scarcely breathing, but her mind was awhirl. Beside her, Beth felt Shona stiffen; the words were obviously hitting home. The music carried Beth as she lost herself in a silent, one-sided conversation with her late husband.

Dougal, Dougal, what could you have been thinking when you jumped off that ship like a stone into a pond? Didn't you realise we'd all be caught up and buffeted in the ripples of your lies? What was so important that you'd risk your life like that? How did you end up on Macquarie Island, and who put a bullet in your back? And why did you keep all those secrets from me, for all those years? Do you realise how much you hurt me? If you hadn't died, I would never have known about Jeremy, or about your secret life. How is that fair, Dougal?

No one heard the main door open and close quietly, or notice a couple who stopped just inside the door at the rear of the chapel. A few, close to the pair may have heard a faint *click* from a mobile phone and the whirr of a small video recorder, but no one took much notice. Their attention was focussed elsewhere.

As the last guitar chord died away, Barry Wray stood once more, and began his eulogy, bringing into sharp focus the reason they had all gathered together that wet, grey morning. Although the two men had never met, he spoke with warmth of Dougal James Kenneth Ferguson, man of science, champion of marine wildlife, valued friend and colleague, loving husband of Elizabeth Bouchier Ferguson, loving father of Malcolm (deceased). He spoke of Dougal's many achievements in his sixty years of life, and the numerous causes he had championed, for the protection of sea creatures everywhere, for the research he had been undertaking at the time of his death into the effects of climate change on marine species, and for the more local causes he had quietly supported since his arrival on the island ten years prior.

Beth sat motionless, but as she listened to the celebrant listing Dougal's achievements and passions, she felt a sense of reluctant acceptance creep into her soul, and for the first time since he had died, she felt she could begin to forgive Dougal for the lies and deceptions he had practised over the years. He *had* been an honourable and a worthwhile human being; her anger with him was justified, she felt, but she could now begin to see a larger picture drawn for her in the words she had supplied to the celebrant. She felt he had taken the bare facts and spun them into a tapestry, the tapestry of Dougal's life; her eyes welled and blurred with tears, but she didn't move a muscle.

At the conclusion of the eulogy, the 23rd Psalm was played; there were tears and surreptitious use of hankies and tissues. The solemnity of the occasion weighed heavily on the room.

The celebrant then called upon Shona Wallace, sister to the deceased, to say a few words about her sibling. Shona rose and went to the podium, where she thanked everyone for coming, and started with her own most personal and nostalgic eulogy for her younger brother. While some may have had trouble understanding Shona's quite thick Scottish accent, they could never have mistaken the love or the depth of feeling she had for him.

Shona told stories about Dougal as a wee boy, of his childhood on Orkney, and his life-long passion for the seals and their kin; she glanced meaningfully at Beth once or twice, but had captured her audience. Here was the *real* Dougal Ferguson, son, brother, and friend.

Shona, like many Island folk, had a natural talent for storytelling, just as Dougal had. She made them laugh with some of her anecdotes, and emotions began to flow, as laughter often precedes tears. When she had finished, and moved to sit back down next to Beth, spontaneous applause broke out; the ice had been broken and people began to relax a little.

Barry Wray moved back to the podium and asked if anyone else would care to speak; getting no replies he then announced quietly that the time had come to say goodbye, and invited people to place their sprigs of heather on top of the coffin before it began its short journey through the dark curtains to the furnaces beyond. Some went and placed their heather sprigs on the coffin, murmuring words of farewell to Dougal; a slide show of Dougal's life began on a large screen off to one side of the chapel; the photos Beth had supplied had been blended together in a tasteful montage. The skirl of the pipes filled the room, as the strains of "Highland Cathedral" began to play. The slideshow ran silently, and the coffin began to move away, to disappear from view.

Beth sat, rigid, knuckles white with panic as she gripped the chair's metal framework; she bit the inside of her mouth and tasted blood, she wanted to scream, she wanted to jump up and stop the coffin, she wanted to *see* him one last time. She dimly heard someone utter a loud, haunting cry, but didn't recognise it as her own voice. She didn't realise she was rocking back and forth until a cool, firm hand gripped her arm; Shona hushed her like a small child, slipped an arm around her shoulders, and together they rocked in mutual grief. Somewhere in the confusion of the moment, Jeremy put an arm around each of the older women and hugged them to him, as the tears flowed, unashamed, unbridled, and unstoppable.

Carrie leaned across and rested her head on Jeremy's shoulder, until the music had almost finished, and the celebrant caught her eye. Carrie nodded, and whispered to Jeremy, "Will you be okay to come out now?" A mute nod told her he had understood.

Jeremy gave his aunt and stepmother a special hug each, and helped them to stand.

Beth and Shona wiped their eyes and noses, then exchanged a hug. Beth went to Carrie and hugged her, then Jeremy in turn, and said, "There are some homemade cookies in the next room if you're interested, laddie…"

Jeremy laughed aloud, and squeezed his little stepmother tight. "You sure do know how to make a guy feel special, you know!"

Beth chuckled, and dried her eyes. "You'll do, laddie, you'll do. Come on, let's get something to eat and drink. I could kill for a coffee!"

***

Vanessa had done her job well, setting out the refreshments. Beth sent Jeremy and Carrie to forage a coffee for her, and a cup of tea for Shona. Beth soon became encircled by well-wishers, people expressing their condolences; many she knew by sight, if not intimately, from the museum and the university. She smiled and thanked them all for coming, inviting them to eat and enjoy the food she had prepared. A small group of strangers approached her and shook her hand; the senior of them said, "You won't know me, Mrs Ferguson, but my name is Peter Gallagher. I was the captain on *Aurora Australis* when your husband went missing, and these are some of the crew members who were with him on that voyage. Your husband was very well-liked and well-respected by everyone he met, Mrs Ferguson. He was a real gentleman. I just wanted to assure you we did *everything* humanly possible to find him, and to tell you how very sorry we all are that we couldn't."

Tears sprang afresh into Beth's eyes for the poor man's obvious distress. "Oh Captain Gallagher, please don't blame yourselves, or distress yourselves further. Dougal could be very... um... *impulsive*, at times." She patted Peter Gallagher's hand, and smiled into his weathered face. "I hope your next voyage is less eventful, sir."

"That was my last voyage on *Aurora Australis*, Mrs Ferguson. I've retired now. Oh," he added, seeing the look of anxiety on her face, "I had already handed in my resignation letter before this happened."

Beth turned tear-filled eyes to his and patted his hand again. "Yes, but it would leave you with a sour taste, though, wouldn't it? Please. Stay and have some refreshments? I baked the cookies and savouries myself. It would be a shame if I had to take them all home again. Jeremy would just have to eat them all, and it probably wouldn't be good for his waistline. Jeremy?" she called, and beckoned the young man over; the captain and his crew renewed their brief acquaintance with the young scientist.

"Shame about your research, lad," commiserated Peter Gallagher.

Jeremy grimaced. "Yeah, well I couldn't really do anything else. Beth's like a mom to me. Couldn't let her down, could I?"

"There'll be other trips for you, lad, I hope," said Peter Gallagher.

"Thank you. I hope so. And thank you so much for all your efforts and your care of the professor and me while we were with you. It means a lot to me." Then Jeremy introduced his fiancée, Carrie, and Beth introduced her sister-in-law, Shona. They were having a pleasant conversation until a rather loud, strident, and high-pitched voice behind Beth said, "Excuse me, Mrs Ferguson? I'm Trinity Trinling from the *Hobart Examiner*. I wonder if we could have a few words, please?"

Beth swung around to face a young, large-bosomed blonde in a dark, tightly fitting cashmere sweater and slacks; she recognised the woman from the morning she had had to jog past her own house and pretend not to speak English, to avoid having speak to her. Shona turned and glared at the interloper; Beth quietly called Jeremy and Carrie to her side, while the brash young woman continued her spiel.

"I'm so sorry for your loss, Mrs Ferguson, but would you mind giving us a statement to go with the wonderful eulogies we just heard about your late husband?"

Beth stared at the reporter and said with great dignity, "If you were present, then you will have all the material you could possibly need, young lady. No, I do not have anything further to add. Would you please leave? You really are not welcome. Goodbye." She turned on her heel, looked to Jeremy and added, "Jeremy dear, would you please escort these people off the premises, and take Carrie with you? She's met this young lady before, I think."

"With pleasure, Beth!" Carrie smiled coldly and walked over to the reporter and the sidekick with the video recorder. Carrie covered the camera with her hand, and smiled sweetly. "Please leave. This is a sad occasion, and you are intruding."

Trinity persisted. "Wait! Haven't I seen you at the house? What's your part in all of this?" Her long-nailed thumb hit Record on her phone screen.

Carrie smiled. "Nice try, but no comment. Now, please leave, before I call your boss." As Carrie was speaking, she and Jeremy were quietly but inexorably herding the newspaper pair towards the front door, gentle but relentless. When the intruders had been escorted from the building, Jeremy locked the front door and dusted his hands. He looked up to find Beth watching him; he grinned. She smiled and blew him a kiss. "Thank you!" she mouthed. "Thank you both!"

***

Beth returned to her duties as hostess of the gathering; there were many who wanted to shake her hand and offer condolences, but Beth felt that she would never remember them all, and was grateful for Vanessa's earlier suggestion that a Condolences Book be provided for the mourners to record their names and any comments they may wish to leave. Dougal's colleagues came and spoke to her, then drifted away; her own colleagues came and offered their condolences.

One by one the mourners came, spoke, then started to take their leave; some would have to return to work, others would take the rest of the day for their own business. A male voice spoke at her elbow as the crowd was thinning. "Mrs Ferguson, dear lady! May I offer my condolences?" She turned. It was Kenneth Finn, Dougal's solicitor. He seized her hand between his own, and looked meaningfully into her eyes; Beth retrieved her hand, indicating the group with it, and turned to beckon her family.

"Ah, Mr Finn, may I introduce you to my sister-in-law, Shona Wallace from Edinburgh, Scotland? And may I also introduce to you my son Jeremy and his fiancée, Carrie?" Jeremy, Carrie, and Shona formed a phalanx around Beth, as they shook hands with the man; she knew they were protecting her from any unwelcome advances; they had obviously picked up her attitude towards him.

"Pleased to meet you all," Kenneth Finn murmured. "So nice to know this dear lady has such a supportive family to see her through this most trying time."

Jeremy answered blandly, "Yes, my mother is much loved and treasured. My father adored her, and *she him*. Thank you so much for coming today. I hope you have had a chance to sample my mother's excellent baking skills?"

Beth trod deliberately on Jeremy's foot, and suppressed a smile as he gave a tiny start.

Oh Dougal, he's your boy all right!

"Quite so, quite so. My compliments on your culinary prowess, dear lady. Now, if you'll excuse me? I must return to my office. Mrs Ferguson, if I can ever be of any assistance, please don't hesitate to call me. So nice to meet you all. Good day." And he took his leave.

Beth looked up at Jeremy. "You are so naughty! Baiting the poor little man like that!"

"Beth, honey, he was looking at you as if you were one of your sugar-topped cookies! He was a total creep!"

"Hush, lad! He was your father's solicitor, and I'm sure he means well. He took care of Dougal's will and legal business very efficiently. Now, I think just about everyone has gone. Let me go and find Vanessa, and we'll take home the leftovers."

Beth found Vanessa, and enlisted Carrie's and Jeremy's aid to pack the left-over food. Beth excused herself to Shona, while she went to speak with Vincent Holden. She found him in his office, and asked him to prepare an account of the expenses, so that she could submit it to her funeral insurance for reimbursement. Vincent Holden assured her that he would have it to her within the week, and thanked her for her business.

While Carrie helped Shona in the kitchenette, and Beth was in the funeral director's office, Vanessa Holden approached Jeremy, an anxious look on her face.

"Jeremy?" As he nodded, she continued in a quiet voice, "Jeremy, I'm afraid there's been an oversight. Mrs Ferguson brought in a bag containing her late husband's coat. It was supposed to have been placed in the coffin with him. Thing is…" She sighed heavily and looked guilty. "Thing is… well, long story short, the coat was overlooked and it's still here!" She looked acutely embarrassed at having made such a grave mistake.

"Crap!" Jeremy muttered, looking towards the closed door of the office. He hesitated, then took her arm. "Where is it now?" he asked urgently.

"Out back, in the storeroom."

"Can you meet me outside with it? I don't want Beth upset right now."

"Okay!" Vanessa exhaled with relief. "Where's your car?"

He told her which one to look for; she went one way, and he slipped out through the front door to the car park, beeping his car unlocked as he hurried across to it.

Vanessa appeared around the corner, clutching a large opaque plastic bag. Jeremy opened the trunk, and stowed the bag away. He thanked Vanessa, reassured her it would be okay, and hastened back inside.

Carrie appeared from the kitchen, followed by Shona just as he entered the foyer.

"Hi, honey, there you are!" Carrie called. "Can you give me a hand with the food please?"

"Sure, let's get them into Beth's car. Where is she?"

"Still in the office. Oh no, here she is now." The door to Vincent Holden's office opened and Beth emerged, smiling and shaking hands with the funeral director. She turned and spotted the tableau; Shona and Carrie with containers balanced in their arms, Jeremy transfixed in the foyer.

"All good?" she asked quietly, looking from one to the other.

"All good, Beth," Carrie answered, giving Jeremy a quizzical look and handing him a pile of containers.

"Ah, we were just going to put these in your car, Beth," Jeremy said, "but we didn't have the keys."

Beth fished in her handbag and produced a set of keys. "Here you are, lad. You could have put them in your own car…"

"No!" he said hastily, then recovered himself. "No, it's a mess in there. They'd be better off with you. I'll have to take Carrie home soon, anyway. She starts her shift at two."

"Oh!" exclaimed Carrie. "What is the time? Hell, we'll have to move, Jezz. Sorry, Beth, I didn't realise what the time was. We'll catch up soon, okay?" She leant down to kiss Beth and whispered, "Sorry, duty calls."

"It's fine, dear. Off you go."

Jeremy took Beth's keys in his spare hand and left the building with Carrie. He returned thirty seconds later, handed Beth her keys, kissed her and walked hurriedly out the front door, calling out, "See you soon, Beth, Aunt Shona."

The two women said their farewells to Vanessa and went out to the car. They were soon on their way back across the river.

Chapter
twenty-seven

Beth and Shona returned to Rose Bay, where they were kept busy carting, stacking, and sorting leftover food. Savoury items went into the fridge, biscuits into the pantry. Shona went off to change out of her funeral attire while Beth was busy in the kitchen, then returned to make a pot of tea for herself, and coffee for Beth while Beth changed out of her sombre ensemble into a warm-up suit of soft plum-coloured velour. Shona had put out a selection of savouries, but Beth headed straight to haul out a bottle of Scotch and two glasses; she poured a generous measure each for herself and her sister-in-law. Handing Shona a glass, she silently saluted their lost one, and swallowed half of the liquid in one gulp.

"Oh, that's better!" she exclaimed, looking across at Shona, who had drained her glass.

"Absolutely! I think I needed that!" agreed Shona. "Warms the cockles of the heart, doesn't it?" The older woman put down her glass and motioned Beth to the table, where she had put the food. "Now, sit ye down, lassie, and eat something before you fall over. You've been so busy, with all the well-wishers, you didn't take a morsel for yourself!"

Beth grimaced slightly, stretched her back and sat gratefully. She selected a few little titbits for her plate, and nibbled them. Her stomach growled demandingly, reminding her that it *had* been a while since breakfast, and she obliged it, eating more keenly now. Between them, the plate was soon empty, and Beth went to fetch more. They ate in silence until the second plateful had disappeared, then Beth pushed her plate away, replete.

"They probably should have been heated," she remarked about her cooking, "but they were just fine, cold."

Shona, finishing her last mouthful, nodded in agreement. "Aye, lassie, they're just fine."

The two women sat, bereft of conversation, each sunk into

reflection and contemplation, sipping their rapidly cooling hot drinks.

"Beth," Shona suddenly remarked, "how is it that you know the Gaelic, lass?"

"Dougal…" Beth choked on her husband's name, cleared her throat and continued, "Dougal spoke it to me quite often, especially in the early days, before…" *Before we lost our boy, and things went wrong between us.* She continued. "He would talk to me in Gaelic, to teach me; little by little I picked up bits and pieces of the language. I don't remember much of my own people's language, except for a couple of old cradle songs my mother sang to me, and I used to sing to Malcolm when he was a baby, so it was important to learn Dougal's mother tongue, to pass it on to our son. We regularly both spoke the Gaelic to Malcolm, and he was becoming quite proficient in the language in his own baby way before he died…." The final word was no more than a whisper. Beth buried her face in her hands and sobbed, shoulders heaving, breath catching as the tidal wave of grief finally overturned her.

Shona started to rise, to comfort her sister-in-law, but sat down and bowed her head. "Och, I'm so sorry, my dear, I didn't mean to upset you so."

Beth shook her head wordlessly but extended a tear-stained hand towards her sister-in-law, who grasped and squeezed it gently. Presently, Beth lifted her head and looked through her tears at her.

"It's all been so *unreal*, Shona, everything that's happened. It doesn't seem long since I was waving to him as he sailed away, and yet it seems that he's been gone *years*. Oh!" She shook her head. "I don't know what to think any more. I knew he was going, and I've become *used* to him going away over the years, and me being alone for months on end but *this*! This is too cruel. I'm so *confused*, Shona! I'm *furious* with him that he had a secret life, and a secret son, but I'm *happy* too, that he can live on, in Jeremy! Does any of that make sense?" she demanded, shaking her head more vigorously, her short dark brown hair swinging to its own rhythm, while stray tears splashed across the tabletop.

"It's been a shock, lass, the cruellest kind, for sure. But you're a strong young woman, and you'll manage. And young Jeremy is a delight, for certain. He's very like his father, but he could be your child too, you know. There's just a *look* about him. Have you never noticed?"

Beth looked sharply at Shona, then across at the photograph Jeremy had erroneously identified, only weeks before.

"I think Jeremy's mother may have been part First Nation like mine, Shona. When Jeremy came here to see me, after he had brought… Dougal… back from Macquarie Island, he asked about that photo over there." She indicated the photo on its shelf. "He asked me why I would have a photo of his grandmother and great-grandmother, which I thought very strange, at the time. I explained that it was a photo of me and my mother, taken not long before we moved down here. It's the last photo I had of her. Anyway, long story short, I think he has First Nation blood in him."

"It's possible, I suppose," said the older woman.

"Yes. But here's the really weird thing, Shona! When he mistakenly identified the people in the photograph, he mentioned their names. And one of the names was Bibi, his great-grandmother. As far as I can recollect, *Bibi* isn't a common name amongst our people, but my grandmother had a younger sister, Biba, who was taken away by the government people back in the early thirties. Anyhow, it started me thinking, and I got Jeremy to tell me of his family history, as much as he could remember. He has some papers, amongst his possessions, that he inherited when his grandparents died, and he showed me those.

"It will probably sound crazy, but I sent away for a couple of DNA test kits, you know the type you can do at home? Anyway, we did them—Jeremy was quite happy to do it, too—and I'm now waiting for the results. I can't really tell you why I did it, except that somewhere in my back of my mind, call it wishful thinking perhaps, the lad and I might be related—apart from him being Dougal's son."

"There are more things between Heaven and Earth than we're ever given to know, lass. Stranger things have been known to happen, as well you might know, from recent events, eh?"

Beth's chuckle was more a watery gurgle, as the enormity of the incredible nature of her husband struck her as funny. She looked at Shona, loving the older woman enormously in that instant for her calm logic and straight talking. Her eyes crinkled up as she laughed, relieved to have been taken seriously about her own hair-brained wishes. The women looked at each other, and both burst out laughing.

"You have to admit, lass," Shona managed to say between her bouts of laughter, "that Dougal was not exactly what you might call *normal*, now was he?"

Beth could only shake her head in mute agreement as she laughed harder. No, Dougal certainly had *not* been normal, it seemed. As quickly as she had started, she toppled off the knife-edge between hysterical laughter and uncontrollable tears, and she was in mourning once more for her lost love.

Shona helped Beth to stand, walked her to her own bedroom, and put her to bed. Beth was grateful to be mothered in this way, lay down, allowed Shona to gently pull the quilt across her weary body, and closed her eyes.

***

What Beth did not and would never know was that nearly 11,000 kilometres away, on the East Coast of South America, another woman also mourned the loss of a husband.

The small fishing trawler *Santa Teresa* had finally made it home to the fishing village on the Argentinian coast, with its sad cargo. Jeronimo and his crew had made good time across the Pacific, despite the winds, but had run into trouble in Chile, where they had stopped for supplies and more ice for his father's body.

The Chilean port authorities were deeply unhappy about the presence of a corpse in the hold, especially as some of the fish had come into contact with it in the rough weather. Jeronimo was forced to jettison all their catch before the port authorities would let them even go ashore. All the men were disgruntled, and their superstitious natures, never far beneath the veneer of their Roman Catholicism, had surfaced with a vengeance. They blamed the presence of the dead man whose body had been unceremoniously dumped overboard for their present run of ill luck.

Their catch was gone, they were detained in port until the officials could be bribed sufficiently to allow them to sail, and their boss's body would need more ice before it started stinking the place out.

"Better," they grumbled amongst themselves, "to have buried the captain at sea."

But Jeronimo had been adamant that his father's body should be taken home, so his mother could grieve properly, and masses could be said for the repose of his soul. So the body remained on board, and the crew grumbled louder. The two troublesome Colombians had escaped as soon as the trawler docked, but none of the men could be bothered chasing them. "Good riddance to bad rubbish," they said.

Bribes paid, supplies and ice procured, *Santa Teresa* eventually left Chile, battled its way through the Straits of Magellan to the East Coast of South America, and made for home in Argentina. Jeronimo had been able to contact his mother so she could start arranging his father's funeral, and the church bell tolled mournfully as the local children shouted out from a lookout that they could see the trawler approaching.

Jeronimo had been dreading the moment when he would have to deal in person with his mother and his extended family. During the voyage, he had become fatalistic about his father's death, and had decided to tell his mother only about a fatal heart attack, and not a murder. The outpourings of female grief disconcerted the young man so that he just wanted to run away, back to sea; he was not used to the cacophony and the endless, repetitive questions he was unable to answer fully. The men and he had sworn an oath of secrecy about the discovery and disposal of the *anglo*'s body, so there was little he could really tell his mother about why her husband had so abruptly died. She would have to be content with the effort it had cost her son to bring his father home for burial.

The whole fishing village turned out for Jorge's funeral; the church bell tolled its sombre tone, the mourners walked behind the coffin to the burial ground, where a hastily dug grave awaited it. Prayers were said, the coffin was lowered into the pit, clods of earth thudded dully on the wood, women wailed and cried loudly, men smoked, shuffled their feet and were helpless in the face of so much grief, although the surreptitious flasks passed amongst them helped bolster their courage.

Jorge Gonzalez was laid to rest in the earth, and the mourners left the gravediggers to fill in the hole which would never be filled in their lives.

Worse still was that there was no money; bribes, ice, and provisions had gobbled up what cash resources the crew had carried. There was no catch to sell, even locally. It wasn't long before Jeronimo had a visit from two 'businessmen' who offered him the same deal they had offered his father, but this time they would not be waiting long for an answer. A few casual questions about his erstwhile shipmates from Colombia made Jeronimo realise that his life and future was in a precarious state. He couldn't report anything to the police; they would want evidence of foul play, and there was none to give. He had asked the men to give him time to think about their offer, so he could consult with his crew. Jeronimo's wife had been of no great help; she had been angry that the children wouldn't have their new clothes and toys, let alone food on the table.

Jeronimo Gonzalez was a deeply unhappy young man; he missed his father's guidance and sound counsel, on more than one level, and he could see a grim future mapped out before him.

***

Back in Hobart, Jeremy Munroe waited until Carrie had gone to work, then let himself into the garage and opened the boot of his car. He pulled out the large plastic bag containing that familiar coat and took it into the house. He lifted the coat from the bag, and shook it out, then held it up. He could see a round hole in the back of the coat; obviously that was where the bullet had passed through, into Dougal's body. It was a puzzle, why Beth would have sent the garment, so dear to her husband, to be cremated with his body.

Jeremy contemplated this for a while, then decided to ask her himself. He found her number on his mobile phone and called. A soft Scottish voice answered his call.

"Hello, Jeremy dear, Beth left her phone in the kitchen when she went for a wee rest. Can I help, laddie?"

"Shona, something really awkward has happened. I don't know the significance of it, but I have the professor's coat here." He hurried on, "Vanessa told me, while Beth was in the office after the funeral, there had been a slip-up, and the coat hadn't been placed in the coffin as Beth had apparently asked for; so she, Vanessa, that is, went and fetched it, and I met her out at the car and I stashed it away so Beth wouldn't see it and get upset." Jeremy stopped to take a deep breath. "Thing is, Aunt Shona, I don't quite know what to do with it now!"

"Calm yourself, lad, calm yourself. I think I need to explain some things to you about your father. I'd ask you to come here, but Elizabeth was mightily overwrought before I put her to bed, and I'd rather she wasn't upset again so soon. She's taken Dougal's death a lot harder than she would admit to anyone. She's such a plucky wee thing, but she reached her limit this afternoon. Could you meet me, say at the end of the street? I'll leave Elizabeth a note saying I've gone for a walk."

"Oh! Okay, if you're sure…"

"Never more certain, lad. Now, away with ye and I'll see you soon." Shona pressed End and replaced the mobile on the kitchen counter. She went to the dresser drawer where Beth had placed Dougal's letter, and laid her hand straight on the folded sheets of paper. Putting them carefully into her handbag, Shona found a pencil and a piece of scrap paper and wrote Beth a short note which she placed next to Beth's mobile phone:

"Elizabeth dear,

I've taken myself out for a long walk. I have the spare keys you gave me, and my phone. Sleep well.

Back soon, Shona.

PS: Young Jeremy rang to ask after you, but I told him you were resting. S"

Shona donned her raincoat, quietly let herself out and walked briskly through the rain to the corner, where she passed the time gazing at the rain-pocked surface of the river until Jeremy's car pulled up.

"Hop in!" he shouted through a partially opened window, "it's too wet to stand outside. Let's go get a coffee!"

Shona hastened around to the passenger door, which Jeremy had courteously leant across and opened for her. He kissed her cheek and thanked her for meeting him.

"Och, laddie, I do believe it was *I* who asked *you*? Now, where can we get a nice pot of tea on a dreary Monday afternoon? I have left Elizabeth a note to say I've gone for a long walk, but I really shouldn't be away too long. She was so very unhappy."

"Let's try the local shopping centre, then. I think there may be a café there, where we can talk out of the rain."

Jeremy eased the car into gear, and they headed for the café he hoped was nearby. If there wasn't one, he could take her to his house and make a pot of tea there, and she could see the coat for herself.

"Actually, Shona, would you mind coming to my place? Carrie's at work, I have tea, and I could show you the professor's coat…" he left the suggestion dangling.

"Splendid idea, lad, splendid idea. And I have something to show you too!"

He changed direction and headed back towards the city, where he and Carrie shared a modest apartment. Jeremy felt awkward at first, until he remembered that the main mess was in the bedroom, and no one needed to go there. He relaxed, and invited his aunt to sit, while he busied himself, making tea in the tiny kitchenette. They kept up a desultory chatter.

"I'm afraid we only have leftovers from the wake, Auntie, if you wanted something to eat…"

"No, lad, they're for you and your lassie. Now sit ye down and tell me what's wrong."

Jeremy sat. "Well, while Beth was in the office doing all the paperwork for the accounts and stuff, after the funeral, Vanessa came up to me and told me that a bag containing the professor's coat, that was apparently supposed to have been put into his coffin with him, had been overlooked and she had just found it! She was afraid to say anything to Beth about it. So I met her in the car park and I put the bag in the trunk, and when Carrie left for work this afternoon, I hauled it out, and I've been just sitting here, looking at it. I saw the professor wearing it so many times, I used to joke that it was like a second skin to him. Strangely, he used to think that was very funny!" His face turned earnest. "But seriously, Auntie, what am I supposed to do with it?"

"What would you *like* to do with it, Jeremy?" asked his aunt, fixing his gaze with her sharp blue eyes.

"I… I'd kind of like to keep it, if that were possible, Auntie. I know I have no right to anything, but that coat brings back memories, happy memories of field trips that I went on with the professor, long before I even knew he was my father."

"Then you should keep it, lad. It's yours by right, apart from anything else. But may I give you a piece of advice? Don't wear it near salt water."

Jeremy goggled at his aunt for a few seconds. He had never heard such a strange request.

"You mean it might shrink or something?" he asked.

Shona fished the letter from her handbag, and spread the pages flat against her lap.

"Let me read to you from the letter your father left for his wife. Now let me see…. Where is the passage? Ah! Here we are!" Shona started to read from somewhere in the middle of the letter; Jeremy sat back, sipped his tea and listened to the musical lilt of her voice.

"'*As you know, I came from the Orkneys, from a long line of fisher-folk; we have all been involved with the sea in one way or another for generations, and ours has always been a deeply entrenched culture of folklore and superstition. You may have noticed this when we lived there, when I was away researching the seals and their cousins…*' We'll skip the next bit, as it's quite personal between Dougal and Elizabeth…. Now, where was the next part you needed to hear? Bear with me, laddie, we'll get there…. Ah yes! Here it is!" And she continued reading to a somewhat bemused young man.

"*… you will have uncovered my greatest secret… I was lucky, or unlucky enough to have been born with this gene; I don't know if Jeremy carries it, but I wouldn't be surprised. You may, by now, have guessed the significance of my old coat, the one you have been so keen to dispose of to the Thrift Shop for so many years, and the one reason I have resisted all your loving attempts to modernise my appearance. It was my means of transformation…; without it I could never return to the form of a seal. I know I told you I couldn't swim well, but that was to protect myself from exposure to prying minds and unanswerable questions. I did **not** want to become a specimen…. Mine was a secret life, and one I was unable to share … go to Orkney if you can and scatter my ashes on the ebb tide. That way they will be carried back to my ancestral home, to the sea stacks of Sule Skerry. Yes… the place really exists.*

Ask … Shona to help you; she lives in Scotland and has always had her suspicions about me and my coat. She was always watching me when I was young; I suspect she guessed long ago. Speaking of the coat, please send it to the flames with me; it must go with me to my final rest."

Shona put down the letter and lifted her eyes to a face white with shock, huge eager eyes staring at her, open-mouthed. She was just about to ask him if he was quite well, when he breathed out one word.

"Cool!"

"Cool?" she demanded, frowning across the table at Jeremy's rapt gaze.

"Really cool!" he declared. "Do you reckon if I put this on and went for a swim in the sea, I'd shape-shift into a seal?"

"Either that, or you'll drown from the weight of it, lad! Enough! Now you know what Dougal was about, why Beth was so adamant that the coat go into the coffin with him. She's going to be none too pleased when she finds out!"

Jeremy reached across the table and grabbed his aunt's arm. "Do we *have* to tell her?" he begged. "Can't I just keep my father's coat, as a keepsake? Don't you *realise* what this could mean for my *research*? How wonderful it could be? Man! I could become one of them, *really* find out what they experience in the oceans! Research from the horse's mouth, so to speak! That's way cool!"

If his face had been anguished before, it was now alight with excitement as he suddenly grasped the huge potential of his new garment, and if the grip on Shona's arm had been firm, it was now almost vicelike. She gently but firmly prised his fingers away with her free hand. He blinked, and came to himself, sitting back with a start.

"Oh! Oh! *Sorry*! I don't know what came over me for a minute. Are you hurt? Oh, I'm *so sorry*!"

Shona rubbed her arm briskly; his grip had been painfully tight. She looked at him quite hard while she thought about his predicament. How *would* her sister-in-law take the news that the coat had escaped the flames? What would she want to do with it? Would it be better just to leave it with the lad, as a memento of his father, a father he had never known as such, only as his mentor. Those thoughts reminded her of a question she had been meaning to ask her only nephew.

"Jeremy dear, what do you intend to do about your thesis, now that Dougal is no longer around to supervise your research?"

"Oh, Auntie, I'll have to search for a new supervisor; someone who would be prepared to take me on as his or her student. There aren't that many here in Hobart, although I might be able to get someone to oversee my work from elsewhere, especially with Skype and emails and instant technology. I'm asking around. Now that the funeral is over, I'll have to start really looking."

Shona glanced up at the wall clock. "I'll have to ask you take me back to Elizabeth's soon, lad. I don't particularly want her waking up and being distressed if no one's there for her."

"She's almost the bravest woman I ever met, Auntie. She has been so strong and caring, even when I've cried like a baby on her shoulder. She is so wise. I'm so very lucky to have her in my life."

Shona smiled. "Yes. She is hoping that you two may actually be blood relatives. She told me about the DNA tests you both did. It all sounds fascinating. I know I'm a lucky woman, to have found a real live nephew so late in my life. Now take me back to Rose Bay, please, nephew of mine, there's a good lad!" Smiling, she brushed her lips to his cheek.

Chapter
twenty-eight

As they were driving back to Rose Bay, Shona asked Jeremy about his thesis. He was happy to talk about something normal, and immediately began explaining his chosen topic, laying bare his passion and determination to do something about the degradation of the oceans.

"One of the things we were going to do on Macquarie Island was to monitor the amount of trash that gets washed up, even in such a far-away place. The professor was very concerned about the effects that plastics and other waste is having on the seal and sea lion populations there." He laughed bitterly. "And as if that wasn't bad enough with them getting tangled up in lines and nets, he was furious about the wastage of chemicals from beauty products and stuff like that getting into the oceans, into the fish they eat. I think he was hoping to monitor how far south the currents were carrying all these poisons. I know he had colleagues at the university here who regularly caught and tested fish for pollutants like microbeads, not to mention the heavy metals from industry."

Jeremy glanced sideways at his aunt, who was staring straight ahead. She must have seen his head turn from the corner of her eye, because she nodded slowly.

"Well, lad, you don't have to go far from home to find the devastation we humans have wrought on our oceans. And you don't have to be a seal to experience it, either. Just ask the local fishermen!"

Jeremy nodded in agreement. The problem seemed insurmountable, but he knew there were people making ground-breaking advances in ways to clear waste from the oceans. He sighed loudly as he also acknowledged that for every really caring citizen in the world, there were two more who didn't give a damn. His aunt agreed. The ideas flowed back and forth, railing against governments who did little or nothing to prevent pollution, against those blinkered people in positions of power around the world who did not believe in the science of climate change, against those who actively sought to pollute and destroy the planet. By the time they had reached Beth's, they had learnt a lot about each other; they looked at each other as Jeremy eased the car to the kerb and shared a conspiratorial smile.

***

Beth was up and about by the time Shona walked in. She was answering emails in the family room, drinking coffee.

"Hi, Shona," she called. "How was your walk? Thanks for the note, by the way. I tried calling Jeremy, but his cell phone was off."

"Hello, Elizabeth, did you have a good rest? You look brighter now." Shona leant over and kissed his sister-in-law on the cheek, ignoring the question, uncomfortably aware of the pages of Dougal's letter wedged into her handbag. "Is the kettle hot, dear?" she asked as she walked into the kitchen.

"Should be!" came the reply. "I only made this coffee five minutes ago, but you may have to reheat the water for tea."

Shona deliberated how she was going to replace the stolen pages without alerting her sister-in-law. She made a pot of tea and carried the tray to the table where Beth was sitting.

"I wondered if I might do a load of washing, Elizabeth?"

"Sure, I'll just finish this email and be right with you."

"I'm happy to do it myself, dear," Shona said calmly.

"I know, but could we do a joint load? I have a few things to wash too."

Beth hit Send and closed the lid. She stood up wearily and went to collect her dirty washing; Shona quickly opened her handbag, strode to the dresser, replaced the letter in the top drawer, and went to collect her own laundry.

Beth returned with an armful of clothes; she stuffed the items into the front-loader and waited for her sister-in-law to return. Once loaded, Beth set the machine in action, and the two women retired to the family room.

"What would you like to do tomorrow, Shona?" Beth enquired. "Do you want to spend some more time with Jeremy, or shall we go out, just the two of us, to do some sightseeing?"

"I'm just fine with whatever you decide, dear," Shona replied.

"Well," Beth began, "we could go out to MONA by ferry, if you like art…. Oh no, they're closed on Tuesdays! We could just go for a long walk around the city itself. Let me see, I'm sure I have a brochure somewhere around here...." She broke off the thread of the conversation as she went into the top drawer of the dresser, and rummaged around in its depths, disturbing letters and paperwork. "Aha!" Shona heard her exclaim as she turned, flourishing a glossy tourist brochure.

"Let's see..." she murmured as she flicked through the pages, "if you want to stay in the CBD, there's the Tasmanian Museum, where I work, Mawson's Hut replica, a number of churches and cathedrals all within walking distance, plus there's Constitution Dock, where the Sydney-Hobart yacht race traditionally finishes, and Battery Point, if we want to climb up to look out over Hobart." She rustled a few pages along. "Ah! There's also the Lark Distillery; they make a very fine Australian malt whisky. The actual distillery is further out, but they have a cellar door, right here in town. So that might be worth a visit and a wee dram or two, do you think?" Shona nodded agreement.

"Aye, lass, it all sounds good. Why don't we spend tomorrow together, just the two of us, then Wednesday, why don't we ask the youngsters to come with us? I'd like to take you all out to dinner on Wednesday evening, if I may? To thank you all for your hospitality."

"Oh!" Beth exclaimed, knuckles flying to her mouth in surprise. "Oh, Shona! I'm so sorry! I didn't even ask how long you were staying, or when you were booked to fly home!" Beth looked so stricken that Shona had to laugh.

"Och, lassie, dinna fash! We've all had other things on our minds, and you particularly! My flight leaves on Thursday afternoon. That's why I want to take you all out for a meal. Do you have anywhere nice in mind, dear?" She held up a warning hand, seeing Beth about to protest. "Or may I have a wee look in that brochure for somewhere suitable?"

Beth meekly handed the booklet across to her sister-in-law, who leafed through it, before exclaiming "Aha! The very place!" She extended the brochure across the table, pointing at an advertisement for a floating seafood restaurant. "What do you know about this one, dear?" she asked.

Beth looked at the advert, then raised welling eyes to her sister-in-law. "That was Dougal's favourite seafood eatery in the whole city, Shona," she whispered. "It has an excellent reputation, the seafood is delicious, and it sits right on the water. That would be lovely, thank you, but I must warn you, it's not cheap."

Shona's eyebrows lifted, then lowered. "Done!" she declared. "Now all we have to do is to invite the children, and hope that Jeremy's young lady is not working that evening."

Beth called Jeremy and asked him to be chauffeur on Wednesday afternoon then bring Carrie to dinner in the evening.

And yes, Jeremy's young lady was not rostered on, on Wednesday evening, but she would be at work in the morning, so he would accompany the older ladies alone.

***

Tuesday morning saw the two women rise and head into the heart of Hobart. Beth parked beneath the museum; the pair grabbed umbrellas and set out on foot to explore. While the rain had stopped overnight, the clouds were lowering and a deep, ponderous grey. Beth looked across to Mount Wellington and was grateful she had not suggested a sightseeing jaunt up its slopes today. The mountain top was invisible, smothered with the same clouds. Silently, she handed Shona a tourist map.

"Where would you like to begin, Shona?"

Shona looked up at the sky, consulted her little map, and suggested that they start down near the dock, then work their way back, while the weather held. "I have a feeling it will be too wet for outdoor pursuits come this afternoon, my dear, so why don't we start at the waterfront?"

"Agreed!" laughed Beth. "Those clouds are not going to be able to contain themselves for much longer!"

In companiable silence they walked down to the Mawson's Hut Replica Museum, faithfully recreated and stocked to show the world how Douglas Mawson, Antarctic pioneer and expeditioner, had lived with his crew and dogs in the bleak fortress that was Antarctica. Shona and Beth moved through the exhibits quietly, almost reverently, only calling the other's attention to some artefact which piqued some interest; Dougal was present in their minds that morning as they took their time, and plenty of photos, stopping to read the plaques aloud to each other.

"Yon Mawson was a brave one, my dear!" remarked Shona at one point. "I'd never really heard much about him. We had the likes of Shackleton, Amundsen, and their ilk in the North."

"I guess I learnt about him when we moved here," Beth replied.

"There were always artefacts and pieces of information about him at the museum. He and Scott are the heroes in these latitudes. The Antarctic is a very unforgiving place." She repressed the shudder which suddenly spiralled through her body.

Curiosity satisfied, they went out into the grey wintry day once more. On their agenda was the Lark's Distillery, which was located right next to the Mawson museum precinct. Once inside, the women spent a very happy half hour, admiring the various offerings on show, and tasting a wee dram of the robust Australian malt whisky. Shona declared herself much taken with the spirit and purchased two bottles to take back to Scotland with her. Beth made a mental note to revisit the shop on another occasion, for her own supplies. Fortified against the icy wind blowing off the water, the pair made their way towards St David's Cathedral. On their way, Beth showed Shona Constitution Dock, where yachts at anchor, high-masted and battened down, bobbed and tossed restlessly on the wind-whipped waves.

"The weather's not going to hold for much longer, Shona!" Beth had to raise her voice to make herself heard against the rising keening of the wind. "Let's get down to the cathedral while we can!"

Shona nodded, and they set off with their backs to the southerly wind and were almost bowled along the street until they reached the lee of the buildings.

"Phew!" exclaimed Beth, swiping her hair from her eyes. "That was a little brisk!"

Shona's short white hair was standing up on end; Beth watched as she made an absent-minded effort to settle it, then decided it was a lost cause.

"Away to this cathedral, then, lass! Which one is this we're going to see?"

"St David's, up on Murray Street. The others are a little far away in this weather."

They walked until they reached Murray Street, where they turned right, into a virtual wind tunnel. Fortunately, the cathedral was not very far along, and much to their great relief, was open to visitors. Beth pushed open the door and they walked quietly in. As they had at Mawson's Hut, each woman went her own way, to look around the imposing building. Each of them, independently of the other, purchased some candles to light as an offering to Dougal's memory; while neither of them were particularly religious, the place demanded awe and respect, and a candle's flickering flame helped to focus scattered thoughts, give strength to the grieving.

After the cathedral, they walked head-first into the sharp teeth of the wind.

"Okay, Shona, it's nearly lunchtime. I'm going to suggest that we have lunch at the museum, where I work. There's a good cafeteria, if you don't mind serve-yourself meals."

"Lead on, my dear! I'm starting to feel a wee bit hungry. The whisky was nice, but it's not warming me through, right now."

Beth chuckled and they strolled purposefully towards the museum. Beth was able to use her swipe key to access the Staff Only entrance, and they quickly found their way to the cafeteria. As they entered, several of Beth's colleagues saw them and called out, inviting them to share a table. Beth smiled in their direction, gently shook her head, and found a small table for two. While Shona went up to select her lunch, Beth walked over to speak with her colleagues.

"What are you doing here, Beth? Aren't you still on bereavement leave?" asked one tall, well-fleshed young gent with pale, freckled skin and ginger hair. His companions hissed at his lack of social skills, but Beth appeared not to notice or care.

"Hi, Stephen. No, I'm not back at work yet. My sister-in-law and I are having a day out in town before she returns to Scotland, and we needed lunch. I figured here was as good a place as any to eat, so here we are. But thank you for the invitation, just the same. Oops, better go. Looks as though I need to go choose some lunch before the hordes descend. See you!"

There was a chorus of "Bye," "Look after yourself," and "See you when you come back to work" as she walked back to their table.

"Och, there you are, lass!" Shona's voice hailed her as they both approached the table.

"Anything good on the menu today, Shona?" asked Beth.

"Aye, lass, plenty. Run along now and make your selection. I've a feeling it's about to become very busy. See yon door?"

Beth chuckled and made good her escape; living with Shona was like having a mom again.

***

By the time they had eaten and wandered through the museum, it was late afternoon. The weather had deteriorated badly and the rain, wind-whipped, was relentless; it stung faces and hands as the two women scampered from the garage to the house.

Beth shook herself and her umbrella just inside the door to remove any raindrops.

"I'm so pleased we brought in the washing to air in front of the fire," she remarked. "It would have been all around Hobart by now if we'd left it outside!"

Shona laughed aloud at the thought of her smalls, as she called her underwear, gaily festooning the Town Hall spire or cartwheeling freely through the suburbs. She shared this thought with Beth, who nearly doubled over in helpless laughter. When the laughter died away from her lips, Beth found she was in tears again. She looked at her sister-in-law, happy in the midst of grief; Beth was suddenly ashamed of the emotions that seemed to flow from every part of her. Shona nodded meaningfully at her and found a tissue for Beth to pat her eyes dry.

"It catches you unexpected, lass. It's nothing to be ashamed of. It's called grief, and you *are* allowed to grieve. You've always been such a stoic wee thing, Elizabeth. I really think it's time to let go and mourn your losses. You've been so busy, ever since I've been here, ensuring that everyone *else* is comfortable, looking after my needs, and young Jeremy's — you've not taken much time for yourself, and I think it's high time you started!"

Beth looked up in surprise at her sister-in-law standing over her, proffering more tissues in her direction. She shook her head and waved them away. It could have been *Dougal* standing there, telling her to get a grip on herself. She sniffed, blew her nose, and smiled at the woman.

"That's exactly what your brother would have done, you know," she remarked quietly.

"I'm gratified!" came the reply. "Now, lassie, what would you like me to do? We've had a long day out, and I must confess to being a little weary, after all the wind and the walking. You'd think I would be used to it, coming from such a cold, inclement climate, but the cold is *different* here; it cuts right through to the bone."

Beth chuckled. "Dougal always said the winds down here were *lazy*, you know. They go through instead of around you!"

"Aye, that sounds like my brother!" Shona laughed. "Now, lassie, what's on the menu for dinner tonight? Come away into the kitchen, lass, and show me what you had planned."

***

The two women spent the next little while preparing their evening meal. As they had both eaten only a light lunch at the museum, they were hungry, and, within half an hour, were both sitting down to a hearty meal of leftovers, which Shona had discovered lurking in the freezer. She chose a beef casserole, while Beth ate a bowl of steaming chilli and rice. The silence was almost complete; both women concentrated on eating; the clinking of forks and spoons against china bowls was the only sound in the comfortable space.

Later, the women talked about Shona's plans for the following day, when Jeremy would be available to spend some time with them.

Shona had thought she would like to see the sights from the top of Mount Wellington, but if that proved difficult because of the heavy weather settling in over Hobart, she thought she would like to go out to Port Arthur.

"It's a grim place, I understand that, Elizabeth, but I've a mind to see it before I leave for home."

Beth was suddenly overcome with emotion again; much as she had secretly resented sharing her space with another woman at first, she had quickly adjusted to another presence in the house. She realised that that was what it had always been like when Dougal had come home from his various trips away. The thought of being finally, irrevocably *alone*, shook her to the core. She cleared her throat.

"Of course we'll go visit it. It's an interesting place to visit. Grim, as you say, but worthwhile seeing. White history is so young in this country, they preserve as much as they can, unless they're ripping it down to replace it with the modern. I haven't quite figured that one out, yet." She shook her head and laughed lightly.

"Done," said Shona.

Chapter
twenty-nine

By Thursday morning, Shona was ready for her flight back to Scotland. The precious bottles of whisky were safe inside two postage tubes, then packed amongst her clothes. Her fine merino sweater was wrapped in tissue paper and laid across the top. The previous evening, she had taken Beth, Jeremy, and Carrie to dinner in an upmarket waterfront restaurant as a thank you to them all for their hospitality. The youngsters had solemnly presented her with a small, hand-made ceramic seal; Shona had been unable to speak, for the tightening in her throat. It was swaddled in socks and jammed inside a walking shoe. Beth had given her a hand-woven Merino scarf in deep blues and greens, purchased from the same woollen mill as the sweater; it too, was packed. Shona had given the saltire from the funeral to Beth, who had promptly taken it to the lounge room and draped it over the couch.

Shona, Beth, and Jeremy had spent their final day together taking a tour of Port Arthur; Shona had expressed an almost professional interest in the grim, colonial penal settlement, and had asked many questions of their guide; she had commented on the memorial plaque, placed there in memory of the visitors massacred in a senseless killing spree some years before, by a mentally deranged man. But she was not unhappy when the tour ended; she felt the atmosphere was psychically challenging.

"Poor souls," she murmured, dabbing at her eyes as Jeremy drove them away. "And to think that some lunatic could smuggle a weapon into there and kill all those tourists. It's the *bairns* I feel for, Elizabeth, such a senseless waste of their poor, wee lives."

Beth had been unable to reply, throat tight, and could only nod in agreement; like Shona, she had been terribly affected by the prison, feeling that abject misery oozed from the stones themselves. Back in Hobart, Jeremy had escorted the older ladies to the ferry, where they had taken a short cruise up the Derwent, taking in the sights. The icy wind and spray had blown away the gloom, and had uplifted their spirits; the late autumn sun had smiled its blessing on them, so that they were able to go out later that evening in a much more positive frame of mind. They had an excellent meal, but their enjoyment was tinged with sadness; Shona would be leaving the next morning and life would resume its rhythm, weighed down by the loss of Dougal.

***

At the airport on Thursday morning, Beth, Jeremy, and Shona made small talk; there was little left to say.

Shona promised to stay in touch with them both, and to make the necessary bookings for a trip to Orkney when Dougal's ashes were released from the crematorium. Beth had confided her intention to travel with those ashes to Scotland, to fulfil Dougal's final wishes; Jeremy had, rather surprisingly, announced that he would accompany his stepmother. And there the matter had rested. Finally the flight was called, and Shona stood, carry-on baggage in her hand. Little was left to say, except *goodbye*. Shona had hugged Beth and Jeremy, whispering in Jeremy's ear before she stepped back from their embrace, then disappeared through the doorway of the Departures lounge.

Jeremy drove Beth home, then excused himself, saying he had matters to attend to; suddenly the house was *empty*. Beth went to make a pot of coffee. The sight of the two rinsed cups upside down in the dish drainer hit her hard, and she buckled at the knees; she staggered to her favourite chair, wrapped herself up in her rug, and broke her heart. Her old life had finally collapsed around her and she realised that she was, now and forever more, alone. Bitter tears streamed down her cheeks, unchecked, and dripped onto the rug.

She sat motionless for so long she was stiff in the knees when she finally stood up. This was so much worse than all the times when Dougal had gone away; *he* was never coming back, his sister had filled the house for a short space of time and now *she* was gone, and Jeremy was behaving a little strangely. He had refused to come in for coffee, had been silent on the drive from the airport, and hadn't given her any indications when he would see her again. She felt abandoned, and that abandonment both saddened and unreasonably angered her.

What is there to stay here for? What will become of me? Who can I turn to?

Not for the first time, Beth rued the lack of a close friend in Hobart; she had always been a private person, and while she got on well with her colleagues and enjoyed their company, there was no one at the museum, or even at the university whom she could count as a close friend. No, she was alone with her grief, and it was threatening to suck her under.

Beth gave herself a mental head slap, made a pot of coffee, and sat down at her laptop to answer the emails that had arrived during the course of the previous week.

***

Beth felt abandoned, raw, and vulnerable, locked in her grief. She returned to work the following week, and deliberately pushed herself to the limit. She worked long hours at the museum, plunging herself into the huge backlog of requests, emails, letters, and the sheer volume of artefacts awaiting attention, that had crept in a slow avalanche onto her desk in the cold basement. She had little time for personal thoughts, and, although she was aware that her colleagues were concerned for her mental state, she was relentless in her labours. She arrived early in the morning and didn't go home to literally fall into bed until quite late in the evening. She lost weight, didn't eat much, and was on autopilot for much of that time; her thoughts, given the chance, would skitter around like a mouse, and she was petrified of losing control. Even the usually pleasant drive to the city each morning became an ordeal to be suffered.

Dougal's death had been a cruel blow, but in the time that had passed, life had been even more gruelling. She was still no closer to discovering what exactly *had* happened to her husband, as the coroner's office was piled high with cases and the police were giving nothing away; she had discovered Dougal's closest-held secrets, and that had shaken her world to its core. Jeremy had all but disappeared from her life, and her world had collapsed inwards until there was only the trinity of work, sleep, and a half tumbler of Scotch every night to assuage her heart's anguish. More than that she could not cope with, at present. The ghosts had to be kept at bay, and she found some solace and amnesia in the smoky amber fluid she downed each night before the nightmares arrived to claim her. She could not remember ever having been brought so low; the underpinnings of her ordered, stable life had been hammered away in a series of pitiless blows.

***

One particular email was a welcome distraction for Beth when it popped up in her inbox a couple of weeks later. She hadn't seen or heard from Jeremy since Shona had caught the flight to Melbourne on her way back to Scotland. It felt like months had passed. She had heard from Shona back in Edinburgh, but from Jeremy and Carrie there had been nothing but a deafening silence.

Beth opened the email and navigated her way through a maze of drop-down boxes and prompts until she arrived at the communication she had been awaiting; she trawled through the material and advertisements, arriving at the lay-out of information. In front of her was a map of the world, with coloured ellipses and circles, many overlapping. She eagerly scrolled down through to the legend on the side; there was her ancient DNA, spread out before her. She marvelled at the breadth of the distribution of her genetic heritage; in many ways she was not surprised to see the overlapping shapes spanning much of the northern Asiatic continent as well as her own country, following the line of the tundra and cold deserts across which her ancestors would have migrated in eons past. She wasn't really surprised, either, by the shapes overlaying the European continent. Her father, after all, had been of French origin before his family had themselves migrated to Canada generations back.

She stared, fascinated, at the colourful display before her eyes, before scanning the page to the site's suggestions on how to join other people who may have been connected to her DNA through their own. There was even a list of possible cousins; she scanned quickly down the list, noting each one's lineage and connection, then stopped abruptly. There was a significant entry; Jeremy Munroe, listed as a possible third or fourth cousin. She released the breath she hadn't even realised she was holding in, and slumped back in her chair, unable to take her eyes from the screen, suddenly aware of the tension that had been gripping her entire body. So, it was true. Jeremy *was* somehow related to her. She scanned the evidence before her, reading and rereading the words. Then she sighed in frustration and sat straight again. There was no mention of *how* he was related; that would be all her own supposition. Beth tapped a pencil thoughtfully against her teeth as she considered her next move. She wasn't fully satisfied; the results were too vague.

Another email from the same site caught her attention and she opened that one quickly; it was the results of Jeremy's DNA test. She had sent the same email address for both tests, so she could look at his ancestry without qualms, possibly without his ever knowing she had peeked. His spread of amorphous shapes was almost the same as Beth's, with the legend on the side giving the percentages of ancient DNA connected to various countries, and the two were very similar. Without becoming too excited by this, Beth scrolled back into her own test results, and read the pie graph once more. Splitting the screen, she was able to look at both tests, side by side; the similarities were amazing, but his circles also extended into Scandinavia and the Scottish part of Britain. Scrolling down to view his possible connections, she noticed her name mentioned, plus other, unknown people whose DNA indicated that they could be far-removed cousins. She decided that neither of the DNA tests were conclusive enough for her to telephone her stepson with the news, but she really wanted to speak to him. She picked up her mobile, letting her finger hover above his number, before deciding against making contact.

There has to be another way around this. It's too nebulous for conclusive proof. If only…

Resolutely, Beth closed the emails, bookmarked them so she could retrieve them without difficulty, pocketed her phone and returned to work. While her surface attention was dealing with her workload, Beth's subconscious was hard at work.

***

Late that evening, curiosity overcame Beth as she picked up her mobile phone once more and dialled Jeremy's number before she could change her mind. She needn't have worried about speaking to the young man; his message bank picked up her call almost immediately and she heard his recorded voice, *"Hey, you've reached Jeremy Munroe. Sorry I can't take your call right now. Leave me a message and I'll get back to you… Bye."*

Taking a deep breath and aiming for a calm, bright tone, Beth spoke into the phone. "Hey, Jeremy, it's Beth. Thought you might like to know I have the results of the DNA tests we did. Call me when you get a chance? Thanks, honey." She disconnected the call, leaned back into her chair, and took a long, deep swallow of the last of the Scotch in her tumbler. She couldn't quite decide whether to be relieved or disappointed by leaving a message, but the sense of loneliness bit even deeper into her soul, and her tears mingled with the few remaining droplets in the bottom of her glass. As she gazed through the bare windows into the clouded emptiness of the night sky, she realised she needed to get a grip on her life; she was losing the fight and the lure of oblivion was seductive. Purposefully, she put away the bottle and took herself to bed.

***

Some days later, she had still not heard anything from Jeremy; she was a little concerned but was still too full of her own grief to exert herself overly much to contact him again. Instead, she picked up her mobile and dialled the funeral home; surely by now Dougal's ashes would be ready?

"Truman Family Funerals, this is Vanessa. How may I assist you?"

"Good morning, Vanessa, this is Elizabeth Bouchier, I mean Elizabeth Ferguson. I'm calling to enquire when my husband's ashes might be ready for collection?"

The young woman's voice was suddenly guarded. "Oh, good morning, Mrs Ferguson. No, they aren't, as we've had a bit of a backlog, but they should be ready in around three weeks or so. How about I let you know when they are available?"

Beth was a little taken aback by the receptionist's slightly awkward tone but agreed to a follow-up phone call. She was a little puzzled, then reminded herself that Dougal's was not the only funeral they would have had to organise, and the solicitude perhaps only extended to current clients. Nevertheless, she was a little peeved that even the formerly friendly young woman had adopted a distant, business-like tone. She sighed at her self-pity, shook her head, and checked the phone for messages. Nothing. Total silence from Jeremy, nothing from Carrie. It was as though the world was avoiding Beth Ferguson…

She chided herself for being a self-indulgent *needy* woman, straightened her back and picked up her mobile phone.

"My name is Elizabeth, and I'm terrified I'm becoming an alcoholic. Help me please?" she pleaded with the message bank, gave her number, and disconnected.

Chapter
thirty

"Ah, hey, Beth?" came Jeremy's voice late one Friday afternoon, two weeks after Beth had left him the message.

"Hey, honey!" Beth exclaimed, relief flooding her voice. "How are you?"

"Erm, I've been better, but I'm coming good now."

"Why?" she exclaimed. "What's happened? Where have you been, and what have you been up to? I haven't heard from you for simply *ages!*"

"Yeah, sorry for that. I had some stuff I had to sort out, and.... Look, Beth, I'm real sorry I haven't been in touch, but I've been away, over on the West Coast, doing some field work."

"That's okay, lad, you're home now. What were you doing over there?"

"Actually, I'm still on the West Coast. Ah, I've been in hospital."

"*What?*" The instant panic showed through her strained voice, and she coughed to compose herself before continuing. "What's happened? Why were you in hospital? Where are you? Can you tell me?"

"Um, I sort of got into a fight with some fishermen over at Macquarie Harbour, and I got a broken collarbone, so I haven't been able to drive for a while, and the doctors wanted me to stay until it healed a little, so I've been stuck here. Didn't Carrie let you know?"

"No, sweetie, I haven't heard a thing from either of you since Shona left." Beth's tone was slightly brusque and petulant, and her voice cracked on the last few words, but she hurried on, "When are you coming home? Is there anything I can do? Is Carrie going over to get you?"

Jeremy chuckled ruefully, hearing the note of stress in his stepmother's tone. "I should be back in Hobart by next week. I'll get Carrie to bring me over to visit. I can't drive at the moment. It's been a bit of a nuisance, actually. I'm so sorry I haven't been in touch. I had a lot of things to think about, and…." He left the sentence unfinished, unsure as to how to explain to Beth the conflicting emotions he had felt since the revelations about his parentage, along with losing the father he had never known, and the secret he shared with his aunt.

"It's okay, honey," Beth soothed. "Now that I know you're okay, I'll stop feeling sorry for myself. I thought I had lost you, too."

"Oh Beth!" Jeremy exclaimed. "Beth, I'm so sorry. I didn't even think…."

"How could you know, lad?" Beth replied gently, mollified by his regretful tone. "I guess Dougal's death hit me harder than I realised. It brought up a lot of unhappy memories, and it's taken me a while to deal with them, but I'm seeing a counsellor now, and things are sorting themselves out, gradually. I guess I feel a little more resigned to my life than I did a few weeks ago."

Beth didn't mention her nightly battle with the bottle, nor the darkest of thoughts that had flooded her mind, despite trying to blot them out with alcohol and hard work. She put a smile into her voice and reflected that she loved and relied on this young man who had been thrust so unexpectedly into her life, perhaps a little too much.

"Anyway, lad," she continued more briskly, "it will be good to see you both when you get back to Hobart. I've missed you." She left those words hang in the air, while a strange silence echoed through the line. "Hello?" she exclaimed. "Hello? Jeremy?"

The young man's voice was weary as he answered. "Um, I've missed you, too, Beth. But I had some stuff to do, and it seemed better to just go and do it, rather than sitting around, feeling sorry for myself."

Beth released her breath with a slight *whoof.*

Have I been sitting around feeling sorry for myself? Have I driven these kids away with my own woes? Crap!

"Probably the best idea, lad. I've been keeping fairly busy myself, at work. Are you feeling any better now?" She could have bitten her tongue off as those words slid out, unintended. Some things you do *not* say to someone in the abyss of heartache. She could have kicked herself, but Jeremy's voice came back, clearly.

"Yes, I guess I'm more resigned to everything now, too. I'm really sorry for running off and deserting you like that. I guess I couldn't face your misery too, after Aunt Shona flew home. Have you heard from her?" he enquired, changing the subject.

"Yes, lad, she phoned to say she was safely back in Edinburgh. She was sorry she had to leave, too, and she said she had really loved meeting you, and that she's looking forward to seeing you if you come with me when I go to scatter Dougal's ashes."

"Oh! Have you heard from the funeral home yet?"

"I phoned Vanessa last week. I must say I thought she was a little off hand about it, but she said there was a backlog, and she'd phone me when the ashes were ready. I guess she's paid to be kind and concerned, but she almost seemed wary of talking to me as if there was something she wanted to say." Beth shrugged, forgetting he couldn't see her. "Anyway, probably I'm reading too much into something that doesn't exist, but she was very business-like and brisk. My fault. I guess I thought she would be the same as I remembered her." Beth's head was beginning to ache, and she started thinking about dinner.

"Uh, yeah, I guess," came the answer, his voice suddenly guarded. "Uh, Beth, did she *say* anything?"

"What? No, lad, she only said that she would call when Dougal's ashes were ready for collection. Why?"

"Uh, no reason, I guess. Well, gotta go. Talk to you soon, okay? Look after yourself, Beth."

"You too, honey. See you soon," she said, but the phone had already disconnected at the other end. Beth looked at the phone, shook her head, puzzled. Just as she put it down, the phone rang again. She snatched it back up, quickly looked at the number and saw that it was the funeral home calling.

"Hello? Is that Mrs Ferguson? This is Vanessa at Truman Family Funerals calling."

"Oh, hello, dear, we were only talking about you a second ago."

"Oh! That must be why my ears were burning," said the young woman, laughing. Her voice suddenly became sombre and business-like. "Mrs Ferguson, I promised I would call when your husband's ashes were ready for collection. They've been processed now, and you can pick them up any time."

"Oh, good. I mean, not good, but at least now I can make the arrangements for their dispersal."

"I do understand, Mrs Ferguson. It's always a sad time when a loved one is taken from us, but this part of the process is another step along the way to recovering from our grief."

"Hmm, I guess. Anyway, Vanessa, remind me of your opening hours again, please, and what time do you close today?"

She noted down the times on a pad, thanked the receptionist and hung up. She glanced at her wristwatch and decided she probably had time to go out to North Hobart today, if she hurried. Calling out her goodbyes, and wishing her co-workers a good weekend, she grabbed her coat and bag from her locker, and scurried.

It was not long before closing time by the time she made it through the late afternoon traffic, and she was slightly out of breath as she hurried through the automatic doors. She stopped and caught her breath, before ringing the bell on the unattended reception desk. Vanessa appeared at the sound of the bell, and greeted Beth quite warmly. The two women made small talk while Vanessa shuffled the final paperwork around for Beth to sign, and found a pen in her desk drawer. She seemed a little preoccupied while she chattered away. Beth had almost tuned out the small talk when her attention snapped back into place at the words "…so sorry about the mix up at the funeral."

"Excuse me, but what did you say?" Beth asked quietly.

"Oh!" said Vanessa, "I was just saying that I'm so glad there was no problem about the oversight at the funeral. I guess your son will have told you about the coat getting mislaid or overlooked, and not going into your husband's coffin, as per your request…. Mrs Ferguson, are you okay?"

Beth had gone stone white; her rings bit into her fingers as her knuckles clenched at the edge of the service counter to hold her up. Her eyes looked suddenly huge in her ashen face, and she seemed to be having trouble breathing.

"Mrs Ferguson! Can I get you a glass of water? You look unwell. Would you like to come and have a seat? Mrs Ferguson?" The older woman had not moved a muscle, still clinging to the counter for dear life. Vanessa was about to call her father when Beth suddenly took a deep breath and fixed her with a fiery stare.

"What?!" Beth roared, sucking in huge juddering gouts of air. "What do you mean you didn't burn that goddamn coat? How dare you!"

"Mrs Ferguson, I'm *so* sorry! I just assumed your son would tell you about the coat getting mislaid… we didn't discover it in its bag until after the funeral… I spoke to your son, as I didn't want to upset you… he assured me it would all be okay… I'm so, so sorry." The young woman was on the verge of guilty tears as the office door opened, and Vince Holden stuck out his head.

"Ness, everything okay? I thought I heard shouting. Oh! Good afternoon… Mrs Ferguson, wasn't it?"

"Yes, Dad. She's had a very nasty shock, and I'm afraid it's all our fault. I have been explaining to her about the coat, and it appears she knew nothing about it." Vanessa and Beth were locked in eye-to-eye combat as the younger woman aimed her words over her shoulder to her father. Neither woman would blink; one was flushed with embarrassment, the other as pale as ice.

Beth had started trembling, a fine tremor of anger ran through her entire body as she clung to the counter with her whitened fists. Vincent Holden stepped towards his client, and diplomatically put a tentative hand to her shoulder; he spoke quietly and calmly.

"Mrs Ferguson, I understand you have had a very nasty shock, and one for which I can only apologise, along with my daughter. If you would like to come into my office, Vanessa will make us a nice cup of tea, or coffee, while you recover from your distress. All right? Would you like to come with me?" Vincent Holden was gently prising Beth's fingers from their strangle-hold on the counter and holding one arm out in the direction of his office. Beth seemed to snap out of her trance, broke her eye contact with Vanessa, who visibly wilted, and fixed the funeral director with her icy stare.

"No, thank you, Mr Holden, I don't think so, but thank you for the offer. I can see that this 'oversight' as you call it may mean little to you, but it was my husband's *last request*. I'm sure you can appreciate the depth of my feelings about this. As for my *son*, he was the *last* person who should ever have taken possession of that coat, but I guess you weren't to know that either. And now, if you don't mind, I'll collect my husband's ashes." Beth's voice had been remarkably calm and controlled throughout, but the anger was thrumming through her, and she just wanted to leave before she really lost her temper.

"A thousand apologies, Mrs Ferguson," grovelled the funeral director. "It was an honest mistake. If there's anything we can do for you, by way of compensation, please let me know. If you want the coat cremated, we could do it for a small fee."

Beth fixed him, basilisk-like, to the spot. "I. Don't. Think. So!"

Each word was a bullet. "For one thing, *you* no longer have the coat, and for another, neither *do I*! Thank you!" she snapped at Vanessa, who had brought the boxed remains in a stiffened black paper bag to the counter, and was offering them to Beth, who took them without even looking inside.

"I trust everything that is supposed to be here, is?" she enquired archly. "Except for the ashes of the coat, of course…. Good day to you both."

With that, Beth and bag departed through the automatic doors on a cloud of indignation, leaving Vanessa and her father to look at each other, slightly shell-shocked. Beth was beyond even thinking about them; just wait until she got her hands on Jeremy. He would wonder what had hit him!

***

The black bag sat on the mantelpiece in the formal lounge room; Beth had not looked at it since she had stormed home and flung it up there. She was still fuming; she didn't want to drown her sorrows in a bottle, so she changed her clothes and went for a long run in the chill evening drizzle. By the time she returned to her house, she was cold and wet, but had calmed down a lot; she had managed to burn most of her anger in the kilometres she had covered, and now she was totally spent. She took a long, hot shower, washed her hair, and climbed into pyjamas and sheepskin slippers, before cooking herself a meal.

She grimaced at the almost empty fridge; where had she *been* these past weeks? She resolved to buy at least fruit and vegetables the next day, then ransacked the freezer, discovering frozen meals from a couple of months before. She even caught herself humming a little tune as she pottered, heating her food. She almost felt normal; whether from the angry explosion or long, exhausting run, Beth had actually felt herself come alive again. Looking at the cold ashes in the combustion stove, she went to the wall and flipped a switch; the central heating would give instant heat tonight. She couldn't be bothered messing around cleaning the fire box.

***

Beth rose early Saturday, and scrubbed her house until it sparkled; *how could I have let it get into such a putrid state without even noticing?* Outside, she was appalled by the overgrown state of the garden; the roses had all blown and the dead flowers hung reproachfully on withered stalks. Weeds were thriving in the winter damp and the whole scene was one of total neglect. She fossicked in the laundry cupboard for implements of weed destruction; armed with secateurs, gloves, a weeding tub, and a kneeling mat, she commenced battle. Three hours later, she was spattered with clods of mud flung up by the wrenched-out weeds, punctured by thorns as she dead-headed and viciously pruned the rose bushes back; she was filthy, her back ached and her clothes were a mess, but Beth's face glowed with an inner satisfaction as she sat back on her heels and surveyed the scene. The tub was full of weeds and rose clippings, the ground was churned up, but at least she could now see the earth beneath and around her precious plants.

Where has my head been? How could it all have run away on me like this? I really need to pull myself together. Right! Time to clean up and go shopping. This is ridiculous, Bouchier! Get a grip!

She lugged the weed-filled tub into the garage and paused on her way back inside to admire her efforts.

***

Sunday, Beth decided to do a further investigation into the mystery of her DNA test results. She quickly retrieved the bookmarked site and started searching. She noticed a couple of emails had bounced into the site for her; the writers introduced themselves as distant cousins from France. Apparently, she was connected to these people through her father's mother's line. One, who had signed himself "Raoul" invited her to go into his family tree through a link, assuring her that she couldn't break anything by looking, but warning that she couldn't add any information either. She clicked on a link and found herself in a whole new world of family connections.

There was her father's name, linked back to his parents and beyond, all through the female line. She wondered, for a second why there was little information about her paternal grandfather's line, specifically, then smacked herself on the head; she would only have the mitochondrial DNA, no Y chromosome for her father's lineage, of course! Peering at the confusing web of names and relationships, she realised that she had *cousins!* For Beth, the only child of an only child, lacking aunts, uncles, and cousins, this was heady stuff!

She wrote Raoul an email, thanking him for his contact and telling him how overjoyed she was to think she actually had *family,* no matter how far removed. She posed a question about how to start her own family tree, as far as she knew, having no idea how to even begin such a process on the site. She was still looking at the names and family ties, when an email pinged into her inbox. Raoul had replied! He explained how to proceed, advising her to use her maiden name. She quickly replied, to thank him for his help, and returned to the site.

She was ready to begin writing her own family history in the new technological age; she just needed the paper version from the locked box in her desk drawer. Beth was suddenly excited; she had found a new interest in her life, and strangely, the future didn't look quite so bleak.

Chapter

thirty-one

By the time Jeremy returned from the West Coast, his shoulder had almost healed. Carrie had collected him and had driven him home to Hobart. She went back to work, so Jeremy, left to his own devices, picked up his mobile and rang Beth. He reassured her that he was fine, that his wound had nearly healed, and that he'd just returned home. Beth sounded very pleased to hear from him, and they chatted, eventually making a dinner date very soon.

It was another week before Jeremy was able to drive to Beth's for dinner. Beth's initial fury over the coat had abated as she delved deeper in the fascinating story of her family tree, and made further contact with distant French cousins, but she still caught herself grinding her teeth occasionally when she thought of Vanessa at the funeral home.

She had cooked a hearty winter casserole, designed to satisfy even the hungriest of young men, that night. She hummed softly to herself as she got the table ready for her visitor. He arrived promptly, offering her flowers and a kiss on the cheek. She hugged him carefully, so as not to aggravate his shoulder, and looked at him; he was thinner, as if he had not been eating properly. For a moment she felt very tender towards him, then remembered Vanessa's words, and her anger flared momentarily. She helped him off with his jacket; his shoulder obviously still bothered him, and he seemed grateful for assistance. He turned and put his hands on her shoulders.

"You've lost a lot of weight, Beth. Are you okay?" Jeremy asked, holding her at arm's length.

"I've been very busy, lad, and I guess I haven't felt a lot like cooking. And you? You've lost weight too, I'd say. Come away through. It's warmer out back. I've lit the fire. The weather's so lousy I needed the comfort of an old-fashioned crackling blaze. Dinner's ready. Hungry?"

"Starved! The hospital was okay, but the meals were, well you know, hospital food...."

"Yeah, I know what you mean. Come on, let's eat. Sit down and be comfortable. Would you like me to serve? I wasn't sure how much use you'd have of your arm, so it's pretty well all cut up."

"It sure smells wonderful, Beth. Yes, please, if you could serve me out a portion?"

"No worries. Here you go. Get that inside you, lad."

They ate in silence; the only sounds were the occasional clink of cutlery against china. When he finally pushed his bowl away after two helpings of the casserole, he leant back and patted his stomach.

"That was absolutely wonderful. Thank you!" He eyed her bowl, still half-full. "You haven't eaten much, Beth. Are you sure you're okay?"

"Well enough, thanks. I've had little appetite recently. But I'm glad you enjoyed it." She offered dessert, which he refused with a rueful groan.

"Couldn't fit in another thing at present but thank you."

"Come sit in an easy chair. I'll make coffee."

Beth started the coffee machine and joined her stepson in the family room. "Now, while the coffee's brewing, tell me what happened, lad. I've been on tenterhooks since your phone call."

Jeremy cleared his throat and began his tale.

"Well, I went across to Macquarie Harbour on the West Coast. There's an enormous salmon farming operation going on there, and I've been reading about the pollution it's been causing in the harbour. Last year, there was an outbreak of disease in the pens, and the government was accused of giving in to the operators by the environmentalists. You must have heard about it? It was on the news and in the papers." Beth nodded, so he continued, "Well, because of the dissolved oxygen levels dropping and the ammonia and nitrate levels increasing, the whole biological system was considered stressed. And the summer's heat affected the dissolved oxygen levels too. There were too many dorvilleid worms in the area — they feed on fish faeces, and they're a really good indicator of pollution."

"Kind of like the canary in the coal mine!" interrupted Beth.

Jeremy nodded. "Anyway," he continued, "the operators announced they were increasing the stock levels, and they refused to accept that anyone else had the right to monitor fish health. The EPA stepped in recently as the regulators of the industry, because the whole operation was on the decline."

"But what possible interest could this be to you, Jeremy? You research seals and other pinnipeds, don't you?" Beth was now alert, a sixth sense prickling at the back of her mind.

"The salmon industry isn't my field, but the seals have become a problem in the harbour, because they're attracted by a plentiful supply of fish, and they're hungry this time of year. Anyhow, the fishermen outside the fish pens, both in the harbour mouth and in the ocean have been complaining about the quantity of seals hanging around and snatching fish from their nets. They've been trying to relocate them away to the north, but they've been a little heavy-handed in their handling of the seals, and some have been injured. Some of the fishermen have been bitten too, so I figure they're out for vengeance."

Beth's sixth sense was definitely awake now. "So… how did you manage to get yourself injured, lad? Not doing anything silly, I hope?" she asked, archly.

Jeremy had the good grace to look sheepish and lowered his eyes. "Um, well," he said slowly, "I kind of had a disagreement with them, I guess, about the way they were handling the situation, and one of them hit me with an oar." He ignored his stepmother's sudden intake of breath. "Caught me on the point of the collarbone and put me out of action. Must have passed out, and next thing I knew, I was in the little hospital in town, strapped up and in a lot of pain." He sat back and smiled warmly at Beth, who was gazing steadily at him. "But I'm here now, Beth, and everything's okay."

Beth gave him a strange look and fetched two steaming mugs of coffee. Jeremy broke the silence.

"So, what did Vanessa have to say for herself, then?"

Beth nearly choked on her drink, recovered, swallowed, and put down her mug. She turned so she was facing Jeremy directly and looked him straight in the eye.

"Actually, she was most informative. I collected my Dougal's ashes and brought them home, but apparently there was a mix-up on the day of the funeral, or the day before, perhaps, and somehow his coat was misplaced and overlooked, so it didn't go into the furnace with him as he had requested in his letter. Naturally, I asked for the coat, and she told me she had given it to you when she discovered the error." She let her words hang heavily between them. He jumped in, to break the accusatory silence.

"Um, yes, she did, but she asked me not to say anything to upset you. She knew she had made a huge blunder, and she was *embarrassed.*"

Beth's voice grew soft and deadly cold. "And when, exactly, were you figuring on telling me all of this?"

Jeremy flinched at the accusation in her voice. "Ah, I guess I wasn't…." His eyes dropped to examine his feet.

Beth stood up and approached him. She put two fingers lightly on either side of his face and tilted it up so he couldn't avoid her eyes. She spoke in an icy, measured tone; Jeremy was suddenly afraid of her; she seemed to swell in size, illuminated by the flickering fire light behind her. A race memory awoke from the depths of his unconscious mind, a memory of magic and shamans and blood. He tried to shake away the image, but his face was held fast in an iron grip. Beth's eyes glittered dangerously; he was mesmerized by their depths. Her voice had diminished almost to a whisper, but her words pierced him like a stiletto as she hissed, "Do you have any idea how absolutely *furious* I am with you? Do you have any idea how *betrayed* I feel? Do you have *any idea*, any idea *at all*?" She abruptly released her hold, and the spell was broken.

Jeremy sat back, still stunned; the towering figure had receded, shrinking down to the small woman who stood before him. He felt an enormous wave of guilt pass through him.

"Uh, sorry, Beth. I don't know what to say…. I figured you'd never find out… I figured you'd be spared the stress… I didn't realise that she would say anything…." He was sobbing now, lungs heaving for breath. "I'm just so sorry…." He shrugged in an age-old gesture of defeat.

"I felt such a fool, out there at the funeral home!" Beth's voice rose as her anger washed through her once more. "They offered to do a separate cremation of the coat, but I didn't know where it was! How could I? I felt like an idiot." She paused to drag in a deep breath. "So, what did you do with it, Jeremy? Where's the coat now? I need it back. I need it to be gone!" Anger was tinged with panic. "It's an evil thing, Jeremy. You need to give it back!"

Jeremy stood up. "No," he said flatly. "No, it's not evil. It's really cool, and it fits real good."

Beth recoiled from him in gathering horror. "No!" she shouted.

"No! You'll end up dead like your father —" She stopped abruptly, fist flying to her open mouth as she stared at him, wide-eyed. "No," she whispered, desperately. "No, you mustn't, Jeremy. Please…"

"Sorry, Beth, as I said, it fits real good. It feels so *cool*, to be able to swim with the seals as one of them. No. No, I'm not giving it back. You didn't want it. You didn't even *like* it! The prof told me you were always on at him to replace it. You had *no idea*, did you!" He was red-faced, shouting, and angry now, anger fuelled by his guilt.

"Listen to me, young man! My husband's explicit wish was for that coat to be cremated with his body." She paused; an unwelcome thought had lodged in her head. "And who told you about what the coat means, *anyway*? I certainly didn't! I only let you see the part of the letter that revealed Dougal's relationship to you. How did you find out? Did you help yourself to my personal property?" Beth was angry again, filled with indignation and a feeling of *violation* as if she had been personally attacked.

"No, I didn't!" came the indignant reply. "I wouldn't *do* that. Someone else showed me, and now I know all about my father, and I think it's really *cool* that he was a shape shifter, no matter how *fantastic* it all sounds. And you know the thing I find most exciting, Beth? *I* can do it too! So, no! Sorry, but I'm keeping the coat."

They stood, glaring at each other, until Jeremy said quietly, "Could you help me on with my coat please, Beth? I probably should go."

"Sure, but tell me one thing. Were you human or… *otherwise* when you were injured?"

Jeremy laughed bitterly. "Oh no, I was very human, Beth. If I'd been *otherwise*, I would have been able to swim out of the way, I'm sure. Nothing much touches us when we're swimming free."

Beth helped him on with his jacket, said goodbye brusquely and closed the door on him. She was not at all sure she ever wanted to see his face again.

***

The following Monday, Beth made travel plans; she booked flights and told her colleagues she would be taking two or three weeks' leave from work, from Friday, to go to Scotland, to scatter her husband's ashes. One of her colleagues offered to collect the mail and water the garden, but Beth gracefully declined and made the arrangements at the post office to have her post held until her return.

She scrubbed and polished the house, even though she knew there would be a layer of dust everywhere when she returned; finally, she packed.

She was used to travelling light; she had perfected it over many years of travelling to far-flung places with Dougal, and one medium-sized suitcase was all she would need for the time away. Dougal's ashes fitted neatly into her small backpack, along with a book and a small Android device. She did not attempt to contact either Jeremy or Carrie, although she organised with the local constabulary to swing past the house occasionally on their regular patrols during her absence. Finally, she phoned Shona in Edinburgh, to let her know arrival times. Shona assured her she would be there at the airport to greet her.

"Bring warm clothes, Elizabeth dear, the weather's on the turn. Our summer's over, almost." Knowing how warm Scottish summers were not, Beth almost laughed aloud. She promised to bring a warm coat and some stout walking boots. If they wouldn't fit into her case, she could always wear them.

Chapter
thirty-two

Beth arrived in Edinburgh late on Saturday morning. Shona whisked her away to a small, well-appointed apartment in the heart of the city. Beth had not visited Shona for many years and was impressed by the location. From here she could walk into any part of Edinburgh's shopping and business precinct, and Beth promised herself a more leisurely visit to the city when she returned from the north. She welcomed a shower and change of clothes, after sitting in the same attire for an entire day. Her skin and hair were dried out from the constant air-conditioning, despite the moisturiser she had lathered onto her skin during the flights. She took her time in the shower, luxuriating in the warmth. Shona had prepared a meal, but Beth, after hours of airline food, had little appetite and apologised for not doing justice to the fare her sister-in-law had laid out before her.

"Och, think nothing of it, Elizabeth dear. I had the same problem not so long ago. Eat what you can, and the rest we'll have for supper."

Beth was reluctant to speak much of Jeremy, but Shona didn't seem curious about Beth being alone; she didn't press the point. When Beth admitted that she and Jeremy had quarrelled, Shona merely shrugged and said, "Och well, my dear, it'll be soon mended, I'm sure."

If Beth found this remark curious, she didn't pursue it. Instead, they spoke of local issues; the weather (always a topic of conversation in Scotland, it seemed), the proposed exit from the European Union by Great Britain and how it might affect Scotland, the renewed push for Scottish independence and what the future might hold, thanks to those in power in London.

Beth commented that she had been out of the news loop for many weeks, working all hours and not watching the television, or reading a newspaper; she realised with a slight jolt that life had been flowing on around her like a river around a rock while she had been trapped in the eddies of her own misery. She quizzed Shona at length about the latest news topics, finally admitting that she hadn't quite been herself since the funeral.

"It happens, my dear, but life goes on, as they say. They'll also tell you that time heals. I'm not so sure that it does, but time and the flow of everyday life swirls around you and in time, Dougal's passing may not hurt quite so much. Och, you'll always miss him, I know, but there will be times of happiness in your grief. I found that when Ruary passed on."

Beth barely remembered her late brother-in-law, who had left Shona a reasonably young widow, but she had never remarried, or even hinted at another romantic interest in her life, as far as Beth knew.

"I know, Shona. I guess it will get easier, but it's been very hard, especially after you left, and… and I have to admit I've probably not been the best company for those around me, recently."

"What would you like to do this afternoon, Elizabeth?" Shona asked, deftly changing the subject. "A nice walk, perhaps? We could walk into town and play tourist for an hour or two. Have you seen our Greyfriars Bobby, the wee dog whose statue is in the heart of Edinburgh? It's a quaint story, about a dog who showed loyalty to his dead master by sitting on his grave for years until the dog itself died. Och, it's a hoax, so the researchers now tell us, but we still love the statue of the wee beastie, just the same. He's a favourite with all the tourists, even if it's a lie. I never tire of seeing him on his pedestal. I think he represents love and loyalty, and that's no' such a bad thing in this harsh world of ours."

Beth blinked owlishly at her sister-in-law; she was in danger of falling asleep in her chair. She stood up.

"Good idea, Shona. If I sit here a moment longer, I think I will fall asleep, and then I'd be awake all night. Give me a minute to collect my handbag and I'm all yours."

The two women spent the rest of the day walking Edinburgh's CBD. They dodged squally showers, took photos, and found a coffee shop where they sat and laughed at other, more dogged souls out in the rain, photographing everything in sight. The women could hear the strident accents through the glass; Edinburgh attracted visitors from every corner of the planet.

By early evening, Beth could no longer keep her eyes open. She almost fell asleep in her supper, excused herself and retired to bed.

She was asleep almost before her head hit the pillow.

***

Next morning, Beth awoke to an empty apartment; Shona had left a note on the scrubbed pine table, along with the makings of breakfast. Beth made coffee, toast and jam, and took it all back to bed. She was drowsing fitfully again when she awoke fully to the sounds of voices emanating from the kitchen. She *knew* that male voice; she quickly dressed and quietly opened the bedroom door. Jeremy was seated at the kitchen table, sipping coffee while his aunt was cooking his breakfast. Beth quickly closed the door again, heart pounding.

What is he doing here? She thought back to Shona's enigmatic comment the previous day about things resolving themselves. Beth was smelling a tall, white-haired rat here, and she wasn't pleased at being set up. Silently she cursed at having given Shona a copy of her itinerary the previous afternoon. She quickly repacked her small case, stood it at the foot of her bed with her backpack, coat and handbag and went to confront her stepson.

"Hello, Jeremy, what are you doing here?"

Jeremy almost choked on his food; he managed to swallow before trusting himself to speak.

"Ah, hmm, hi, Beth. I just got in this morning. Didn't Shona tell you I was on my way?"

Beth glared across her stepson's head at Shona. "No," she said angrily. "No, she did not! And I'll ask you again, what are you doing here in Edinburgh, Jeremy?"

"I've come to visit with my auntie!" came the saucy, jaunty reply. He looked up at Beth and grinned. "And I've come to help you scatter my father's ashes on Orkney. You promised I could before Shona left Hobart."

Beth took a step towards the young man, brown eyes almost black with anger. Her hands were curling into fists, and she badly wanted to hit him, just to wipe that complacent smile off his face. She took a deep breath, loosened her fists, and replied smoothly, "That won't be possible, I'm afraid. I've decided to go alone."

"Oh Elizabeth!" Shona protested. "You canna stop the laddie… He's set his heart on it."

Beth stared coldly into Shona's eyes. "I can, and I will, thank you very much, Shona. It's really no business of yours. And…" she continued, "while we're speaking of other people's business, how did

Jeremy find out about that wretched coat, hmm? *I* certainly didn't tell him. *He* swears he didn't steal the letter from the top drawer of the bureau. So, I guess that just leaves *you*, Shona. You're the only other person who knew where I had put it for safe keeping. So, when did you two get together for your little pow-wow? And why keep it such a deep, dark secret from me? Don't you think I had a right to know that the coat still existed?" Beth's voice had risen to a shout.

"It's his birthright, lass," Shona stated coldly. "It's about family and birthright."

"Dougal didn't even want the boy to know he was his son! Don't talk to me about family! Your brother obviously was prepared for Jeremy never to know that he even had a father who cared. How fair was that to his son? You were a guest in my house, Shona. How could you *do* such a deceitful, underhanded thing?"

"And you're a guest in *my* home, Elizabeth. I dare say the neighbours won't be taking too kindly to your shouting."

Beth snapped. "Well, I shan't stay and drag down the tone of the neighbourhood for one more minute, Shona. I'll collect my things and be on my way." She moved quickly into the bedroom, picked up her suitcase, backpack and handbag, and headed for the door. "Thank you for your hospitality, Shona," she said politely. "I'm sorry it had to end this way. Goodbye. Goodbye, Jeremy."

She opened the door, but Jeremy had bolted out of his chair to stand in front of her to bar her exit. She looked up at him coldly.

"Get out of my way, please, Jeremy. I do not wish to hurt you."

The young man laughed at her threat. "Wait!" he shouted. "If you'll just wait, I'll come with you."

"No thank you, lad" Beth replied softly, but firmly. "I'll go alone. Enjoy your visit with your auntie — I'm sure she'll be pleased to show you the sights of Edinburgh. Now, please step away from the door, Jeremy, I mean it."

Jeremy caught at her arm, but she shrugged his hand brusquely away and stepped out into the hall, closing the door quietly behind her. As she walked to the elevators, she could hear raised voices coming from behind the closed door. She shrugged; what her sister-in-law did with Jeremy, Beth no longer cared. She squared her shoulders and took the elevator down to the ground floor with her case, where she asked directions to the car hire firm she had booked from Hobart. Although it was only a ten-minute walk away, Beth hailed a cab and was soon signing the paperwork for her hire car. After consulting maps, and listening to two people's different directions, she was on her way out of town, heading north.

Chapter
thirty-three

Westray, Orkney, September

Beth burrowed her face into her windproof jacket as she slogged along the short distance from the Loup Head lighthouse to the edge of the cliff top. The only blessing about the force nine gale howling at her was that it kept the tiny biting insects at bay, at least on the windward side. Jeremy pounded along the grassy plateau alongside her, clutching a small cardboard box in his hand. They were liberally smothered in insect repellent, on every exposed part of their bodies, but the midgies, as Shona called the minuscule tormentors, almost seemed to relish the scent of citronella.

They'd had to leave the ancient Land Rover at the lighthouse and walk the last few yards; but the view was spectacular. The afternoon sun was in their eyes as Beth stood on tiptoe and screamed into Jeremy's ear; he shook his head — he couldn't hear a thing. Beth shook his arm and pointed away to the west. It was one of those gloriously deceptive early autumn days, full of sunshine and hope, but with teeth of ice in the wind. Jeremy nodded and followed the line of her outstretched fingers; in the distance he could just discern the smoky outline on the horizon that was the sea stack known as Sule Skerry. She dug into her rucksack and handed him a pair of binoculars; the hazy apparition suddenly became clear. The sea stack was obviously of a decent size to be visible from so far away. Beth was shouting again but the wind stole three words in four and she had to resort to mime.

In her frustration, Beth was dancing around like a demented toddler, tugging at Jeremy's sleeve. She pointed at the box under Jeremy's arm, mimed throwing the contents into the wind, mimed choking and brushing at herself as the ashes would come straight back into their faces, and finally pointed down towards the sea. She was pulling him away from the cliff face and pointing energetically at the lighthouse; he was almost doubled up in laughter at her antics. She carefully walked her fingers along her sleeve, then pointed at the break in the tough grass, and beckoned to Jeremy to follow her. He caught her meaning and complied.

Under the lee of the silent sentinel, although the wind was still blowing into their faces, it was a little easier to talk and be heard.

"If we scatter Dougal's ashes from up there," Beth shouted, "we'll end up wearing him!"

Jeremy was forced to bend down to catch her words. He grinned at her and yelled back, "Good point, Beth, do you have another option?"

She grinned back and nodded. "Come on, lad, let's go. Did you see Sule Skerry, way out there to the west?"

Jeremy nodded. "Yeah, is that the same place as in the song?"

"Yes. Come on, laddie, before these midges leave nothing but bones behind. Let's get back to the car."

They turned on the cliff top for one last look before they sought a more sheltered spot; Beth suggested the ashes should be scattered onto the ebbing tide. Suddenly, Jeremy clutched Beth's arm and pointed down; she gasped when she spotted the familiar shapes. Below them was a pod of orcas making its way past this north-west point, travelling south.

Watching them closely through the binoculars Jeremy had thrust back into her hands as they passed, Beth could have sworn that the leader, a female leading her pod to warmer southern waters for the northern winter, looked up at her and *winked*. Beth heard the *whoosh* of the whale's breath on the wind as a plume of spray erupted from her blow hole; the eye then regarded Beth with a solemn, penetrating gaze. There was an indefinable message in that scrutiny; the woman stood transfixed, until the pod had gambolled its way around the point and out to sea. She could almost feel their urgency, to migrate before these waters became too cold, and the *joy* they would take in the journey.

Beth and Jeremy returned to their borrowed vehicle and found their way along a rutted track down the side of the promontory until they had left behind the sheer cliffs and were within walking distance of a shingle beach further south. The wind was less fierce down at sea level, but they would certainly wear the ashes if they tried to release them into the air. On the short journey down the bumpy track, Beth told Jeremy what she proposed; the tide was turning and would carry the ashes away to the west, as Dougal would have wanted, so they would carefully scatter his remains onto the water and let the tides take them home to Sule Skerry.

***

From Thurso, Beth had booked accommodation for herself for two nights at a farmhouse not far from Pierowall. After clearing Edinburgh's traffic, she'd driven as far north as she could go on the Scottish mainland, still smarting at the explosive interchange between herself, Jeremy, and Shona. She had taken the car on the overnight ferry from Thurso across to Stromness on Orkney's main island the previous day, and had driven out to see the Ring of Brodgar and Skara Brae before heading for Kirkwall in time to park up the car and take the last ferry to Rapness on Westray.

Beth had been in her element at Skara Brae, indulging her memories as she revisited the ancient site, humming almost happily as she drove across the island towards Kirkwall. She had decided to leave the car on the main island, so she could take the ferry, scatter Dougal's ashes on the tide, then fly back to Main Island to pick up the car before heading south again. She had been promised the loan of a four-wheel drive vehicle to take her out to the lighthouse the following day, and she knew there were regular buses to Pierowall from the ferry terminal at Rapness. She had contacted the owner of the farmhouse B & B and would be collected from the bus stop in the town.

After she had secured the car in the fenced-off area at the terminal, she thought she heard her name on the wind when she set off for the ferry but shook it off as fantasy; no one knew her here, not after so many years. She put her head down and walked towards the gangway, pulling her little case behind her, ticket in hand. As she neared the gangway, she heard her name called again; she looked up and stopped dead in her tracks. Jeremy was leaning against the bollard at the entrance. He looked quite white, very young and terribly vulnerable in that moment. He also looked incredibly guilty.

"Beth, I can explain!" he pleaded, taking a tentative step towards her. "Please! Please, will you listen to me? I *so* want to come with you to say goodbye to the professor, and I feel *wretched* that I've made you so unhappy.... Please, Beth?" There was a decided wheedle to his voice.

She glared at him, picked up her small suitcase and marched towards the gangway. "What are you doing here, Jeremy? I thought we had said quite enough to each other back in Edinburgh, you, and your aunt."

"Oh Beth! If only you knew! When you stormed out with your stuff, Shona and I had a terrible fight. She was so angry with me for not keeping you in the loop about the professor's coat, even though it was she who told me about it in the first place. She accused me of selfishness and being arrogant. She shouted at me that in Scotland, family is everything, and I had just destroyed my father's honour and memory with my actions, and told me I may look like him, but I wasn't a patch on him!" The young man sighed and shrugged wearily. "And you know something, Beth? She's right. I *am* selfish and arrogant.

"I thought I was having a really good laugh at both of you, and proving how clever I was, keeping the secret. And now it's all backfired. My aunt's so angry, she never wants to see me again, and *you* hate me, which leaves me with exactly no one to care about, except maybe for Carrie, and *she's* not talking to me, either! Says I'm a prize idiot, that I have to grow up and sort this mess out if I ever hope to marry her!" His young voice, normally so strong and sure, wavered on these words, and a tear of pure self-pity welled up in his eye.

"I've been waiting here for you since yesterday. I didn't want to miss you. Please?" he begged.

Beth stood and looked at him, unmoved; she could see the attendant at the top of the gangway gesturing to her. She held up a finger and smiled pleadingly; *one minute?* The attendant rolled his eyes and threw his hands in the air, tapped his wristwatch meaningfully, nodded briefly and started the preparations for pulling in the gangway so the ferry could depart.

She faced her stepson. "Look, lad, I *don't* hate you, for what it's worth. I'm pissed off with you, that's for sure, but I have a ferry to catch, and they aren't going to wait much longer. I already have accommodation booked for the next two nights, and I'm not losing my deposit. So, stay or come along as you choose, but I have to go! I have things to do, and I'm getting on that ferry!"

Jeremy picked up his backpack, slung it onto his shoulder, grinned at her and said, "Well, *Mom*, what are we waiting for? Let's go!" and bounded up the gangway.

Beth shook her head as she followed, muttering, "*You devious little shite*! Don't think I've forgiven you, no, not for one moment, Jeremy Munroe!"

***

They'd arrived on Westray in the morning and caught the local bus to Pierowall where the farmer's wife, Morag Campbell, had met them. Beth explained away Jeremy's presence, and asked if the lady had another room free. The middle-aged, solidly built and rosy-cheeked woman with the familiar sing-song Orkney lilt had agreed immediately, looking from one to the other, with the telling comment, "Aye, it's easy to tell you're mother and son!" She'd whisked them away out of town to the farm, where she showed them to Beth's room with an apology to Beth and a stern, but twinkling admonition to Jeremy.

"I'm sorry, young man, your room isn't quite ready, as we weren't expecting you. Put your luggage in here for now and I'll move it for you later."

Their hostess plied them with Westray Wife, a local unpasteurised cheese, her home-made chutney, and freshly baked oatcakes for lunch before giving directions so they could set out on their grim mission. The farmer had already agreed to lend Beth his battered old Land Rover for her afternoon adventure on the rough tracks, as he would be working close to the farmstead that day.

Beth had managed to find the lighthouse without too many wrong turns, and now they were *here*; neither of them spoke as Beth took the small, heavy box that had sat on Jeremy's lap for the drive, and cautiously opened the lid. She had borrowed a pair of scissors back at the farmhouse and cut open the hermetically sealed plastic bag holding Dougal's ashes. The wind picked up the top layer of ash in its mischievous fingers and flung it at the pair, which made them cough and splutter. Jeremy took the box, and squatted down on the beach, turning his back to the wind to shelter the contents as he pried the lid off fully. Walking backwards towards the water, he looked back at Beth, who nodded. He removed the lid a little more, turned and carefully sprinkled some of the contents onto the tide.

"Goodbye, Professor. I wish I could have known you sooner. I wish I'd known you as a father..." A soft voice suddenly whispered in his ear and a warm, gloved hand patted his shoulder.

"He knew who you were, Jeremy, and he loved you, I'm sure of it. I know he was very proud of you." Beth had joined him at the water's edge, and took back the box, tipping out the remaining ashes to join the others.

"Go in peace, Dougal love. Go home now and rest." Tears, partly from grief and partly the fault of the biting wind, sprang into her eyes and she felt them slide icily down her face as she watched the waves suck at the ashes and carry them out to sea.

Beth and Jeremy brushed the ashy layer from their clothes, closed the empty box and stood, gazing at the grey layer as it sat on even greyer seas like a slick, before breaking up and sinking.

"Come on, Beth, it's done. Time to go now. You're going to freeze out here."

"I'm stronger than I look, laddie." Beth smiled tremblingly through her tears, sniffed loudly, and wiped her face. She had found a handkerchief in her pocket and cleaned herself up as much as possible. She looked up at Jeremy, whose sudden hoot of laughter echoed around nearby cliffs and set seabirds screaming angrily when he saw her grimy face; he was overcome with tenderness for his little stepmother and felt genuine remorse for treating her so badly.

"Oh Beth," he spluttered, "you look like you're wearing war-paint!"

"Have you seen your own face, then, lad?" she countered, laughing, and feeling an instant release, like that of an over-wound clock spring, as tension drained from her body. The worst was over now; she had farewelled her husband, made tentative peace with his son and now she could get on with her life. As they stood there on the shingle beach, Jeremy shouted and pointed out to sea again.

"Look, Beth!" he shouted, sounding ridiculously young. "More orcas!" Her breath caught in the back of her throat at the childlike excitement in his voice; for one bizarre moment she heard Malcolm's piping toddler's voice in his half-brother's words. As she beheld the new pod, she felt strangely blessed, as if her clan's totem had come to salute her. A strange ripple of homesickness wound through her guts as she watched them pass.

Beth and Jeremy stood observing the pod as it made its way along, then turned resolutely back to the car.

Chapter
thirty-four

At supper that evening, Jeremy asked their hosts about the whales.

"Ay, lad, they migrate south each autumn to feed and breed. But it's unusual for them to be so far west. They usually go around the East Coast. Mind you," the farmer confided, "the waters here are warm enough, for all we're so far north. That's why we can farm and grow our cattle and crops. The Gulf Stream helps to regulate the climate. And there's an abundance of seals this season. Perhaps that's why the whales are following this route. Now, if you'd gone to Shetland—" The man devoured a large mouthful of cheese and oatcake. "--you'd not have the mild weather as we do here. That was lovely, mother." The old man belched softly and patted his stomach. "You've done us proud, as always." The farmer's wife smiled; her eyes twinkled in Beth's direction, eyebrows raised.

"Yes, thank you, it was truly delicious. And I love this cheese!" Beth exclaimed. "But I couldn't eat another thing right now."

"You'd be Americans, then?" enquired the farmer, Alasdair Campbell, unexpectedly.

"No, no, we're Canadian, my son and I," answered Beth quickly, glancing sideways at Jeremy who nodded, still munching. Where he put all that food into such a lean frame, she would never know. "We came to send his father's ashes home to Sule Skerry. Dougal was from Orkney, you see, and those were his wishes."

Alasdair looked up at them sharply under grey, beetling brows, piercing dark eyes giving nothing away, glanced meaningfully at his wife, and nodded silently. "Oh, aye…" he muttered.

"So…" his wife quickly broke the sudden silence, "have you any other plans while you're here on Westray?"

"Yes!" Beth exclaimed. "Yes, I believe there are some wonderful archaeological sites on this island, just as on the rest of Orkney. I remember visiting some on Main Island when I was here with my husband many years ago, but I'd never had the opportunity until now to visit the sites on Westray. Do you have any suggestions?"

Her question diffused the tense vibes she had been getting from the farmer since she mentioned the sea stacks away to the west, and the local couple were happy to chatter on about *their* sites of interest, with offers of maps and the loan of the battered Land Rover again.

Beth felt moved, but almost embarrassed by the couple's generosity, and said so, but the discussion ended with both Beth and Jeremy agreeing to borrow the ancient vehicle the following day, to do some sightseeing. The Westray Heritage Centre had artefacts, but would probably not be open to visitors this late in the season, nor Noltland Castle, located near Pierowall. Maps were unfolded, and the four of them leant in to sketch out a route for the visitors to take.

"Noltland Castle," said Jeremy. "I'm sure we passed it on our way to the coast this afternoon, Beth."

"Aye, lad, you would have. It's very famous," said Morag. "In 1560, Adam Bothwell granted the lands of Noltland to his brother-in-law, Gilbert Balfour, who built the castle. Balfour was Master of the Royal Household to Mary, Queen of Scots, you see, and was involved in the plot to kill her husband, Henry Stuart, Lord Darnley." Beth nodded as Morag spoke; the woman's passion for local history was obvious. "But he lost the lot when Mary was imprisoned, and the property was given away to someone else, then restored to the family much later. You know what these royals are like…. Anyhow, during the Wars of the Three Kingdoms in 1650, Royalist officers occupied the castle after their defeat at the Battle of Carbisdale. Local Covenanters captured and burned the castle. By 1881, it was described as a ruin, and was given into state care by the Balfour family in 1911. Historic Scotland maintains the ruin now. It's worth a look."

Beth looked at her hostess, amazed. "Wow!" she exclaimed. "You sure know a lot about the local history."

Morag blushed and smiled at Beth. "I was a schoolteacher before I married Alasdair and had to leave. Married women weren't allowed to continue teaching in those days, so I took up making cheese and chutney, and looking after our four children. I've always loved history. I can't get enough of it. The children are all grown and flown the nest now, so these days I volunteer at the Heritage Centre, where you're going tomorrow. I'm one of their guides."

Beth smiled. "Times sure have changed now. I'm still working, children or not." She smiled at Morag and turned slightly to wink at Jeremy. "I'm pretty interested in history, and pre-history, too. At present, I'm working at a university in Tasmania, Australia. I work with prehistoric artefacts, but from *their* indigenous culture. I'm sure glad you had room for us here, Morag, Alasdair. It's been so interesting talking with you about this. I wonder if we would have found out so much if we'd stayed elsewhere."

Morag positively twinkled under Beth's compliments and promised to look out more books and brochures for her. "Och!" she added, "If you're interested in looking at the dig, I'll see what I can arrange for you, you being in the business, so to speak. Leave it with me."

***

That night, snug in a floral wallpapered room at the top of the farmhouse, Beth listened to the wind howling across the flat landscape, around the stone building; she dozed and dreamed. She dreamt of tall, dark, whispering pines, and lakes the colour of a peat bog, where only the surface reflected back the blue skies of summer. From the pine forests came the howls of wolves, yipping and yodelling to the moon before a huge orca emerged from the lake, coming to rest in front of Beth, one eye fixing her in its gaze; there was a deep message in that all-seeing eye, a silent communication between two females of different species. Jeremy came running through the forest, clad in his father's black coat, heading for the lake as if to dive into its depths; Beth opened her mouth to warn him of the danger but had no voice. It hit her then; *orcas kill seals!* She was rooted to the spot in her dream as her body tossed and turned in the narrow single bed, transfixed by the eye of the whale. *Don't interfere with the boy*, came the unspoken message. *He is as he is. This is his journey, not yours. What will pass, will pass. It is his destiny alone. Leave him be, and return to your roots, daughter of the Orca.*

Beth woke with a start, gasping and reaching out for the glass of water she had placed on the bedside table. What a dream! That would teach her to eat so much cheese before bedtime! She lay in her bed, listening to the wind as it breathed heavily outside her window, and longed for home.

***

When she woke in the morning, the wind had died away a little, and Beth could smell the aroma of frying wafting up the stairs to her

305

nostrils; suddenly she was *ravenous!* She washed and dressed quickly and clattered down the stairs to the kitchen. Morag was busy at an Aga stove, deftly collecting and combining ingredients in a huge casserole dish, while watching the breakfast that had aroused Beth's hunger. She turned and smiled, then looked past Beth to greet Jeremy, who had been similarly woken and drawn to the kitchen.

"Well, good morning to you both! I hope you slept well? Breakfast won't be but a minute more. Do you take toast? And would you like tea or coffee with your breakfast? Or juice? We have both."

"Good morning, Morag. The food smells delicious! I'll have coffee, thanks, and a glass of juice to start with. Oh!" Beth turned as Jeremy tapped her on the shoulder. "Good morning, lad, did you sleep well?"

Jeremy bent and planted a filial peck on his stepmother's cheek before replying. "Yes, thank you, I did. Good morning, Morag, breakfast smells *good!*"

Morag smiled at his boyish enthusiasm and invited them to sit so she could serve their meal. Beth felt a little awkward about being waited on, but the farmer's wife had it all under control; glasses of juice, toast in a rack on the table, and two plates heaped high with freshly cooked eggs and crispy bacon. While they ate, Morag chatted to them about the morning's agenda.

"Alasdair's had to go away up to the cattle this morning, so he's taken the Land Rover and his dinner, but I'm free today, so I'll be your guide, if that would suit you?"

Beth quickly looked at Jeremy, then nodded. "That would be grand, thank you, Morag, but only if it's not inconveniencing you…"

"Och no, supper's almost in the pot, ready for the oven, and I'd be delighted to show you around. Your own personal guide, you might say. Give me thirty minutes or so, and we'll be away. There's plenty to show you."

On the way across to the Heritage Centre, Morag told them a little of the history of the place.

"If we go across to Noltland to see the ruins of the castle, I'll show you what's left of the dig site at the Links of Noltland. There were a lot of Neolithic and Bronze Age buildings discovered there but the sand dunes that protected them have been continually eroded and the site has been in danger of destruction. In our museum at the centre," she continued, "we are lucky enough to have the Westray

Wife—not the cheese, you understand," she added with a laugh, "but a tiny figurine. It's only four centimetres tall. They say it's the oldest carving of a human figure ever found in the British Isles. It came out of the dig at Noltland back in 2009. Since then, the archaeologists have found more artefacts and they're also in our museum at the centre." Morag spoke with passionate pride about her island.

"We also have the Westray Stone on display there," she continued, warming to her role as tour guide. "It's a Neolithic carved stone from a chamber tomb. In 2015, the diggers got very excited when they discovered a subterranean building dating from the Bronze Age. They think it may have been a sauna. Just imagine!" she exclaimed. "I'll take you over to Tuquoy and Quoygrew if we've time, if you're interested in the Viking history of Orkney. You are?" She smiled at Jeremy's and Beth's nods. "Excellent. We might manage Langskaill too, then. They're all interesting sites."

***

Between Morag's enthusiasm for the history and pre-history of Westray, and the tourists' desire to see everything they could, they were out for most of the day. Jeremy begged off the archaeology, saying instead he'd rather go hiking. Beth eyed his backpack suspiciously, and murmured quietly into his ear, "Going swimming, laddie? What do orcas eat? And you're still not forgiven, by the way, so watch your step. Don't get too cocky, buddy!"

Jeremy had the good grace to redden fiercely, hang his head and stammer out, "Touché, Beth! There's nothing in my pack except essentials like insect repellent, your binoculars and my phone, plus a wind-proof jacket. I didn't even bring it!" he whispered. "I figured it wouldn't have been a real smart move." Beth nodded.

Beth and Morag returned, tired but elated after a day spent amongst artefacts, dig sites and stunning scenery. They'd toured along the cliffs and stopped to watch countless thousands of seabirds wheeling, screeching, and jostling for roosting places along the cliffs on the east of the island. Beth had been able to recognise kittiwakes, puffins, and gulls, but she was ignorant about many more species that she had seen. Morag pointed out some, but without the field glasses it was impossible to identify the teeming hordes easily. Beth had asked her hostess if the bed and breakfast trade was brisk on Westray and asked what sorts of visitors they would have during the year. Morag confided that in spring and summer they accommodated walkers, birdwatchers, sightseers, and the occasional few archaeologists who opted to stay apart from the main group. She confided that some of the university students who came to dig often liked to party hard, and that some of the older members of the team preferred to able to sleep at night.

"Hard enough to sleep in the summer when it never gets truly dark," she remarked, "let alone being kept awake all night by rowdy, drunken teenagers."

Beth had smiled over some of Morag's pronouncements, but she had to concede the woman was a fount of local knowledge, and she considered herself lucky to have found such an accommodating and entertaining guide.

Jeremy had found his way back to the farm without mishap, none the worse for his adventures on the wild wind-battered terrain, apart from multiple insect bites; at supper that evening, Beth asked if one of their hosts could take them to the airport at Aikerness the following morning, or whether they should book a cab. Morag offered without hesitation, drawing from her husband a quiet smile.

After supper, pleading tiredness and the need to pack, they managed to escape to the relative quiet of the upstairs rooms. The wind had picked up during the day, and by evening it was howling a westerly gale again. Beth reflected that it was no wonder there were few, if any trees on Westray, given the severity of the wind rushing across the island twenty-four hours a day. She listened to the moaning wind lamenting outside her window again, but tonight it lulled her into a deep, dreamless sleep.

Chapter
thirty-five

Southern France

It took a dead vine leaf falling and kissing her hair to bring Beth back to her surroundings. Snatches of conversations ebbed and flowed around her, everyday lives under discussion... the harvest and the price the grapes would bring this year... the teething, grizzling baby, poor thing... the coming marriage between two families... a girl's secret admirer not so secret after all.... So many conversations in French, some so rapid-fire that at times Beth could not keep up.

She had chided herself more than once for allowing her father's language to wither with disuse, but as she relaxed with a glass of wine and let the babble flow over her, many words sprang from her memory, and she was able to follow, if hesitantly. Fortunately, no one assumed she could speak the language; all questions were addressed to her in English. Everyone seemed keen to practise the language! Beth was relieved; understanding and speaking were two very different creatures, and her rusty French conversational skills were almost non-existent.

As she shook her head to dislodge the leaf, a hand reached across the table to pluck it gently from her hair and lay it in front of her.

"You were, as they say, miles away, *n'est-ce pas*, Elizabeth?" A deep masculine voice anchored her abruptly into the reality of the *now*, and she looked up sharply at its owner. A pair of dark, twinkling brown eyes, set in a sun-tanned, square-jawed ruddy face, gently sculpted by age and the elements was regarding her solemnly, while a mouth, half-hidden beneath a luxuriant white moustache was twitching with amusement at her expression.

"I was thinking about the cave paintings at Pech Merle, and Lascaux and wondering how far away they are, and whether I could hire a car to go there tomorrow before I leave. I would hate to have come so far, only to go without having seen them. So yes, I guess I was miles away, Raoul. So much to think about, so many things have happened." She gestured at the long table, scattered with the detritus of a hearty meal. "So much kindness and generosity, so many people...." Her voice faltered, as, suddenly unsure, she looked around.

"Ah the family extended!" he proclaimed. "So good to have the family all together but" — he lowered his voice to a stage whisper — "so nice when they all go home, also!" he announced. Two pretty, dark-eyed girls sitting alongside him to his left giggled and poked him in the ribs.

"*Papi*! You say the most shocking things! Anyone would think you did not love having us home to lunch!" one laughed outright at him.

"It is true, Sandrine! You make your grandfather's head spin with all your chatter, chatter, chatter, like the magpies in the trees! I am always glad when you go home!" But he caught her around the shoulders with his free arm, and bestowed on her head a loud, whiskery kiss. Beth heard him whisper softly, "But I am always so glad when you come home to see me, *chérie*. And I am so proud of you!" He remarked across the table to Beth, "This one is my eldest granddaughter, Sandrine. She will be a fine doctor, I think. She is already at the university. I am a very blessed man." He squeezed the girl's shoulder then released her, smiling tenderly.

Beth didn't know what to say in the face of so much open affection; her own life had been so very different. She bent her head slightly, so the tears that had sprung into her eyes would not be noticed or remarked upon, or, worse still, misinterpreted. She picked up a crisp bread stick and twisted it around in her hands, crumbling it gently onto her empty plate.

"You are from *Australie, madame*?" a female voice enquired. Beth quickly looked up, hoping the tell-tale too-bright shine in her dark eyes wasn't too noticeable. The young woman sitting next to Sandrine was gazing at her, curiosity sketched across her open, heart-shaped face.

Beth cleared her throat. "I live in Australia, yes, but I'm not from there originally. I'm actually Canadian, although my husband and I have lived in many places around the world, wherever his research work and employment has taken us."

The girl's face clouded over. "But where is your husband now, *madame*? Could he not come with you today? Oh *madame!*" she exclaimed as Beth's face paled. "Have I said the wrong thing? Are you not well?"

"*Alors, Chantal, ça suffit!*" her grandfather growled. "That's enough!" he repeated. "You are embarrassing our guest with your impertinent questions. Go and help your mother make the coffee!" He made a shooing motion with his hands.

"But *Papi*," she wheedled. "Please?"

Beth intervened. She stretched a hand across the table, to lightly touch Raoul's. "It's really okay, she's just curious." She smiled brightly at the girl, who had subsided a little under the rebuke, but returned Beth's smile readily enough.

"My name is Elizabeth, Elizabeth Bouchier. I was born in Canada, on Vancouver Island. My father, Jacques, was of French descent, which is how it turns out I have cousins right here in France, through his mother's line. I've been living in Australia, in Tasmania, for the past ten years with my husband. He…er…died earlier this year, and I've just been to Orkney, north of Scotland," she added, in case the girl's geography was sketchy, "to scatter his ashes as he requested in his will. My stepson went with me," Beth added.

The girl's eyes had gone wide with the simple version of the tale and her eyes had filled with tears.

Oh no! thought Beth. *If she starts, I won't be able to stop!* She reached across the table with her other hand and touched the girl's. "Chantal, please don't cry. Because if you cry, I will too!" She smiled pleadingly at the teenager.

Their bright, tear-filled eyes locked across the table, then Chantal nodded at Beth, withdrew her hand, and reached for a handkerchief. Turning away from the table, the girl discreetly blew her nose and dabbed at her eyes.

Beth looked back to find Raoul gazing at her intently. She blinked slowly, deliberately, to swipe away her own tears, then looked again. The intensity of the look was still there, but there was a gentle smile beneath the white moustache. He reached out and clasped her hands.

"You are a very kind, very generous woman, *cousine* Elizabeth. I am so glad you decided to accept our invitation to visit. Thank you for your kindness to Chantal. She is young, and not very, how shall you say, *tactful*, at times."

"She is young, yes. And you are so lucky to have her." The tears were threatening again; she cleared her throat. "Would you excuse me, please, I have to visit the bathroom. Chantal?" The girl looked up. "Could you show me where the bathroom is, please, my dear? I seem to have forgotten already."

"Certainly, *madame*. This way."

"Excuse me for a moment, Raoul. No, no, please don't get up!" She held out a hand to stop him, but he was already on his feet. He smiled and held Beth's hand to help her negotiate the bench seat.

Thank God I wore trousers!

"Your stepson, *madame*, he is handsome, *non*?" Chantal asked, by way of conversation as she led the way. Beth laughed aloud. Behind her, heads turned in her direction at the sound of her laughter, then smiled at the reply she gave the young woman.

"Yes, he is very handsome, his name is Jeremy and he's on his way back to Australia right now. And Chantal? My name is Elizabeth. Okay?"

"Oh, Jérèmy. *C'est cool!*"

It was all Beth could do not to laugh aloud.

***

Evening brought more food, more wine, and candlelight. By then, most of the family had departed for their own homes; babies and toddlers needed their beds, the teenagers had ridden their bicycles down the winding driveway or taken a shortcut through the rows of vines. Tomorrow, the week would begin again, with school, university, and work: all the everyday chores. The quantity of food had decreased, but fresh dinnerware and full bottles appeared on the table. Beth knew she could not possibly eat another thing, after such a long and leisurely lunch; it seemed to have gone on all afternoon. She sat in a kind of happy stupor, reflecting on the overwhelming kindness of these strangers who had made her welcome; suddenly she burst into tears.

To have a family! A noisy, bubbling, energetic crowd who had all embraced her, physically as well as emotionally, and welcomed her into their world. She felt overwhelmed and the tears flowed unbidden.

"My *chère* Elizabeth! What is wrong?" Raoul had materialised at her side and had caught her unoccupied hand. "Is something the matter?" He looked worried.

"No, Raoul, nothing is wrong. It's all so… unexpected! To be made so welcome, when none of you know anything about me — it's just a little overwhelming, I guess."

"But you are our *cousine*, my dear! Our blood! How could we not make you welcome in our little family?" Raoul cocked his head to one side, patting her hand in a comforting way and looking at her intently.

"I guess I've never been a part of anything so — large — as this. My own family was small. I was an only child, and my husband's family was also small. And my sister-in-law is very, ah, reserved, I suppose you could say. Displays of spontaneous affection are not in her nature. My late husband was sweet and quietly loving in his own way, and I loved him dearly, but he was not given to romantic outbursts, either. It's just all a little *foreign* to me, I guess." She smiled at him through her tears. "Does that make sense?" She sniffed, and was fishing in her pocket for a tissue, when Raoul produced a clean white handkerchief from his pocket with a flourish. She almost giggled; he was *sweet*.

"*Oui*," he answered gravely. "I cannot imagine such a lonely existence. My family is so important to me, especially since my beautiful Celeste passed away. Come. Sit with me; we'll drink a toast to our dear ones, *non*? After dinner we will fetch out the old family Bible. Then we will amend the records to reflect our good fortune in our new *cousine*."

He filled a glass with a dark, blood-red wine that soaked up the candlelight. Beth tasted it; it was smooth, luscious, and fruity. It spoke to her of the earth and the sun kissing the vines; she could taste the love and pride that went into making this vintage. She sipped a little more, then placed the glass on the table.

"Yours, of course?"

"*Oui, bien sûr, ma chère*. But of course! It was a good vintage, this one."

"It's absolutely exquisite, Raoul, but I don't think I could drink any more at present."

"As you wish, Elizabeth. Come! Eat something. It will cheer you up, I think."

Beth wiped her eyes and blew her nose. She would have to replace Raoul's handkerchief. She stuffed it into her pocket and smiled at her host.

"Surely you don't dine like this every day, Raoul?"

"But of course not, my dear! During the week, we are all so busy with the vineyard and the presses, we have only a simple repast in the evening. However, Sunday is a special day. If the family members are home, then it is good to meet together under the vines and celebrate life. Life is too precious to waste, *n'est-ce pas*?" He raised his glass and saluted her before drinking.

"Life certainly *is* precious, Raoul, which is why I have been so angry with my husband for throwing his away!" She shook her head. "I don't know what happened out there at sea, and I'll probably never know for sure, but somehow he got caught in the wrong place at the wrong time, being *foolish*! And I'm still angry with him for dying." She turned haunted dark eyes towards him. "Oh! Does that make me a selfish creature?" She stopped abruptly, hand over her mouth. "Please excuse my outburst, Raoul, I think I've had a little too much to drink. My mouth is running away with itself."

Raoul opened his mouth to say something, but his words were drowned in an outburst of chatter from further down the table, as Pierre, Elizabeth's other cousin, Raoul's younger brother approached them. With him was his wife, Celine, and Raoul's sons Henri and Jean-Claude.

"The girls will be along in a minute, Papa," said Henri. "They've gone to freshen up after dinner. Perhaps our new cousin Elizabeth would like to go and join them? You really are selfish, Papa, you have managed to monopolize this lovely lady all afternoon! We would *all* like to get to know her a little better..."

Beth suddenly felt that the younger man's words were quite barbed; did he suspect her of some dark motive for accepting the invitation from Raoul, or was he flirting with her? Certainly, nothing had been said at lunch, but the older son looked a little the worse for the wine he had consumed; was he jealous? Did he think she was out to snare his papa? Nothing could be further from the truth! She rose abruptly and faced him.

"Thank you, Henri. Just so. I was just saying to your father that I really could not eat or drink another morsel, and that it is probably high time I retired for the night. It has been a very long day for me, and I must prepare my baggage for the flight home. I would like to thank you all for the wonderful and warm welcome to your home and table. Good night."

Raoul kissed her on both cheeks and watched her walk away. As Beth went, she could hear the older man speak sharply to his older son. Their conversation was rapid, but vehement; in the last few hours, Beth had remembered quite a lot of French; she was able to pick out enough words to realise that the younger man was being insulting, questioning her right to be there and calling his father an old fool. At the final insinuation, the older man had obviously had enough and this last outburst was punctuated by a sharp *crack*; the resounding slap echoed through the tiled walkway as Beth was closing her bedroom door. She wedged a chair under the door handle just to be sure. Her cheeks were aflame; she had not felt so humiliated in a very long time. She crawled into bed, fully clothed, and cried herself to sleep.

***

Morning brought a splitting headache and a cotton-wool mouth; *no more wine*, she thought sternly. She stood under the steaming water in the shower until she felt human again. She scrubbed herself raw with a sun-stiffened towel; she almost rejoiced in the tingling of legs and arms as the scratchy fibres gave her a brisk massage while she dried off. She chose a dull-gold short-sleeved top, and a long navy-blue cardigan to complement her trousers; layers, perfect for an early autumn day in the south of France. Hair brushed and face moisturised, she was ready to face the world.

"Bonjour!" came a chorus from the family assembled at the breakfast table. "What would you like to eat this morning, Elizabeth?" Celine, Pierre's wife gave her a kiss on either cheek.

"Just a juice if you have any, please, and perhaps a piece of toast? I ate so much yesterday I really don't see how I could fit any more in."

Celine laughed and darted away to fetch breakfast. Beth felt awkward; she would have offered to help the woman, but Henri was there, wolfing down his breakfast, a sullen look on his face. Any move she made would be misinterpreted, she was certain.

Raoul came into the large kitchen, wiping his hands on a towel.

"Bonjour, ma petite!" He smiled and greeted her the same way as Celine had. Beth nearly giggled; his moustache tickled her cheek. "You are looking radiant this morning, Elizabeth! I 'ope you had a good rest. Was everything to your liking?"

Beth caught Henri's look from the corner of her eye. "Yes, Raoul.

Thank you for asking. I was most comfortable." She cleared her throat. "While you're all here, I would like to thank you from the bottom of my heart, for your kindness and the warmth of your welcome to me. I know you don't know me at all — after all, I could be anyone." She threw a glance at Henri, then looked back to the others. "But I have felt welcomed as a cousin. It has meant a lot of me, especially after the shock of losing my own dear husband so recently, in trying circumstances. I brought my laptop with me, so that Raoul and I could look at the family trees, in order to enlarge yours a little, and mine, a lot, I hoped. This was a side trip, on my way back to Australia. I'm supposed to be back at work in two weeks, and I have responsibilities at home. Thank you all again for your kindness. Perhaps I could extend to you all the same hospitality if ever you decide to visit Australia. Thank you." And with that, she sat down.

Henri's face had darkened as she spoke; if he was feeling remorseful about things he had said, then it was no more than he deserved. If he still harboured evil feelings towards her, she knew no words would ever convince him otherwise. The best thing she could do, would be to leave, that day.

Chapter
thirty-six

Raoul, however, had other ideas; he would accept no argument, or excuse that Elizabeth had to leave today. He was obviously still angry with his son from the previous night, and he had noticed that his guest's beautiful dark eyes were red-rimmed, and slightly puffy. He was certain that it was not from his excellent vintage.

"Lascaux is closed, unfortunately, Elizabeth, so we are driving to Pech Merle. I have booked a guided tour in English for you."

***

In Raoul's estate car, she gazed out at the landscape. They were climbing into the hills north of Toulouse, zooming along narrow roads with sheer drops into deep gorges on her side. She hoped she would not be ill and concentrated on the horizon. *Don't look down, don't look down…*

"You are very quiet today, Elizabeth. Has something happened to upset you? Your stomach, perhaps? You did not make a good breakfast this morning. Perhaps we should stop and have an early lunch; I have packed a picnic for us."

"I'm fine, thank you, Raoul, just a little thirsty. I'm not accustomed to drinking wine anymore. No, I'm just enjoying the beautiful countryside. I'm so happy I decided to do the DNA test. I have found cousins I never even knew existed. But that's not the reason I did it."

And suddenly she found herself talking, really *talking* to Raoul; she chattered away, gazing out the car window all the while. Somehow it made it easier to talk, without having to meet his or anyone else's gaze while she marshalled her thoughts. She told him about Jeremy, how she had learnt of who he was, about Dougal's letter, or at least the 'Jeremy' part of it, how betrayed she had felt; she told him about the DNA test because of Jeremy mistaking two people in a photograph for his own kinswomen; she told him that she had had the results for Jeremy's as well as her own DNA, and that he had turned up as a cousin too. She found herself unburdening to this kind and generous man as he drove them along the narrow, twisting roads winding up the hillsides of the Midi-Pyrenees. She told him about her lost son, her husband's job that took him away so much, her job at the museum in Hobart, and about how lonely she hadn't realised she had been until coming to France.

Raoul listened, eyes fixed on the winding road, but nodding as he acknowledged her words. In turn, he told her about his wife's cancer which had taken her from the family two years previously, after more years of suffering than he cared to remember; how the children had rallied around him since then. He told her how protective they were of him and his interests. "As if I were in my dotage!" he huffed at one point, making Beth chuckle.

He chanced a very quick glance at the woman beside him; her face was lit from within when she laughed, he noticed. Watching the road, he told her all about the vineyards and the winery, the method they used for pressing the grapes, and promised her a tour of the property when they returned. At the mention of the winery, Beth stiffened, and Raoul noticed a change in the atmosphere in the car. At last, they reached the small town of Cabreret, and Raoul pulled off the road onto a grassed area.

"Here we will make a small snack, Elizabeth. You are quite hungry now, I think."

Beth realised that her stomach had settled, but that it was now growling in a most alarming manner; Raoul must have heard the grumbles. She laughed.

"Yes, my stomach is demanding, like a wild beast!" She laughed at his sudden hoot of laughter; the two of them sat there on the grassy verge, laughing and filling baguettes with cheese, pickles, ham, and salads from the picnic basket.

"Did you pack this?" she demanded through a mouthful of home-made baguette, waving the half-eaten delicacy towards the basket.

"But of course!" Raoul exclaimed. "I was just preparing it when you arrived for breakfast this morning."

"Well, it's delicious! Thank you so much for taking time out of your busy schedule to take me out to Pech Merle, too, by the way. It means a lot. It's my field of expertise, so to speak."

"No, my dear. Thank you for coming to see us. Pierre and Celine and I have certainly appreciated the opportunity to meet you. And it gives me a wonderful excuse to leave the winery for a day out—something I don't get a lot of time for in the summer and early autumn. No. The boys can manage very nicely without me. It's time Henri got a chance to shine in his own right, without his papa looking over his shoulder all the time."

"Does Henri like the idea of becoming a vintner? He hasn't chosen any other profession for himself?"

"*Non*! The boy lives and breathes the grapes, much as I did at his age. He has a good nose and shows talent for blending the grapes to produce the right bouquet and taste. My younger son, Jean-Claude, he also has a head for making wine, but… but I don't think he will want to inherit the winery when I retire or die. I think he is more interested in life outside, away from his older brother. A shame, because my elder son needs his moods tempering by another, calmer head. My son-in-law Thierry, Sandrine and Chantal's papa, now *he* is a good worker. He tends the vines, does all the soil testing and the agriculture, and assists Henri in the blending process. My daughter Madeleine does the farm accounts and runs the office. My younger daughter Claudine, she has her hands full with the little ones at present, but she will return soon, to tend the cellar door. It is a family concern, you understand. Everyone works, even me." Raoul popped the last piece of his baguette into his mouth, wiped the crumbs from his moustache with the back of his hand, and stood up.

"*Alors*, if you have finished, I think we must now hurry to join the tour before it departs underground."

"Sure!" Beth hopped up nimbly, dusting crumbs from her trousers.

She helped Raoul repack the remains of the picnic—he had brought enough for a small army—and they set out for the final climb to Pech Merle.

"Raoul, I've noticed vineyards with the word 'Pech' on them. Does it mean something special?" Beth asked as they drove the remaining distance.

Raoul laughed. "*Mais oui*! In *Oc*, the ancient language of this Occitaine region, 'pech' means hill. So 'Pech Raoul' for example, would mean simply 'Raoul's hill'. In French, 'merle' means 'blackbird'. So perhaps Pech Merle is simply Blackbird Hill." He smiled at Beth, chuckling as the realisation dawned on her and she smiled widely.

"Oh!" she exclaimed. "How simple, after all." She clambered out of the car as soon as they stopped, before he could come around to open the door. "What're we waiting for? Let's go!"

Raoul laughed and shook at his head. He rather liked his new-found cousin. He didn't care what Henri had said. And he didn't believe a word, either.

***

Pech Merle was everything Beth had hoped it would be, and more. She marvelled in the sheer *antiquity* of the place, the size and depth of the caverns. Following the guide from artefact to artefact, Beth was in awe of the dedication of those people who would have had to brave the darkness to worship their mother goddess and seek her help, armed only with a dish of animal fat and a crude wick, and the soft ochres for making paint for their sacred images.

It was as close as Beth had ever come to a truly religious and spiritual experience, there in that cave.

She forgot about the petty jealousies of Raoul's family; she forgot about Jeremy and Shona. For a short while, she even forgot Dougal, then felt a surge of guilt as she remembered him, but such was the magic of the place itself, that she forgave and immersed herself in it.

The guide kept them moving along, but not so fast as to make the visitors miss the important paintings and natural wonders. There were the cave pearls, strange stalagmites which had formed into large balls of shining limestone. The cavern sounded with the ever-present drip-drip of the limestone-saturated water as it seeped slowly through the rock above, to deposit another layer, a micron at a time as it had over countless millennia.

Beth gasped in awe as the guide pointed out the slash marks on a far wall, made by a cave lion when they still existed. She shuddered as she thought about those intrepid ancient people; not only did they have to brave the sacred darkness of the cave, but they had to contend with huge carnivorous beasts in order to make their offerings and paintings to ensure a good hunt, or simply leave a handprint, outlined in spat-out ochre, to say 'I was here'.

Beth's heart absolutely melted when they rounded a rock in the vast cavern, and there, on the facing wall was something she had only ever seen in reference books. Picked out in ochres, with the outlines of several other beasts behind and around it, was the spotted horse, two horses in fact, overlapping and facing in opposite directions, powerful hind quarters but scant forelegs, bodies almost perfectly proportioned but with smaller heads. The artist had left his handprint signature as a calling card for the goddess so she would favour the clan.

There was almost absolute silence in the cave as the small group stood in awe, while the guide explained the artwork. The group then moved along, to stop in wonder at the mammoth depicted on another wall. Not so talented, this person, or perhaps one in haste or fear for his life; the mammoth was more an outline, with straight lines for the hair and only a hint of the trunk and tusks, but the *intent* was clear enough for the earth mother to read. This time the hind quarters were minimal, but the forequarters and shoulders were massive; the artist was praying for a large mammoth to slaughter for meat and hides against the winter's blast in that glacial landscape.

Beth went cold with the enormity of it all; she shivered and pulled her long cardigan around her protectively. She felt a jacket being slipped around her shoulders, and a reassuring pat on the shoulder told her that Raoul had noticed. The party moved on, stopping at a roped-off area of petrified mud; in the mud, the guide pointed out a footprint. Beth's breath caught in her throat; it must have been a child or small woman who had ventured down into the womb of the earth. The thought of her child going into a dark and dangerous space made her shudder. Raoul's hand lightly touched her shoulder again; she acknowledged the gesture with a pat of her own hand and gave him a ghostly smile. He nodded; the place was special to him, too.

Finally, they climbed the stairs, into the warm reception area, where a new group was waiting. Beth gave Raoul back his jacket with thanks.

"Would you mind if I look in the museum while we're here?" He accompanied her, exclaiming at the size of the cave bear skulls and the cave lions' claws and teeth. Beth took many photos on her mobile phone, including maps of the areas where the ancient peoples had sought shelter and sustenance in an Ice Age world. She stopped in the souvenir shop and purchased some large prints of the spotted horse and mammoth, as well as some smaller postcards of the various wonders she had seen.

Once outside, Raoul retrieved the picnic basket, and they sat on some logs under the trees. Raoul strolled over to the kiosk and bought them each a can of soft drink when Beth declined the carafe of wine he had produced from the basket.

"Is there a bottom to that basket, Raoul?" she asked. "It seems to have a never-ending supply of food and drink in there."

He smiled, a little indulgently. "It is efficient packing, Elizabeth. *Et voilà*, there is enough space inside this basket for a three-course picnic for a family." He opened the basket with a flourish and demonstrated his claim. Beth laughed at his dramatic flourishes; he seemed to like her laughter, because he smiled very broadly at her.

"Is there anywhere else you would like to go today, *ma chère cousine?* Would you like to have a look around Toulouse on our way back to the *vigne?* It is not out of our way, at all. In fact, perhaps you might like to see Carcassonne? Is this a little modern for your expertise, perhaps?"

"No, not at all, Raoul. Carcassonne would be wonderful to visit if you think we have time…"

"We have all the time in the world, my dear. *Allons-y!*" He held out his hand to Beth and together they walked back to the car, Raoul carrying the picnic basket. He solemnly opened the door for her. She watched him; he was shorter than Dougal, but comfortably taller than she was. He was thickset across the chest, but there was little fat around his girth. His arms were well-muscled, from years of physical labour, but his hands were not all calloused. Apart from his large moustache, he was clean-shaven, and a shock of white hair covered his head abundantly. She was glad she had responded to that initial email he had sent her through the genealogical site.

She was still smiling when he got into the car. "Something amuses you, Elizabeth?" he enquired.

"I'm so pleased you wrote to me through that site, and that I replied. Otherwise, I might never have met you or your wonderful family. It's given me a warm and comforting glow in my soul to know that I actually *do* have some family in the world."

"Ah yes, you have been alone a long time, I think. Too long, perhaps. Solitude is pleasant when we choose it, but it can be a burden when it comes unbidden. As for me? I am very happy that you responded to my email, and even happier that you accepted the invitation to visit us. Now, *ma petite.* Carcassonne?"

"Yes please."

***

At the end of an amazing day, Beth felt *alive*, dusty, tired, and *happy*. She sat down with Raoul and the family for a 'simple' supper that evening; Henri was still withdrawn and watchful, but his aunt monitored his behaviour towards their guest. Celine and Pierre were eager to hear about Elizabeth's exploits, and her impressions of Pech Merle; they were impressed, they said, by her stamina for visiting Carcassonne in the same day.

"My time here is so limited, Celine, I felt Raoul's offer was too good to refuse. Who knows if I'll ever get back this way. And yes, it was tiring, but *so* worth it. I really loved the horses with their crocheted sun hats to stop the sun burning their ears! Raoul has been very patient with me. I could not have asked for a better guide!" Beth smiled at them all, and especially at Raoul, seated across the table from her. "Thank you so much, Raoul, from the bottom of my heart, for a wonderful day. Thank you all, for making me so welcome! I have so enjoyed being a part of a family; you have all been wonderful!" She lifted her glass, and saluted them all, before taking a sip of the delicious, fruity vintage. "*Merci à tous!*" she declared, hoping that was the correct way to say 'Thank you all'. Judging from the smile and salutations from them, she'd got it right. Wine glasses were waved in her direction, toasts were drunk, and Beth went to bed that night a lot happier than the night before. The only tinge of sadness was the thought that next day she would have to resume her journey back to Australia, and to her solitary existence.

Beth found that she was hopeful that she might hear from her new cousin, Raoul, again.

Chapter
thirty-seven

Beth buckled herself in. By lift-off, no one had claimed the middle seat, so she and the other passenger in the same row shared some extra room. Once the plane was in the air, headed for Dubai, and the seatbelt sign was off, Beth closed her eyes and thought back over the past two weeks.

She had returned the hire car once she and Jeremy had completed the long drive south from Kirkwall, across the strait, and down through Scotland to Edinburgh. Jeremy was returning to say goodbye to his aunt. Beth had nothing to say to Shona, so she declined his invitation to accompany him. Besides, she had received an email from her distant French cousin whilst they were on Orkney; she had said nothing to Jeremy. There was the chance he would tell Shona, and she was still dubious about her stepson, despite their cheerful outward appearances. *Her* father's family was none of Jeremy's or Shona's business.

She kissed her stepson and wished him a safe journey home to Australia. When he had raised an eyebrow, she brushed the unspoken question aside, saying she had business to attend to, workwise, before she too flew back to Hobart. She promised she would be along directly. "No more than a week behind you, lad! Now off you go! See your aunty, make your peace with her, then get home to your girl!"

The email from Raoul had been chatty; in it he had invited her to visit him and his family at their winery near Montpelier if she ever found herself in the Northern Hemisphere. She had laughed aloud, considering the exquisite irony of the timing; she had written back, explaining that she was, at that moment, in Scotland on family business, and making it clear that if the invitation was mere courtesy, she would understand. In a swiftly answered email, Raoul had insisted she would be very welcome; his entire family was agog to think they had an *exotique* distant cousin from the other side of the world. If she would like to accept their invitation, someone would meet her at the airport in Toulouse, should she decide to fly in.

***

Beth had gone straight to the airport, purchased a cheap ticket to Toulouse and had departed Scotland the following morning before she could change her mind. She had sent Raoul a message to say she was coming, and he was there at the airport, true to his word, to greet her. They had chatted on the journey southeast to his family vineyard, deep in the Languedoc region, where she had been welcomed by the whole family, or almost all....

In his office after dinner on the final evening, she and Raoul had pored for hours over his large, complicated family tree, as he explained her connection to him and the rest of the family. With Raoul's assistance, she had created a family tree for herself on her laptop and was encouraged by her white-haired cousin to copy his notes and insert the names of all her new-found family members in their appropriate places.

Raoul had driven her back to Toulouse airport the following morning; he had shrugged expressively when she suggested she could take a cab, and gallantly refused to be swayed. He farewelled her in a very Gallic manner; kisses on either cheek, followed by a huge hug. Beth was perilously close to tears again. She had not cried so much in years.

"Come back and visit us again, Elizabeth. I have really enjoyed our time together. I will email you soon. *Bon voyage, ma petite!*"

Tuesday afternoon, Beth was back in Edinburgh, where she swallowed her pride, and went to make her peace with her sister-in-law. Spending time with her French cousins had brought home the realisation that family was *everything*; something she had craved since the death of own small son. Jeremy had gone a little way to filling that void, but Beth had been unsettled and, she had to admit ruefully, *jealous* of the camaraderie that had sprung up between Jeremy and his natural aunt.

It was not the most encouraging meeting she had ever gone to, when she rang the doorbell at Shona's apartment; Shona was wary, but gradually relaxed as Beth explained some of her fears and misgivings, and confessed to having feelings of envy of the easy relationship between her sister-in-law and her stepson. Shona had relented and hugged her, scolding her for a 'silly wee thing'.

"Och, and don't you know how much he adores you, silly girl?" After that, the ice was thawed completely; they laughed and cried together.

Beth was able to assure Shona that Dougal's ashes had been scattered in accordance with his wishes, she told her of the ashes blowing into their faces on the wind, and how Jeremy had remarked she looked like she was wearing war paint. Shona laughed so hard at the mental image, she cried. Beth said that she and Jeremy had had time to talk at length about many things, including Dougal's coat.

"So, I decided it's really none of my business, what the lad does with Dougal's coat, Shona. His path is not mine to walk."

"I think that's very wise, Elizabeth dear. After all, it might simply be a keepsake of his father; it might not work at all."

"Oh, it works, apparently! He's told me so, himself."

Shona had the good grace to look a little shocked by this revelation, but Beth repeated firmly, "It's not my path to walk, Shona, nor yours. What will be, will be."

***

Beth dozed, waking for meals and drinks, and necessary bathroom visits. She was very happy to be able to disembark some hours later when the plane touched down in Dubai; she welcomed the opportunity to stretch her legs and go for a wander around the terminal building. She picked up a text from Jeremy, to say he was finally home in Hobart, and that he would come to the airport to meet her on her return. She sent him back a quick message, thanking him for the offer; she sent love and promised to text again from Melbourne.

She gravitated towards the shopping area, and purchased some small, lightweight souvenirs; some to send as thank you gifts to the family in France, and some to take home to Australia. She found exquisite scarves for Carrie, Celine, Madeleine, Claudine, and the two youngsters, Sandrine and Chantal, small soft toys for Claudine's babies, and monogrammed handkerchiefs for Raoul, Pierre, Henri, and Jean-Claude. She permitted herself a little chuckle; she hoped Raoul would get the joke of the hankies.

Back in the air, Beth stayed awake; she watched movies or read most of the way. It was a fourteen-hour direct flight, and she was exhausted when she reached Melbourne. Fortunately, she had a little time to wait for the connecting flight to Hobart and was able to send

Jeremy the promised text message with her arrival time. He answered almost immediately, while she was drinking a coffee, assuring her that, yes he and Carrie would be at the airport to meet her and sent her their love.

***

Hobart was beautiful in the spring. Beth had begun to feel she would never get there! She felt admiration and gratitude for Shona, who had made the trek across the world to farewell her only brother. She was pleased her sister-in-law had come, even if events had taken a turn for the worse for a while in Scotland. She had felt easier in her mind since she had visited Shona's apartment and had made her peace. Beth felt calmer and more in control of her life than she had since April, when she had seen her husband off on his journey for what turned out to be the last time. Her life had spiralled seriously out of control since then; her emotions had corkscrewed around since Dougal's disappearance and death, and all the subsequent drama and revelations about his life.

At the airport in Hobart, Beth waited for Jeremy to arrive. She waited over an hour. She was desperately tired, and would have liked to go home straight away, but he had promised he would be there. She watched through the plate glass windows as sudden cloudy rain showers swept across the airport, and smiled to herself at the capricious nature of spring. The precinct was glary in the afternoon sunshine after the rain and she was happy to be inside the terminal; she had packed her sunglasses in her case. She was not really bothered; she was able to use the bathroom at leisure and freshen up. She whiled away some minutes buying and drinking another coffee and checking her messages, but as time dragged on, she decided to call him. There was no answer, so she left him a voice mail, telling him not to bother coming out after all; she was exhausted and would take a cab home.

Outside there was the usual line of cabs; she walked down the race to the first one. The impeccably dressed turbaned driver jumped out to hold the door open for her, and take her baggage to the boot. She buckled herself in and gave the driver her address.

"I'm sorry, madam, but there is a hold-up in the traffic at present. We are having to use a slightly alternate route. It will take a little longer to get to your destination."

"Oh!" Beth said, conversationally. "Roadworks?"

"No, madam, a traffic incident, I think."

"Oh well, these things happen," she said, hating herself for the cliché as it slipped unbidden from her mouth.

"Indeed they do, madam. I was talking to some of the other drivers who had come in behind me. They were saying to me that the roundabout at the entrance was almost completely blocked off by police, and ambulances and tow trucks. Some poor unfortunate has apparently had an accident at the roundabout." The turban waggled slightly as the driver spoke.

"Well, no wonder my poor son couldn't make it to the airport to meet me!" Beth's tension eased. "Ah, that explains everything! I was beginning to worry about him. It's not like him to be late." Beth realised she was starting to burble on and made a conscious effort to stop. She must be more tired than she supposed.

The cab driver negotiated the labyrinth of the car park, taking an alternative exit, directed by a police officer on point duty. Off to the right, Beth could see flashing lights in blue, red and amber, with emergency workers in their hi-vis vests at the scene. Tow truck operators were winching a couple of mangled cars up onto the flat beds of their vehicles; three ambulances came screaming down the road behind them, lights and sirens in full use. Her taxi driver kept well to the left and reduced his speed, as the emergency vehicles raced past them; soon they were out onto the highway. Beth thought about the last time she had driven this way; it must have been when she and Jeremy had farewelled Shona a couple of months ago. *Was it only that short a time ago? It seems like years.*

"It looks like there were only two cars involved, madam," said the driver. "I can see no other vehicles." And suddenly the bottleneck of traffic was over, and the driver sped up. They were away. Beth spared a thought for the 'poor unfortunates' who were on their way to hospital. Obviously, there must have been more than one casualty, or more minor casualties who could fit inside two ambulances. *But they always send a backup, just in case.*

Once home, Beth unpacked, started a load of washing, and made coffee. The aroma of coffee mingled with the slightly stale aroma of 'closed-up house'. She opened windows onto the late afternoon sunshine, took in lungsful of clean spring air, and surveyed her little world. It was good to be home.

After tending to the washing, she had a coffee, heated some pie from the freezer, and tried Jeremy's mobile phone again, several times. No answer each time. She tried Carrie's. No answer. Eventually, frustrated, she sent them each a message that simply read: "Home safe. Call me when you can. See you soon. Love you. Beth."

***

She was awoken early the following morning by the doorbell. She struggled stiffly and groggily to her feet; she had fallen asleep in her armchair. She opened the door a crack; two strangers stood there in the soft grey half-light of the dawn; she flipped the outside light on, and saw they were two uniformed police officers.

"Just a moment," she called hoarsely, dry throat cracking with the effort as she closed the door, released the safety chain, and opened the door wider.

"Good morning. Can I help you?" she asked, running a hand through her tousled hair and clearing her throat.

"Elizabeth Ferguson? I'm Sergeant Greyton and this is PC Jennings." Warrant cards were produced and waved in front of her nose.

"Yes, Beth Ferguson." Beth blinked. "Is something wrong? I've been away, and just got back yesterday."

"May we come in please, Mrs Ferguson?" asked PC Jennings, a slight brunette.

"Sure, if you'll tell me what this is about."

"We'd prefer to talk inside if that's okay. Would it be okay if I sat down? You might like to sit down too?"

"Not particularly," said Beth. "I've been sitting for hours. You'd better come through. I'll make a coffee. You sure look like you could do with one. I know *I* could. This way." And she set off, leading them to the family room out back. She bustled to start the coffee machine.

A gentle but firm hand clamped onto Beth's shoulder. "Let me do that, Mrs Ferguson. The sergeant needs to talk to you, and he does prefer it when he can sit down to talk." The young PC's voice was quietly confiding in her ear.

"Well, okay, all the stuff is there. I just wish you two would spit out whatever is bothering you. I've had a long, tiring flight from Scotland, and I'm really not in the mood for riddles. So, spit it out, sergeant, what's up?"

"Do you know a Jeremy Munroe, Mrs Ferguson?"

"Sure! Jeremy's my stepson!" She looked around at the young woman making coffee in *her* kitchen, and back at the man seated in front of her. "Why? What's he done?" she asked, suspicious.

"I'm afraid there's been an accident, Mrs. Ferguson. May I call you Elizabeth?" She nodded. "Thank you," he continued, clearing his throat.

"What kind of accident?" Beth demanded. "What in the name of all that's wonderful has happened?"

"Ah, Mrs Ferguson… Elizabeth… I'm afraid your stepson was involved in a traffic accident yesterday afternoon."

A worm of unease started to uncoil in her belly. "That explains why he's not answering his phone. Is he okay?" Beth looked at the officers and their expressions took her breath away. She turned a white face, all hollow cheeks, and dark, round eyes to focus on the sergeant. "Is he okay?" she repeated in a hoarse whisper. Her stomach roiled in fear.

The sergeant cleared his throat uneasily. This was the one job he really, really hated about being a police officer.

"Mrs Ferguson, your stepson, Jeremy Munroe, is in hospital. He sustained some nasty injuries in the collision. We found his ICE details in his wallet. He named you and his fiancée as his next of kin. The hospital did try several times to contact you by phone, but there was no answer." Beth's eyes flew to her phone. She picked it up and peered at it; the battery was flat.

"Here, Mrs Ferguson, drink this." A mug of freshly brewed coffee was placed on the low table in front of her. PC Jennings sat down beside her on the couch.

Beth jumped up. She was stunned, bewildered, yet galvanised into action. She paced up and down the room. "What? How? When? How? What happened?" She sat back down just as abruptly and looked at them.

"And have you told Carrie yet? She'll need to know! Carrie! His fiancée! She's a police officer too, you know, but just at the minute I can't remember which station she's at. I'll get my phone. No, it's flat. My address book! That'll have her number. I'll get it for you. Does she know yet?" She jumped up again and scrabbled through her handbag, which was sitting on the dining table. She started flipping through the pages, babbling on to fill the awkward silence as she leafed jerkily through the book.

"Sure, I know it's kind of old-fashioned to keep an address book, but I have the phone as my back-up. She should be in here somewhere... what was her last name again? Give me a sec, I'll find it..." The book was gently taken from her, and she found herself being guided back to the couch by the young PC, who sat down beside her. The two uniformed officers were looking at her intently, shooting each other guarded looks. The sergeant resumed his role as the bearer of bad news.

"Elizabeth, I'm sorry. DC Carrie Harkaway... was with him in the vehicle at the time." He held up a hand as Beth gasped and turned even paler. "She's in the intensive care unit at the Royal Hobart Hospital. They're doing everything they can for her."

Beth looked at the police officers and said quietly but quite lucidly, "Oh no! Not Jeremy! We've just been to Scotland to scatter his father's ashes!" She looked at them again, scrutinising their faces, seeking the truth in their eyes. "Where did it happen? The accident... and how?"

"Our traffic incident officers have been working to establish what happened, but it appears from the marks on the road that another car slammed into the vehicle they were driving at a major roundabout near the airport. We'll know more when we can interview your stepson and his fiancée." *If they ever regain consciousness...*

Beth stood up. Her face had lost all colour; she looked grey, and slightly blue around the lips. She whispered hoarsely, "Will they be okay, Sergeant? Will they pull through?"

PC Jennings cleared her throat and answered, "Ah, Mr Munroe's condition is stable, but the hospital has been trying to contact you all night. They only had your mobile phone number from Jeremy's wallet. So, we've come to take you to the hospital, to be with him. As for DC Harkaway.... She's in an induced coma until the swelling around her brain has reduced. She hit her head pretty hard when the other car hit them. When she wakes up, we'll be able to ask her exactly what happened."

"I'll just grab my coat and keys. Just give me a minute..."

Beth grasped futilely for something to steady her as the room started to spin, and her last thoughts before the wooden floor reared up violently to meet her were "Jeremy, I'm so sorry!" And after that, all was blackness.

Chapter
thirty-eight

Beth sat at Jeremy's bedside. She felt dirty; her face felt grimy, her eyes gritty and swollen. Her head still hurt from hitting the floor when she fainted, but she was more concerned with the still figure in the bed in front of her. He looked so *young*, so *vulnerable*, that she couldn't stop her scalding tears. Beth chafed the hand which was not hooked up to IV tubes and the oxygen monitor, and talked softly to him.

The doctor in ICU had told her to talk to him, to help him wake up, but she was dubious. They had come via the emergency department before allowing her to visit Jeremy. The resident on duty had pronounced her fit to sit with her stepson.

"If you start feeling dizzy or nauseous," he had told her, "ring for the nurse, but we think you're okay for now."

The doctor in charge of the ICU had come and sat with Beth and told her that Jeremy's condition was serious but stable. "We've scanned him for brain trauma, Mrs Ferguson, he hit the air bag pretty hard. He has some internal bleeding, which we've stabilised. Sit and talk to him." When she asked about his injuries, the doctor had shaken his head and started talking about severe concussion, internal injuries, and a broken arm.

"The other vehicle smashed into the passenger door, Mrs Ferguson. I'm afraid that your son's fiancée took the full impact. She's on the critical list. I'm sorry I can't tell you more at the moment. Anyway, I'll take you to him now. Call if you need us."

And so she sat, and talked to the motionless figure in the bed, through tears of guilt and remorse.

"Jeremy, you're all I have right now. I'm so sorry, lad. It's all my fault. I shouldn't have asked you to come fetch me from the airport. I'm so sorry!" She sat, weeping for them both. *Jeremy, you mustn't die!* She squeezed his hand and changed the subject.

"Guess what, lad? I got the results of the DNA tests back and it looks like we *are* related after all, just as I suspected, when you mistook my mom's picture for your grandmother's. Isn't that great? I'm so sorry I didn't tell you at the time, but I was hurt and kind of resentful because you had formed such a close bond with Shona, and I felt afraid that I would be shut out of your life.

"But we had a good time on Orkney, didn't we? And a lot of laughs, too. I'm so glad you made it home to Carrie. Oh, Carrie!" she exclaimed, looking at his expressionless, unconscious face. "Carrie's in another room up here, too, you know, lad. She got banged around in the accident, as well. She's still unconscious, so she doesn't know you're in here too, but the medicos told me that her mother has been notified and she'll be flying in from Sydney as soon as she can get away.

"You haven't met Carrie's mom yet, have you? She'll be pleased to meet you — I bet Carrie has told her all about you, you beautiful boy." She lifted her hand to stroke his hair but was afraid to cause him further pain. She contented herself with stroking his hand; *how could this happen?* She continued talking to him, telling him about the visit to France, how she'd discovered some cousins on her father's side of the family, and how she'd managed to visit the prehistoric caves at Pech Merle.

She realised she was rambling on, filling the small room with sounds other than the beeping monitors. It was extremely difficult to conduct a one-sided conversation with someone so thoroughly *not there* and she found herself starting to doze off, still holding his hand. Fatigue finally caught up with her, and she fell asleep to the gentle rhythmic beeping, head resting on the side of Jeremy's bed.

Beth woke up to a feather-light, insistent pressure on her hand. She raised her head and looked owlishly at the slim figure squinting sleepily at her.

"Jeremy!! You're awake!" She jumped up and kissed him gently. "Oh, my dear, dear boy! How are you feeling?"

"Pretty rotten at present, but I'll live, I guess. How's Carrie? And is the baby okay?" His face clouded with concern.

"Baby? What baby?" Beth sat down with a thump and looked at him, shocked. "What baby, Jeremy?"

"Oh, Beth! I only just found out when I got home from Scotland! We were going to tell you when we met you at the airport, but..." His voice trailed away. He said, very quietly, "Maybe it was our fault, the accident, you know… we were busy talking about having the baby and getting married, and then, BANG! And I woke up here."

***

By the time Beth left Jeremy's bedside she was exhausted, physically and emotionally. She wanted nothing more than to return home and sleep forever. But she had no car, and she needed fresh air before she called a cab. When she emerged into the sunshine through the main door, she realised with shock how far the shadows had moved—it was already late afternoon!

As she stood in the sun, soaking up its rays, a cab arrived on the hospital forecourt. A woman, in her late fifties or early sixties emerged from the back seat. A tall, elegant woman, with beautifully coiffed blonde hair blending artfully into grey, eyes hidden behind designer sunglasses, in well-tailored but slightly crumpled clothing. She hardly spared Beth a glance, looked pointedly ahead and almost ran in, dragging a small suitcase behind her. Beth hailed the same cab before it departed and sank into the back seat as the cabbie drove her home.

***

Beth contacted her boss to say she was back from overseas, and guiltily asked for more personal leave time, while Jeremy recovered in hospital. Her head of department had seen the footage on the nightly news already.

Beth was back next day, sitting with Jeremy, chatting about inconsequential nonsense and having serious talks about the lad's future. Carrie was still in ICU, immediate family only; staff were tight-lipped in Jeremy's room. He begged to be allowed to visit, and two days later, he was given permission, Beth pushing his wheelchair.

As they approached the door to the ICU, the tall blonde woman who had passed Beth days earlier, emerged. She was visibly upset, shaking, and blotting at her eyes. Beth suddenly registered why the woman had seemed familiar during their brief encounter at the main door; she must be Carrie's mother. The familial resemblance was striking.

Beth approached and said quietly, "Excuse me for asking, but are you Carrie's mother? Can I help somehow? I'm Elizabeth Ferguson, Jeremy's stepmother. I think we may have crossed paths when you arrived the other day."

The woman looked contemptuously at Beth, then started yelling.

"You have a nerve, showing up here! You have a lot to apologise for. If it hadn't been for you, my poor girl wouldn't be lying in there, dying…. Why couldn't you take a taxi like everyone else?"

Beth was stunned; Carrie was *dying*? *Oh no! No, no, no!* She reached out a hand to touch the woman's arm, only to have it smacked viciously away.

"Don't you *dare* touch me! This is all your fault! And *you…*" she screeched, turning on poor Jeremy in his wheelchair, "you've killed my precious girl, you mongrel bastard! I could *kill* you myself!"

Jeremy wasn't quick enough to dodge a hefty slap across his face; it snapped his head around, and he groaned in pain. His distress only seemed to enrage the woman more, and she moved like a snake to strike him again. This time he managed to get out of the way, but Beth wasn't quite so lucky; she took an open-handed slap to the face. The weal it left was a dull red.

Two security guards appeared; they had heard the yelling and witnessed the assaults. They quietly stepped in and used their bulk to isolate the furious woman from her victims, taking an arm each, while asking if Beth and Jeremy were okay.

"*Let me go!*" the woman screeched. "Let me go! My daughter is *dying* in there! I have to be with her! Let me go, *please*?" As fast as the woman's fury had appeared, it dissipated, and she sagged against her captors, sobbing her heart out.

Beth said quietly to one of the guards, "Can I talk to her for a moment, please?" Without waiting for a reply, she stepped up to the bereft woman and touched her lightly on the arm. She spoke very quietly.

"I'm so sorry, I don't even know your name. My name is Beth. Would you like to come and sit down? I wanted to tell you how much we love Carrie. She's become very dear to me in these past months. You're a very lucky lady, to have such a wonderful daughter. Come, sit down with me for a moment."

The woman looked at Beth; her voice was lower now, but the words were bitter.

"I don't think so. This is your fault. Why couldn't you have taken a taxi like other people do? Now, if you'll excuse me, I must get back to my daughter. She needs me." And to the guards she added haughtily, "You can let go now. I'm not going to do anything stupid."

She shrugged them off, straightened her clothes and walked back into the ICU.

Jeremy looked helplessly at Beth; his face bore a similar red welt. He was in tears.

"Please, Beth? I have to see her! I have to see my girl! I can't lose her, not now! I don't know what I would do without her…. She can't die!" He grabbed Beth's arm and howled into her sleeve like a wild man. Beth was helpless; she stroked his hair and repeated, "Let it out, lad. Let it out."

***

Some minutes later, the door opened, and the ICU nurse beckoned them in, saying to Jeremy:

"She's in a very poorly way, but she'll know you're there. Go and sit with her. Talk to her. Don't mind her mother, the poor lady's beside herself with grief. Would you like me to take you in? She can only have two visitors at a time. Sorry," she added to Beth. "I'll see if we can get Ms Marsh to take a short break so you can see Carrie for a moment or two. Leave it with me."

The nurse pushed Jeremy's wheelchair through the doors, and Beth was left, standing alone, thoughts racing. There was a noise behind her, as two uniformed police and a couple of plain clothed officers entered the waiting room. Beth recognised Gavan Hopper, the DI who had come with Carrie when Dougal had disappeared; the uniforms were the same pair who had brought Beth to Jeremy's bedside.

"Hello again, Mrs Ferguson," said Gavan Hopper, extending his hand to Beth. "How is Carrie?"

"Not brilliant, I'm afraid. I'd like to visit with her, but her mom has been pretty upset and a bit physical. I think she's calmed down a little now. I'm waiting for the nurse to bring her out for a couple of minutes so I can see Carrie. Jeremy's in there at present. There's a limit of two visitors, apparently."

"Everyone at the station wanted to come and see Carrie. She's a very popular girl. We'll wait." They sat down and picked up some magazines to leaf through, to pass the time.

Presently, a nurse escorted Carrie's mother out and beckoned Beth to go in. Beth received a hostile glare, but the woman was obviously aware of the uniforms in the waiting room.

Beth approached Carrie's bedside and whispered to Jeremy,

"How are you bearing up? Was she nasty to you?"

He whispered back, "She pretty much ignored me, Beth. I just want Carrie to wake up, but no one will tell me anything. She's so *still.*"

Beth squeezed his hand and turned to the figure attached to tubes and machines; there was no sign of life, except for the lines pulsing across the monitor screens. She put her hand onto Carrie's and whispered, "I'm so sorry, sweetheart. Come back to us. We miss you."

Chapter
thirty-nine

From a local Hobart newspaper:

Collision claims second victim

'Police Media confirmed today that a second person has died from injuries sustained as a result of a two-car collision at Hobart Airport on Friday last week.

The victim has been identified as Carrington Megan Harkaway, 28, a resident of Hobart. Ms Harkaway, a Detective Constable at South Hobart Police Station, transferred to Hobart eighteen months ago from Sydney. Her fiancé, Jeremy Munroe, who was driving the car at the time of the accident remains in hospital recovering from his injuries. His condition has been described as serious but stable.

Senior Sgt Kane Cookson, Police Prosecutor, has confirmed that Mr Munroe will not be charged with any offences on the death of his passenger, as the collision was caused by another vehicle failing to slow down or give way at a roundabout near the entrance to the airport, according to eyewitnesses. The other driver, who died at the scene has been identified as Bogdan Milcic, 39, unemployed, of Glenorchy. Police sources have confirmed that Mr Milcic's car was unroadworthy at the time of the accident when it skidded on the wet road due to bald tyres and faulty steering. Police have urged motorists always to drive to conditions and to ensure their vehicles are made roadworthy for the approaching festive season.'

Carrie's funeral a week later was a moving, well-attended occasion. Most of her colleagues attended and six officers carried her coffin; members of her netball club turned out in force, in a show of solidarity, but she had no family other than her mother and Beth to mourn her. Beth draped the scarf she had purchased in Dubai across the white coffin.

Jeremy was still in hospital, recuperating, and Shona could not make another long flight across the globe. Sarah Marsh, Carrie's mother had decided that her daughter's body should be cremated, and she would take the ashes back to Sydney. Jeremy was terribly distraught when he heard that news. Sarah had also demanded that Jeremy's belongings be removed immediately from Carrie's apartment. Beth could understand the other woman's grief and anger, but not such utter vindictiveness.

As the young man was unable, Beth collected his stuff and took it home to Rose Bay. Dougal's coat she hung back in its old place, behind the front door. It was comforting, somehow, to have it home again. Once more, Beth's world had narrowed to a focal point; between her work and hospital visits with Jeremy as he recovered, she had little time to brood.

She had to break the news of Sarah's unreasonable demands to Jeremy, but assured him he had a home with her, that his gear was secure. The police had interviewed him at length about his role in the fatal collision, but he had never been charged; eyewitnesses had come forward to corroborate the forensic findings, and Jeremy was exonerated.

After a session with her therapist one hot December day, Beth had an epiphany; she realised she had nothing to stay here for. Jeremy was now home and slowly recuperating, but he was snappy, prone to bouts of anger or morose silence, and very depressed. He blamed himself thoroughly for Carrie's death. And his student status had changed, as he had dumped his studies, and he would have to return to Canada. His depression seemed to deepen. Even Beth's announcement that she too was returning to Canada didn't seem to move him at all.

Beth looked across at the browning Tasmanian hills and landscape, caught already in the fire-prone throes of the Australian summer heat, and suddenly longed, with all her heart, for the forests of spruce and the deep, peaty lakes of her homeland.

***

Beth had written a series of long emails to Raoul. Most of them she had deleted, but one or two managed to find their way to the other side of the world.

From: Bouchier.Elizabeth@googlemail.com
To: Raoul@vigneDupont.fr

My dear Raoul,
I really don't know if I should tell you, but I miss you all. I didn't realise how important a family could be until I met yours.
When I returned to Australia, as you know, my stepson's fiancée was killed in a car crash on their way to collect me from the airport. I have felt the pain and the weight of that guilt ever since; that somehow I was the architect of her death. I know this is a foolish notion, but it's there, lodged like a boulder in my heart. Jeremy has always scoffed at the idea that it was my fault, but I blame myself.
I've always been very independent in my life. As I told you that day on the way to Pech Merle, I spent many years alone with my work, curating in various institutions around the world while my husband was away with his research, and never admitted to feeling lonely. But since Dougal's death, and now Carrie's, I seem to have lost my shield of invulnerability, and it is a very frightening and bewildering thing to have my emotions and fears stripped so bare. The sense of longing I have started to feel since returning to Australia, the need to be a part of something bigger than myself, is growing stronger every day.
And so, my dear cousin, I have come to a decision about the rest of my life. I have decided to move back to Canada, specifically to Vancouver Island where I was born. Perhaps I will find some work in the museum in Victoria, if I am lucky, working with the artefacts of my mother's people.
Jeremy has lost his student visa, as he has completely abandoned his studies, so he will have to return to Canada soon. He came from Ottawa, on the other side of the country, so I guess he'll return there; I'll probably not see him again. I must confess, Raoul, I'm very worried about the lad's mental health, but I cannot seem to reach him. It's as if he died with Carrie, in some ways. The fact that he had just learned that he was to be a father has hit him doubly hard. And I just don't know what to do for him – I feel there's nothing I can do, except be there for him.
When I told him I had decided to go back to VI, he just nodded and continued to stare out the window.
I feel that I am living in a house full of ghosts – except that one

of them is still living.

I am so sorry to unburden myself to you like this, but I felt, when we met in France that we had something in common, some connection. I'm not normally like this... in need of reassurance... but this past year has completely knocked the stuffing out of me, as they say, and I'm trying to reassess who the real me is, after so many years, and where my confidence and certainty about the world has disappeared to.

Anyway, my dear, thank you for listening to my endless miseries. Send a kiss to each of your delightful granddaughters from me, please?

By the way, did you receive the small gifts I purchased for you all in Dubai? Amid the uproar and upset of Carrie's sudden death and Jeremy's injuries, it was good to be able to do something nice, something pleasant for someone again.

Write to me when you can? I always look forward to your opinions and to hearing the news of life in your beautiful part of the world. My best wishes to your children and your brother.

Until next time, au revoir mon cher cousin,

Elizabeth xx

Beth sat down to check her emails one searing January afternoon, and received a pleasant surprise. She had already made some tentative job-related enquiries to the Museum of British Columbia, located in Victoria, the largest city on Vancouver Island. The director had written her a polite reply, inviting her to forward her CV to them; they would keep her name on file, and should she relocate in the foreseeable future, they would be pleased to receive a call from her. Beth sat back, smiling broadly. It wasn't *Yes* but it wasn't *No*, either.

There was also an email from Raoul. She opened it eagerly.

De: Raoul@vigneDupont.fr

À: Bouchier.Elizabeth@googlemail.com

Ma Chère Elizabeth,

Ma belle, my heart is truly full of pain for you. You have suffered more than your fair share of grief this year, I think.

You are a strong person, Elizabeth, but even the strongest oak tree will break in the tempest. Perhaps you are learning now to bend a little like the reeds? Perhaps this way you will also survive the storms? And like a supple tree, fate twists us into interesting shapes, much as the vines are shaped by training them onto their supports as they grow.

You know you can write to me and talk about anything, my dear. I too felt a connection when we met. I rarely speak about my beautiful Celeste with strangers – the fact that I could speak so freely to you about her meant a lot to me. I felt we were on the similar wavelength also, that day.

Your beautiful gifts arrived in time for our Christmas celebrations. You could not have arranged delivery at a better time! Père Noël himself must have delivered them I think. The girls are all in raptures over their silk scarves; you are altogether too generous, chèrie! The children loved their soft toys, and we men have all appreciated some fine new handkerchiefs. Thank you so much!

Is the weather warm in Australie now? Here it is cold and the fire is crackling merrily in the hearth tonight, but it is not as cold as in the North. Paris has been very cold – there has been a lot of snow, and we have even had small snow showers here. The vines are all asleep at this time of the year, so they take no harm from the cold – in fact a little nip of frost can do them good! But only a little nip, you understand! The loggia where we ate our family feasts is open to the skies now; the bare trunks of the vines stretch like protective arms across the top.

Elizabeth, I feel you are making a wise decision, to return to your roots. If you truly feel you have nothing and no one to stay there for, and you are not happy, then it is best to move on. It is important, especially as we age, to feel connected to a place, somewhere that has meaning to our lives. And as you are making your decision for yourself, not for anyone else, this is positive. I wish you a good price for your house, and that the move goes smoothly.

*When the solitude becomes uncomfortable, please remember you are always welcome to come visit and sit and eat with us among our vines; there will **always** be a seat here at my table for you, chèrie.*

I send you large kisses, ma petite, from us all,
Raoul.

***

Suddenly it was autumn again, and Beth found it hard to believe it was almost a year since Dougal had died. She looked around her house. All her precious belongings—artefacts, ornaments, photographs, and books—had been packed carefully into sturdy boxes, and were stacked up in the empty front room, awaiting collection for shipping. Most of the furniture had been sold or given away to the thrift shop. She had donated much of her clothing to charity. She had secured an excellent price for the house; it would be more than enough to pay for her move and find some decent accommodation on Vancouver Island while she set about finding work.

In two separate crates were Jeremy's worldly possessions. She couldn't bear to throw them out, so they were going home with her. It was now nearly two months since Jeremy had gone out one summer morning, taking only his car and his father's sealskin coat; his gear and a note for Beth he had left in his room. When she read that note, Beth's heart had shattered completely.

She'd jumped into her car and driven to the coast, searching. She had screamed his name to the mocking wind… only the seagulls screamed a reply.

The police eventually found Jeremy's abandoned car but impounded it, pending an ongoing investigation into his disappearance. The last thing she did before she caught the plane for Vancouver was to sell her car to a local used-car yard.

Victoria, Vancouver Island, BC.

The coroner's report into Dougal's death contained no surprises for Beth, just more heartache.

Record of Investigation into Death (Without Inquest)
Coroner Act 1995
Coroners Rules 2006
Rule 11

I, Keith Lloyd-Jones, Coroner, having investigated the death of Dougal Ferguson
Find that:
The identity of the deceased is Dr Dougal James Kenneth Ferguson;
The deceased died as a result of an attack by person or persons unknown;
on or around 30 April 2015 in the waters of the Southern Ocean; and was born in Orkney, UK, 20 April 1955, aged 60 years at the time of his death; was married with no surviving children, was employed as a Professor of Marine Sciences at the University of Hobart at the time of death.

In regard to the evidence gained in the investigation into Dr Ferguson's death and the police report, the following has been recorded: an opinion of the forensic pathologist as to cause of death, expert forensic reporting, police and witness affidavits and relevant documents. Based on this evidence:

Circumstances surrounding death:
Between the hours of 23:00 Wednesday 29 April and 07:30 Thursday 30 April, Dr Ferguson went overboard from the icebreaker *Aurora Australis,* headed in a south-easterly direction en route to Macquarie Island at the time of Dr Ferguson's last known sighting.

His disappearance was not discovered or reported until 07:30 Thursday 30 April. His cabin mate and student, Jeremy Munroe, reported the disappearance to the ship's captain, Peter Gallagher.

Captain Gallagher (now retired) immediately ordered a thorough search of the ship. On failing to find any trace of Dr Ferguson, he then contacted the relevant authorities, and an air and sea search was instigated. Despite an exhaustive search, Dr Ferguson's body was not found.

The body of a man was located on the shoreline of Macquarie Island on Saturday 2 May. It was later identified as Dr Ferguson by Mr Munroe, (now himself missing presumed dead). It was collected and repatriated to Hobart.

On 15 May 2015, Dr Julius Macfarlin, forensic pathologist, conducted an autopsy on Dr Ferguson's body. He observed a bullet hole in a coat which the deceased had been wearing at the time of his disappearance; ... corresponded directly with a bullet later retrieved from the spinal column of Dr Ferguson. He formed the opinion that although Dr Ferguson's death was ultimately caused by drowning, this would have been exacerbated by the debilitating wound inflicted before his death. There was bruising consistent with the deceased being in prolonged contact with a fine mesh netting. The pathologist was unable to determine time of death, or whether the gunshot wound was responsible for Dr Ferguson's disappearance overboard. I accept the opinion of Dr. Macfarlin as to the cause of death. Toxicology testing revealed no drugs or alcohol in Dr Ferguson's blood.

The actions of Captain Peter Gallagher in orchestration of a full search and rescue effort at sea are commendable.

No indication was given as to how Dr Ferguson's body

arrived at Macquarie Island. It is the conclusion that his body was transported to that location by person or persons unknown.

No weapon has been recovered, either from *Aurora Australis*, or from Macquarie Island.

I commend the actions of those on Macquarie Island who first discovered and recovered Dr Ferguson's body and the comprehensive investigation and report provided by the Australian Maritime Safety Authority and the Tasmanian Police Force.

The circumstances of Dr Ferguson's death are not such as to require a further enquiry.

We extend sincere condolences to the family and loved ones of Dr Ferguson.

Dated: 26 September, 2016, at Hobart in the State of Tasmania
Keith Lloyd-Jones
Coroner

Beth pinched the bridge of her nose. There it was, in black and white. The story of Dougal's demise. Suddenly she felt drained, empty.

She fetched a coffee, then sat back down and re-read the email. She put the document into a separate legal file. Scrolling down through the remainder of her inbox, she picked up an email from Gavan Hopper.

From: hopper.gavan.g@taspol.gov.au
To: Bouchier.Elizabeth@googlemail.com
Subject: Missing person

Dear Mrs Ferguson,
Just touching base to let you know there has been no sighting of your stepson or a body to date. His car was investigated thoroughly, and I can now tell you there appears to have been no evidence of foul play in his disappearance. However, forensics were able to recover some unusual fibres from the vehicle's back seat, which analysis showed were animal in origin. Is it possible

Mr Munroe was carrying an animal or something made of fur?
The vehicle has been placed in the holding lot. Please advise what
you wish done with it. Mr Munroe appears to have had no
family, apart from you and his late fiancée.
Kind regards,
Gavan Hopper, DI

***

From: Bouchier.Elizabeth@googlemail.com
To: hopper.gavan.g@taspol.gov.au
Subject: Jeremy's car

Dear DI Hopper,
Thank you for the update. As to the car, do you still conduct
auctions? If so, could it please be sold at the next available
opportunity? Any money it makes, I'd like to donate to the Police
Widows and Orphans fund if your force has one.
I still live in hope that Jeremy will one day reappear, but I'm
probably grasping at straws.
Thank you all for your kindness to Jeremy when Carrie was
killed, and for your friendship to them both.
Will there be a Coronial enquiry into Jeremy's disappearance
eventually? And will you let me know, please?
Kind regards,
Elizabeth Bouchier Ferguson

Beth hit Send, and looked at the clock. Her stomach reminded her it was lunchtime. She grabbed her coat and handbag, and tapped softly on the door of her supervisor's office.

"Hi, Amy, I've finished for the day and I'm off now. See you tomorrow, yes?"

Amy Pleasance looked up and smiled at Beth. "Sure thing, Beth. See you tomorrow. Have a nice day!"

"Will do. You too. Bye."

Beth closed the door and walked down the stairs to the main entrance. She could have taken the back stairs, but the shopping precinct was closer through the main door, so she headed that way. The receptionist at the front desk looked up and said, "Oh hi, Beth, I was just trying your extension. There's a gentleman here to see you.

He's sitting over there," and indicated a corner setting by the large windows. Beth frowned at her.

"For me?"

The girl nodded, smiling. "Specifically asked for you." She smiled, and whispered, "He's nice, kinda cute in a grandfatherly kind of way."

Curiosity piqued, Beth slowly turned her head. Heat flooded her face; her grieving heart skipped a guiltily happy beat. She turned back to the receptionist. "Thanks, Emily. He's a friend from overseas."

"I figured that, he has a very strong accent. Is he French? He looks French…"

Beth nodded, blushing; she hoped the girl would not have noticed, but a knowing smile told her otherwise. She gave Beth a thumbs-up gesture and a huge grin.

"Thanks, sweetie." Beth put a finger to her lips, turned, and approached the chairs. The man, who had been engrossed in a magazine, glanced up at the sound of her heels on the mosaic floor. A huge smile engulfed his entire face as he saw her walking towards him. She was beautiful; a small, elegant figure of a woman, whose answering smile filled his heart.

"Hello, Raoul! What are you doing here?"

She was suddenly enveloped in a huge hug, momentarily lifted off the ground and kissed thoroughly on both cheeks. She returned the hug with more enthusiasm than she would have believed possible. Raoul finally held her at arm's length and looked her up and down, quite critically.

"But you are wasting away, *ma petite*! I have come to see *you*, of course, *ma mie*! Who else?"

Beth was at a loss for words; she stood and looked at him in amazement. His email of a few weeks ago had held no hints of an impending visit, but she was suddenly *delighted* he was here. Her feelings threatened to overwhelm her for a perilous moment; she managed to stammer a reply.

"I'm so happy to see you, Raoul! I can't believe it's almost a year since we last met. How have you been?"

"I have been well. Better than you, I suspect, little one. I have been thinking of you much, *chèrie*. Your emails have broken my heart in sympathy with your pain. So, with harvest complete now, and the boys all occupied in the presses, the place is in good hands. Pierre and Celine are in charge while I'm away. In fact, it was Celine who suggested that I should visit you, instead of, how did she put it, pining for your company, worrying over each email, and driving her mad, speaking of you so much. *Et voilà*, here I am! But, this is your lunch break, *non*? Here I am, chattering away like a magpie, when you should be eating before returning to work. You are altogether too thin, *ma petite*. May I take you to lunch?"

Beth gurgled with laughter amid these revelations; he had *missed* her! And, she realised with a jolt, looking up at him, she had missed him too.

"Actually, I've finished for the day, Raoul. I was just on my way home. I have a small apartment quite close by. I walk to work most mornings, these days. It's so nice, not having to drive, or look for parking spaces; besides, I love to walk. Would you like to come home for lunch? I don't know what's in the fridge — I was going to call in at the market for some meat and salad, but you're welcome to join me."

"I have a better idea, *ma petite*. Allow me to take you out to lunch, yes? That way, someone else can prepare the food, and we can relax and talk, over a glass of wine. *C'est une bonne idée, oui*?"

Beth tucked her arm into his and gave a little chuckle when he brushed a whiskery kiss across her cheek. She gently squeezed his forearm, and returned his kiss.

"Yes, my dear friend, it is *indeed* a good idea. I have much to tell you. Let's go!"

THE END

Information sources

Wikipedia

Lonely Planet

www.maritime-executive.com/editorials/the-new-human-rights-at-sea-debate

ABC News website

The Australian National Antarctic Research Expeditions (ANARE) website

ANU Research School of Earth Sciences (RSES) website

www.magistratescourt.tas.gov.au

www.antarctic.gov.au

www.medicinenet.com

www.betterhealth.vic.gov.au

www.aph.gov.au

L'Officiel du Canal du Midi – edition 2014

Centre de Préhistoire du Pech Merle, Cabrerets, France

Acknowledgements

I would like to acknowledge the following people for their help to bring this story to fruition:

My long-suffering editor, Amanda Pederick, of The Picky Bitch Editing, for her expertise, help, willingness to brainstorm, endless patience and professional advice.

My good friends and mentors, Margaret Jamieson and Josephine Williams, without whose encouragement this story may simply have remained an idea languishing in my brain.

Andrew Penna for his expertise and knowledge of emergency radio procedures and police roles in emergencies.

Carol Dunk, for medical advice.

Stephanie Corsetti, ex-ABC Radio journalist for her advice on how the Press and Police tackle thorny newsworthy issues and the procedures for informing next-of-kin.

Julie Stephenson, walking buddy, for her patience and help in finally nailing the title.

I'd also like to thank the following people for their willingness to help me wrangle a lengthy, not-quite-right-yet manuscript and to give their feedback and comments as readers: Josephine, Margaret, Lisa Holt, Colleen Biggs, Kym Goodman, and Josephine Harris.

Thank you all.

Sasha Penno

N.B. All the places are as faithfully accurate as I can make them; all the characters are totally fictitious and any resemblance to persons living or deceased, is purely coincidental.

If I've played with distances and times for the sake of the narrative, *mea culpa*, but they won't be changing.

Naturally, any, and all mistakes will be mine.

About the Author

Sasha Penno's career has been long and multi-faceted.

Born in South Australia, Sasha spent a year in the West in her late teens with her dog, living and working on a sheep station, before returning to Adelaide. She worked with overseas students, and in private enterprise before deciding to become a teacher.

Later, she moved to Victoria where she has pursued her life-long love of history and languages whilst teaching adolescents and adults, as well as indulging in her fascination with archaeology, pre-history and alternate therapies, along with broader interests including gardening, silk-painting, and soap-making.

With a wealth of ideas demanding to be released, and after many years of writing short stories, Sasha turned her attention to more serious writing, particularly Australian historically based fiction. She is now permanently based in South-West Victoria, Gunditjmara and Bunganditj country, when not travelling the world or around Australia.

Also by Sasha Penno

The Tides of Longing

Paperback: ISBN 978-1-923102-07-1

On a remote northern beach, a young man is washed up on the incoming tide, injured, alone, and lacking any ID.

Further south, a widow, still grieving the loss of both husband and stepson, receives an email that brings her hope.

Accepting an invitation from distant cousins to spend the festive season at their vineyard in the south of France, she little imagines how her life will be turned on its head once more, but learns that, in the end, the tides of longing pull us home, to where we belong.